CONTENTS

ROAD'S END
AND OTHER FANTASIES

By Brian A. Hopkins

When they surrounded him in the stables, she was still clinging to his arm, begging him to flee. He pushed her tly aside and placed his hand on the hilt of his sword.

"No!" she screamed. "They'll kill you!"

The smile that tugged at the corner of his mouth and the m set of his eyes said that he didn't fear the twenty-four rds that had him surrounded. Nor did he fear death. The e that his fingers tapped out on the hilt of his sword was a iliar one. His hands had at last found something they knew v to do.

"Please," she begged him. "Don't do this. I could not bear to ch them kill you."

The circle of guards drew tighter. The Turtle Knight paused, ecisive, his blade drawn just inches from its scabbard. A iliar song trilled in his blood, pounded in his ears, twitched g the tendons in his sword arm. But the princess had placed hand on his wrist. The warmth of her burned through him.

"Put down your sword," she begged. "They won't hurt you. se.

"Do it for me."

And that's how he came to set his sword down in the dust surrender to the prince's guards. They knocked him down. ed him senseless. Stripped him of his armor. Bound him in ns.

And caged him in the dungeons.

ROAD'S END

A moonless blanket settled over the cold, grey stone of Dunbarton. Against the pitch-black sky, her four towers were slender lances of white. The River Clyde reflected back the night's inky depths, spotted here and there with the flickering shine of winter stars. In the woodlands bordering the castle's southern wall, the starlight cast an army of umbrageous shadows, crouching like sinister sentries beneath tree and shrub.

One shadow moved.

The fleeting form was darker than the gloom in which it sought to hide. Starlight hinted of ivory fang and claw; otherwise, the sleek shape was all but invisible. Had the guard atop the southeast tower not been asleep at his post, he might have seen the beast move with cat-like grace and speed from the overhanging boughs of Müirwood Forest, across the glen, and thence to the banks of the castle moat.

At the water's edge, the beast missed not a stride to hesitation, but leaped, sailing full thirty feet to land on the narrow strip of ground between moat and castle wall. There, eclipsed in the complete darkness cast by the sixty-foot-high wall, it was imperceptible, just another thin dagger of night.

Following the contour of the wall, the intruder proceeded to the main gate where a wooden bridge spanned the moat. On the bridge were two men-at-arms. Their lances left somewhere within, they seemed focused on the placid surface of the moat.

"I kin a time when we had a proper bridge," said the taller of the two. "One fit to be drawn up when needed."

"Aye, but the moat 'twas a wee bit more functional then. Clyde keeps 'er clean now."

"By God, your chil'ren dinna use to swim in 'er! Look't 'er now; fit to drink."

"Best no' be mocking Alaric's peace, Kilbearn. 'Tis been good to you and yourn for more years than you can count."

"Aye, tha' it has," the one called Kilbearn admitted. "Still, I miss—Gods! What...?"

The black that was not shadow suddenly leaped from where it crouched beside the open gate. Unlike any animal they were familiar with, this one attacked in utter silence.

Only Kilbearn saw it at first. From his peripheral vision, he saw it launch like some black cat, claws extended, ears laid back flat against a skull that was in no way feline, lips curled back to reveal fangs set in a mouth one might encounter on a swamp dragon. One massive paw caught Kilbearn as he stumbled back from the bridge railing. Talons met light mail and soft human flesh, both of which parted. In a shower of blood and broken silver rings, the tall guardsman threw up his arms and spun about, his body turning nearly end over end before it flopped lifelessly to the floor at his comrade's feet.

The stouter guardsman got off one scream, one blood-curdling scream the likes of which should never be heard from a man—leastwise not a man who had followed King Alaric into battle.

The scream echoed through the cold courtyards, awakening the southeast tower guard. It drew two more whose duty was patrolling the battlements above the main gate. Abandoning a dice game, they gathered up their crossbows and rushed to the parapet. Before they reached the wall's edge, the scream was followed with a splash.

The two sentries leaned over the parapet, catching one brief glimpse of a fleeting shadow disappearing into the woodlands, but nothing else. Below them, one body lay crumpled, a dark stain spreading fast on the pale wood of the bridge. There was no sign of the second gate guard, save the starlit ripples expanding in the moat.

Alaric mac Cullen, hair tousled and eyes still full of sleep, wrapped in a heavy cloak that might have been the spread from his bed, rested a hand on the cold iron and peered through it to the dark-shrouded bridge beyond. A crimson moon was just beginning its ascent. Bathed in this morbid red glow was the body of the guardsman, Kilbearn. Trickles of steaming blood radiated out from the corpse, meandering across the hoof-polished surface of the bridge, following cracks and joints to ultimately strike a slow cadence from the surface of the moat. To one side of the corpse, shadowed from the moon's eerie pallor by the bridge railing, lay a small object. Glittering in the starlight, it commanded Alaric's attention.

"M'lord King, whoever slew Kilbearn and Dunkeld could still be close," warned the Captain of the Guard. "A skilled archer wouldna have trouble putting an arrow through tha' portcullis."

Alaric stood silent for a moment, the bitter wind flapping the heavy cloak about his ankles, then he stepped back from the red tinted iron.

"Thank you, Sire. Now, I'll send men—"

"Raise it, Captain Cannich."

"Sire?"

"Raise it."

Seeing the look on his king's face, Cannich decided not to protest. He motioned to waiting soldiers. "I want a hand of archers on either side of us when we go out." Men moved to obey him.

"Raise the portcullis," Cannich called to the watchtower. Chains rattled as they were drawn taut, followed by the protest of wooden gears under immense weight, then the thump and groaning of wheels and cogs as the portcullis began its ascent.

When the base of the massive grating reached chest height, Alaric ducked under it and strode out into the moonlight. Cannich cursed under his breath and followed, his archers flanking them on either side.

"Watch the treeline!"

Encircled by archers, Alaric and Cannich knelt at the fallen soldier's side. While the captain turned over his crumpled guardsman, Alaric examined that which had held his attention since arriving at the castle gate. There were actually two items, one set to hold the other in place against the brisk wind that swept across the bridge. By some trick of fate, the fast-spreading blood had diverged around the items, leaving the tattered scrap of parchment and the shard of violet crystal which weighted it down untouched.

"'Twas no man did this to Kilbearn mac Dalry, Sire."

Alaric collected parchment and crystal, then turned to look upon the corpse. A set of six parallel lacerations, bone deep, ran from lower abdomen to face. Intestines and other internal organs—even whole ribs—were torn from Kilbearn's body. His face was beyond recognition.

"No blade did tha'," commented one of the archers.

"Six," muttered another. "Devil's number."

"Eyes on the trees!" Cannich bellowed at them.

"The other man—Dunkeld you named him … Where?"

"The sentries on the wall heard a splash." Together they rose and looked over the railing at the water.

"'Tis too dark. Send for lanterns."

Cannich sent one of his archers after the lanterns. King, captain, and the nine remaining archers stood in the moonlight and waited.

And they watched the dark-shrouded, red-leaved treeline of Müirwood.

While they waited, Alaric examined the items the midnight assailant had left. He held the violet crystal aloft in the moonlight, watching as the moon's glow lent it a crimson hue.

"What is it, M'lord?"

"A memento," the king answered. "Given by me—many years ago."

"Given, M'lord? To whom?"

At that moment, the archer arrived with lanterns. Alaric reached for one, but Cannich stayed his hand. "Tha' lantern makes a bonny target, Sire. Let me." He took the lantern and extended it out beyond the bridge such that it cast a white luminance over the water.

Several yards out from the bridge floated the missing guardsman. Face down in the dark water, it was impossible to see how he had died, but every man on the bridge ι Kilbearn's eviscerated corpse.

"Bring them in," Alaric commanded softly and started toward the castle.

"Sire."

The king turned, his face tired and old in the moonlight.

"The crystal. Who did you give it to?"

"My wife, the Lady Rosewick. I gave it to her long ago ... long before she died."

Glaston set another log on the fire. Though it hurt his twisted knee, he knelt by the hearthstones and studied his master where he sat nearby. Alaric the king was known to many. Alaric the man was known to a very select few. Glaston was one of those few.

When he'd waited several long minutes without Alaric commenting on his presence, Glaston cleared his throat. When this brought no response, he spoke. "Rumors are, 'twas a demon took those two men tonight."

The king remained silent.

Glaston sighed and sat down at the hearth, taking his weight off the old battle wound. Though insulated with heavy tapestries, the room was bitter cold. *The old girl's getting drafty,* he thought, as the stone hearth stung through his leather trousers.

The tapestries hung in profusion about the Great Hall depicted the many battles fought to win and hold Alaric's kingdom. The older tapestries told of the fall of the Tyrant King, Tiroth Cann. There was Alaric mac Cullen standing over the vanquished king's body and donning the ivory circlet Tiroth Cann had stolen from an older Cullen, the color of the piece long faded. Newer tapestries showed Dunbarton armies forcing northern raiders back to their ships. On a beach strewn with bodies stood heroes of Clan Cullen, Glaston himself among them.

But the newer hangings were far from new, and the older ones were ancient.

"If you're no' going to talk with me, I may as well take my bones back to bed."

Alaric ran a hand through his long, greying hair, realizing for the first time that it had come loose in his sleep and framed his face in disarray. From his robe, Alaric withdrew the note, which he'd already read, and the violet crystal, a one-time gift to his wife. He held out the crystal so Glaston could see it.

"Recognize this?"

"Rose's?"

"Aye," answered the king. "I'll tell you a story. Once there was a bonny lass whose attention was sought by two young lads. These men were the best of friends. One was an orphan, taken in by the other's family."

"Yourself and Rorvik."

"And Rosewick," the king conceded. "I found a jewel which I planned to give her at Harvest Feast, but I lost it swimming in Loch Lomond. Rory found the jewel and swore he would make it *his* harvest gift to her. We fought o'er the crystal, but in the end our friendship won out. We took it to Rose and told her tha' we'd place it atop Raven's Crest. At her command, we'd climb and the first to reach the crystal won it, the right to give it to her, and her hand."

Alaric shrugged his massive shoulders, a smile on his face. "We were young and romantically, hopelessly in love. We thought such promises of love as binding as the blood oath we'd sworn each other the day Father gave us hunting knives." He closed the crystal tightly in the palm of his hand as if to squeeze the rest of the tale from it. "I won the contest. And, though the contest dinna decide it, I also won her hand."

"And you found tha' crystal tonight?"

Alaric nodded. "Along with a message commanding my presence at Gairloch Crail."

"Tiroth Cann's fortress?"

"Aye."

"But it lies in ruins. Has for nigh thirty-four years. And who would be so bold as to demand *your* presence?"

Alaric took a deep breath. "The message is signed by Nordric Kril."

Glaston shivered. He remembered Cann's necromancer standing atop the smoking ruins of Gairloch Crail's main tower.

Dressed in swirling robes of black, Kril had looked down to the beach where they stood over Cann's mutilated corpse and set a curse on them all.

"We should have hunted tha' whore's son down."

"We tried. Remember?"

Glaston got to his feet and paced the room, his limp prominent. Finally, he spread his arms and laughed. "So? Come dawn, we ride out and finish what we should ha' done long ago. We finish Kril and leave him for the gulls."

"No."

"Why no'?" Glaston demanded.

"Kril's message is clear. I am to go alone."

"And why honor tha' request?"

Alaric showed him the crystal again. "You remember when Rorvik left us eight years ago?"

Glaston nodded. "Too damn peaceful around 'ere for him."

"Rose loved both of us, Glaston. It broke her heart to see him go." He paused, studying the crystal where it lay in his weathered palm, glittering in the light from the fireplace. "When he left, she gave him this."

Alaric stroked the warhorse's corded neck. Pleased to see its master, the shire nuzzled Alaric's cheek. The horse caught the scent of oiled steel and stamped excitedly. Its eyes were wild in the lamp light, eyes that had seen more than they cared to of this stable.

"Steady, Darnaech," Alaric bid. The cream-colored dun tossed its head and drew back. Accentuated by the flickering light of the stable's oil lanterns, muscles rippled as the horse pranced about the small stall. Darnaech threw back his head and whinnied in eagerness to be on the road. The call was exhilaration, warning, and promise of service, all in one.

Alaric felt like throwing back his head and repeating it.

It was early and the stablehands were not about, thus Alaric enjoyed the simple pleasure of saddling the stallion himself. It'd been too long since he'd last readied his own mount.

Darnaech stood 18 hands in height and a broad eight feet in solid girth. The shire's back was short, strong, and heavily muscled. The hindquarters were long, wide, and likewise well-muscled. There was a fine feather on all his limbs. His mane was thick—just brushed, for this was, after all, the king's horse. Long of leg, with large, wide feet, the animal looked cut from stone. Descended from the horses of William the Conqueror, Darnaech bore a lean face with a slightly Roman nose.

Alaric loved the animal second only to friends such as Rorvik and Glaston.

As Alaric was adjusting the final straps, Glaston arrived carrying a long shirt of chain mail and a shield—all the armor the master-at-arms had been able to convince the king to take. Setting aside the heavy, fur-lined cloak he'd worn to the stables, Alaric slipped the mail over his head and under the broad leather belt from which he had hung his broadsword. Then he drew the cloak back over his shoulders and tied it closed. Taking up the shield, Alaric frowned at the crest of Clan Cullen bolted to its face.

"He'll be knowing who's coming with or without tha' coat-of-arms," Glaston remarked.

Alaric tied the shield to the shire's saddle, then turned to his friend. They stood beside the anxious stallion for several long moments, neither of them knowing how to say goodbye to the other.

"I could go—" Glaston tried one last time.

"No." Alaric reached up and removed the circlet from his brow. He forced it into Glaston's hesitant hands. "For the people. In case I dinna return."

Eren watched the stag bend to drink from the swift stream. It dipped its muzzle, drank briefly, then raised its head, nose high as it tested the wind. The woodsman waited patiently, bow in hand with arrow nocked and ready. This was the same stag that had eluded him for three consecutive years. More than twenty points adorned those massive horns. The deer had to weigh at least 180 pounds, more meat than he and Gwen would eat all winter.

Just lower your head for another drink, Eren coaxed the animal.

A flick of the ears and it did just that. As its head dropped, Eren drew the longbow, one smooth motion taking no more than a heartbeat. Once drawn, he held the arrow anchored firmly, broadhead protruding an inch from the bow's riser, fletching snug against his lower lip. He knelt there, waiting for the deer to finish its drink and raise its head. When its head went up, presenting him with the broad surface of its white chest as target, he would let fly the arrow.

The deer and he heard it at the same time: something large coming through the forest. Magically fast, the deer was gone. Too tense to do else, he let the arrow fly. It ricocheted off a tree and disappeared into the heavy foliage.

Eren dived into the underbrush, sliding a second arrow from his quiver. He had no way of knowing what had scared off the deer; just last year, there had been a rogue bear in Müirwood. But what burst through the dense undergrowth was no wild bear, but a man astride a massive warhorse. The horse was a dun-colored shire, well equipped with good leather and metal trappings, a small parcels bag, bedroll, and a shield strapped to the saddle. The man was tall and dark of hair, features shadowed by the high collar of a heavy fur cloak.

They went straight to the creek where the horse bent to drink and the man slid from its back. As the stranger alighted, his cloak parted and Eren thought he caught the glint of metal within. As the stranger knelt to drink, a long broadsword was evident at his side.

Years of living in the deep forest had left Eren wary of strangers. Men did not often journey through this part of Müirwood when there were easier routes. Eren had Gwen to think of, not to mention the child she was carrying.

The horse suddenly stopped drinking. It raised its head, snorted, and tested the wind. Ears pricked forward at full attention, the horse stamped in the soft mud of the creek bed. Eren knew horses. And he knew what this one was signaling.

The dark-haired stranger rose from the creek and lay a hand alongside the tall shire's neck. "What is it, Darnaech?"

At first Eren thought the breeze had shifted and the horse had somehow gotten wind of him. Then he realized that the wind was still strong in his face and that the horse's attention was directed across the creek.

The stranger leaped effortlessly into the saddle, left hand firmly taking up the reins, right on the hilt of his sword. The horse backed away from the creek, probably seeking more reliable footing. The rider didn't have to initiate the move; this was a horse trained for war. As it moved, Eren caught a glimpse of the shield and the crest it bore.

A crash of brush and something came hurtling across the creek, too fast to determine much in the way of detail. It was black; it was huge, half as high as the warhorse and equal in body length; it had unnaturally long talons and teeth; and it didn't belong in his forest.

The cat—he found nothing else to call it—struck the warhorse head on, fangs sinking in equine flesh. The horse screamed. As it stumbled backward, one massive black paw swept over the horse's head and dashed the rider from the saddle. Sword half drawn, the stranger crashed into the underbrush, a piece of rent cloak floating in the air where he had been. The horse went down beneath the silent hellcat.

Regaining his senses, Eren clawed at the bow he had dropped. In his panic, he couldn't find the arrow he had held at ready mere seconds ago, so he pulled another from the quiver on his back. As the cat went mad, rending horse flesh in an insane shower of blood, Eren nocked the arrow.

The stranger was on his feet. A shaft of noonday sun flashed off his sword. He rushed the cat, unknowingly blocking Eren's shot. The cat rose from the feebly struggling horse, crimson running from its reptilian face. The swordsman swung a blow meant to take off the foul creature's head, but it ducked, unbelievably fast, and struck a blow of its own. Talons rang off chain mail and the stranger was hurled back. Sunlight sparked off several chain links as they spun away.

As the stranger fell, Eren drew his bow and sighted on the broad chest of the hellcat. Across the short distance separating them, their eyes locked just before he released the arrow. Under that searing gaze, he felt for a moment as if it marked him, recording his actions for later retribution; then he released the bow string.

The arrow seemed to fly in slow motion. Or perhaps it just

seemed that way relative to the reaction speed of the cat. Once it knew his intention, once it knew Eren would fire, seemingly before he even knew it himself, the cat moved. The arrow struck it not in the chest, but high on the shoulder where it glanced off bone and caught in the thick cords of muscle there. The cat turned and was gone as swiftly as it had appeared, carrying the arrow with it.

A silence settled over the forest, broken only by the labored breathing of the downed horse. Eren stood trembling, another arrow nocked and drawn without even realizing he had done so.

The stranger got unsteadily to his feet, gave the woodsman one unreadable glance, then turned to the horse. The shire had given up struggling and lay in a spreading pool of blood. Setting aside his sword, the stranger knelt at the horse's head and gently stroked its face. As Eren joined him, the horse's breathing stopped.

The stranger's hand went to his sword as he looked up from the dead mount. Eren slid his arrow back into the quiver and showed him the empty bow. "'Twas a fine animal."

The stranger looked at his hand, covered with the shire's blood. "A good friend. An *old* friend." There were tears in his eyes and Eren decided right then that he liked the man.

The stranger gathered up his shield and rose to his feet. There was blood running from his shoulder where the chain mail hung in tatters. Eren caught him as he stumbled. "You're injured. My home is no' far." Gwen would have his hide, but he was determined to know more of the creature he had seen and shot. Besides, the man bore the crest of Alaric. He was either a thief or one of the king's own soldiers.

"The wounds are no' tha' serious. I'll just be needing a minute to catch my breath."

They sat against the trees that lined the shallow creek. The stranger held his sword, still unsheathed, across his lap. He closed his eyes and seemed content to just rest. Eren nervously scanned the surrounding forest, certain that the hellcat would not have gone far.

"You live in these woods?" the stranger asked.

"Aye. Name's Eren."

"Kilbearn," the stranger returned.

"A soldier?"

"I've *been* a soldier."

"Grim business, soldiering. Myself, I live here in Müirwood, content with the peace Alaric has given me." Eren was silent a minute, waiting to see if Kilbearn would volunteer anything about himself. Finally, he asked, "You serve the king?"

"Seems like I've served the crown all my life," Kilbearn answered in a tired voice.

"And now? You're a good four days from Dunbarton. Seems rather far for a hunting trip or afternoon ride."

"I follow my own path now," Kilbearn answered.

"And tha' thing follows you?"

"'Til I kill its master." He got to his feet, wincing at the pain in his shoulder. "Toward which end, I need to be moving." He held out a hand to Eren. "You saved my life, woodsman. For tha', I'm in your debt. But I'm afraid I must ask one more favor of you."

Eren gripped the offered hand firmly. "Let me take you back to my home and my wife can tend tha' shoulder."

"No. Tha' demon will be back. I'll no' endanger you and your family by leading it there. The shoulder will be all right for now. The favor I need is a simple one. Show me the quickest way to the forest's edge and the Cann Road."

"The road to Gairloch Crail." It wasn't a question, more a statement that hung in the chill, pine-scented air like there was more to follow.

Kilbearn nodded. "It's to Gairloch Crail tha' I go to stop this thing."

Eren frowned, seemed about to speak, then motioned upstream. "I can show you where to pick up the road. This way."

They followed the creek for about fifty feet more until it crossed a game trail disappearing uphill in the deeper woods. The woodsman took the slope without hesitation, using his bow to push aside intervening branches. As they started the climb, Kilbearn finally sheathed his sword. Twenty feet up the slope, he paused to discard his shield. A stride or two further and he tossed aside the heavy fur cloak. "I'd rather freeze than bear tha' weight." He hugged his left arm tight to his side.

They walked without talking for thirty minutes, then Kilbearn called for a rest. He slumped to the ground, back against a massive oak. "No' as young as I used to be."

"And tha' wound's no' making it any easier. You should let me look at it."

"I'll manage," he replied stubbornly. "Before, when I told you my destination, you were about to say something."

"There've been strange things afoot at Gairloch Crail. The ruins have a new tenant."

"You've seen this *tenant?*"

"No. But I know tha' he arrived several years ago."

"These *strange things* started then?" Kilbearn asked.

"Aye. A tower tha' appeared overnight. Strange lights from the windows of the tower. Fires tha' burn an eerie green rising from the rooftop. Howling. Gossamer shapes on the wind. Things like tha'. I've meant to carry word to Dunbarton, but ne'er seem to get tha' far from home. There're very few travelers through here—no' much chance of anyone else spotting it."

"You said *several* years ago. How many exactly?"

Eren shrugged. "Three. Four maybe."

Using the tree, Kilbearn pulled himself to his feet. "It's important, Eren. When?"

"Would have been the winter I built the new woodshed for Gwen. I was sick the winter before and she couldna reach the old woodshed for all the snow, so I—"

"When?" Kilbearn demanded impatiently.

"Three winters ago."

A cold, hard stare came over the soldier's face. His hand went to his sword and gripped the hilt, knuckle-white.

"What is it?" Eren asked, getting to his feet.

"Show me tha' road."

Müirwood ended drastically, forming a treeline straight as an arrow. From there, a field of knee-high grass ran to the bluffs overlooking the sea. Midway between the forest's edge and the deadman drop to the sea, lay a stone road, the road built by

Tiroth Cann in the days of his empire.

Eren pointed to the ribbon of stone bisecting the swath of green. "Runs from the fields of Doriath where Alaric turned Cann's forces back, up through the hills below Dunbarton, into the highlands where it skirts Müirwood, and then down to the sea and Gairloch Crail."

"I know where it leads."

Eren looked at the stony face of his companion. "Aye, I guess you might at tha'. Were you there when Alaric stormed Gairloch Crail?"

"I was there."

"Then I owe you a great debt."

"You owe me nothing, friend. 'Tis I who owes you."

"Gwen and I couldna live free as we do in Müirwood, were it no' for what you and thousands of others did thirty-four years ago. We owe Alaric everything."

A brief, irritated frown crossed Kilbearn's face. Then he reached beneath his shirt of mail, dug for a moment, and pulled out a violet shard of crystal. He handed it to the woodsman. "For your lady."

"I dinna understand."

"This Gwen you speak of. Tell her you found it. It'll make her happy, make her smile."

"But it must be very valuable."

The soldier shrugged his uninjured shoulder. "The value is in the giving, friend. I want you to have it. Again, I thank you. You're an honest man, Eren of Müirwood."

"I could go with you," Eren blurted out.

"I wouldna allow tha'. No' with tha' woman waiting alone in Müirwood."

"But tha' beast—"

"Will no' trouble you again. You have my word on tha'."

"At least take my bow."

Kilbearn showed him the injured shoulder. "I couldna draw it."

The two men stood in silence for a moment, each certain he'd never see the other again. Then the woodsman pocketed the crystal, nodded in resignation, and turned back to Müirwood.

In mere seconds, the forest had swallowed him without a trace. The king turned and walked alone through the tall grass.

The road ran uphill for another twenty minutes, then it leveled out and followed the edge of the sea cliffs. Here Tiroth Cann had been forced to clear back the forest when he'd laid the road. In many places, Müirwood was now reclaiming its own. Brush and saplings lined the swathe between road and forest proper with a miniature Müirwood. Alaric noticed fresh cuttings, scores of stumps whose sweet sap permeated the cold air, as potent as the smell of the sea below.

Walking to the cliff's edge, he looked down. There, anchored in the calm waters in the lee of the peninsula on which Gairloch Crail was set, was a vessel. From this distance, it was hard to be certain, but she looked to have suffered some hull damage. Perhaps she had run afoul of one of the many reefs that lined the coast.

On the white sand beach, he saw men shaping timber they'd brought down from the highlands. Finished planks were ferried by longboat out to the anchored ship. He watched them a few minutes, wondering what business they were about. They might legitimately be merchants put in for honest repairs. Or they might be pirates forced in after a battle.

Finally, he realized he was wasting what little daylight was left to him. And every minute he wasted was another minute Rorvik spent in the hands of Nordric Kril. He got to his feet, drew his sword, and began looking for a good straight sapling, all the while intentionally not looking up ahead where the road ended and, already visible, lay the ruins of Gairloch Crail.

Ruins that is, save for one resurrected tower.

The tower looked to have been haphazardly assembled from the surrounding ruins. The stones were poorly set and incongruently blackened from the fires that had raged thirty-four years ago. There was no door, merely a rough opening in the stone.

At first glance, the tower looked empty. Then his eyes adjusted and he spotted the scattered array of splintered bones in the middle of the floor. Some were animal: deer, rodent, and several farmers' cows. But the majority were human bones.

Sacrifice? Blood for the casting of spells? He wasn't sure he wanted to know.

A stairway, also of rudely stacked stones, fit against the wall and spiraled upward. Alaric's gaze traveled the length of the stairway and found that it ended at the top before a rough-hewn door of wood.

Alaric set his foot on the first step and began the long climb to the top. His shoulder continued to throb. His breath was coming in ragged gasps. Though it was cool, even in the tower, his face was coated with a fine sheen of sweat. His mind seemed to wander, recalling another day, another climb, another prize to be won...

And if I reach the top first, the crystal is mine to give her?

"Aye," Alaric answered the childhood memory.

And though she marry me, and we have many fine, strong sons, and live happily ever after, we'll still be friends?

"Always."

From the halfway point, he looked down, a fall of at least forty feet.

"It's no' nearly as high as Raven's Crest, Rory," he called up the stairs. His challenge echoed round about, ringing off the ambivalent rock.

Nothing. Silence. The only sounds were his footsteps and labored breathing.

An older, bored Rorvik: *We're growing old, Alaric. Getting fat and lazy. There are lands yet to conquer, still kingdoms ripe for the picking. If it's justice you need like the old days, we'll find another tyrant. Surely there's blood tha' needs letting.*

"I canna leave Rose, Rory."

Then I'm sorry. But I've got to go. One day, when you're ready—

"When I'm free of these responsibilities."

—you can follow me. We'll do it all again, brother.

He stopped at the door. Softly: "I'm here, Rory. I'm ready to follow you."

He leaned the cut sapling to the right of the door, took a deep breath, and kicked with all his might. The door crashed open, slammed against the inner wall where it tore free of its old hinges and thundered to the stone floor. Alaric stepped forward, standing in the threshold.

The room was empty save for a single throne, Tiroth Cann's throne, now battered and ancient, stained with the rust red of old blood, blackened like much of the stone from the conquering fires of yesterday. On the throne sat the old sorcerer. At his feet, sat the black cat-thing. The cat eyed Alaric intensely, but neither moved nor made a sound. There was no sign of the wound Eren had inflicted on it. From within Kril's robes of black, emerged a weathered hand. He motioned Alaric forward into the room.

Alaric stood his ground. Except for three windows spaced evenly about the circular wall and the doorway in which Alaric stood, there were no other exits from the room.

"Where is he?" Alaric demanded.

Kril smiled, a toothless grin that further wrinkled his ancient face. Kril had been old when Cann fell. Time hadn't overlooked him in the years since. The lines in his face were miles deep. At his feet, the hellcat's tail thrashed in irritation, its leathern scales making a dry scraping on the stone floor.

"You've already murdered him," Alaric moaned, blood pounding in his ears.

"I've waited a long time for this." Kril rasped, his voice nearly a whisper.

"Why wait any longer?" Alaric taunted.

The toothless grin again. "I've been here for many years, King Alaric. Right under your nose. I've taken *everything* from you. Now the time has come to take the kingdom that should have been mine long ago."

"Yours? Cann would have killed you eventually. He dinna tolerate any threat to his power. You were an oaf then; if he'd known you'd one day possess power, power to summon something like tha'—" He pointed to the crouching beast. "Then he'd have slit your throat long ago."

Kril laughed, his rheumy eyes as tight and black as the hellcat's. "Tiroth Cann was a puppet. In time, I'd have crushed him. Just as I've crushed you."

"Forget the speeches, Kril. Send your cur for me. Or are you brave enough to try me yourself?"

"In a moment. Before you die, you must understand how I've

brought about your demise. Surely you've guessed most of it."

Through clenched teeth and lips curled back in a snarl: "The sickness tha' took Rosewick. 'Twas you."

"And the reason she never bore you any children?"

So, there were things he hadn't already guessed. Alaric reached out and gripped both sides of the door frame, holding himself back. Every fiber of his being called out to lunge at the grinning sorcerer and strike his head from his shoulders. But between Alaric and his nemesis lay the salivating beast. Alaric forced himself to wait.

I'm sorry, Rose. Gods, but I'm sorry. A child's light might have kept you alive, might have brought you out into the sunshine, out into life. It might have given us tha' last piece we needed to be happy. I ne'er knew...

"I've been around all these years, Alaric. I've made sure your kingdom prospered—for one day, it would be mine—but I've made sure you left no heirs to the throne. And when I felt the time was right, when I had finally located the last thing you cared about, your friend Rorvik, when I'd drawn about me all the power I needed to exact the vengeance I wanted, I came here. A few spells and your lovely Queen took ill and died."

Alaric tasted blood in his mouth. His teeth were clenched so tight, he thought they must surely shatter.

"I even took away that silly horse—"

"Enough!" Alaric screamed. "You want me? Here I be!"

Kril smacked as if tasting a tart wine. His lips, stretched thin over barren gums, looked tainted with blood. For a moment, he savored the hot hatred radiating from the king in the doorway, drank it in with a sigh of animal satisfaction; then he smiled.

"Very well then. I've one thing more to take from you." The sorcerer raised his hand from where he had been stroking the demon's scaly head.

The cat-thing came alive like a compressed spring. A scrape of claws and it hurtled through the air, crossing the room in a single leap meant to end with Alaric beneath fang and talon.

So fast was its leap that Alaric was almost too slow to react. He clawed back outside the door and to the right, taking up the straight young sapling he had cut. Swinging it into the room, he braced its butt against the stone floor and screamed in terror and battle-lust as the cat-thing met the sword-hewn point.

Eight hundred pounds of demon struck the sapling squarely, the makeshift lance impaling the beast through the chest. For the first time, it cried out. The bestial roar of anger, surprise, and pain shook the tower.

Alaric was forced back nearly off the landing and down the steps as the cat-thing struggled against the lance. Then he regained his footing. Leaning his weight against the lance, he forced the howling demon back into the room. He knew he had only a few more seconds before he lost his capability to hold it off. Already, its claws had nearly torn apart the sapling. But every second, its struggles grew weaker, as its blood pumped out onto the cold stone.

The cat's jaws clamped down on the shaft, and even over the din of their conflict, Alaric could hear the wood splintering. Only the fact that the tip of the lance was buried deep in the demon's breast allowed him to use it as leverage. Strength fading fast, he forced it back through the doorway, clawing for footing every step of the way. Once beyond the threshold, he lowered the butt of the lance, braced it against the wall to one side of the doorway, and went for his sword.

As his sword cleared its scabbard, the sapling snapped and the hellcat reared on its hind legs, front claws outstretched to embrace him. Like the prow of a ship, the shaft stood out between the reaching claws.

Alaric struck with all his might. The blade just barely missed the demon's head, cleaving off one scaly ear, and then sinking with a solid thud down through its shoulder and into its chest. With a gurgling roar of protest and pain, the beast sank to the floor. As it fell, Alaric's sword parted like tired parchment, leaving him holding only the hilt in his two tightly-clenched fists.

From the floor, the beast reached out with one bloody paw and sank its talons into Alaric's calf. He looked down, amazed that the beast had any fight left. Even as he looked, the claws seemed to shrink back on themselves, withdrawing from his calf muscle.

Before Alaric's eyes, a horrifying transformation began to take place.

Across the room, Kril rose from his seat and cackled with glee. "Now, Alaric! Now I've taken everything from you!"

At Alaric's feet, the demon changed. The talons retracted, shortened, became fingers of normal human flesh. The tail seemed to wither, and then disappeared completely. The body, cat-like and black, shrank, taking on human contours and proportions. Thick black hair became breeches and a shirt of dark leather. The head, long and serpentine, shortened. The face became human. Where no hair had been, there grew a thick mop of sandy brown laced with grey.

Only two things remained the same after the transformation: the wooden shaft of Alaric's hand-made lance standing out from a bloody breast and the shattered blade of his broadsword buried in a ghastly wound that ran from one side of the neck deep into the chest cavity.

Alaric fell to his knees and touched the face of his dead friend. "Rory, I—"

"*Everything!*" Kril cackled. "All that remains is your own life. And that is also mine to take." Nordric Kril started across the room, one hand raised over his head. In that hand burned a witchfire of emerald green. The green radiance lit the entire room, casting a shadow Alaric out and down the stairway.

Slumped over the bloody corpse of his friend, Alaric paid the sorcerer no heed. The fight was gone out of him. Physical and mental exhaustion were all that remained; neither a fit weapon for the madman crossing the room to finish him off.

"How I've waited for this," Kril sighed. The witchfire pulsed now, its incandescence turning the grey stone green, so bright there were no longer any shadows in the circular room atop the tower. A wind came up out of nowhere, whirling up and about the sorcerer, fluttering his black robes about him like the wings of a bat.

"Look at me, great king. Look at me!"

The muscles in Alaric's neck bunched and strained with resistance. His head shook with a palsy that affected none of the rest of his body. His head turned, against his will, to look up at Nordric Kril.

"Now you are mine, Alaric mac Cullen."

Kril had become a swirling force of impenetrable black, a whirlwind of evil with but one anomaly: the green fireball in his right fist. The green phased to a brilliant white, pulsed, began to grow. The burning white arced out, crossed the short span separating them like a bolt of lightning, struck Alaric and hurled him across the room.

Alaric rebounded off the tower wall and crumbled to the floor. His head was reeling, darkness swirling about his mind, threatening to suck him down into a black whirlpool. He was dimly aware of blood trickling into his eyes. Somewhere distant, he heard Kril laugh.

Then from the doorway came the *sluagh ghairm*, a war cry not heard since the days when Gairloch Crail stood besieged. At this sound, the green witchlight, which had suffused the entire room now in not only brilliant light, but a stifling closeness as well, faltered, sputtered, seemed for just a moment as if it might go out.

In that brief span of time, Alaric heard the hum of a bow string and a silver shaft hissed across the room to disappear in the swirling black robes of the sorcerer. Alaric's first thought was of the forester, Eren, but the shaft was too short and fast to have come from a longbow. Weakly, he raised his head to find Glaston in the doorway. Hurling aside a crossbow, the Dunbarton warrior pulled a heavy battle axe from his back and charged into the room. The echoes of the battle cry that had signaled Tiroth Cann's defeat were still reverberating throughout the small room as warrior and sorcerer met.

The axe swung viciously, its blade throwing back green light. From where Alaric lay on the floor, it looked as if the axe passed right through Nordric Kril, but that was impossible. Wasn't it?

Kril made a grand sweeping gesture with his arm, leaving a green arc burned across Alaric's vision. Even though no actual contact was made, Glaston was lifted by the blow and knocked rolling across the floor, helm dashed from his head, pieces of plate armor broken free and sent banging off the walls.

But Glaston hadn't come alone. Dunbarton guardsmen crowded the doorway. Other short, sleek quarrels sliced through the suffocating green air to disappear into the maelstrom of power that Kril had become.

The maelstrom weakened. The witchfire sputtered, dimmed, held its own, but at a much weaker intensity. Kril returned to form. Then he sprouted wings.

"Alaric, he's going to escape!" Glaston howled from where he lay against the far wall.

Kril lunged toward a window, dark wings tucked tight against his back for a dive to the open air beyond.

Surely there's blood tha' needs letting...

Rory's words echoed in the room—or was it only in his mind? The shattered sword was still clutched in the King's hand, had been ever since he'd used it to slay his best friend. He rose and in one fluid motion hurled the sword hilt. The ruined weapon spun through the air and struck Kril a glancing blow in the head. The sorcerer stumbled, blood gushing. Concentration shattered, the eerie fire in his hand sputtered and went out. He staggered a few feet and then went to his knees in front of the open window. The wings extended as if of their own accord.

Kril reached out with an uncertain hand, caught the edge of the window and began to pull himself up to his feet. Wiping blood from his eyes, he looked back over his shoulder. His eyes gleamed a viscous black. His lips, blood red, parted to reveal yellow teeth.

"Dead now slain by brother's hand, no grave shall hold thee in this land—"

Glaston lurched to his feet, caught up his battle axe.

"—power mine to life thee give. Rise and walk, for you now live!"

Rorvik's corpse began to twitch.

The axe whistled end over end across the room and cleaved off one outstretched wing. Kril threw back his head and howled at the ceiling. The bloody wing flopped on the floor for a moment, then suddenly was no more. It simply vanished, gone so fast Alaric wasn't sure it had ever been there.

As Kril screamed, Rorvik's corpse fell still, whatever foul incantation remained to complete the spell abruptly cut off with the inhuman wing. Kril's other wing also vanished. Then he lowered his head again and opened his bloodshot eyes—and met the anger-twisted gaze of Alaric mac Cullen.

The King took a handful of Kril's dark robes and shoved him back against the window ledge. Kril struggled. One claw-like hand flailed at the stone window facing, the other dived into the dark robes for a weapon. Alaric caught his wrist as it emerged with a jeweled dagger. Kril pushed with all his strength, striving to drive the blade into his opponent's side, but Alaric held him fast.

Alaric turned the dagger in Kril's hand until the tip of the blade lay against the sorcerer's stomach.

"Alaric. Wait, I—"

"There's no' a thing you could say," Alaric interrupted.

Kril screamed as his own dagger slid into his gut. He screamed again when Alaric twisted the blade. Then Alaric shoved him backward, and Kril screamed all the way to the ground. There was a sickening slap when Kril hit the rocks below, then silence throughout Gairloch Crail. Alaric looked out and down once, by no means certain he'd slain the sorcerer until he actually verified it with his own eyes. Nordric Kril lay spread-eagle on the scattered rocks below, silent crimson trickles tracing lines in the dust about him.

Alaric went back to his friend, removed the weapons that had stolen his life, and then gathered him in his arms.

Silently, the Dunbartons in the doorway parted for him and Glaston. They carried their friend several hundred yards out from Gairloch Crail, away from the aggravated ghosts that haunt those shattered walls. With his bare hands, Alaric scooped out a shallow grave while Glaston watched, knowing not to offer assistance.

When the grave was finished, they gently added the body, then covered him with rocks to keep away the predators. Behind them, at the base of the tower, the gulls had already found Nordric Kril. Their lonely cries echoing over the ruins and the soft solemn roar of the sea below were the only sounds as the king wept for his dead friend.

"I told you no' to follow me."

Glaston tossed aside the last piece of his battered armor and stood hugging his arms against aching chest and ribs. "I ne'er was very good at following orders. You know tha'."

Alaric made no comment, just stood looking down at Rorvik's cairn. The stones were all small, untouched by the fires that had brought down Gairloch Crail; they'd been careful to gather them all well away from the castle ruins.

"I figured it safe if we followed far enough behind you."

Alaric let out a long sigh. "Just as well. Were it no' for your interference, I'd be dead."

"Aye. And *tha'* I couldna live with." Glaston started toward the waiting soldiers. "Let's go home, my king. You can ride double with me."

"You havena asked how he died."

"What?"

"You havena asked me how Rory died."

"Kril killed him."

"I killed him, Glaston."

"I dinna understand."

"Nor do I. I only know by reacting as Kril predicted I would, I slew the man who had been a brother to me."

The old soldier lay a hand on his King's shoulder. "Let's go home. We'll sort it out there."

"No. I canna go back, Glaston."

"But—"

"I can no'. It'll kill me, old friend. What scares me is tha' Kril and I are too much alike, both products of our ambition. Lust for power and revenge forged the monster we just slew. Likewise, my desire for peace and comfort have made me what I am. I have grown soft. It's only by going back, by finding what Rory left to find, that I can find myself again. What remains of my life is the only legacy I have for Rory. I must finish the things he set out to do."

"Then I'll come with you!"

"No. I need you to go back and make sure there's an orderly and fair transition of power. See tha' the crown's passed on to someone worthy of it and tha' the people accept the successor. When things have settled down, you can follow if you like. I shanna be tha' hard to find."

"But where will you go?"

They spotted him first as he scaled down the steep cliffs. More alarming than the one man's descent was a line of horsemen that appeared on the cliff's edge. At this distance, it was impossible to tell, but they looked to be uniformed soldiers.

For a time, they stopped loading their timber and watched.

"Comin' down from tha' tower, 'e is," one of them commented.

"I'll no' be trusting 'im then."

The first mate shoved them back toward the long boat they were supposed to be loading. "Back to work, or I'll be feeding the both of you to the sharks."

Then the mate set to watching the stranger's descent.

It took forty minutes to reach bottom. When he did, he crossed the beach without hesitation. As he approached through the loose sand, the mate studied him carefully. The stranger was a big man with unbound hair of black and grey. There was blood in his hair and on his face. He moved like he was more accustomed to a horse than a ship.

Near as the mate could tell, the stranger carried no weapons.

The mate set his hand purposely on the heavy falcata at his belt and nodded toward the tower. "You came from up there?"

"Aye."

"We've seen strange things these past few evenings from up there."

"You'll be seeing no more."

The mate didn't catch the meaning in that. "True enough," he said. "We'll be pulling out after a few more loads."

"Name's Kilbearn. Where're you bound?"

"That'd be the business of our cap'n."

"Pirates?"

The mate grinned, showing blackened teeth. "You've a problem with tha'?"

"None."

"Friends of yours?" the mate asked, indicating the line of horsemen on the cliffs.

"They followed me out of Dunbarton," Alaric answered without looking back. "King's guard."

The mate arched an eyebrow. "You've enemies in high

places, friend." He stepped closer, hand still on the hilt of his weapon. "Truth be known, we lost several men 'fore we put in 'ere to make repairs. Know anything about the sea?"

"No' a thing. But I can learn."

"Perhaps," the mate sneered. "We'll see. But know now tha' if you dinna learn, there's no turning back. We'll toss you o'er the side."

"Fair enough."

The mate leaned close. He reeked of brine and dead fish. "And wha' I say is law. I'm the first mate."

Alaric smiled. "Aye."

Time enough for you, Alaric thought. *And after you, your captain.* A salt breeze tossed his hair as he looked past the first mate to the long, shallow currach sitting on the turquoise sea— and beyond the ship, to a new horizon.

IVORY IN THE BLOOD

Gerek heard their approach. The tranquil morning air distinctively carried the sounds of warharness and armor, yet he rose and went to the yard unarmed. Though he had lifted no weapon in more than eight years, it still felt uncomfortable to greet any visitor thus. More so with visitors such as these who were obviously not interested in good fellowship and ale.

The riders drew to a halt, destroying much of the yard he had worked so hard to cultivate. One horse sidestepped into the flower bed, trampling the flowers Aelfraeda had planted years ago. The rider forced the horse back to the yard, doing more damage than if he'd held his ground. Once they were stopped, the nearest just short of trampling Gerek where he stood, there was an eerie silence soon broken by the lead rider. His voice was powerful, stern, and direct. Even the horses stood fast while his breath smoked in the morning mist.

"If Gerek ap Aodhan be your name, then I have business with you in the name of Owein Skaga, Lord of Caer Glas."

Gerek braced himself, knowing full well the type of man he baited. "I speak with no man through helm, nor with whom I know not."

The mounted warrior's hand went immediately to the longsword at his side; habit, that much Gerek could tell. This was not a man accustomed to belligerence. For but a moment, mail gauntlet rested on hilt, then he seemed to retreat somewhat in the saddle. The hand left the sword and went to the visor.

The faceplate lifted with no sound at all; a man who cared for his armor, or one who could afford new when he chose, or one whose armor had never seen the outdoors. Gerek ruled out all save the first when he saw the steel grey eyes of his visitor. This was a man of war. Moreover, this was a man who had *seen* war. And perhaps something else as well; there was a weariness back of those grey orbs that went beyond mere bloodshed on the battlefield.

"I am Rhys, Commander of Lord Owein's armies. I've been sent from Caer Glas to find ap Aodhan, he they call the Dragonslayer."

"If it's the slaying of dragons you're after, then you've come to the wrong place."

Leather creaked and the warhorse snorted as Rhys swung down from the saddle. "Are you, or are you not, Gerek ap Aodhan?"

"I am he."

Riders shifted in the yard, nigh twenty men flanking left and right as if they thought he would attempt something. Gerek was both amused and annoyed to learn that his reputation was animate even after an eight-year lapse. Rhys reached up with both hands and completely removed his helm. Bracing it under his right arm, he crossed the short distance separating them and offered his left hand in greeting.

The left hand, leaving the right free to draw sword or longknife. These thoughts passed through Gerek's mind like recollections of old friends. Gerek chose to ignore the offered hand, both to bait the man, and because a handshake through the mail gauntlet irritated him as much as talking through the helm. Rhys withdrew the hand and retreated a step. *Sword's reach,* Gerek thought to himself.

"It would appear that legends leave out details such as rudeness," Rhys remarked sourly.

"You've not come for my hospitality," Gerek fired back. "You bring men of war. Men who have obviously failed at something you hope I will succeed at."

Rhys frowned. "Direct then?"

"No other way."

"We have a problem at Caer Glas—"

"Obviously."

"—for which we require your unique talents."

"Have the peasants finally risen against your tyrannical Lord?" Though Gerek had never met Lord Owein, he had ample experience in dealing with feudal lords. There were exceptions to the rule, but most were pompous and unjust, supported by the peasants unlucky enough to fall within their domain.

There was a shuffling of weapons and several curses from the warriors in their semi-circle of steel. Tyrant or not, they were loyal to this man Owein. Perhaps Gerek's arrow had flown off target with that remark.

Rhys surprised him completely by laughing. "You don't leave many outs for yourself, do you, Dragonslayer? Once you've done with insulting us and our Lord, we'll be ready to kill you if you refuse to help. As it stood before, you might have had some chance of refusing us and keeping your head on your shoulders."

Gerek swallowed that and realized eight years of peaceful solitude had yielded an appreciation for life. "Ask, then."

"No," Rhys responded. "Lord Owein requests your presence. Whatever aid is asked of you, he will ask it. Get what you need."

Gerek shrugged. "I need only the clothes on my back."

"I think not, Dragonslayer."

"What then?"

"Whatever weapons and armor you'll need."

Though he knew, and had known since the sound of their approach had echoed up through the canyons, Gerek asked anyway. "What weapons?"

Rhys smiled. "Why, whatever weapons you use to slay a dragon."

It loomed dark in the distance, a towering, malignant structure. Grey Castle. Caer Glas in the Celtic tongue. Visible for an hour before they actually reached its gates of black iron.

"Don't see how a dragon could bother you much in there," Gerek remarked to his companions.

"It's not us it's bothering," Rhys answered. "It's the peasants."

Score another one for this Lord Owein, Gerek thought to himself. *He cares about his serfs. Aelfraeda, my love, how have I become so cynical over the years?* Of course, there was no answer; she'd been dead nearly two years now. Sometimes, he still caught himself talking to her.

Behind him, the wagon creaked as it hauled his weapons and armor. Rhys had insisted that the gear be hauled in a wagon they had brought. Armor, sword, and lance had all been retrieved from their resting place beneath the floor of Gerek's house. Rhys' men had been adamant that Gerek not have the opportunity to touch anything. Despite their curiosity, Rhys had seen to it that none of his own men had opened the oilskin-wrapped items.

At the castle, Rhys was hailed from above and, once identified, the gates swung open and an iron portcullis was hauled up. Gerek remarked on the castle's defenses.

"There was a time when we saw many wars in these valleys, Dragonslayer. There's been peace for the last five years, but we don't lessen our vigilance." Gerek made no comment and Rhys continued, "Caer Glas has withstood four different sieges since it was built."

"And one dragon has you at a loss?"

"It's hard to fight something that moves only at night and lives beneath the ground."

"Then you know of its lair?"

Rhys drew his horse to a halt in a courtyard, ignoring the question. Stablemen rushed forward to take both their horses. Gerek noticed the soldiers took care of their own mounts. He awarded them some small measure of respect for that.

Dismounting, Gerek patted the horse's neck. It was a good, strong warhorse; no Riagan, but a good horse all the same. He longed for the companionship of his old friend nearly as much as he longed for Aelfraeda. However, Riagan wouldn't be needed this time, since Rhys obviously knew of the dragon's lair. This would be no mounted charge in the open. It would be your typical cave encounter: go down, find dragon, irritate it enough to get it to charge, brace lance, and let it do the rest, while you hoped and prayed your armor withstood the heat. Later, burnt and blistered, he'd take the head up for the people.

It took a minute before Gerek realized he was suddenly

thinking in terms of actually fighting this dragon. Why? Years ago, he hid his weapons beneath the floorboards of his cottage and retired. *Keep your wits about you, old son,* he told himself. *You're too old and much too soft for this kind of work.*

"This way," Rhys interrupted Gerek's thoughts.

Gerek followed him through an archway, across a smaller courtyard, and from there up a series of stone steps leading to Lord Owein's audience chamber. Owein had evidently been told of their arrival, for he was waiting. He rose and extended his hand to Gerek. Gerek surprised himself by taking it. Owein was a strong, amicable looking fellow, not at all the tyrant Gerek had envisioned Caer Glas would produce.

Gerek decided it was time to make amends. "M'lord Skaga, I am Gerek ap Aodhan. How may I be of service?"

"Please sit over here and I'll have wine brought in. You must be thirsty after the ride." Owein led him to a large table to one side, away from the formal audience area. "Rhys, send the wine in on your way out."

Rhys frowned at the dismissal, but left all the same. Gerek and Lord Owein seated themselves at the table. "A loyal man, Rhys Breandan, but he has failed to deliver in this matter. Oh, not for want of trying, mind you; I have no complaints."

The wine was brought in by an older woman dressed in simple, but sturdy clothing. She poured for them both, serving Gerek first. He waited until she had left before repeating his question to Owein. "M'lord, I was brought here under some duress. I must insist that you explain."

Owein took one long drink of his wine, leaned back in his chair and began. "Three months ago, there was a tremor in the foothills east of here. Those tremors unearthed something. Perhaps it had been waiting there for many years to escape, or perhaps the avalanches that followed the quake simply awoke it. I've heard tales about them hibernating for centuries." He looked Gerek dead in the eyes. "We are speaking, of course, of a dragon."

"Eight years ago," Gerek replied, "I scoured the land in search of dragons. Your own father was one of the half dozen or so men who funded the search. I found nothing. At the time, we were convinced there were no dragons left."

"And you retired, the last of the dragonslayers."

"By that time, the only dragonslayer who had lived to retirement."

"The evening following the quake, several farmers reported missing cattle. We assumed it to be thieves. The thefts went on. A week later a young peasant woman disappeared. Days later, a shepherd and half his flock vanished. It continued, with Rhys and his men investigating every step of the way. In time, they laid traps and eventually one paid off; it came."

Gerek saw it in his mind, not Rhys and his men specifically, but others who had set traps for something they didn't understand. They staked out cattle or sheep, with the men trying to remain hidden, but oh so visible to an airborne beast with hawk-like vision. They would be bored, for this would not be the first night they had watched the trap. Nor would it be the first night the dragon had watched them. It would know the trap on first sight and it would wait, knowing the nature of man from eons of watching him evolve. In the dark mist of early morning, the dragon would strike from the air, killing those who didn't flee quickly enough. Sure, they would fight, but with weapons they used on other men: crossbows with quarrels that would bounce from reptilian scales and swords whose edges were meant to turn other blades. Better to fight him with a skinning knife that would at least scratch the hide, than bludgeon him with a blade meant to pound armor. The dragon would feed that night on human flesh, ignoring the tethered bait. How many times had he heard such tales? Had his fee ever been exorbitant enough that they need try it on their own?

Owein seemed to sense that Gerek knew what had happened and didn't go into the details of their failure with the trap. "Less than half escaped that night. Rhys' own brother was among those slaughtered. For him, it's been a personal battle ever since. A vendetta that has paid off, for Rhys followed it back to its lair."

"Forgive me if I seem skeptical, Lord Owein, but that is not an easy thing to do. No horse I've ever seen can keep up with a dragon in flight."

"This dragon doesn't fly. It is old, so old that the wings

have atrophied. I've never seen anything so huge—yes, I was there that night and I saw it. Nor would I have ever thought something that big could move so fast."

"They will surprise you," Gerek patronized.

"No, I've seen others. I even saw you slay one about sixteen years ago. You hunted it for Lord Daren of Cornwall. I was among those who watched from a distance when you ran it down. The Dragon of Cornwall could have sat with ease upon our dragon's knee."

Gerek wanted to laugh, but couldn't. "Surely you jest, M'lord. I recall the encounter, unique in the fact the dragon chose to fight in daylight, thus providing theater for hundreds, yourself among them. But that was a mature dragon. Hell, the beast was so big and brown he would have been mistaken for a fair-sized hill had he gone to ground somewhere. That was no small green I slew in Cornwall that day."

Owein swallowed the last of his wine. "I know. Cornwall's dragon must have gone—what, three rods? Our dragon is nearly twice that long."

Gerek said nothing, setting his empty goblet aside. Owein continued. "Rhys and thirty men tracked it to its lair. Rhys and twenty of them went down after it. Hours later Rhys came out, dragging two wounded. The rest perished. It was then we sought you."

"I can tell you what I know of slaying such beasts, Lord Owein."

Owein seemed not to hear him. "I want you to kill it. We have checked; you are the last man alive who knows their weaknesses. You are the last with the skill to meet it and succeed."

"M'lord, for more than eight years, the battles I have fought have been in my garden. I am an old man. Dozens of old wounds prevent me from moving freely before mid-day. I cannot go in there after your dragon."

"Then we are lost. We have encountered the last dragon, but there is no last dragonslayer after all." Owein half rose from his seat. "Must I show you what's left of those who've fallen to this nightmare? Is it the money? Name your price, man! I'll pay anything for the safety of my hold and people!"

Gerek ran his finger idly around the rim of his empty wine goblet. His mind drifted again and he saw other meetings, meetings where fees had been discussed long before anyone cared where the dragon was or what the dragon had done. Meetings where princes and barons seeking adventure had hired him to simply hunt down a dragon. Never mind whether the dragon had ever done anything. It was game, like a deer or fox, and Gerek had served as huntsman more often than he cared to recall.

But here was a man struggling to protect his people.

Here was a dragon rumored to be nearly twice the size of any Gerek had ever encountered.

Here was a dragon that had gone from slaughtering cattle and sheep for food to killing peasants.

Here was the last dragon.

And here was the last man alive who had ever slain one.

The wagon creaked to a halt, and Rhys pointed up to a crumbled ridge. "There," he said. "Look to the right of that fallen spire. See it?"

Gerek forced back an involuntary shudder. Dragons like the entrances to their lairs to be tight fitting. He'd seen dozens of them that had piled rocks around the entrances until they could just barely squeeze through. They did this to make their lairs easier to defend. If this one followed suit, then it was one hell of a big dragon, easily twice the size of the Dragon of Cornwall, as Owein had said.

"I see it."

Rhys jumped down from the wagon. "Let's get started."

Gerek looked back at him and frowned. "One thing needs to be made clear now or I stay in this wagon. I'm going in there after that ugly brown bastard. Alone."

Without answering, Rhys dropped the tailgate on the wagon.

"Do we have an understanding?"

"Yes," Rhys mumbled. "But one thing you should know. He's gold, not brown."

Gerek swallowed that with everything else he'd heard about this extraordinary last dragon. Everyone knew young dragons were green. What they looked like at birth was anyone's guess since no one had ever managed to track down a lair with young. It was assumed from studies made on the reproductive organs of dead dragons that they were egg layers. Gerek had always dreamed of finding a cache of dragon eggs. It had never happened. As the dragon matures, the green eventually darkens and becomes a rusty brown. The brown eventually reaches the color of rich mud in the mature dragons of about three to four rods in length. Or at least in what Gerek had always assumed was a mature dragon. Perhaps with age, the brown faded to gold. Perhaps adolescent dragons were all mankind had encountered. Until now.

The dragonslayer swung down and joined Rhys at the rear of the wagon. Rhys handed him the longest of the oilskin-wrapped packages which had been hauled from Gerek's home in the mountains. Gerek unwrapped it.

The lance was longer than any Rhys had ever seen before, measuring a half rod or more. The package had been deceptive since the lance was wrapped as two pieces, shaft and blade. The blade itself was eight hands long. Rhys watched as Gerek mounted the head over the shaft and then inserted pins to hold it in place. The pins took some hammering, for which they used Rhys' dagger. When the lance was assembled, Gerek extended it to Rhys and the Caer Glas Warlord took it in reverent hands.

"Not the sort of weapon one would carry into battle," Rhys commented as he felt the slender blade. "Any heavy weapon would shatter this blade. Why's it so thin?"

"Feel the edge."

Rhys ran his finger carefully over the edge and yelped. "Sharper than anything I've ever seen before. Can't even touch it without cutting myself."

"A dragon's hide is scales, tougher than your own armor. This blade is razor sharp and thin enough to slide through those scales and find its heart. You get one chance, one thrust. If the blade turns, or shatters, or misses its heart, you're a dead man. With one claw, it'll crush you like a bug, or those mighty jaws will lock around your body and bite you in half. Or, if it's feeling particularly playful, it might just roast you alive. Most dragonslayers died because they missed with the lance."

"This is long enough to reach its heart?" Rhys asked, indicating the eight-hand blade.

Gerek frowned. "It's long enough to kill any normal size dragon. As for our overgrown friend in there..."

Next, the dragonslayer unwrapped his sword and withdrew it from its plain leather sheath. Like the lance, it was different from anything Rhys had ever seen. The blade was wider than that of even the stoutest broadsword. Very thick and heavy in the center, the blade then tapered down to the thinnest, sharpest edge imaginable. Gerek slid it back into the sheath. "Your own weapon would shatter the edges of this blade if I were to attack you with it. It was ridiculous of you to keep me from them when we left my home."

"I had no way of knowing."

"No matter. I like a man who takes every precaution when confronting the unknown." Gerek handed the sword to Rhys. "Careful if you unsheathe it. That blade is made for cutting a dragon's neck."

Gerek continued to unwrap the rest of the packages. They proved to be armor not much different from Rhys' own, albeit heavier by about 40 pounds. There were other subtle differences: like the double visor, the inside one being slotted for vision, while the outer was solid to protect the eyes. Or the hooks on the inside of the greaves, which Gerek explained were used to cling to a dragon in battle. As he suited up, the dragonslayer explained other differences to Rhys Breandan. Rhys didn't realize it, but what he was watching, no one would ever see again.

Armored, Gerek ap Aodhan belted the sword about his waist. Though he was a tall man, the tip of the blade nearly reached the ground. He took the lance from Rhys, collected a torch from a pile of them in the wagon, and looked up the hill. "Do not follow me in, Breandan, no matter what you hear. Understand?"

Rhys nodded. With the hilt of his dagger, he struck a spark

from a piece of flint, lighting Gerek's torch.

"If I don't come out, either we have slain each other, or it has won. Probably the latter. Your best bet then is to try and seal the cave." With that, Gerek ap Aodhan turned and began the short ascent to the entrance of the dragon's lair.

He remembered the first time he had stood thus before a dark cavern's entrance. He had been nine years old and with Aodhan, his father.

"Son, what I do now, I do for the sake of those townsfolk back there. Never think there is any glory in this profession. I don't do it for fame; and, as you well know, I only charge enough that you and your mother may live comfortably. There's an evil on this Earth, son, and we've been given the power to remove it." The tall Celt had looked down at the youth that just barely topped his waistline. "I know you don't understand, son. But that creature down there is one of the devil's minions. It's my duty to destroy it."

Aodhan had emerged from that lair, dragging behind him the severed head of a rather small brown dragon. He'd rolled it down the hill to the waiting townsmen, who'd stared at it in terror as if it still had some power over them. Then their stares had gone from terror to awe as they looked up the hill to their deliverer.

Gerek tried to recall how many times he had stood before the entrance to a dragon's lair since that first time. He couldn't. This time was only marginally different. The dragonlance was clutched in his left fist and the dragonsword hung at his side. The differences? There was no Riagan waiting below to carry him home. And there was no Aelfraeda to dress his wounds when he got there.

Both visors were up and he felt the wind on his face. He smelled flowers nearby. What was it that his father had once told him?

"Son, every time I go down into one of those holes, I think what a fine day it is to die."

He had never been sure what his father meant by that until the first time he had gone down alone. Before he went down, he had stood, tasting the windborne essence of life, and understanding had come in a rush. It was indeed a good day to pass from this world to the next.

Lance and sputtering torch held out before him, Gerek ap Aodhan entered the lair of the last dragon. There had been times when he had to take the lance down in parts, but not this time. There was plenty of room. This was an immense opening.

The damp dark of the lair enveloped him.

The great head rises from its resting place on the stone floor. Golden eyelids go up, revealing emerald orbs. The dragon's eyes scintillate in the glow from the cavern's natural skylight. The tail thrashes in irritation, then is abruptly still. Nostrils flare, emanating wisps of sulfureous smoke that curl languidly in the still cave air.

He has come.

Though it has felt fear before, the dragon feels none now. This is destiny. The dragon has been awaiting this moment for a decade.

Minutes later, the dragon can hear him as well as smell him. For a human, he moves with incredible stealth; yet he is only a man, and an armored one at that.

A long, forked tongue lashes out and a few drops of liquid flame bespatter the nearby rock. The dragon rises on silent feet and turns to face the cavern's southern entrance. Here the cavern meets a natural tunnel. The walls are covered with dried blood and the cave is littered with dented metal, remains of those who came hunting before.

This man is different.

He is not the first. Others of his calling have met this dragon on a variety of battlegrounds. All those are dead. This man is the last. Fate has brought them together at this point in time. A predestination set in motion when first their races met and exchanged blows.

The final confrontation has come.

Warm air rose to meet him. After a few moments of descent, he lowered the first of the helm's visors. The air was moist. Perhaps a natural spring lay somewhere deep beneath the surface, kept warm by that which swam in it.

It waited.

Somehow, he knew it was aware of him, even when he was sure the sounds of his approach had not yet reached it. There was a sensation within him that he had never felt before. As he was sure the dragon was aware of him, he was just as aware of it.

The dark tunnel twisted and turned, yet he had no trouble navigating it in the dark. He felt as if he could as easily have tossed aside the torch. It was as if he had passed this way before.

With a shudder, he realized it was somehow calling him. The dragon, not he, had passed this way many times, knew every turn in the dim passageway. But was it guiding him, or was he somehow one with the beast that waited?

There was a sound from below, something reptilian sliding across rock and the click of claws. It had turned to face him.

How did he know this?

A gust of hot air against his face, and he knew it wasn't far away. A few more turns, he would meet the maw from which that foul breath issued. His foot rocked something metal. He looked down to find a battered breastplate. Beneath it lay a halberd, shaft broken. The halberd was unbloodied; the same could not be said of the breastplate.

The next turn in the passageway brought him to what was a small alcove to the lair and the scene of a massacre. Strewn about the cavern were the battered remains of armor and the blackened bones of a score of warriors.

Now visible was the last turn. Around that, he knew the dragon lay in wait. He could feel its breath wafting around the bend. The walls ahead reflected lambent fire that did not originate from his torch. He knew it was laughing.

Laughing? Why?

Gerek dropped the torch and gripped the lance firmly in both hands. Did the dragon know something about this predestined encounter that he did not? For a moment, he had the strangest feeling that he had been here before. This was a cavern he had walked more than once, maybe not in this life, but in a myriad of others. He had turned that corner before and it had always been the same.

He would turn the corner...

Move forward, just place one foot ahead of the other.

...with the lance extended and ready...

One hand ready to drop the second visor to shield his eyes if need be.

...coming face to face with the dragon, golden nostrils flaring and emerald eyes penetrating to the core of him and...

Turn the corner.

...the dragon would say:

"And so, he has arrived."

Gerek braced the butt of the lance. The sense of deja vu had left him, and he was now in his element. *Charge*, he bid the golden monstrosity before him. But the dragon rested casually, tail curled around and over its forelegs, content to see what the intruder would do. This was unlike any lair encounter he had experienced before. Typically, dragons attack upon invasion of their domain. It was this characteristic which all dragonslayers used to their advantage: the charge, the braced lance, the impaled dragon, and then the hacking with the sword.

This dragon followed none of the norms. And what's more, it had talked to him!

"Welcome, Gerek ap Aodhan."

He lowered the lance and raised the helm's visor. "You know my name," he stammered.

"The last dragonslayer. How could I, the last dragon, not know of you?"

"You knew I was coming."

"Before you did, human," the dragon replied.

"And you know why I've come?"

"Better than you do, human."

Gerek ignored the cryptic answers and chose instead to examine both the dragon and the cavern in which it rested. Both were huge, but there the similarities stopped. The cavern was dark, black igneous rock born of fire. The dragon was gold, aureate brilliance born of sunlight.

The worm was indeed bigger than any he had ever seen, easily measuring the six rods attested to by Lord Owein. As Owein had said, the wings were atrophied. If this dragon could fly at all, it would be for short distances only. The head was a broad triangle, horns of silver, eyes of emerald, and fangs of ivory that dripped a liquid conflagration. The dragon's pupils were pools of tenebrous gloom. Its claws were penumbras ebony, worn little by the rocky cavern floor.

The cavern itself had two points of access: the tunnel at Gerek's back and another, similar opening, which lay beyond the dragon. Roughly circular, the cavern measured approximately 20 rods in diameter. Room for several more dragons—even ones this size. Gerek, however, had his hands full with just one.

He realized he'd been gawking for several minutes while the dragon waited patiently. Where was the demon he had come to slay? Where the beast his father had raised him to fear and hate? "I ... don't understand," was all he found to say.

"You've come to slay me," the dragon responded bluntly. "What don't you understand about it?"

Sweat trickled down his back. It was hot in the lair, and the armor was becoming damn uncomfortable. He decided to be more assertive and took a firm grip on the lance. "You've overstepped your bounds, worm! Cattle and sheep are one thing, but the peasants are something else."

"Ah, the farmer's daughter that disappeared."

"And the young shepherd—"

"Who can tell you more about her whereabouts than I'll ever be able to."

"What do you mean?"

The dragon sighed, causing Gerek to jump as flames sputtered forth. They splashed harmlessly to his left, though, and he was left somewhat embarrassed for his reaction. Lance lowered again, he listened to the dragon's answer.

"Why was it so easy to steal sheep from that young shepherd?" The dragon did his best impression of a human's grin. The attempt, however, was wasted on Gerek. "Because he was busy sneaking off from his flock every night to see the farmer's daughter. The two of them got tired of bedding in the farmer's barn and finally ran off together. Hence their disappearance."

Gerek surprised himself. "Why do I believe you?"

More flame, this time a laugh which even Gerek recognized. "Perhaps before this night is through, you can answer that question yourself."

The dragonslayer looked down at his lance and frowned. *What am I doing here?* He moved to the cavern wall and leaned the lance there, the dragon following his every move. Sweat ran into Gerek's eyes, and he again cursed the armor.

"Take it off," prompted the dragon.

"That'd certainly make it easy," he replied sarcastically.

Again, the strange sound of a dragon's laughter. "If I wanted you dead, ap Aodhan, dead you'd be."

That sank in. This beast was nearly twice the size of the largest dragon Gerek had ever killed, the Dragon of Branwyne. The lance hadn't been long enough to reach that dragon's heart. How could he expect it to reach this one's? There was the dragonsword at his side, but it had barely triumphed over Branwyne's dragon.

Time to decide, he told himself. *Do I hurl myself at this dragon and try to take him with me to hell? Or do I see where all this is leading?*

What would father have done?

And then fast on the heels of that last thought: *Father's long dead.*

He removed the helmet, eyes on the dragon at all times. This set aside, he unbuckled the belt holding the sword about his waist. The sword he unsheathed, pleased as something he judged as nervousness passed through those emerald eyes before he leaned it beside the lance. He sat down then and began the job of removing 120 pounds of armor without assistance. The dragon lay its head across its forelegs and seemed content to watch for a moment, then abruptly it asked, "How many of my kind have you slain?"

Gerek looked up from the greave he was unbuckling. Why the hell was he removing his armor in front of this monstrosity? "Thirty-seven. The last more than eight years ago in the hills of Northaven." Why did it feel like a confession?

"And your father before you?"

"Some say he slew over a hundred dragons in his lifetime. I think the actual figure was around seventy. He never would say." Then, accusingly: "A dragon friend of yours ripped him limb from limb when I was only fifteen." Both greaves off, Gerek set them aside and started on the buckles above his knees.

"There were more of us in those days," the dragon reminisced. "You humans breed like vermin. A dragon takes hundreds of years before he reaches maturity and seeks out a mate. Time was on your side, human."

"We had to protect ourselves," Gerek countered.

"And we had to eat," was the quick reply.

"It didn't have to start as it did. Somewhere, hundreds of years ago, when man and dragon met for the first time, the dragon could have spoken up."

"Was he given the chance?"

"But thirty-seven times I've confronted one of you and not once did a dragon say, 'I think there's been some mistake.'"

"Maybe there was no mistake," the dragon mused. "Maybe our two races were destined to war, mine to lose, and the two of us to meet here, where I guard a treasure beyond belief."

Gerek's eyes darted to the opening behind the dragon. Treasure? It was a myth, a peasant's daydream. Never had he found anything of value in a dragon's lair.

The look did not escape the dragon. "In due time, human." Armor set aside, Gerek sat back against the cavern wall, both more and less at ease without the 120 pounds of steel weighing on his body. If the dragon made its move now, he was a dead man. But had he ever been otherwise? For whatever good it would do him, his sword was within reach, as was the now useless lance.

"You leave today with no weapons, Gerek ap Aodhan," the dragon hissed, reading either his mind or his intentions. "You walk out of here more than a warrior today. More than the slayer of dragons that you were."

"Explain."

Flames of irritation. "When—no, *if*—you leave these caverns, you leave without that armor, without those weapons, without my head."

"All this in exchange for...?"

"The treasure behind me."

Gerek rose to his feet. "Seems I should take a look at this treasure."

The dragon also rose, more movement than Gerek had yet seen from the beast. It didn't move to block his path to the lair's second exit; rather, it seemed to be moving to a vantage point from which it could watch Gerek enter the treasure room.

Gerek realized as he approached the dark entrance that he was now out of reach of his weapons. Small concern, however, since the dragon's movement had effectively cut him off.

He was forced to duck to enter the dark antechamber. As he crossed the threshold, the dragon extended one forelimb and rested a claw the size of Gerek's forearm on his shoulder. "Harm her and you'll not die a quick death, ap Aodhan. That I promise you."

He entered. It was a small cave, lit only with light from the larger chamber reflected by the golden dragon. Shadows concealed everything, and he was about to turn about, when the dragon moved and with it moved the reflected light. A shaft of that golden light fell across the floor, and there she lay, purest white on a cloth of velvet black.

"She's real?" Gerek managed to get out.

At the sound of his voice, she raised her head, dispelling all doubt. Dark eyes met his, and he read some small measure of fear there. He showed her empty hands, glad to be rid of both weapons and armor for this meeting. "Does she have a name?" he asked, eyes locked with hers.

"She hasn't said," the dragon answered from behind him.

"She's beautiful."

"Magic. Stuff of legends, like myself. The three of us are the last of our kinds. You, the warrior of old, born of honor and courage. Life wagered time and time again for the peace and quiet of farm folk and overfed lords. Me, last of a race born ten thousand years before man. Destined in the end to perish at their hands because we are not as prolific. And her, last of a race nearly as old as my own. Cursed by human mythology to be something she's not and to die for it. The last—"

"Unicorn." Gerek scarcely breathed the word, mind still refusing to accept what his eyes saw. They had been legend all his life. He had never believed they existed. Until now.

The foal got to her feet. Coat of purest white, matching hooves, mane and tail the same, long and full, looking just brushed a thousand strokes. Eyes that echoed impenetrable depths, matching black nose testing the air, and a horn that should not, by all laws of nature, be there. This was the treasure that confronted him. She was so small, couldn't be more than a few weeks old.

"Where did you—"

"A story that'll never be told, ap Aodhan. Suffice to say, she was entrusted to me. She is the last."

"What will you do with her?"

"Give her to you."

He spun about to confront the golden face that peered in at him and the unicorn. "Give her to me?"

"That's what I said."

"In exchange for armor, weapons, and your life?"

The dragon laughed, some of the resulting flames coming dangerously close to Gerek's feet. He did not, however, back up for fear of startling the fragile creature behind him.

"I'm changing your life, human. Take this frail creature and do what I cannot. Raise her. Perhaps in years ahead, you'll find a way to curtail her species' extinction. For all I know, she'll breed true with your own horses." The dragon paused. "My life, however, was never part of the bargain. Mine will continue to its own predestined end. Yours, on the other hand, will change. That change precludes the need for those items you've left in my lair. I am giving you a reason to live."

Gerek turned back to face the spindly-legged apparition on the velvet spread. He extended a hand, and she first sniffed carefully, then nuzzled it. Her muzzle was soft and new, bringing unwelcome memories of himself as a child and Riagan, this size, given as a present from his father.

"I'm offering you a chance, ap Aodhan, to right some of the wrongs you have done in your life. Help this creature. Show me your race is more than butchers."

He knelt. The unicorn moved against him. Seconds later, she melted into his arms.

"You'll take her?"

In answer, he enfolded the unicorn in his arms and got back to his feet. "What will you do?" he asked. "Caer Glas is bound to hunt you and—"

A warrior's scream of attack, the dragon turning on claws that tore loose chunks of solid rock, the foal squirming loose to run for the shadows of her small alcove, and the bright flicker of flame in the lair, all seemingly at once. Gerek whirled about so fast, he turned an ankle on loose rock and went sprawling. As he scrambled to his feet, he heard the voice of Rhys Breandan and the roar of the dragon as one.

"Die, worm from hell!"

Rhys had the dragonlance clutched in his hands. Nearby, a discarded torch sputtered hungrily on the rocky ground. He dived at the dragon, not knowing the technique was to set the lance and let the dragon come to you. His aim was true and the lance met the dragon behind the left shoulder blade where one might hope to reach its heart. However, Breandan hadn't counted on the aureate scales of gold. Tougher than any armor, they turned the blow. Rhys, with eighty pounds of armor, crashed into the side of the dragon amidst the flying shards of both blade and shaft.

The dragon whirled and one great foreclaw swept the Caer Glas warrior aside. Rhys flew across the cavern and slammed against solid granite. He hung there against the wall for a second, one gauntlet dropping to clatter to the ground along with several small clasps and such which had torn free of his armor; then he sprawled forward and was still.

Gerek reached the dragon's side, limping on the turned ankle. Dragon blood ran to form a pool at his feet. The lance had penetrated before it shattered. From the amount of broken blade on the ground, Gerek estimated half its length must be in the dragon's side. The dragon turned to look at him, and there was fire in those emerald eyes.

A moan from across the room and Rhys was on his feet. As Rhys drew his broadsword, Gerek saw blood running from mouth, nostrils, and both ears. His helm was dented as if it had been hit with a poleaxe. His visor hung to one side, twisted. Drawing back the broadsword, he lunged at the dragon.

"No!" Gerek screamed, but it was too late. Rhys was in motion and the dragon's mouth gaped, flames smoldering hotter than any hell. No choice, Gerek also moved, rolling under the dragon's belly to reach the dragonsword.

Rhys struck. The blow caught the dragon squarely across the snout. Sparks and blood flew. The dragon roared and Rhys was enveloped in flame. The force of the blast lifted the warrior and hurled him back a full rod, where he landed, somehow on his feet. His screams, as fire consumed those areas not covered by armor, jarred loose stalactites that had hung for thousands of years.

Even as the flames erupted from the dragon's mouth, Gerek struck. The dragonsword bit with a solid *thunk* into the beast's neck and held there. The dragon spun about, snapping the blade, and slamming its head full into Gerek. He saw the shattered sword hilt spinning away just before he struck the cavern wall.

Everything went black.

Sometime later, hours or days he couldn't have said, he felt something nuzzling against his side. He opened his eyes to gaze into those of the unicorn. The side of her white muzzle was streaked with red blood. *Shattered innocence*, Gerek thought to himself.

He rolled to a sitting position, crying out as broken ribs grated together. His head spun. For a moment, he almost went back under; then the cavern quit spinning, and he was able to stay up by leaning on the foal. Vision cleared, he looked upon the carnage.

The mess against the far wall had been Rhys Breandan. A few flames still licked hungrily at the remains. Nearer, lay the dragon. Its head was stretched full upon the cave floor, the emerald eyes watching him intently. From the wound in the neck pumped a river of blood. Gerek discovered he was sitting in the continuously spreading pool of dragon blood. The unicorn's hooves were red with it.

The dragon spoke first. It was no longer the powerful voice to which Gerek had grown accustomed. "Not what I had expected from a dragonslayer of your reputation, ap Aodhan."

Gerek crawled closer, aware of the fact that he'd already be dead had that been the dragon's desire. In moving, he discovered one leg was broken. He moaned with pain, but crawled anyway. The same leg had been broken before.

He reached the dragon's head and surveyed the damage there. The dragon would raid no more flocks. "I—"

"Moved to protect the other man," the dragon said it for him. "Instinct. Even as when I torched him. We are both driven by those instincts. It's the only way both of us have survived to become what we are. The last."

The emerald eyes shifted to the unicorn, which waited, uncertain of her own fate in this haven turned slaughterhouse. "Take her, Gerek ap Aodhan. She has none of the warrior instincts that have allowed both of us to survive."

"Is there nothing I can do for you?"

"Nothing, human. Asking that shows me I've at least changed you from the man who came in here for my blood. Leave me now while I have the strength to seal these caverns behind you. I'll not have the peasants down here after my head when I'm gone."

Dragging the bad leg, Gerek found the largest piece of the spear's shaft and used it for a crutch. Slowly, in great pain, he got to his feet and made his way toward the lair's exit. At the tunnel, he turned back and called for the unicorn. The fragile creature looked to the dragon, and some unspoken communication passed between them. The unicorn trotted through the blood to join Gerek.

Gerek turned to leave, but the dragon called him back.

"Do me one favor," it bade him.

"Name it."

"The others will forget. Humans have never wanted to believe in things of magic—dragons, unicorns, faerie elves—but you know different. Remember me as I was, ap Aodhan."

"I will."

ONE-EYED JACK

(with David Niall Wilson)

John Chance preferred honest work when he could find it. There was somethin' about using his hands for more than shufflin' cards that appealed to him. Blisters were like trophies; aching muscles, sweet memories of youth.

There were other things he could do with his hands—things not so legal, or at least not so innocent, things he'd let slip those many drunken nights I'd had him in my bed—but he'd set those occupations aside as well. I've seen him do everything from sweepin' floors to blacksmithin' to buildin' coffins. Once he even repaired a Gatling gun for Custer's 7th, though that night I had to listen to him curse himself for a damn fool for gettin' so close to the military. Custer never asked how a nameless handyman came to know about Gatling guns. He was more interested in putting plenty of distance between himself and the Indians who'd chased him from the Little Bighorn. Chance said that the 7th were cowards and cornholers and rapists, every one, and that the West would be a lot better off if Sitting Bull or Crazy Horse would take every curly lock from the top of old George Armstrong's head. There was some fear that the Sioux and Cheyenne might hit Golgotha, but they passed us by. Chance said that the black market operating out of Golgotha had been indiscriminately supplyin' both sides of the war for years. Destruction of the town would hurt the Indians as much as it would the whites.

So Chance did odd jobs, earning enough to afford meals, liquor, and, occasionally, me. Because honest work was as hard to find in Golgotha as honest law enforcement, he didn't make much. When Chance's pockets came up empty—as they so often did—and there was no work to be found, he was forced to find a game. Problem was, John Chance's reputation preceded him. Players in a game with Chance never forgot, rarely forgave, and often warned everyone else even remotely connected to the green tables.

But this particular night, there were strangers in town. Maybe they hadn't heard about Chance. Or maybe they had. There were three of them, as mean a lookin' trio as ever blew into Golgotha—and we'd had more 'an our share. Chaps and spurs and the kinda' hats on which daisies might grow with the right amount of watering. The biggest one had a scar that buried most of one eye and revealed the molars on one side of his mouth. His teeth were dog piss yellow and his hair was comin' out at the roots. The other two were uglier. They settled at a table in the Lucky Lady, a table with two empty chairs, and motioned me over.

It was a slow night. I had twenty-five dollars from sellin' old Sam Morton a poke the night before. When they motioned to one of the empty chairs, I figured what the hell ...

That was before Chance entered the saloon.

Most of the saloon fell silent when he swung that one eye around to check the place out. Don't know how he knew the strangers would be waitin'. It was like he could smell 'em from outside, like he'd tracked 'em down by the sound of the double eagles jinglin' in their pockets. Didn't matter. He walked over and made a sort of sweepin' motion at the other open chair. As grand a gesture as any dandy from St. Louis, but it was as out of place in the Lucky Lady as checkered table clothes. Ol' Scarface sneered at Chance, but he nodded, too. They were there to take some money; if they took it from a sissy-boy, that was fine by them. They should've looked closer at John's shoulders, at the way the muscles rippled and played beneath his clean white cotton shirt, before they made such a judgement. John winked at me, and I rolled my eyes. I had any sense, I'd a up an' left right then. Never been known for my brains though.

I saw one of the ugly ones checkin' out John's patch, and I

felt my blood run cold. Didn't do to be mentionin' something like that, not to Chance. Not in a game. Things were goin' to get ugly enough without gettin' him riled.

It was unnerving, that patch. He never acted like he had any sort of handicap, not in anythin' he did. At night, it was as if he was walkin' in daylight. When he looked at me, sometimes, I saw his good eye swing to the side, sort of like it wasn't payin' attention, but I still felt him starin', or someone starin'. I never was sure if Chance and whatever was behind that patch were of one mind.

John took the seat and set his money on the table in neat piles. He was like that. Everything in its place. He smiled around the table, and Scarface started to deal. Straight poker. Nothing wild. Dollar ante. John nodded, but he never took his eyes off that man's hands, and I knew he thought he was about to be cheated.

I never knew what he saw. His smile changed some, though, after that first deal. The ugly men had pairs, each of them. John drew three deuces. I fell short of my straight and folded, happy to be shut of the whole mess. I watched John, no way I could do anythin' else. John put those deuces on the table, but he never reached for that pot. Never twitched. He watched old Scarface, that smile plastered thick over his face, like molasses. Scarface dropped his cards. Flush. He reached slowly for the pot, but he was watchin' John too. Somehow, I realized, he'd cheated. John knew it, the ugly men knew it, and Scarface knew, now, that John knew it. It was a tense moment, let me tell you.

By this time, we'd drawn a crowd of Golgotha locals and drifters. There was Billy and Bobby Dupree, twin brothers that ranched a small spread outside town, "Colonel" Darian Brown, limping around the side of the bar with a full glass of rye and his free hand gripping the snake's head on his old wooden walking stick, and several of the other ladies that frequented the Lucky Lady, upstairs and down. Sarah, Sally, and a tiny little thing with peroxide hair that called herself Fifi. If she was from France, I was the Queen of England, but she could take a poke with the best of us. Like me, they were holding their breath.

Scarface started flippin' the cards slowly through his fingers, shufflin' without glancing down, watching John, and waiting. John Chance met that stare, but he kept his peace. So it seemed. Some things, and some men, are *never* what they seem.

As Scarface went to deal the cards, John said carefully, slowly, enunciating each word like he was in a grammar test, "Around these parts, it's customary to pass the deal around the table."

Scarface cocked one mangled eyebrow, a broken-backed caterpillar there by the cleft some brutal wound had left in his forehead. His buried eye looked like it was about to burst free of the wad of scar tissue and roll out across the table. "That so?"

Chance smiled. "That is, of course, unless you're playing by Missouri rules, in which case, he who wins the hand wins the deal." Chance's words sounded sincere, but his smile told me there was no such thing as Missouri rules. Poker was poker, Missouri or not.

Scarface placed the deck on the table in front of Chance. If he knew Chance was blowing smoke up his ass, his face didn't let it show. "Did I fail to mention the rules? Sorry. Cut?"

John Chance reached out and tapped the top of the deck. "I trust you, sir." I counted my twenty dollars as lost. It generally only took one touch. He didn't even have to be the one doin' the dealing.

"Seven card stud's the game," Scarface announced. "And just for the hell of it, one-eyed jacks are wild."

It was an obvious goad, but Chance only had an eye for the cards. We anted up again and Scarface dealt. Two cards down. One up. Chance's face card was the ace of spades. Mine was the queen of hearts. (But, knowing Chance, I could have told that without looking.) The uglies got deuces. Scarface dealt himself the six of clubs. Everyone but Chance checked their hole cards. Mine were worthless.

"I believe," said Scarface to Chance, "that it's your bet."

"Five dollars."

"Without looking at your cards?"

Chance merely smiled.

Scarface shrugged. "A fool and his money are soon parted."

I called. So did the ugly brothers.

"See your five and raise you ten."

Chance tossed in a ten. Me and the uglies followed along. I was down to five dollars, but wanted to hang on one more round. Chance would give me some of the money back tonight—for services rendered, of course.

Scarface dealt. The ace of hearts joined Chance's ace of spades. The queen of diamonds joined my queen of hearts. The two of diamonds picked up the queen of spades. The two of spades picked up a seven of diamonds. Scarface gave himself the queen of clubs.

"Pair of aces, pair of queens, nada, nada, and a possible flush," Scarface announced. "It remains your bet, One-Eyed Jack."

I winced.

"That is what they call you, isn't it?"

"Sometimes," Chance whispered.

"How the hell did you lose that eye anyway?"

"Five dollars," Chance said, tossing in his money.

"Wasn't cheating at cards, was it?" The two uglies cackled. "Me, I got this—" He ran a dirty finger down the length of his disfigured face. "—fighting the Comanche. You ever fight Indians?"

"Looks like I'm going to be short a few queens," I cut in, "and a girl's got to have money for toilet water." I tucked my last five in my cleavage. "Gentlemen, I am out."

Scarface made a playful grab at the five I'd tucked away, but I leaned back out of reach. "Tha's all right, sweetheart. You'll be hollering for me later … when I'm the only one in this dump with the money to pay you for a poke." He peeled back the corners on his two hole cards, shielding them with his other hand so only I could see. "You aren't the only one at the table coming up short." He had Chance's other two aces.

The first ugly brother looked at his two and his queen, looked at his two hole cards, looked at what money he had in front of him, and tossed his cards into the pot with a grunt. The second ugly threw in his five dollars.

"Raise you twenty," said Scarface.

Chance slid his money into the center of the table with a

quick, fluid flick of his wrist. Scarface never let his gaze slip
from Chance's face, watching like some sort of hawk sizin' up a
mouse for dinner. If Chance noticed, you couldn't'a told it.

Ugly Number Two looked over at Scarface reproachfully,
eyeing the pile of bills he'd already tossed into the kitty, then
turned his cards down. "Done," he said shortly.

"Just you and me," Scarface grinned, his smile turnin'
sneaky.

He flipped up Chance's next card. The jack of clubs. Scarface
smiled. "Looks like your brothers are hidin', Jacky boy," he
crowed.

He flipped the next card onto his own stack. Three of clubs.
Three clubs showing and the ace of clubs in the hole—possible
flush. I wanted to get away from that table pretty badly, 'cause I
knew what was coming, but there was a kind of energy cracklin'
in the air. I couldn't pull myself away. Chance had that one
eye of his locked onto Scarface's two, and it was the damndest
Mexican stand-off I'd ever seen.

"Your bet, Jacko," Scarface said softly.

"Five dollars." Chance replied, refusing once more to rise to
the bait. He was smiling slightly, but otherwise you'd 'a thought
he was asleep. He was that quiet.

"And fifty," Scarface countered.

Chance slid his money in once more, but I could see that his
pile was dwindlin'. It was gonna come to a head soon, one way
or another.

"Heard tell once," Scarface started in, real conversational
like, "of a Cheyenne brave that knew how to play poker."

Chance's one good eye narrowed the slightest bit. The
others might have missed it, but I knew him. I'd seen that look
before, when he was concentrating real hard to sight a plane on
the edge of a coffin, when he was sharpening his knife, when
a couple of Custer's boys had asked him if he'd ever had any
squaw pussy.

"You ever run across such a thing?"

"Deal the cards," Chance whispered.

Scarface shrugged. "Read 'em an' weep, One-Eye," he
barked, tossing the last face card onto Chance's pile. The jack

of diamonds. The two royal faces stared up at Chance, as if mocking him with their twin sets of good eyes. Scarface's smile widened. He tossed his own card casually atop his stack. Another club, the ten. One card short of a flush and he and I both knew about that ace of clubs.

"Looks like you might be in a bit of trouble there, Jacky Boy," he sneered. "Flush is some mighty good cards ... a sight better'n two pair." He talked cards, but when that mean son of a bitch said "pair" he was lookin' straight at Chance's eye patch. I felt a shiver run up my spine, and I thought about just walkin' over to the bar before that last card went down. I thought, and then I sat. Seems I was stuck to that chair good—no hope for it now.

"Five dollars," Chance said softly.

Scarface chuckled. "Sure you wouldn't like to take a look at those two hole cards?"

"I know what they are."

"Magic, eh? The kind an old Cheyenne might teach you if you traded him something of value?"

"What would I have that a Cheyenne would want?"

Scarface only smiled. "Raise you fifty."

Chance counted out what amounted to the last of his money.

"Last card," Scarface announced. "Strongest hand showing always takes the last card face up." When Chance made no reply, Scarface sucked at his yellow teeth and added, "Missouri rules, don'cha know."

The card was the two of hearts.

"Pity." Scarface looked at his own card and set it face down on the table. It hardly mattered what it was, since he already had his flush, but he let me see it anyway, blowing me a little kiss as he did so. King of hearts, mate to the queen still in front of me. "Don't we make a pair, darlin'?"

Chance had to stand up to get at his pockets. He dug around, came up with three crumpled dollars. Quietly, he placed them on the pile in the center of the table.

Scarface grinned so wide, I saw three empty sockets where molars should have been. "I see your three," he drawled slow and deadly, "and raise you—" He made a show of counting what money remained in front of him. "—a hundred and twenty-seven."

Chance was broke.

I had five dollars rolled up nicely in my cleavage and maybe fourteen upstairs in my room. I couldn't help him.

"Looks to me," said one of the uglies, "like someone's a wee bit short."

"Looks to me," echoed the other, "like we got us a forfeit." He said the word "forfeit" like it was some kinda' furry animal he'd drug out of a hole and was about to put a bullet into, as if he'd been wantin' one for dinner all along.

Scarface cocked his eyebrow so that his mangled eye crossed with the other one. It made him look more insane than before with that wild bauble gleaming out from beneath the broken brow. "You got the cash, my one-eyed friend?"

Chance's lips drew tight.

"You know, I like you. And I sure hate to see a man fold with two pair showing like that. I'm gonna make you a deal, Mister One-Eyed Jack. I'm gonna let you trade something for the difference in the pot. How's that sound?"

"Me," I blurted out, unexpectedly. "He already paid me and I was gonna sleep with him tonight. I'll—" I suddenly found myself staring down the muzzle of a Colt. No doubt about it, Scarface was fast. This wasn't the first time I'd stared down the business end of a gun, but this time I was really scared. Scarface looked mean enough to pull that trigger.

"You're gonna be real quiet, whore. Real quiet. There ain't no doubt that I'll be poking you tonight. Hell, the size of this pot, I might just buy a turn for Joe and Shifty here. But right now, right fucking now—" He cocked the gun so that there was no mistaking his intentions. "—you're gonna be real quiet, so we menfolk can finish our business. Understand?"

I nodded very slowly and very carefully.

"Good." He eased down the hammer and set the revolver on the table, his hand casually resting on the handle. The barrel was pointed at Chance.

"Seems maybe I do recall a Cheyenne who liked to play poker," Chance interjected in the silence that had suddenly eclipsed the entire saloon. "Problem was, he wasn't much good at it. He asked me to teach him a few things."

"And what did he give you in return for these poker lessons?"

Chance tapped the eye patch. First time I'd ever seen him touch the thing. Far as I knew, he never took it off, not when we'd made love, not when he'd slept over in my room, not even when we'd bathed together in the creek out north of town.

"Show me."

"Collateral," Chance replied. "The eye patch is collateral."

Scarface frowned. I suspect he didn't know what the word meant. "You show me what's under the patch, I forget about the money you're short. We turn over our cards and somebody takes the lady upstairs for a good time." A sidelong glance told me who he believed would be taking me upstairs.

"We turn the cards," Chance countered. "You win, I show you what's under the patch. You lose, and I keep it on."

"Now what the hell kinda' deal is that?"

"Missouri rules."

"Missouri rules, my ass. You show me—"

"I thought you were certain of your hand."

"Course I'm certain of my hand."

"Then what's the difference?"

"Difference is … Oh hell, one way or the other I'm looking under that fuckin' patch, pretty boy." He cocked the Colt again and aimed it at Chance's head as if he might shoot the damn eye patch off. "You understand what I'm telling you? You want to play this out, we'll do that, but in another minute you're taking that son of a bitch off or I'm putting a bullet through your other eye.

"Are we clear on this?"

"Clear as the Missouri River. Show your cards."

"There ain't but one you need to see." Scarface used his left hand to flip over the ace of clubs and carefully lined up the five dog paws side by side. "Flush beats two pair under any rules." The uglies laughed in unison. Scarface's gun wavered ever so slightly, but did not return to the table top or its holster.

"But one thing it doesn't beat," Jack replied, "Aof is four of a kind." He turned up his two hole cards, which until that moment no one had seen, and laid them beside his aces and jacks.

One-eyed jacks. Both of them.

They all got quiet then. Scarface was starin' at those cards, and you could almost see wheels a turnin' in his head. He was goin' every shade of red, headin' toward purple, like he might explode, but he never moved. His face twitched, right there along the scar tissue over his eye, and his lips were pressed together real tight.

Chance hadn't even looked at his cards. He was watchin' Scarface. He didn't make a move toward that pot either, but he started talkin' real soft. I could tell, even past that twitch, that Scarface was listenin'.

"Looks like I win this one, friend," he said. "I don't play cards for a living, as a rule. Make coffins—that's what I do these days. I was thinking about a bit of wood I got in just last week. It was brought to me by a small band of Cheyenne braves—yellow fir. That's the tree it came from. Yellow fir."

The twitch was becomin' more pronounced, and I saw the uglies backing away from the table. They were listenin' to Chance, but they were watchin' Scarface.

"You holster that Colt," Chance concluded, "and I'll forget you drew it on me. If it remains in my face much longer, I'm going to be fitting you to one of them yellow fir boxes."

Scarface blinked. "Them ain't the cards I dealt you."

"How's that?"

"Them ain't the fucking cards I dealt you!"

"You saying I cheated?" Chance asked softly. "That'd be kinda hard with you doing the dealing and all. Be a tough call to make with you saying you know what you dealt me."

Scarface looked back at the two uglies. "Sumbitch is taking me for a fool, boys."

At that moment, with Scarface's attention diverted back over his shoulder, Chance slapped the Colt out of his hand. Chance moved so fast that I don't believe anyone actually saw him. I know I didn't, and I was sittin' right there next to him. First anyone knew, Scarface's gun just clattered across the saloon floor, somehow not going off, though the hammer had been at full cock. Wasn't a real bright move, though. Maybe Chance didn't think it through. Maybe he was just tired of looking down that Colt's chute. Snake-slippery fast, Joe and Shifty's guns hissed out of their holsters.

"You are one dumb sumbitch," Scarface acknowledged. He reached out and raked in the pile of money. "You're also a cheat. The pot's mine. And that patch is coming off." He motioned back to the uglies. "He don't take it off in the next five seconds, shoot him."

Chance glanced at me and there was real pain showing in his good eye. "Whatever happens," he whispered, "don't look."

"Huh?"

"Don't look, darlin'. You have to trust me on this." I read such a strong mixture of fear and worry reflected there with the pain, that I knew he was serious. If I valued my life, his good eye beseeched me, I must not look when the patch came off.

So I didn't. Oh, I was tempted. At one point I even started to turn my head and I would have looked, but I felt his grip, strong as one of those vices at the smithy's, on the back of my neck. He kept me facing forward. I couldn't even look away as terror rose on the faces of Scarface and the ugly brothers. I could have closed my eyes, but in everybody there lives a gawker. In everybody there rises the need to watch true horror when it's encountered. The child's mangled body caught in the hay bailer, the Indian left squirming on the impaling rod by Custer's 7th, the farmer gored by his own ox, the wagon overturned on the pregnant woman. We all stop and look. We can't help ourselves.

Scarface tried to push back from the table, the money from the pot a sudden explosion of green as it scattered out of his hands. Both uglies fired. I looked later and never found where those slugs went. They didn't hit the table or the floor. They didn't hit the wall behind Chance or the ceiling or the gaudy chandelier overhead. There's only one place they could have gone. Only one explanation why they didn't kill John Chance.

Whatever terror he revealed when he removed that patch, it was a damn sight more powerful than those two lead slugs. It drank them bullets down as surely as it drank the souls from those cowboys' eyes.

I saw them come out. The whole place started shaking, like a thousand drums were bein' pounded at the same time, and there was a rushing sound, like the wind through the trees when a storm sweeps in off the desert. Scarface heard it too, and I could see in his eyes that he wanted to turn around, to search out the sound and its source, but he couldn't do it. He stared at Chance, and then that man started clutching his throat and bulgin' at the eyes. I tried to step back as he lurched forward, falling to his knees, but Chance held me still as stone.

Scarface's head was bulging, like somethin' was a pushin' at it from the inside. His eye popped out like a Walleye'd Pike. I saw something poking through that scar, bursting through that eye, and it was there —whatever essence made him who and what he was—bein' hauled out and sucked into the vortex of force that was spinnin' about the room and robbing me of my breath. It didn't want to come, that thing, but it did, and I managed to tear my eyes to the side to see that the same thing was happenin' to the uglies. Their spirits were being ripped out through their eyes, though they tried their damnedest to drag themselves back in, rippin' and clawin' at their bodies as if the hounds of Hell itself were on their tails. I reckon maybe they were.

There was a snap of energy when those spirits broke free. The howlin' nearly drove me out of my mind with its fierceness. The three of them swirled together, molding into a single bright spot of spirit stuff, and they whirled over my head, wailing and crying and screaming all at once.

And that wasn't the end of it. It wasn't just those three. Colonel Brown, the Dupree twins, Sarah and Sally, they was all drawn in. I saw each of them fighting, clutching at themselves, saw the hell that stood behind me reflected in their terror, and I saw them ripped free and sucked out through their eyes like over-ripe grapes, leaving behind nothing more than empty sacks of skin.

The tears were running down my cheeks, blurring my vision. I felt myself sinking to the floor, felt Jack take me in his arms. Sometime durin' those long moments of darkness and confusion, Jack musta put the patch back on, 'cause there was nothin' but silence when I opened my eyes back on that room. Silence and the muted squeaking of Old Brody the bartender's cloth over a beer glass. He'd never looked up from that glass, though what he'd seen in its reflection I'd wager he'll never forget. Still wasn't lookin' up. Fifi had fainted straight off when Scarface pulled his gun—she never saw a thing. The others were gone. Their flesh remained, but nothing of what had dwelled within it.

Jack turned me to look at him, but I averted my eyes.

"It's all right, Lily," he said softly. "It's all right now."

But it wasn't, and it never would be, and he knew it. I looked up then, catching the pain as it flickered across his face and sank down into depths I couldn't even begin to follow.

I think he needed me at that moment, more than he'd maybe ever needed anyone in his life, but I couldn't meet his gaze. Stiff, unyielding, I couldn't melt into his arms and let him console me. Likewise, I couldn't hold him and try to absorb some measure of his pain. There were eight dead people litterin' the floor of the Lucky Lady, and not all of them deserved to be dead. More importantly, none of them had deserved to die ... that way.

"I'll be seeing you, Lily," he lied, letting me slip away. "It's going to be a long night." His gaze swept the room at floor level. "I've got some coffins to build. Come morning ... come morning, I'd best be moving on."

"Chance, I—"

He pressed a finger against my lips. "Don't say it, Lily. Ain't no use in being sorry for something that can't never be changed. Whether it's in the cards or out on the streets, Fate's a cruel dealer. I've folded my share of friendships, and the best thing to say is always just plain old goodbye."

He let that finger trail back along my jawline and down along the side of my neck. For a moment, I remembered his touch, so knowing and gentle, and I almost asked him not to leave. But then I remembered the cold, still bodies that just moments ago had been living, breathing people.

"Goodbye, John Chance."

He collected the money which Scarface had scattered across the floor, and then he walked out without lookin' back. I never saw him again, but I hear stories about him from time to time. Stories about a strange gambler who never plays a room more 'an once. Stories about the strange things that happen when he touches the cards. Some nights I hear stories about that damn eye patch. On those nights, I curl up under the covers alone and try to remember him the way he was in my bed, the way he was when he was John Chance. I try not to think about that night when he was One-Eyed Jack.

ONE CHANCE IN HELL

A ONE-EYED JACK WESTERN

(with David Niall Wilson)

Slippery McGee shot first. Everybody knows that. Everybody knew the stranger with the eye patch didn't stand a chance, that he was as good as dead 'cause McGee was faster 'n a rattlesnake and twice as mean. Even a ten-year-old dirt farmer's son like me knows that.

Pa told me once how he'd watched McGee shoot an Injun to pieces, taking off his thumbs first so he couldn't work no spells or hold his six-shooter, then whittling away at him with those forty-fives, all the time lecturing about God and consorting with prairie devils and how white men was superior to *all* the colored races: the blacks, the injuns, and "them goddamn stinkin' chinee." McGee shot the Injun through the ankles, snapping the bones so he couldn't get up and run away. He broke his arms with bullets. Shot off his ears and the tip of his nose. Punched holes in his sides. Reloaded several times, says my Pa. Sheriff Cooper watched most all of it, having come out after the first few shots echoed through town. Finally, after what musta been twenty rounds of torture, Cooper just walked over and stared at McGee for a minute, then finally told him, real quiet and cautious like, "McGee, I'm getting tired of hearing that damn Injun screaming. If'n you don't go on and put a bullet in his head and shut him up, I'm gonna have to arrest you for disturbing the peace." So McGee went on and finished the old redskin off. No telling how long he might have gone on like that if Cooper hadn't come out. Ever after that, though, he'd glare at Cooper and kinda finger the handle of his Colt whenever the Sheriff walked by. Cooper avoided him like the plague.

Anyway, it came as a real surprise that Cooper would come out, with McGee there bleedin' in the dirt, that one-eyed stranger standin' over him, and say something I don't rightly reckon I ever heard him say.

"Drop that gun right there. You're under arrest."

See, Sheriff Cooper, he'd been wanting McGee dead for years, ever since McGee decided to make Hades his home. Hard to imagine Cooper arresting the man who'd just done him a favor. Not to mention that Cooper wasn't much better'n McGee (who, by this time, had stuffed his thumb in the hole in his neck and was trying to drag himself over to his gun), and most times he'd shoot a man in the back before he'd arrest him.

All in all, it was shaping up to be a mighty strange day, starting from the moment that stranger walked up and insisted that McGee not hang that drunken Chinee laundryman. McGee only had one response for folks what put their nose in his business.

And McGee shot first. Everybody saw that. Lightnin' fast, his Colt slipped out of that low-slung holster. He was a hip-shooter—that's what my Pa called him anyway, one of them kinds that don't have to aim, just draws and lets 'er rip from the waist. So, his Colt slips out smooth as Mama's butter and barks like thunder, long 'fore the stranger cleared leather. Everybody saw that.

What they didn't see, cause most didn't have the angle, and most had their eyes on McGee—he was somethin' to watch when he drew down on a man, sheer poetry in motion—what they didn't see was what the stranger did. I was watching the stranger. I was watching so's I could see McGee's bullets open him up, so's I could memorize the little dance steps he made when he went backward. (Pa always said, wearing that scornful frown he reserved for such statements, that I was a bit too fascinated with such things. Morbid, he called me, it sounding like a sin.) While the stranger drew his own gun, real slow and purposeful like with his left hand, he was reaching up to that eye patch with his right hand. He flicked it up for just a second—revealing *what*, I can't say, cause his hand blocked my view. McGee's gun barked and that forty-five slug went *somewhere*. (Don't ask me!) And by then the stranger had his own gun out. He raised it to eye level, sighted, and shot McGee right through the throat.

Now the question was whether the stranger was gonna try 'n gun down the Sheriff. Cooper clearly had the upper hand on him, but we'd have all said the same thing about Slippery McGee. The tension hung in the air for only a few seconds, though. Then, with a deft twist of his wrist, the stranger reversed his gun and extended it to Sheriff Cooper. "I'd consider it a personal favor if you'd let me take that Chinese gentleman down from there before you lock me up, Sheriff."

Cooper just stared at him like he was some kinda new bug found a'crawlin' through his eggs. Like me, and everyone else in Hades, it'd been some time since we'd heard someone talk like that. Reminded me of a visit once from my aunt back east.

"Come again?" Cooper finally spit out.

"As you can see, he's balanced rather precariously. If he should slip…"

By this time, McGee had gotten his hand on his Colt and everyone up and down the street started hollerin' to point this out. In his present condition, McGee was likely to start blazing away, stripped of his usual marksmanship, and there's no telling who he'd kill. So Cooper, he snatches the stranger's offered six-shooter, steps around him, and kicks McGee's gun out of his hand. "You just go on and bleed to death now, McGee. I don't want no more trouble outta you."

Slippery McGee tried to say something, but nothing but blood came outta his mouth.

"I was aiming for his shoulder," confessed the stranger.

Cooper frowned at him. "Well, you're a damn poor shot. Now march your ass on down to the jail there 'fore we see how good *my* aim is." He gestured with both his own gun and the stranger's to show he was serious.

"What about the man with the noose around his neck?"

Cooper swore some then, using words my Pa says I gotta

grow into. Then he ordered Milt Branson, the stableboy, and Henry Guthridge, who used to run the general store before the bank foreclosed on him, to get the Chinee down and untie him. "Satisfied?" Cooper asked the stranger, but rather than wait for an answer he gave him a couple stiff jabs in the ribs with them there pistols and started him marchin' toward the jailhouse.

I was supposed to be fetching a roll of bailing twine for my Pa back at the farm and would probably be in for a whupping for being so late, but I followed along. Behind me, the undertaker started measuring Slippery McGee for a box, McGee growling at him and slapping him away with them blood-soaked hands for a few seconds 'fore he decided to go on and die.

The sheriff and the one-eyed stranger disappeared into the jailhouse, and I decided it was worth one of Pa's tannings to find out what was going to happen. McGee was a whole lot less interesting now that he'd quit flopping about. The crowd on Main Street (our *only* street) was already gathering outside the jail. I figgered they'd all be wanting a lynchin', the stranger having murdered a citizen and all—even if it was McGee—but I was wrong.

I heard Mae Belle Rainey mumbling to Preacher Thompson that it shore was a shame they couldn't give ol' One Eye a medal for what he done. I recalled that McGee had made free with Miss Mae Belle's sashayin' hind quarters more than once, and figgered it was personal with her. Then I heard the others. All of them grumbling and calling out for Sheriff Cooper to let that boy go and bring him around to the Silk Slipper for a drink.

Behind me I heard the excited jabber of the Chinee laundryman thankin' the men what hauled him down. I supposed he'd done learned his lesson about overstarchin' a man's shirt, especially one as mean-tempered as McGee. Weren't for that stranger, he'd be the one getting measured and planted today.

I watched the jailhouse door expectantly, but no one came marchin' out. I knew it was time to get to the general store and back home. Pa would want to know what had happened—I just hoped I got past the whuppin' to tell him.

Pa went in to town the next morning, having gotten over my

prolonged absence more quickly than I'd dreamed possible on account of my news that Slippery McGee'd been gunned down. Pa and McGee had a history—not pretty, and not somethin' we talked about. Pa had backed down hard, choosing life over pride one drunk night out at the Slipper. Pa had very nearly turned gunslinger hisself, about a million years afore I was born, but in the end he'd traded in his gunfightin' skills for a farm and Mama. Often's the times he'd told me that any man can be a gunfighter, the kinda man that roams about and don't choose his fights. Pa said a gunfighter's fights are chosen for him. And the only fight worth taking up, he'd say, is the good fight. But I expect he wished he was more'n a farmer that time McGee backed him down. And I know he weren't sad to see him shoveled under. Now it seemed he felt McGee's death deserved another good drunk. To my surprise, he let me tag along. The south fence needed mendin', but somehow Pa seemed to have let it slip his mind.

We rode in through the dust and the silence to find that the crowd had gathered again at the jail. Mae Belle was at the door, arms loaded with platters and utensils, bangin' on that door with her foot. Nothing. No sheriff. No one-eyed stranger. Pa rode right on up to the Slipper, tied off his horse, and walked up to Mae Belle with a grin.

"That one-eyed feller in there?" he called out as he approached, "feller who took down Slippery McGee?"

Mae Belle spun on him, mad enough to spit bullets, and Pa wisely backed away, staring at her like she'd gone crazy—which I figgered she had.

"He is," she spat, "but you wouldn't know it. Sheriff Cooper's had him locked away tighter'n a drum since the shooting."

Pa blinked and thought a bit. I could see him addin' it all together in his head ... murder, Slippery McGee and the line of dead men he'd left behind, Sheriff Cooper. When he was done, I could see it hadn't ciphered any better for him than it had for me. Made no sense. The sheriff should have made that stranger a deputy, not locked him up.

Pa went right up to that door and banged on it hard, a lot harder than Mae Belle had managed, even with her foot. At first nothing happened, but I knew my Pa—and apparently Sheriff Cooper did too. Just when I saw Pa lookin' around for an axe or something else to get after that door, it swung open. Pa stepped back a pace, blinkin' in surprise, and Sheriff Cooper stuck his head out, frowning.

"What do you want, Wilbur Morris? And you, Mae Belle, what in Hell's name is all of this nonsense?"

Pa wasn't backin' down this time. "You let him go now, Cooper," Pa said, loud enough so's I reckon everyone in Hades could hear him. "You let him go."

"Man murdered a citizen of our town," Cooper replied, not dropping his eyes from Pa's gaze. "Figger to take him 'fore the county judge tomorrow morning."

"Figgered wrong," Pa said matter-of-factly.

The crowd was moving forward all ugly like, and I could see that the Sheriff wasn't too happy about it, but he held his ground, opening the door enough to let everyone see the sawed-off he was sporting for the occasion. "I have a job to do," he grated, voice rattlesnake soft and hard. "I mean to do it."

"You ain't done your job in a month of blue moons," Mae Belle shrieked, stompin' her foot. She had a head of steam, now, and I reckoned, if'n I was the Sheriff, that I'd have gotten clear. "You let McGee do whatever he wanted 'round here, and now he's stopped—no thanks to you. You let that Godsend go!"

"That's right," someone in the crowd yelled, "God sent that stranger to Hades!"

"God sent him to set us free from the likes of Slippery McGee!"

"Let him go!"

Sheriff Cooper just shook his head, muttering 'bout how God hardly needed a one-eyed gambler what can't shoot straight to do his dirty work. Then he ducked back inside, and we all heard the grating of the bolt as he flung it tight on the far side of the door. It got real quiet for a minute then—real quiet. Pa grumbled as to how he was going to the Slipper to do some thinking. Most of the other men were already heading in that direction. I reckoned it was gonna take a considerable bit more liquoring 'fore they were fired up enough to actually do anything.

I took that moment to slip 'round behind the jail and up to the rear window—the one that joined the stranger's cell. I knew he'd be there 'cause there only was one cell. Standin' on my toes, I could just get my chin to the sill of that window and look inside. From that angle, I couldn't see the stranger, but I could see Sheriff Cooper pacing outside the cell.

"Look here, Chance, if'n those dirt farmers swill enough of the Slipper's finest, they're gonna try and storm this place. A lot of 'em are gonna get kilt. Hell," he took off his hat and wiped the sweat from his forehead, "I might get kilt myownself. I gotta tell ya, Chance, I ain't real partial to that."

"Seems to me that you could solve your problem by letting me go, Hubert."

Cooper frowned. "I asked you not to call me that. I changed it, Chance. I told you I changed it. Told you more than once. Call me Dakota." He gripped the bars of the cell and puffed up like a bristly ol' porky-pine. "It's Dakota Cooper now. You call me that or you call me Sheriff Cooper. Got it?"

"You were Hubert Cooper when we snuck away from the Seventh that morning after the Sioux massacre."

"Damn it, Jack! I told you not to be mentioning that either!"

"For living in a country founded on the principles of freedom of speech, Hubert, you've got some peculiar rules."

The stranger named Chance laughed then, like he enjoyed baiting Cooper, like he knew all Cooper's secrets. He obviously knew more'n anyone else in town. In the last two minutes, I'd done learned more than in the five years since Cooper'd showed up in Hades and accepted that tin star what nobody else wanted. Why hadn't he ever told anyone that he was there when Custer slaughtered them heathen Sioux in retaliation for the whuppin' they gave him at the Little Bighorn? And why had he a run off afterward? Hell, last I heard, they were still hangin' them's that had deserted, them's that couldn't stomach killin' all them squaws and babies along with the braves. Pa said it was a "necessary evil"—like when God killed off everything and everybody in the flood, 'cepting them's as Noah took, of course. And Pa said them squaws is actually the meanest when it comes to black magic, that they'd a sure 'nough put spells on every white man what rode away from there. I dunno though. Sometimes I think about all them babies. Them babies didn't do nuthin' bad. Don't seem right killing somethin' what never had a chance to grow up and be one thing or t'other. Pa just scowls and asks me what the hell the Cavalry was gonna do with a buncha babies and no mamas to take care of 'em.

I see his point, but I still don't know. Musta been a terrible thing. Terrible enough to make a man turn deserter, I reckon.

There was a space of silence 'tween them then; until, finally, Chance said, "I guess I can just call you Coop, like I did in the old days."

Cooper kinda eased back from the bars and let out a long sigh. I saw the blood return to his knuckles. Saw some of the meanness go outta his eyes. "Look, Jack, you know what I want. I know that Cheyenne you saved taught you some magic. I dunno what it is, whether you say some kinda magic words or smoke some of that peyote weed and dance nekkid in the moonlight, but I know I gots to have it." He reached into his pocket and pulled out a deck of cards, started shuffling them against the bars of the cell. "I've heard stories about you. Knew it was you on account of the missing eye and all. They say you can change a card by touching it. They say billiard balls do strange things when you're in the room and roulette wheels—"

"A lot of things get said, Coop," Chance interrupted. "A lot of things get blown out of proportion. Legends start that way." His voice went all soft and thoughtful like. "Couple years ago, I ran into William Cody. You know what those damn legends did to him. They turned him into some kind of carnival freak."

"I ain't talking 'bout no damn legends, Jack! I'm talking 'bout what I need so's I can get out of this outhouse of a town. I'm talking 'bout what you can do to help me. I'm talking 'bout what I can do to help you."

Chance got up from his cot then and stood with his back to me. His was a tall man, broad at the shoulders. Looked to have seen a lifetime of hard work, like my Pa, but somehow that work didn't sit the same on him; it didn't bend him over like it did my Pa. His hair was black as the ace of spades, gathered in the back and all knotted up with the strap of that eyepatch. He crossed the cell and placed his hands on the bars, leaning close to the sheriff as if they was old friends, as if they might hug if'n them bars wasn't 'tween them.

"It's not a gift, Coop. The Cheyenne knew that when he gave it to me. He knew it, but he gave it to me anyway, because cheating's what they do when they feel they've been cheated first."

"You didn't cheat that young brave, Jack."

"Yes I did, Coop. He wanted to die. I stopped him."

"You saved his life!"

"It wasn't mine to save."

"That's a load of bullshit and you know it!"

"Look," Chance said, and he took the deck of cards from the sheriff's hands. "Even if I *could* give you this," and he slipped a card from the middle of the deck, "this so-called *luck...*"

Cooper let out a little gasp. I couldn't see the card, but I didn't need to. I could guess.

Chance cut out another, adding it to the first in Cooper's hand. "You wouldn't want it, Coop." He cut another. And another. Cooper held them up, fanning them out in his hand. Four jacks.

"You let me be the judge of that," whispered Sheriff Cooper.

That was when the pounding resumed on the front door. Pa's voice came through, loud and clear. "Cooper, we done had us a town meeting down at the Silver Slipper. Seems you just been voted out as sheriff. Open up!"

"It's probably not the right time to be stubborn, Coop," Chance said softly. "I believe your townspeople are serious."

Something not quite right happened in Sheriff Cooper's eyes about then, something I've never seen in a man's eyes since, and hope I never do. They went all narrow, like a snake's, and his hand went to the gun hangin' at his belt. Chance weren't armed, that much I could see, but there was no rabbit in that 'un. He stood his ground as calm as they come, watching that six-shooter raise up and point right at his heart, as if he was watchin' the preacher on a Sunday morning.

"I mean to have that magic, Chance," Cooper said softly. The pounding at the door was louder. I could hear footsteps rounding the corner of the building toward me. Cooper ignored everything but the man in front of him. I heard him draw back on the hammer of his gun, the distinctive four *clicks* of that Colt loud and sudden.

"Take your shot then, Coop," Chance said softly. He didn't have a gun, but I saw him reach up kind of lazy like toward that eyepatch. My heart caught in my throat, rememberin' he'd done something like that the day before, and that he should be dead, but was starin' down the sheriff instead...

Things got kinda crazy just then. Strong hands grabbed me from behind, pulling me down and away from the window. I scratched at the sill, trying to keep my position, to see what would happen next, but it was no use. I was dragged clear. A loop of heavy rope was passed through the bars and tied off with a hasty knot. As the men scattered, leavin' me standing to one side, the rope snatched taut, dust motes springing into sunlight all along its length. A horse whinnied with strain, and then the whole back wall of the jailhouse was coming down, rock and mortar spilling out into the alley.

Something caught my ankle and I fell. By the time I got back to my feet, choking on dust, the sheriff was standing there in the gaping ruin of the wall, holding the one-eyed stranger by the collar with one hand and pressing his forty-five against the back of his neck with t'other.

"Now hold on just a goddarned minute!" Cooper bellowed.

The townspeople crowded the alley, shoulder to shoulder. Some had sticks. Some had guns. Several of them had bottles. Pa was in the front.

"Let him go," said Pa.

"Wilbur, this here is destruction of town property," Cooper said. "I'm gonna have to place you under arrest."

Pa slipped his old Navy cap 'n ball out of where he'd tucked it in his belt that morning. "Ain't nobody gettin' arrested today, Cooper. Leastwise, not by you. You're fired."

"Fired?" The sheriff sounded almost childish, like little Brett Stavory whenever I push him down after school. "You think you can just fire me?"

"We can do more'n that if we have to," Pa said, raising his six-shooter.

Cooper laughed, a high-pitched girl's laugh, the kinda laugh a man makes when he's done snapped a rein in his head. Then he started shooting.

The whole alley erupted in gunfire. My Pa was one of the first to fall. He didn't do no fancy dance steps. He just crumbled, like a puppet that's done had its strings cut, folding to the ground with his knees up around his face and the barrel of his gun pointed at his crotch. My own survival instincts put me down among the crumbled ruin of the wall. The one-eyed stranger—Chance, the sheriff had called him—twisted away from Cooper and dived to the side of the alley, stumbling over the debris and falling to his knees. Cooper recoiled as several bullets punched holes in his shirt, but he didn't go down. I realized that his gun was empty when the hammer clicked on nothin' for the second or third time. From the other end of the alley, things got quiet. There was moaning and several cries for God, but the shooting had stopped. Cooper swayed on his feet, the holes in his shirt blossoming bright red flowers. For the longest time, the whole scene just stayed that way; even the gun smoke seemed frozen in time.

Miss Mae Belle stepped over several bodies and approached the sheriff. "Now look what you've done, Sheriff Cooper."

Cooper ignored her. He glanced at Chance. The one-eyed gambler seemed to be in shock.

"What the hell were you thinking?" Mae Belle demanded.

Cooper snapped open the gate on the side of his six-shooter, put his index finger on the extractor rod, and began punching out his empties, swaying there, his shirt growing redder and wetter by the second. The loudest sounds in the alley were his brass cartridges ringing on the rocks and a whistling noise coming from one of the holes in his chest.

My Pa groaned.

"Help him!" I told Mae Belle.

She looked at me, her eyes as sad as an old hound I once saw run over by the stage. She pulled her hands away from the front of her dress and showed me where it was bright with blood. "Need some help myownself," she muttered. Then she sat down hard on her ass.

Cooper was slipping new rounds from the loops in his belt and stuffing them in his gun. "You're a dead man," he told Chance.

Chance was trying to get to his feet, but he was moving awful slow. I saw that there was blood on his arm, and I realized that he'd taken one, too.

When I pried the gun outta Pa's hand, he looked at me and tried to say something. I'll never know what it was, cause that was the last moment I ever saw him alive, but I like to think he was trying to warn me, trying to tell me that I was about to start down a very hard road, a road that made men like Slippery McGee.

Cooper raised his gun, cocked it, and pointed it at the one-eyed stranger's head.

That's when I shot him. His hat lifted off the top of his head, taking most of his brain with it. For a moment, he stood there, his head open like a busted egg, then he pitched forward like a fallin' tree. I'll never forget the sound his face made when it smacked the ground.

Chance looked up at me.

"Help my Pa," I said, as the gun slipped through my fingers.

He put two fingers against Pa's neck, held them there a few seconds, then shook his head. "He's gone, son."

"Miss Mae Belle?"

Her head had slumped forward on her breasts. Her hands were crossed in her lap, one turned up so that it cupped a tiny pool of blood. Chance checked for her pulse. "she's gone, too," he said.

I hugged my Pa and tried to figure out how I'd explain it all to Ma. Chance stood to one side, quiet and uncertain, wondering perhaps what he could possibly say to me. I finally let him off the hook.

"Wasn't right," I said, "McGee trying to hang that Chinee."

"No," he said. "It wasn't."

"And the sheriff … wasn't right him arresting you."

He didn't say anything.

"So my Pa's a hero. He fought the good fight."

"He did."

I nodded, sprinkling the top of Pa's head with my tears. "That's all that matters, then."

When he didn't reply, I looked up for his approval, but he was gone. I never saw him again, though I often heard stories told about him. One-Eyed Jack they called him. An old Cheyenne had taken his eye in exchange for what some called a gift, but others called a curse. They say that under that eye patch was nuthin'. Absolutely nuthin'. But it's a hungry sort of emptiness, and every now and again, One-Eyed Jack has to feed it. They say he's a gambler. A gunfighter. A handyman. A cleaner of stables and a sweeper of boardwalks. The stories make him out to be many things. Our paths often crossed, but never met again.

In the years after Ma died, while I was still working my way west, earning a name for the quick draw and leaving a trail of dead men behind me, I learned that every man is a gambler, but not every man is as lucky as John Chance. Luck's a fickle lady. She'll love you one minute and leave you wonderin' the next. Sometimes you ain't got one chance in Hell of avoiding the shit that's been planned for you. Sometimes all a man can do is roll the dice and wait on the snake eyes...

PURE CHANCE
A ONE-EYED JACK WESTERN

(with David Niall Wilson)

Sometimes the sun beats down so hard on the desert that you can't really see the horizon. The waves of heat just rise from the sand and shimmer like some sorta warped mirror, hidin' what should be seen and showin' what should not. Sometimes a man sees a thing that ain't there. Sometimes somethin's there, but there's a door deep inside that same man's brain that slams shut and refuses to let it through. Maybe that's best.

And sometimes, every great now and again, fate, pure chance, or the workings of the devil puts a man where he can't help but see a thing ... whether he wants to or not. Such things are apt to change a man's life. Forever.

There were no clouds in the sky the day the stranger came trottin' his horse outta a stand of trees just the other side of town. I remember 'cause Clem Bates and I were sittin' on the stoop out front of the Dry-Gulch Saloon that day, boots propped pretty-as-you-please and hats tipped down just far enough to divert the flies. You couldn't miss him. Even from a distance you could sense something wasn't quite right.

Something glittered beneath his shirt, and my first thought was *lawman*, though that didn't set quite right. His horse was edgin' out of the trees kinda spooked-like, side-stepping so's it seemed the man was gliding side-wise across the sand like a desert rattler. I turned and kicked Clem, but by the time he snorted and sat up, half-pissed off and half fallin' out of his seat, I'd turned back, and there was nothing there. Sand was blowing in little clouds over the frypan ground, and that shimmer was in the air. Too hot. It was too damned hot, and there was nothing there.

I nearly jumped out of my skin when the horse snorted not three feet away from me.

Clem and I ain't what you'd call graceful at the best of times. Fallin' and standin' all at once was probably a right entertaining sight. If so, the stranger didn't show it. He sat there on his horse, waiting until we were upright, me with a hand out-stretched in welcome and Clem with his hat in his hands, fiddling it in a circle like he always does when he's nervous. The stranger just sat his horse, leavin' my hand wavering in the still air 'tween us. I s'pose I should say something 'bout that horse right off. If I don't, you won't believe what comes later. The horse was our first clue, though neither me nor Clem realized it at the time.

It was a big old mare, gray as a Confederate officer's overcoat, with red-rimmed eyes and lips that curled back from the bit all cracked and dry with not even a spot of spittle, as if that horse hadn't drank since last Christmas. Its hooves were weathered and split like old fence posts. Vicious red sores peeked out from around the edges of the saddle blanket, weeping pus down along the animal's sides and along where the cinch strap crimped its swollen belly. But them saddle sores weren't the worst of it. There was this gash, this monstrous wound that stretched from under the mare's jaw down to her right foreleg and across her chest. Laden with maggots and crawling with flies, it stank like a possum some coyotes had buried two weeks ago. If'n you looked hard—hell, even if'n you didn't—you could see bone down in the green'ing meat of that wound.

How that horse could be standing, let alone have hauled this fella across the desert, was beyond me. It was then I noticed the horse's sides. They weren't heaving like they oughta been. They was still. Still as the dead.

"I'm looking for a man," the stranger said, voice smooth like the oily sheen on a pool of tainted water. "A man you may have seen. He wears a patch over one eye. Likes a good game of poker."

When we didn't answer right off, he continued.

"Men call him Chance. Or sometimes ... One-Eyed Jack."

I'd never heard of a man named Chance, myself, but even if I had this wasn't the sort of fella I'd have tossed that knowledge to without a question.

"What do men call *you*, stranger?" I asked, fighting off the quiver that tried to weaken my voice.

The man stared at me. His eyes had a glaze over them, like a sand-scratched window pane, but they were intense. God, were they intense. I've stood on the desert at night, when the wind whips along so hard it can flay a man alive and the air is cold enough to freeze the blood in your veins. That moment was colder. Little chips of ice glittered behind his glazed eyes, and something washed through me. That's how it felt. Something hit me like a wind that ignored skin and bone, slid on through, touching everything, watching and stealing like a mongrel dog at a campfire. Then it was gone. And when it left, his coat fluttered, just enough to catch that glint of metal beneath, but not enough to see what it was.

By the time my mind cleared, he was nearly done talking, and I found I'd lost all stomach for conversation.

"Name's Cole," he said softly. "This man Chance ... he took something of mine. And I aim to have it back." He leaned forward in the saddle, a difficult task because the saddle was scarred and blackened like it had been in a fire, and there weren't a lot of it left. The saddle horn was completely gone, the leather there all curled back like burnt jerky. His right leg hung free where that stirrup was missin'. Cole's weight bowed the horse's head so that I got a look up its nostrils. They were cracked like an old river bed that hadn't seen water in decades. Bone glistened along the ridge of the horse's nose where the hide had peeled back. "And I'll kill any man comes between me and what's mine. You understand?"

Clem and me nodded, neither of us capable of findin' voice.

"Now, he's either here now or he will be soon. So I'm gonna ask again. Have you seen him? Have you seen this John Chance?"

"No, sir," I said, and Clem mumbled somethin' decipherable only by the frantic shakin' of his head.

Cole chewed on that a minute, the dust in his beard crackin', the crow's feet around his eyes deepenin' to a point where I expected to see blood. "You got a sheriff in this town?"

I pointed. "Next to the general store. Jim Bauer's his name."

With a savage jerk on the reins, Cole turned his horse and started up Main Street. As he did, I saw what was under his coat. It wasn't a badge. A badge would need something to pin to. And Cole wasn't wearing no shirt. 'Cept for a heavy layer of dirt—the kinda dirt you'd find caked on the belly of some old dog that oughta be took out and shot—his chest was bare. But part of his chest was missin', replaced by a chunk of metal bigger'n my hand with all my fingers spread out hard. The skin around that metal was puckered and blue, weeping little trickles of fluid that might be red or might be yellow, but was now just the color of that grave dirt. It might have been a frying pan buried in his chest. It might have been a cannonball. But it's for damn sure there weren't no room left in there for a heart.

Clem clawed my shirt sleeve. "Dead," he wheezed. "That fucker's already dead..."

I shrugged him off. "Don't be stupid, Clem. Dead men don't walk and carry on conversations."

"That'un did. What d'ya think he wants with Sheriff Bauer?"

"I don't rightly know."

But we only had to wait a minute to find out. Bauer musta been watchin' from his window, 'cause he walked out on the veranda to meet the stranger. Cole never said a thing to Sheriff Bauer. He just drew the Colt strapped to his thigh and shot Bauer dead. Four times in the head, tracking the body as it jerked this way and that, brains and skull bone splatterin' across the door and its blue lettering: SHERIFF. Bauer was dead 'fore he hit the ground—hard to be otherwise with so much of your head gone—but the stranger pumped the last two rounds into him anyway, aiming for the head again. When the smoke cleared and the last of the echoes left the street, there wasn't nothing left of Bauer's head but jelly. He lay there with his boot heels facing skyward, his toes scratchin' at the boardwalk the way a dog's hind leg'll do when you rub its belly, a red puddle spreadin' from the stump of his neck.

The town was silent save for the sound of brass cartridges tinklin' to the ground as Cole reloaded. It couldn'ta took him more'n a few seconds, the fingers of one hand all nimble on that extractor rod whilst the other hand seemed to float new shells from his cartridge belt and slip 'em easy as you please into the cylinder. When he was done, he gave that Colt's cylinder a spin, slapped shut the loading gate, and then snaked it back into leather. From the time Jim Bauer tipped back his hat and made ready to say "Howdy, stranger," to that Colt slippin' back in the holster … God almighty, it couldn'ta a been a whole minute.

Cole turned his horse back to where me and Clem was frozen in place.

"You go and you gather up everyone in town," he said. "You bring 'em to the saloon. Them's that does what I say'll live. Them's that don't are gonna die. Understand?"

We both nodded.

"Go on then."

The Dry Gulch Saloon was dark inside. Any other day of the year, there'd a been candles on the tables and oil lamps flickerin' their yellow light down from the walls. It seemed that Cole didn't take much to the light. Clem and I stood for a long time on the boardwalk, watchin' the doors swingin' from the last man to pass through and figurin' our odds of hittin' saddle leather and the edge of town before that Colt spit lead.

They didn't seem good.

I pushed the doors wide, and we slipped inside all quiet-like, steppin' to one side of the door and gettin' a good view of what was going on. That was the second time that day that the world sorta stopped being normal. There were folks at the bar, leanin' in close to whisper amongst each other, drinkin' whiskey, but doing it without the usual jests and laughter. The piano was quiet, though Bertie Parks, the piano man, was sitting right where he always did. Judi, the whore I'd vote most likely to make enough money to one day leave town for someplace like San Francisco, was sitting at the end of the bar, left alone for the first time in history. Doc Bloom was there, though he was known to avoid the saloon on account of his near-death experience with some tainted liquor. Miss Tate from the hotel sat with her husband and three young'uns. McGruder from the livery was there. And even Reverend Lancaster, perched in the corner with his face all screwed up like he done gone and caught a whiff of an outhouse. Looked to be the whole town ... which is what Cole had asked for.

I've been in and out the doors of that saloon more times than most men, and I've never seen less'n four games of poker goin' at once. That day, there was only one. Cole was sittin' at the poker table, his hat tipped down low over his eyes, cards held loose, and a glass of whiskey to one side. I watched the game progress, him slidin' more and more money to his side of the table at each shuffle of the cards, but I never once saw him lift that glass. He played like he hadn't a care in the world, but the pile of money by his cards just kept growin'. He didn't seem worried by the fact that there was guns a'plenty in the room. I was wonderin' how long it'd be before someone decided they wanted to leave. My money was on one of the drifters at the bar, one of the cowpokes with his own six-shooter strapped low, or maybe Pike Roberts, the town's banker and a reckless womanizer, who was known to carry a holdout gun at the small of his back.

The whole thing was like some made-up story in a back-East playhouse, acted out by a bunch of people who'd forgotten their lines and didn't want to be in the play to begin with. Clem and I made our way to the bar, as there weren't nothin' more we *could* do, turnin' our backs on the insanity.

"Couple'a whiskeys, Ace," I called. The bartender turned away from where he'd been listening to Tom Ellerton bitch about his cow of a wife (who was seated with her two boys at the table near the Reverend) and his dead-dog farm. Ace gripped that whiskey bottle so tight I thought he'd crush it in his bare hand as he hurried over.

"Afternoon, Josh. Clem. Hell of an afternoon."

I nodded, glancin' over my shoulder. Cole was watchin' me, as if he'd known in that split-second he would catch me staring back at him, and my heart went cold. I turned back to the bar. At least if he shot me from behind, I wouldn't have to see those eyes.

"That it is," I replied, watchin' the golden liquid flow into the glass in front of me. "You can put that on my tab."

"No need," Ace said, voice waverin' slightly. "It's taken care of. All of it."

I took the glass and downed it in one quick swallow. "Hit me again, then," I wheezed around the fire in my throat. "I got the feelin' I'm gonna need it."

The sun was slipping lower, and the shadows were getting hard to sift through.

"Light some of those candles," Cole called out. "Not too many, though. I like it dark."

Ace slipped around the corner of the bar and hurried to do as he'd been told. I wondered what kind of lesson Cole had given them all to get such obedience from grown men. I suppose the flies buzzin' around Bauer's headless corpse might have been enough.

Outside, the sound of a horse whinnying floated in; the street echoed with hoofbeats.

Cole came to attention, but a second later relaxed. It was as if he could sense that this wasn't the man he was lookin' for. "Someone tell that cowpoke to get on in here," he said. His voice echoed, hollow-like. Like it didn't belong in this world.

Being closest to the doors, Doc made like he was going to comply, but then a cowboy shoved his way on through, whippin' his hat off'a his head and slappin' it again' his chaps with a great cloud of dust. "Woo-hee!" he declared, "I am glad to see the sun set, cause that's gotta be the hottest dang day of my life! I—" He surveyed the room. "Who the hell died 'round these parts? Y'all look fit to..." His voice trailed off as his eyes settled on Cole. It didn't take a genius to see the entire room was arranged with Cole as its focus.

"Anyone else ride into town with you?" Cole asked.

"Just me," the man replied warily.

"See anyone on the way in?"

"There was some stranger out by Washita Creek. Stopped to water his horse and wash some of the sand outta his eyes, I reckon."

"Tall, dark-haired fella?" Cole set a finger to the side of his eye. "Wearing a patch?"

The cowpoke nodded. "Yeah. That'd be him. Probably be along in thirty minutes or so. Friend of your'n?"

Cole nodded. "You could say that. Ain't seen him in a few years. We'll be celebrating when he gets here. Slide on up to the bar and have a drink, cowboy. Liquor's on me tonight."

"Don't mind if I do!" And he jangled up to the bar so's Ace could set him up.

"How long we gotta stay here?" asked Pike Roberts.

"Long as it takes," said Cole.

"And if'n we decide to leave?"

Cole nodded toward the door. "That door swings any way but in … and the man that goes through it'll be dead."

Roberts got to his feet, straightening his forty-dollar smoking jacket. "I don't think you realize—"

"No," Cole said so soft as to make you wonder how he could interrupt the other man's speech, "I don't think *you* realize." His hand slipped beneath the table. "Your hand moves any closer to that hideout gun, I'll shoot you dead."

Roberts swallowed, his apple bobbing like he'd gotten his boot lodged in his throat. His hands went to his sides.

"Smart man." Cole smiled, but cold, like a snake. His teeth were brown. Decay or dirt, I couldn't tell. "You just keep thinking about your sheriff." He pushed back his chair, got to his feet, and surveyed the room. "All of you … just keep thinking about that sheriff if'n you want to live through this night."

It was the Reverend that had the nerve to ask the question that was on all our minds.

"What do you want with this man … this … One-Eyed Jack?"

Cole spun on him. "Damn good question, Reverend! Seeing as how we got some time to kill, why don't I tell you a story. It'll be just like church on Sunday." He laughed, a mean-spirited sound. Like a fox toyin' with a half-dead rabbit. He walked to the bar, tippin' his hat in a grand, sweeping gesture, bowed to the lot of us (and there was that flash of metal from his chest again, winking silver in the candlelight). Before he replaced his hat on his head, I saw patches where his hair had fallen out and his scalp lay bare and sickly gray.

"Once upon a time," he began, "in the badlands of the Dakotas, three brothers came upon an Injun and his squaw hunkered down in some hills where they could hide and work their evil spells on white folk. Injuns was something the brothers knew all about, see, cause they'd ridden with Custer. They'd seen the things those red bastards could do with a fire and some wolverine blood and the moon sitting just right. I could go on about those things, about how an Injun can cut out a white woman's womb and cultivate somethin' not of this world in it, about how one of them devil squaws can suck out a white man's soul with the hole 'tween her legs, about how an Injun can paint himself with the blood of a wolf and walk about at night in the shape of that wolf, slipping into the camp of his enemies and ripping out throats whilst good men sleep ... I could tell you many a tale, but you wouldn't believe me unless you'd seen these things yourself.

"But you're seeing me now, ain't ya? So you'll believe this." He pulled open his coat, drew his Colt, and tapped the barrel against the metal embedded in his chest. *Clink. Clink.* "Pure silver. The finest of silver from Mexico. Sent by Santa Anna when he aimed to buy back Texas. But we all know that Santa Anna's silver disappeared somewhere, that Mexico blamed us and we blamed them. And we all know about the bloody war that erupted on account of it. But no one ever found that silver.

"No one 'cept that Injun and his squaw."

A coyote set to callin' about then. I couldn't help that chills went up my back. Clem was shakin', too, the shot glass in his hand sloppin' out and paintin' the saw dust on the floor.

Cole spun his revolver a few times as if reluctant to holster it, as if he loved the feel of it in his hand, then he stepped over to Judi, caught her by the hair and pulled her head back so's her breasts arched all white and creamy from the top of her bodice. He kissed her there, pressin' his filthy lips to the firm contour of her bosom, and made a great smacking sound like a child with a candy stick from the general store. He laughed, a deep, throat-clotted sound like a man with consumption.

"Any of you boys ever suckle at the teat of a red woman? Ever taste the peyote and sage that oozes from her private places?" He spun Judi (who looked ready to swoon) away into the nearest arms and laughed again. "Oh, she tried to hex us, all right. A squaw knows a million spells she can put on a man. But we tied her hands and Orley cut out her tongue. We staked her out on the ground and took turns on her all night long, whilst her man watched. Calvin wanted to kill him, but me and Orley wanted him to watch, wanted him to know what we'd done before we kilt him. We tied him up with that squaw's tongue in his mouth, wrapped some old saddle leather round his face so he couldn't spit it out and couldn't talk neither. We weren't taking no chances.

"It was long about midnight when one of us found the bar of silver wrapped in his blankets. It was stamped with the flag of Mexico and Santa Anna's personal seal. We all knew where it musta come from. But that damn Injun wouldn't tell us where he found it. We cut his squaw up in front of him, put her heart in his lap, but he wouldn't talk. We cut off all the fingers on one of his hands, but he just clamped his mouth shut and shook his head. I took a stick from the fire and burned out his eyes. I peeled the skin back from his arm and let his meat sizzle over the fire. I put cactus needles through his balls. Nothing. He wouldn't say a word about where that silver came from."

The saloon had gone deathly quiet, each of us swallowin' whatever bile, whatever comments, whatever outrage we might be feelin'. None of us were fond of Injuns, each of us having seen our share of relatives scalped in the wars that Custer brought to an end, but none of us had ever heard such pure savagery described with such relish.

Then, in that silence, there came the sound of hooves from outside, *thump-thumpin'* on the hard-packed red clay of Main Street.

Cole turned to the doors of the saloon, his mouth drawn in a rictus grin. "We tortured that damn Injun all night long, but he wouldn't talk. Come morning, we'd run out of ideas and was just figuring to shoot him in the head and take that one bar of silver. It wouldn't make us rich, but it would buy one hell of a drunk."

The hoof beats drew nearer.

"It was then John Chance rode into camp."

Cole shifted so he was square to the swingin' doors, shoulders hunched, eyes narrow and focused, hands danglin' at his sides, fingers tappin' the butt of his Colt.

"We never heard him coming," he said without lookin' away from the door. "He slipped up on us like he floated on the wind ... stopped at the edge of our camp and sat there, watching."

The hoofbeats stopped outside. There came the creak of saddle leather as someone dismounted.

"We had that damn Injun bound over a fallen tree trunk, his buckskins down around his ankles. Calvin had been makin' some jokes about using him like we'd done his squaw, but we finally decided to shove a piece of dynamite up his ass. We were all set to light the fuse and leave him there when something made me stop and turn. Don't know what it was. A change in the wind. The smell of a man that didn't stink of blood and squaw juices. So I turned ... and I saw him."

There came the thud of a boot on the veranda outside.

"I reached over and pushed Orley toward the other side of the fire. Same time, I grabbed iron. I was always fast with a gun. Hell, some said I was quick as William Cody. But I never cleared leather before a bullet set me back on my ass. More shots rang out. There were suddenly pink pieces of Orley's brains runnin' down my cheek. He fell with what was left of his head in my lap. Calvin, never much for a shootout, tried to reach his horse, but the stranger shot him as he tried to swing up into the saddle. I saw Calvin's bandanna hang up on the saddle horn and the horse go to jumping and bucking with Calvin flopping there, his face all blue and his tongue hanging out, his hands alternating between the bandanna that was choking the life out of him and the hole in his back that was pumping out all his fluids. I know'd he was done for.

"I was dying, too. Blood was oozing out of a hole in my chest and pooling in my lap around Orley's shattered head. Chance stepped into the firelight, his six-shooter still smokin' in his hand. I tried to lift my Colt, but he kicked it away. 'Wait here,' he says, as if I was an old friend that he wanted to visit with some more. Then he walked over to that half dead Injun and started untying him."

The doors swung open and a tall man stepped through. He wasn't wearin' a hat. His unruly hair was long and black, shot through with gray, bound in the back with the same leather thong that held an eyepatch over his right eye. His good eye was the color of storm clouds and had that same yellow, threatenin' glow. There weren't sound one in that saloon. Standin' beside me, Clem appeared to not even be breathing, and I realized everyone was holding their breath, waiting for Cole or the stranger in the doorway to slap leather. But the two men just studied each other, silent, eyes dead and mouths set.

"What'd that Injun ask you for, Chance? What'd he want when you finally had him untied?"

Chance blinked, the storms in his eye softenin'. There was a sadness about the man, a somber mantle that said he'd seen it all and then some, a weight on those broad shoulders that had nothin' to do with age or fatigue.

"He wanted to see her one last time," said the man with the eye-patch.

"See her? Who? That dead squaw bitch?"

"His wife."

Cole laughed, pointed at the patch. "So he took your eye so's he could do it. Now that's some kinda gratitude!" He threw back his head and roared with a laughter shared by none of us in the saloon. We were still numb, shaken by the story, shaken by the presence of these two men, one of whom seemed larger than life … and another who had obviously cheated death.

Pike Roberts saw it as an openin'. He pulled his little thirty caliber holdout gun and fired at Cole. The gun was incredibly loud within the confines of the saloon. The range was point blank. There was no way he could miss.

Bertie Parks flailed back against his piano, the ivory keys janglin' as bright red blood sprayed from Bertie's throat. Judi screamed. Doc Bloom rose from his seat and tried to stem the flow of blood, but Bertie was flailin' about too much.

Pike's second shot veered off in the opposite direction, shatterin' bottles behind the bar. His third punched a hole through the ceiling. And his last, which seemed to almost walk a circle about Cole, who had still not stopped laughin', punched clean through the side of Tom Ellerton's head, droppin' him without a sound except a brassy clang when his hand slapped the foot rail, shattered the empty whiskey glass in the hand of our late-arriving cowpoke, and buried itself with a meaty *thunk!* in Clem's shoulder.

And that was that; Pike's little four-shot holdout gun was empty.

Cole drew—his hand a blur, like the striking of a snake— and shot Pike in the right kneecap. Before Pike could drop, Cole fired again, and the dandy's other kneecap vanished in a spray of red. Pike Roberts fell with a howl of pain.

The saloon was in chaos. Tom Ellerton's wife was screamin' and would have charged across the room, but Reverend Lancaster was holdin' her back. Clem was hangin' onto me, his shoulder soaked with blood. Bertie Parks was down on the floor, his feet thrashing and his eyes wild, while Doc Bloom, bloody to the elbows, struggled in vain to stem the flow of blood from his neck. One of the drifters tried to make it through the door. Cole shot him in the back; the man collapsed at John Chance's feet.

Chance had drawn his own gun, but stood there with a look of unaccustomed dismay on his handsome features. He didn't know what to do. We'd all seen what had happened to Pike's four point-blank shots.

"Quiet!" I yelled. "Nobody move! And for God's sake, nobody try to shoot him again!"

Cole looked over at me. For a moment, I thought he might kill me, but then he gave me the slightest smile and a nod, the kinda look a schoolteacher gives her brightest pupil.

Pike Roberts was cryin' like a baby, rockin' back and forth on the bloody floor, his useless legs folded under him, his knees a red pulpy mess.

"Shut up," Cole said, raising his Colt to plug Roberts in the head.

"Wait!" said Chance.

Cole cocked an eyebrow at him.

"It's me you want. You let these people live and—"

"What makes you think *anyone* gets to live, Chance? What makes you think I can't just kill the entire town?" He shot Pike Roberts right between the eyes. Pike's head snapped back hard again' the floor, central point for a spray of brains, blood, and bone chips.

"Nobody move," I repeated, surprised that my voice was now a quiverin' whine, like a schoolgirl who's had a frog set on her lap. I cleared my throat and tried to say it again with more authority, but nothing more would come outta my mouth 'cept for an embarrassin' little mousey squeak.

Even so, the saloon went quiet again. There was nothin' but the sound of Ellerton's wife sobbin' on the preacher's shoulder. Bertie was still there on the floor, but his struggles had ceased. Doc stood nearby, Bertie's blood dripping from his hands to speckle the floor. Clem was clinging to me, shaking so bad now that the shot glasses on the bar were trembling.

Nobody moved. Nobody said a word. There were four dead men in the room. No one wanted to be number five.

Cole tapped the silver embedded in his chest with the barrel of his revolver. *Tap. Tap. Tap.* "You want to give it a try, Chance?"

The stranger with the eyepatch holstered his weapon.

Cole laughed. "So you saved this Injun's worthless hide and he repays you by witching out your eye. You stupid son of a bitch."

Chance said nothing.

Cole looked over at me. "Never trust a red man, Townie. They'll fuck you every time. I damn near got out of there, you know that? Whilst our good Samaritan here was thrashin' about and screamin' over the loss of his eye, I was a'crawling for my horse. I managed to get myself up in the saddle, thinkin' that if nothin' else I could at least crawl off and die somewhere's peaceful—hell, no telling how long that bloody Injun would make me suffer for what we'd done to his squaw. I no sooner got my hands around the reins than that Injun ups and lights that stick of dynamite and tosses it at me. My horse took most of the blast, but I caught more'n enough to do the job. The saddle-horn was hurled right through my goddamn chest.

"I was dead 'fore I hit the ground."

Reverend Lancaster gently pushed Ellerton's wife aside and stood, clasping his hands together and beginning a prayer. "Dear Father, deliver us from evil—"

Cole swung his gun in Lancaster's direction. That was all it took for the preacher to sit down and shut up. Whatever faith he had in his God, the gapin' muzzle of that Colt was a far more obvious presence in the saloon.

Cole smiled at Chance. "So the Injun takes your eye. Hates you for what he finds when he can see again. He'd rather be dead. But he owes you. So he makes it a trade. He puts something in that empty socket, something you keep hidden, something with incredible powers. Hell, it's only been a year and it's already the stuff of legends. One-Eyed Jack they call you. Man can draw four aces from a deck without stackin' it. Billiard balls run circles at your command. Roulette wheels know your name. The finest of blackjack dealers push away from the table when you approach. All on account o' what lies beneath that eyepatch." He cocked the Colt and leveled it at Chance's face. "Show me."

Chance crossed his arms across his broad chest. "But you haven't finished your story."

"Oh?"

"Tell them how the Indian dragged your corpse into the firelight, melted that bar of silver down and poured it into the cavity in your chest. Symbol of your greed ... what better item to serve you as a new heart?"

Cole stroked the silver with his free hand. I wondered what he thought of the trade, if the silver had been worth it, if he preferred his new heart over his old.

"He brought me back from the dead so's I could find you," Cole told Chance. "So's I could get back what was mine. That's my own black heart under that eyepatch. The Injun gave you the only thing there more powerful than hisself, the only part of me he knew he couldn't destroy. When it's mine again ... I'll be alive again."

Chance shook his head. "The Indian snatched something from the night sky, Cole. Something darker and heavier and even meaner than your evil core. He snatched it from the sky and he set it in my skull. It's a curse. Payback for having saved his life. A guarantee that every time I try to help someone again, only ill will come of it." His voice was laden with guilt. A good man whose good intentions were fated to turn out poorly. Where could he go? Who could he call friend? "And each time this thing in my skull drinks down some other evil, I'm left to carry on with it, to see it in my mind, to hear and feel and smell and even taste the foul black ichor of it."

Cole gestured with his gun. "Bullshit. Take off the eyepatch."

"Not until the story's done. Why did the Indian raise you from the dead?"

"I told you already!"

"You killed his woman. Tortured and mutilated him. I can't imagine he wanted anything less than an eternity in Hell for you, Cole. Why are you walking the Earth?"

Cole looked confused. His gun wavered. He stroked the silver again.

"Where's the Indian now?"

"Dead! I kilt that sumbitch! He did his witching and then passed out from loss of blood. I caved in his skull with the iron pot he'd used to melt that silver. Pushed his face into the fire. Held him there whilst his brains boiled, his hair burned off, and his face peeled back all black from his skull."

"Before he could tell you what he really wanted."

"He wanted me to take you back to Hell with me! That's why he brought my horse back, too. Now shut up and take off that damn eyepatch!" Cole screamed, leveling the Colt again. The rest of us flinched, but Chance didn't even blink. Cole took a step forward, the gun trained on Chance's face.

"Shoot me and it dies with me," Chance said calmly. "Step outside and I'll show you." He took a step backward, his shoulders hitting the doors.

"Don't move!" Cole screamed, spittle flying.

"Outside." And Chance's shoulders shoved the doors open as he took another step backward.

"I'll shoot! Goddammit, I'll blow your head off!"

"Outside," Chance repeated, the doors now slipping past his shoulders and swinging freely.

Cole lunged forward, hit the doors so hard it's a wonder they didn't break off their hinges, and then he, too, was out on the boardwalk. The townsfolk in the saloon let out a collective sigh. Tom Ellerton's wife dashed across the room and threw herself on her husband's lifeless body. Judi ran for the stairs and the safety of her room.

I leaned Clem against the bar. "Wait here," I told him. "Doc will take care of you." Then I started for the door.

"Don't do it, Josh," Clem said. "Don't go after 'em. Some things a man's not meant to see."

But I went to the doors and looked over them, looked out at the two men squared off on the boardwalk, Chance with his back to me and Cole with his coat thrown open and that bar of silver gleamin' in the last bit of sunlight.

"That's far enough," Cole raged, the gun shakin' in his fist. "Give me what's mine!"

Chance reached up past the stubble on his face and set his fingers to the eyepatch, then hesitated. "This is even darker than your heart, Cole. Darker than the Hell that Indian must have had in mind for you when he brought you back from the dead."

"Just show me, you son of a bitch!"

Chance nodded. "I'll show you. My only regret is that I'll be watching you suffer for the rest of my life." And he raised the patch.

Had he been facing me, I don't know what I would have seen when that eyepatch went up. I don't reckon I'd be alive today to tell you this story. Cole's fate would have been mine. Was it pure chance that the stranger with the eyepatch had placed his back to the saloon? Probably not.

I saw Cole scream. Saw him pull the trigger on his Colt. Once. Twice. Then he came up empty, the hammer clicking several times on spent cartridges. I don't know where those two bullets went, only that they were aimed at John Chance's face.

A great wind seemed to swirl up around Cole. The Colt was sucked from his hand, flew toward Chance and vanished. His hat left his head and the ragged wisps of hair on his skull soon followed. His coat shredded, its bits and pieces fussin' and flappin' like deranged crows as they hurtled toward the maelstrom that was buildin' about Chance. Everything was sucked forward and simply ... vanished.

Cole screamed ... and screamed ... as his eyes bugged out and the flesh was sucked from his face. As the meat flew from his bones. As his organs shredded themselves coming through his ribs. His eyes left his skull. His tongue and his teeth and even his fuckin' esophagus climbed outta his mouth and hurtled across the space between the two men. Everything was sucked into the vacuum of John Chance, into whatever unholy well waited in that empty eye socket. Bones snapping like kindling, screams dying on that eerie wind, Cole disintegrated ... until there was nothing left except that lump of silver, which hit the boardwalk with a heavy thud and sat there rockin' back and forth for a moment in the eerie quiet. John Chance, whom many call One-Eyed Jack, let the eyepatch settle back down and stood with his shoulders hunched and his hands hanging at his side.

"Lord God A'mighty," I whispered.

He looked back over his shoulder at me, his good eye full of pain and guilt and surrender. "God has yet to play his hand in this game, friend." He stepped to his horse and swung up into the saddle. "Perhaps the stakes still aren't high enough."

Then he turned and rode off, leavin' me standin' there in the doorway of the Dry Gulch Saloon, a fortune in silver at my feet, a grievin' town at my back...

...and Cole's dead mare snorting blood and pus, watchin' me with those Satanic red eyes from where it was tied to the hitching post.

TELL ME A STORY

THE SAGA OF THE TURTLE KNIGHT

This one's for all the perfect little princesses … and,
more importantly, for the love of turtles.

From: Lara Oakland
Sent: Tuesday, October 30, 2001 8:33 AM
To: Brian A. Hopkins
Subject: Good Morning
I don't feel like doing any work today … tell me a story. :-)
Lara

From: Brian A. Hopkins
Sent: Tuesday, October 30, 2001 8:35 AM
To: Lara Oakland
Subject: RE: Good Morning
Your wish is my command, Princess.
Bah

— THE PRINCESS AND THE TURTLE KNIGHT —

There was once a kingdom called Oakland, populated by a princess, inquisitive squirrels, tragically romantic tilt-at-windmill types, the occasional court jester (not always discernable from the aforementioned tragically romantic types), and other assorted characters who will walk in and out of our story without being fully developed ('cause I ain't writing a damn novel here, ya know!) but one must assume they're present to fully operate the kingdom, pamper the princess, and so forth.

The Princess of Oakland thought she had everything. She'd worked hard for this little piece of deceptively perfectopian castleburbia. Behind her walls, she told herself she was completely happy. She had her prince (Okay, so maybe they should be king and queen, because prince and princess makes it sound like they're brother and sister or something, but just go with it, okay?) and thought him perfect, even if he did rattle the bastions and portcullis of her castle with his snoring at night. So what if his schedule, so askew to her own, left them little time together? So what if he spent his days making war on the neighboring kingdoms and spent his nights surfing Internet porn sites and watching Skinamax while she slept? (They could not sleep together because of his atrocious snoring.) She had her cat and her Oakland night clubs and her peanut butter crackers (which she loved, even if the squirrel that had recently invaded her closet did not, a fact she'd discovered when he ignored the bait in her traps) and people to clean up after her and some expensive art hanging on the walls and so many other things to occupy her time. Princess Lara had everything she needed.

Or so she thought.

He came to the castle one day riding a turtle, which she thought was pretty preposterous, not realizing he was a preposterous sort of fellow. Vagabond, warrior-poet, trail-blazer, skirt-chaser, and hopeless romantic. He was all of that. His armor was considerably tarnished and it was obvious from wear that his lance had seen more than one windmill. He might have passed her by, intuiting that her squirrel-infested closet still held cheerleading outfits (which she could still fit into, no less!)—and cheerleaders had always been beyond his reach—but she was bored and she asked him in for a sip of wine. Nothing else, mind you. Just a sip to wash the dust from his throat. Give his turtle a little time to rest before galloping off into the sunset. (Okay, so turtles don't exactly gallop, but this is, after all, a Disney-type fairy tale. It ain't reality. It could never happen. Which actually makes it all the more poignant, doesn't it?)

She was bored (a plague that eventually infests every utopia) and he was rather dashing and she thought what-the-heck and she invited him in. Somewhere between the wine and the music of her voice, his eyes went dreamy and he made the mistake he always makes.

"Lady," he said, setting his sword at her feet, "I would know thee."

"*Know me*, Sir? Why ... no one knows me. Knowledge requires trust, and I've been burned by your type before."

He would have bet his very last nickel and even the saddle off his turtle that she had, in fact, never met his type before, but he let that pass and said, "Princess Lara, do you believe in love at first sight?"

She actually laughed at him. "Romantic nonsense, Sir Knight!"

"Then you don't believe in romance either?" he asked, trying not to let her see the great sadness that had come into his eyes. If she were to see it, she would misinterpret it. She would think him sad for himself, when in reality he was sad for her.

"Romance? What childishness is this, Sir Knight?" And she gave him the line he'd heard so many times before. "Grow up!"

She didn't believe in romance. She didn't believe in trust. Could never understand how these were the very essence of his being. He collected his sword and turned to leave ... but she called him back.

"You haven't finished your wine."

Though it was bitter, he drank it down. Smiled. Thanked her.

"What do you do out there," she asked, "there in your world of adventure and romance?"

"Mostly," he replied with all honesty, "I tell tales."

"Oh? Then sit and tell me one."

So he sat, while his turtle-steed rested and the sun painted the top of the western wall and her prince slept, unaware of the incursion, and his heart ached for what she professed she couldn't feel. He sat and his heart was exposed, as it had been exposed so many times before. And he tried to tell her a story about things she professed not to believe in...

– THE KNIGHT AND THE QUEEN –

...and this is the story that the Turtle Knight told Princess Lara:

Once, in a kingdom far, far away (imagine these words scrolling *Star-Wars*-wise across your screen), there lived a king. He was an old king, long secure in his kingdom (which had succumbed quite some time ago to the same plague that was just beginning to nip at the heels of our fair princess), long of tooth and weak of will, retired and quite set in his curmudgeonly ways. For a queen, he took a younger woman, because that seemed the best way to brighten his otherwise drab existence. As for the queen, she accepted his offer because she'd been burned by younger suitors many times before. She hadn't lost her belief in romance, she hadn't totally given up on happiness or love, but she had decided that neither were quite so important as a safehaven. The king might have even reminded her of her father, though she would never have admitted that to anyone, not even the knight who stole her heart—but I'm getting ahead of the story.

Being a queen is nearly as difficult as being a perfect little princess. The king expected much of her. Hers was the job of running the kingdom, while he mostly slept and saw doctors about a certain medical problem (which ought not to have much bearing on our story, but, alas, the queen was only human, after all). She was unsure of herself. Had doubts as to her abilities. When she met with the kingdom's advisors and councilors and every petty little bureaucrat with his thumb in the king's pies, she wondered if it was wise to speak out. They might label her a bitch or perhaps even ridicule her ideas. She could defer to their recommendations and boringly sage advice, thereby sparing herself the embarrassment. She was, after all, very uncertain of her capabilities. Perhaps her ideas *were* stupid. Make no mistake, it was a man's kingdom and most of the kingdom's officials believed that her place was the king's boudoir (even if he couldn't exactly take care of business in that department).

She found solace in a lowly knight. It started simply enough. There was a meeting. She was confronted by several gentlemen who were actually selling her a bill of goods, a line of bullcrappa, a proverbial pig in a poke. And they thought she was too stupid to see that. The truth was that she did see through their charade, but she was uncertain how to proceed.

"P*ssstttt*..." came the tinny rasp of air through a visor during one of the meeting's breaks.

"What? Who?"

"Here," said one of the knights set to guard the door. He jiggled his hauberk so that she would know which one he was.

"And why are you *pssssttting* me, good Sir Knight?"

And he told her what to tell the slingers of bull to put them in their place.

"They'll throw me out on my ass, Sir Knight!"

"No they won't. You're the queen. Believe in yourself. Stand up to them."

"They'll slip poison in my wine, undermine my credibility with the king, call me a bitch, and predicate everything by mentioning PMS."

"They'll listen," he told her, "or else."

"Or else what?"

"Just trust me."

Through the narrow slits in his visor, the queen studied the knight's eyes, and whatever she saw there was solid and true and worthy of her trust. So she trusted him. And she did as he had instructed. And when the men in the meeting rose to argue against her, before a derogatory word could slip their thin lips, the knight stepped forward and with one mighty blow of his hauberk split the conference table in two. "Gentlemen!" he roared. "Let us not forget that this lady is the queen!" And they saw in his stance and the fire in his eyes that it would not be wise to utter the words that lay on their tongues. Their heads could be as easily split asunder as that table. They acquiesced to the queen. Left the meeting. And from then on, they listened to what she had to say and treated her with the respect warranted not only by her position but by her wit and wisdom.

And afterward? The knight removed his helm and stood before her, sword at her feet.

"Why have you done this for me?"

He removed his gauntlet and touched her face. It was answer enough. She pressed herself into his arms, weeping for all the loneliness she had been feeling since marrying the old king. It had been so long since she'd felt strong arms around her. It had been so long since she had trusted someone. So long since she had bared her own heart. She swore she loved the old king, but there was room in her heart for another love, room for the love of this dedicated and romantic knight.

...that's the story the Turtle Knight told the princess. And when he reached this point, the princess laughed her pretty little laugh and said, "So then the king found out and had the knight's head removed. End of story!"

"No," said the Turtle Knight, sadly, wistfully, "that's not how the story ends. Perhaps that would have been easier for him..."

– THE PRINCESS'S GARDEN –

That evening, while the Turtle Knight slept beneath a tattered blanket in the stables with his mount, the princess lay in her feather bed, with her three finely-crafted, oh-so-warm-and-snuggly comforters wrapped around her and her prince snoring loudly in another room. Her hair had been given a thousand strokes of the brush by one of her many handmaidens. Her nails (fingers and toes) were just so. Her lingerie was exquisite and expensive (if somewhat under-appreciated, being as how she was sleeping alone). She had applied a fresh daubing of expensive perfume behind her ears and in the soft-as-silk valley between her perfect breasts.

"It's a stupid story," she told her cat. "On the morrow, I shall bid him mount that ridiculous turtle of his and be gone."

The cat merely yawned and stretched its claws.

"And you, you silly cat, you should be catching that squirrel in my closet!"

Another yawn from the cat.

When the sun rose again on Oakland, the knight packed his things and saddled his mount. The turtle was anxious to be off, for rarely had she known an idle day—and turtles are well-known for their wanderlust. But the knight couldn't bring himself to ride through the city gates without seeing the princess one last time. So he went to see her ... merely to say goodbye, mind you. He found her in her garden, admiring the beautiful flowers and shrubs planted and maintained for her by her gardeners. He stood for a moment mesmerized by her beauty, by the way the sun gleamed on her hair and accentuated the sweet contours of her gown. The rose lent its color to her cheeks. The periwinkles, gardenias, and dragon lilies gleamed in her eyes. It seemed as if the entire garden was arranged around her, all its colors circling her like a kaleidoscopic mosaic. Every leaf, every branch, every supple petal and bud seemed to strain toward her beauty, there in the center of the garden, in a spotlight created by the sun focused down through the trees. The knight gasped and held his breath, afraid the slightest whisper of air from his lungs would shatter the scene.

When she saw him, the princess could not believe that her heart skipped a beat. "Don't be silly!" she told herself. He was patently ridiculous, with his breastplate and greaves, his gauntlets and spurs. Such things had gone out of style years ago. With a sidelong glance at him over her rose bushes, she said, "Oh. You're still here?"

"I came to say goodbye, fair lady."

"But you haven't finished your story yet," she blurted out. She immediately chastised herself. What was she doing? He was a silly, romantic, Don-Quixote-ish buffoon. There were probably dragons that needed slaying or completely non-PC damsels in distress (which she certainly was *not*, thank you very much!) that needed rescuing or children who needed told a bedtime story or someone somewhere somewhen who probably had need of his ridiculously antiquated services. She certainly didn't need him. She didn't even like him!

"Would you have me finish?" he asked.

"Yes!" she answered, her heart being quicker-on-the-draw than her mind.

So they sat on a bench, while the birds sang and bees buzzed from one flower to the next. With a heavy sigh, the turtle lay down in the grass. She had seen it all before, of course, and knew they wouldn't be leaving today. As it watched the two humans through drooping eyes, the turtle noted how close the princess sat beside the knight, saw how she laughed at his words and studied his eyes and every now and then would gently touch him with her hands. The knight breathed deep of her perfume, touched her when and where he thought he could get away with it, and searched for the right words to expose her carefully guarded heart. The turtle watched and the turtle listened ... and the turtle knew that in the end there'd be nothing but heartache for her master. But being just a turtle, there was nothing she could do but wait...

– SCRABBLE IN THE CLOSET –

That afternoon, while Princess Lara strolled along the Oakland avenues being entertained by the Turtle Knight, the cat and the squirrel sat down for their usual tea and crackers in the princess's closet. A half-finished game of Scrabble lay between them. It was the cat's move, but he didn't have any vowels.

"I say," said the squirrel, who had adopted a British accent to make himself appear important, "whatever is your lady friend doing with that vagabond-looking chap?"

"I think," said the cat, "that she's falling in love with him."

"Poppycock!" exclaimed the squirrel. "You're off your milk, Kitty. That lady of yours has a heart the size of a walnut." Mentioning the nut set the squirrel to salivating and he hastily gobbled a peanut butter cracker, chasing it down with a sip of Earl Grey. His pinky was extended ever-so-properly as he drank his tea.

Irritated, the cat swept several crumbs away from the word CORN. "You don't know her like I do," said the cat. "She bottles her feelings up inside. Doesn't let them show. Thinks it's *purrrrr*-fectly acceptable to hide her true self."

"Well, that's hardly any way to live, now is it?"

"She's got issues," acknowledged the cat.

"Haven't we all? And what about the knight? Did he finish his story?"

"He did." And the cat told the squirrel what the Turtle

Knight had told the princess in the garden. How the queen and her knight had been happy for a time. Eventually, however, the knight had asked her to leave the king. And she had refused.

"So he bloody well rode off into the sunset in search of greener pastures, eh?"

"No. He stuck around, hoping she'd change her mind." The cat used its "H" and "P" to bridge the words CORN and MEOW. "Hope," said the cat. "Don't forget my double letter score." The cat drew two new letters from the sack, the "Q" and the "Z," and hissed a curse or two under his breath.

The squirrel licked the point of a pencil with the tip of his quick little tongue and jotted the score down on a notepad.

"But the queen didn't budge. She would call him up and meet him for what the knight described as 'long, lazy afternoons abed,' but she had no intention of leaving the king for a lowly knight. More and more, he came to understand that while he loved her with all his heart, she was merely using him."

"Stud service," said the squirrel. "There are worse ways to make a living." He flicked his tail, remembering how in his younger days it had attracted many a foxy lady squirrel. These days, its brilliant red had mostly gone gray and there was considerably less hair than there had been. Another year or two and his tail might resemble that of a rat. Suddenly self-conscious, he tucked it away beneath him.

"He began to see less and less of the queen," the cat continued, "until eventually the memory of her was an open wound, nothing more. Clearly, she'd forgotten him. Evidently, he'd never been that important to her at all. Then one day, she sent word that she was leaving the king, leaving for some other kingdom where she'd met another man. Though she'd told the knight that she would never leave the king, she was doing so now … just not with him. For some unexplained reason, she thought the knight should know."

The squirrel paused with several Scrabble tiles in hand. "Well, there you have it. Don't you see? She must have felt something for the knight. Otherwise, why would she have taken the time to tell him this? She wanted him to stop her. Did he go after her?"

"No. He let her go." The cat shrugged. "Pride maybe."

"Or maybe he'd finally seen what her heart was made of," said the squirrel. Using the cat's "H," the squirrel placed his tiles, using all of his letters to spell HEARTACHE. "Triple word score," said the squirrel. "I think you've lost this game, Kitty."

The cat shrugged. He was used to losing to the squirrel.

"Do you think the princess knows?" asked the squirrel.

"Knows what?"

"That the Turtle Knight is the same knight in the story."

"Oh. Maybe. The question is, does she care?"

"What difference does it make?" asked the squirrel.

"It makes a difference in whether she plans to break his heart, too."

"Oh. And the turtle?"

"What about her?" asked the cat.

"Do you think she knows how to play Scrabble?"

— THE GLASSBLOWER AND HIS LADY —

"And did this knight also tell stories to his lady love?" asked the princess, her voice a sweet sound to the Turtle Knight's ears … even in mockery.

They were strolling the marketplace of Oakland, sampling the sweets from confectioners' stands. The princess had a thing for candy corn. The turtle followed a short distance behind them, carrying the knight's helm, lance, and sword so that the knight's hands might be free to sneak a second or two of princess-contact here and there. He would touch her hand, though he couldn't actually hold it lest someone in the marketplace see. And every so often he would put his palm to the small of her back. Once he'd even managed to touch her hair. The turtle thought him a pathetic sight.

"Yes, he did," the knight answered.

"What sort of stories?"

"Oh, all sorts of stories, but mostly stories about the life they could have together."

"Tell me one of his stories," the princess commanded.

The Turtle Knight thought for a moment. They'd left some

of the noise of the market behind and the jingle of his spurs was now a merry tune, undercut by the deeper melody of his armor plates clanking together. The wind lifted the hair from his forehead and ruffled the old bit of lace brocade pinned to his shoulder piece (another story altogether). "Once," he said, "the knight and the queen were standing before a glass shop, watching as bowls of molten glass were scooped from the furnace and gathered in glowing orange orbs at the ends of the glassblowers' pipes, looking for all the world like the smoldering staffs of some powerful wizards."

The turtle let out a sigh and settled down to rest her feet. The turtle had heard this story the first time around and really didn't care to hear it again. The knight needed a new act. With some polish and maybe a bit of training in the art of juggling, the two of them could be making real money in Vegas. But, *nooooooooooo*, the knight had to waste all his time entertaining spoiled princesses! The turtle shut her eyes, blocked out the story, and thought about all the stuff she could buy on a Las Vegas entertainer's salary.

"Watching the glassblowers work their magic—blowing into their pipes, rolling and shaping the glass as it cooled—the knight told the queen the story of a new glassblower come to work at the shop. This glassblower was a lonely man who lived all alone, having never found his true love. Oh, there'd been women for him before, but none had been *the* woman. None had been capable of returning the great depth of love that he carried in his heart. And, so, in time, like so many others, the glassblower had just given up on love—"

"Like the queen's knight did?"

"Oh, no. Never for one minute believe that the queen's knight gave up on love. It's not in my—er, I mean, *his* nature to surrender. He's out there still," said the Turtle Knight, "searching for that one woman who will understand the true nature of love, as he understands it. Others before him quit the quest or settled for less than they wanted, but this knight, this one true knight, his quest goes on."

The princess laughed, though precisely why, even the turtle (who had popped out of her day dreams just in time to snort at the knight's little bit of romantic nonsense) couldn't say.

The knight flinched, but ignored the princess, pressing on with his (uh, that is to say, *the queen's knight's*) story. "Though the glassblower worked very hard, all of his work was flawed. He didn't understand what was happening. In the city he had just moved from, he had been known as the finest glassblower in the land. His work was valued above that of all other glassblowers, and he had lived quite well on his income. But here ... it seemed that every piece of glass he blew contained ripples and swirls and uneven surfaces and ... well, it was completely, inexplicably flawed. He had all but resigned himself to taking work cleaning out the troughs at the vomitorium, when another glassblower took a vase from his hands and held it up to the light. 'Look at this,' he said. 'It's not flawed. There's a face there.'

"Of course, the glassblower couldn't believe it. He looked at the piece himself. Sure enough, there it was: the face of a woman. It had to be a fluke. He dug through the shards of previous work which hadn't yet been shoved back through the glory hole and into the furnace. Holding these shards up to the light, he could see other parts of the same face. Here was her nose. Here the lobe of an ear. Here the delicate curve of her jaw framed by a wisp of her long hair. Here was her eye captured in a glass fragment that was sapphire blue. He blew a new piece, a large glass bowl like might be placed in the center of a table and filled with fruit. The bottom of the bowl refused to run smooth. When he held it up to the light, there she was again. He blew another vase. There she was. He blew an intricate glass handle for an umbrella, twirled it in the light and watched her face rotate in three dimensions within the solid center of the cylinder of glass.

"She was in everything he created.

"'I am cursed,' thought the glassblower, but he refused to give up. Now that he could see the pattern to the flaws in his glass, he could work with it. He brought out the features of the face within his glass. She became more distinct and clearly-wrought with each new piece that he created. And she became more beautiful. Hers was the face that he had sought all those years. This was obvious from her eyes, which contained more depth and compassion and understanding than mere glass could possibly convey. There was some great magic at work here ... and the glassblower knew that such magic would not have been worked without some reason.

"This was the woman he was meant to find."

"And did he?" asked the princess.

Had the turtle been capable of speech, she would have said, "D'uh..."

The knight smiled patiently. "The glassblower's work and the face that each piece contained became quite popular in the kingdom. Before too long, he had more work than he could possibly find time to do. The waiting list for a piece of his glass was very long. He worked day and night, rarely leaving the shop—even though he knew he should be scouring the city for the woman whose face had become his art. Art is like that, though, taking over a man's every passion, leaving little room for the normal pursuits of life. Many an artist has forgotten to eat, to sleep, to take care of his or her most rudimentary needs. True art is like that. True muses are merciless."

"So he *didn't* find her?" said the princess with much exasperation.

"Did I not say there was magic involved here, m'lady? True magic, like true art and true love, cannot be denied. He was working one day, bent over a glorious centerpiece of glass, when he heard a woman's voice. 'There,' said the voice, 'didn't I tell you it was you, Sarah?' The glassblower looked up and found two women studying a piece that he had created just that morning. 'That's your face in the glass,' said one of the women. And the glassblower saw that she was right. The other woman, Sarah, was the one he had been looking for."

"And they fell in love and lived happily ever after," snapped the princess, "she though he spent all his time working in his stupid shop, slept in a different room altogether, and rarely gave her the attention she needed."

"Oh, it wasn't like that at all," said the knight. "She didn't believe him at first when he told her that he loved her. It took a great deal of work for him to convince her."

"And then they lived happily ever after?"

"Yes, but there's more. So that she wouldn't be bored, so that they could spend more time together, he brought her to the shop and taught her to blow glass."

"And together they made the most beautiful glass in the world," said the princess. Her cynicism was really beginning to annoy the turtle, who was suddenly remembering how much the queen had enjoyed this story when the knight had first created it for her.

"No," said the knight. "The glass that they blew together was flawed."

"Flawed?"

"Yes. Flawed. But when they held it up to the light, they saw the face of a beautiful child, a lovely girl with her mother's eyes and her father's smile."

Despite herself, even though she had already heard the story and knew its denouement, the turtle smiled at the ending and for just a second her calloused turtle heart beat a little faster.

Who knows what the princess might have said about the story, for at that very moment an out-of-breath messenger came running up to them.

"Oh!" said the princess. "A note from the palace. The prince must have returned!"

The knight's heart dropped into the pit of his stomach as the princess tore the imperial seal from the scroll and unrolled it, waving off the messenger who was trying to catch his breath enough to tell her something. "Begone," she said dismissively.

"The prince works so hard, you know," said the princess to the knight. "It's been days since I've seen him for more than a few minutes at a time. I'm sure this is a note from him—"

The knight bit his tongue. Tasted blood.

"—telling me to rush right home so that we can spend some time together." Her eyes scanned the message … and the smile faded from her face.

"What is it?" asked the knight.

"It's not from the prince," she stammered.

"Who is it from?"

"My cat."

"Your cat?!?!"

"Yes. And it's addressed to your turtle."

The turtle raised her head.

"It seems she's been invited over for tea..."

– HEARTS LAID BARE –

The cat scratched his head and studied the Scrabble board, in particular the perplexing word that the turtle had just created. The cat hated to be perplexed. The closet where the three were playing was dark, but the squirrel had brought along his flashlight. He'd even installed new batteries that morning. The steam from their tea made lazy curlicues in the beam of the light. A heavier and sweeter-smelling cloud hung over their heads, permeating the princess's gowns and lingerie and musty old cheerleader outfits. Outside, they could hear water being drawn for the princess's bath. Word had arrived that the prince was coming home, and she wanted to be all clean and sweet-smelling for him when he arrived.

"Empath?" asked the cat. His eyes were bloodshot, because in honor of their guest the squirrel had broken out some really fine weed, rolled a joint, and they'd been passing it around for the last ten minutes.

"Empathy," said the squirrel, as he took a toke, his British accent long since replaced with a marijuana slur that had a slightly south-of-the-border ring to it, Ais the understanding of another person's feelings, the *tuning in*—if you will—to someone else's emotions." He held the smoke in, his squirrel face all scrunched up and his whiskers standing at porcupine-quill attention. His eyes were jet black marbles in the gloom of the closet, beady as a rat's. He was, of course, cousin to rats and field mice and possums and skunks and other varmints that the princess had long since run out of her city, but he'd have denied the lineage even unto death. Or at least unto the threat of death. Like most of his kind, he'd squeal in the end, spill his guts, sell out his best friend. (Never trust a squirrel with a secret.)

The turtle, who couldn't speak, bobbed her wrinkled head up and down.

"Well, then," said the cat, accepting the doobie from the squirrel, "she needs a Y."

The turtle shook her head back and forth.

"No. Empath is a word, too." The squirrel frowned at the turtle. "Though I'm not at all sure they exist, so perhaps we shouldn't allow it. You're not saying that *you're* an empath? You … a turtle?"

The turtle merely blinked.

"What's an empath?" asked the cat—and, under his breath as he exhaled: "Damn, that's some good *sheeeet*." And he did that vibrator thing that cats do, which set the Scrabble tiles to rattling.

"An empath is someone with an extremely well-developed sense of empathy, someone able to tune in another person's emotions, thoughts, hopes, dreams…"

"A mind reader?"

"Not exactly," said the squirrel. "At least not if I understand it correctly. If our shell-toting friend here was an empath, she couldn't pick your next Scrabble word from your brain before you laid out the tiles—that'd be mind-reading. She could, however, feel your excitement at having found the word."

The cat, staring suspiciously at the turtle, placed his next word on the Scrabble board. FLEA.

"Well," said the squirrel sarcastically, "even I picked up on the excitement for that one." He studied the board for a moment in silence, as the cat passed the joint to the turtle, while outside they heard the water stop and the princess fussing at her handmaidens to stir the bath and make more bubbles. Then he placed his next word on the board, using the cat's "L" and the turtle's "T" to create CHARLATAN.

"Huh?"

"It's when someone is not what they claim to be," explained the squirrel, glancing sideways at the turtle. "Don't forget to count my double word score," he added (it was the cat's night to keep score), preening his scraggly tail the way he always did when he was pleased with himself, Aand I think I also get a bonus for using all my letters."

The cat computed the score, which was subsequently

corrected by the squirrel, and then it was the turtle's turn again.
VERITAS.

"Huh?" said the cat again, becoming more and more agitated with certain guests who felt the need to make their host feel stupid.

"It's Latin for truth," said the squirrel. "But you can't use foreign words." And he flicked the tiles away with his tail. "Besides, how could you prove such a thing?"

"Prove what?" asked the cat, not realizing that the turtle, lacking the ability to speak, was conversing by way of the game.

"How could she prove she's an empath," explained the squirrel.

The turtle retrieved some of her letters, rearranged the others, and added a couple from her rack: CONDUIT.

The squirrel didn't wait for the cat to ask what it meant. "A pipeline. A mode of transmission from one thing to another." He squinted through the haze of smoke at the turtle. "You're saying that not only can you tune in someone else's emotions, but you can serve as a conduit for those emotions? You can share them with someone else?"

The turtle did her slow, ponderous nod again.

"You're full of shit," said the squirrel.

"Prove it," said the cat.

The turtle took a long, leisurely drag from the weed, the squirrel and the cat protesting as the last half-inch of joint disintegrated to a fragile, smoldering twig of ash right before their bloodshot eyes. She held the smoke deep in her substantial lungs (turtles have massive lung capacity, which is what allows them to sleep on the bottom of the ocean for so long and to be such excellent saxophone players) and closed her eyes, smoke curling languidly from her nostrils, her tiny little turtle tail tapping annoyingly against the side of one of the princess's high heel shoes. As the other two Scrabble players waited and watched, their every nuance and poise indicating skepticism, the turtle's attention folded in on itself, to a place where the marijuana swirled in psychedelic colors about her brain stem, to a place where her third eye winked like a sly whorehouse favorite ("You won't regret picking me, no sir!"), to that inner sanctum where her empathetic awareness could sweep out over the city.

And she did that thing she knew how to do, that parlor trick left over from one of her previous lives (which is another story altogether).

Miles away, the Turtle Knight had climbed to the crown of the highest tower in Oakland and there he sat, his head back, the moon lending an unfamiliar pallor to his tanned face, his eyes focused on something more distant than the stars, his heart barely beating. There hung about him an aura of tragedy, a sense of the wanderer, the failed poet, the misunderstood dreamer, the martyr. It wasn't an obvious thing. More intuitive than visual. But it was there in the way the moonbeams struggled to shine from his tarnished armor. In the set of his shoulders. In that single strip of lace pinned to his shoulder—which, at this moment, even the breeze failed to touch. It was a glaze applied over the scene by the absolutely lost cast to his eyes, the lackluster lay of his hair on his forehead, the subtle way his ankles were crossed, the gnarled callouses and pale scars on his hands and how they hugged his knees but were so painfully, obviously empty. These were hands meant for a task or a companion. Lacking either, they simply lay in waiting—but in their waiting was such a set of hopelessness ... well, it was as if it would be better to cut them off and burn them than leave them laying there with no purpose. But more than these subtle visual cues punctuating the scene, there came over the psychic-turtle-airways the empathetic ones, which the turtle absorbed with her usual nonchalance—she was, after all, quite accustomed to feeling everything the knight felt—and passed on to her two companions.

"Oh, man," the squirrel muttered. "That's sad. I think I just lost my buzz."

"Sad?" said the cat. "It's *purrrrrr*-fectly pathetic. He oughta just throw his ass off the tower."

They all three felt it. The great empty longing that lay at the core of the knight. The black weight of his famished heart. The dead tingling in hands that longed to feel her skin. The olfactory ghost of her perfume. The eyes that picked out her hourglass shape in the constellations. The mouth that shaped her name. The ears that believed they caught her laughter on the wind. The endless loop of her playing over and over in his mind. The desire. The hope. And the misery.

And, more, they felt how this was just the knight's latest episode of hopeless torment. They saw the line of women that had preceded the princess. Saw their smiles, their sweet caresses, their betrayals and rejections and fare-thee-well-good-sir-knights. They felt the unappreciated sacrifices. The romantic notions disregarded or made light of. Saw the sword of love raised on high and lowered a thousand times ... and felt with what absolute dejection it was sheathed again and again.

"How does he bear it? It's too much for one lifetime," whispered the squirrel, tears running down his furry little cheeks, and, as soon as the statement was out, both he and the cat empathized the awful truth: that it was more than just one lifetime. That this was the knight's curse. That he was the eternal lover, the immortally hopeless romantic, the sacrifice made to keep love, as it was understood by ten thousand princesses, safe. Without the Turtle Knight's suffering, none could love, because love would be measured not in hasty, passionless kisses, empty endearments, selfishness and self-serving facades, but in true sacrifice and commitment and ... forever and evers. It was the Turtle Knight's curse to understand true love. To feel true love, again and again.

And to never have it returned.

But the turtle's empathy didn't only touch the knight. It touched the princess. And they saw her, powdering and primping before her mirror, making herself ready for the prince who was due at any moment. She was already planning what item of lingerie she was going to wear. She would meet the prince at the door wearing something that would actually be more enticing than if she were to answer the door buck-nekkid. She'd already rehearsed her lines. "I have a problem," she'd say coyly, batting her carefully prepared eyelashes, cocking her hip just so, drawing back her shoulder blades and elevating her chest to accentuate nipples that she'd pinched just before opening the door. She'd purse her painted lips and arch her highlighted brows. "Think you can help me with it?" And the prince would sweep her in his arms and carry her into the bedroom and do what his hormones told him to do. The princess would moan and gasp ... and it would all be over rather quickly because she hadn't been this aroused in years. She'd really been missing the prince lately. He'd been far too busy with the kingdom and his wars, and he hadn't been paying her enough attention. No sir, not at all. But she'd show him. She'd remind him why and where they were so good together.

Why ... she'd fuck his royal brains out!

"She loves him *sooooo* much," purred the cat.

"Oh, sod off!" said the squirrel, because he had seen through the charade. He'd read the princess's subsurface emotions as if they were newspaper print bleeding through the backside of the page. "Can't you see what she's hiding from herself? This passion wasn't inspired by the prince. This passion belongs to that bloody damn fool, that Turtle Knight!" (The loss of his buzz had returned his faux British accent.)

And it was true. Somewhere deep inside, perhaps the princess knew the truth. But she'd locked it away and would never admit it. What she felt ... the passion, the longing, the libido ... well, it belonged to the Turtle Knight. It was he who had aroused her so. And she was giving it to the prince, who would blissfully suck it up, smoke a cigarette afterward whilst congratulating himself on being every bit the stud, and then go back to business...

...while the Turtle Knight sat atop a tower and contemplated his insignificance in the cosmos.

And then the turtle, because she was high on the squirrel's really, really excellent weed, screwed up big time. The emotions that she'd been channeling in one direction suddenly broke the dams in her mind and flowed in all directions. The princess was suddenly privy to the emotions of the squirrel, the cat, the turtle, and the knight. The knight, likewise, was privy to all of their feelings. It was like a confessional in which the curtains had suddenly been ripped aside.

There lay the knight's unrequited love for the princess, his undying sense of chivalry and commitment and sacrifice, his hopelessly romantic heart in all its hoary naked glory. "Oh, grow up!" thought the princess.

The knight, given the knowledge that what the princess felt for him and the passion that he had inspired in her heart would be given to the prince, felt his heart crack for the ten thousandth time. He opened his mouth and wailed. His cry echoed over the walls of the city, resounded from the alleyways and courtyards, setting all the neighborhood dogs to barking. He understood it wasn't real love that she felt for him, but it was at least a physical desire—something that he could have built on if she'd chosen to share it—and the loss of it was nothing short of physical pain. A knife had been driven through his heart. The world had been pulled out from under his feet yet again.

The turtle threw back her own head and howled ... not the howl of a turtle (because there is no such thing as a turtle howl), but the howl of a wolf. The howl terrified the cat, who shot through the squirrel's hole in the ceiling and vanished into the attic, leaving half his hair fluttering down on the Scrabble board. It caused the squirrel to faint on the spot, because he had suddenly seen that there was indeed a charlatan in their midst (for this was only a turtle because an ancient spell prevented them seeing it for what it really was) and knew how tasty his little squirrel ass must appear to a certain species. The squirrel's furry little body thumped down on the board, scattering the tiles, several of which rearranged themselves (completely of their own accord) to spell the word WOLF.

The princess dashed across the room and yanked open the closet door. "What the hell is going on in here?" she screamed, whereupon she caught a full whiff of the marijuana, saw the fainted squirrel and the howling turtle, and starting screaming for her servants.

While, across the city, atop the tower, the knight rose to his feet, his toes hanging out over the edge of nothingness, spread his arms, and felt himself lifted by a breeze that had at last appeared, a breeze that bore with it all the misplaced trust and petty falsehoods and jealous sorrows ever employed in the name of love.

– CAGES –

The prince had indeed been on his way home and chose that very moment to enter his wife's boudoir, where he found her screaming and chasing the turtle about the room. The turtle managed to slip through the open door, elude the guards stationed outside, and dart down the stairs. (Turtles really can dart when they must.) The prince might have given chase, but the princess was quite vocal about a "monstrous beast" waiting in her closet. The guards might have chased after the turtle, but they were far more concerned with guarding the prince's back. (He wasn't known as the most capable of swordsmen.) Thus, the turtle made a clean getaway.

After charging into the closet to see what dreadful foe awaited him (guards close on his heels, of course) and finding naught but a fainted vermin, the prince sent for a cage. In short order, the squirrel was locked up tight.

"Now," said the prince, his knuckles white on the hilt of his sword, "I think I'm due some explanations here. Who is to blame for this mayhem? Where did that turtle come from?"

"I don't know," the princess lied. "I found the turtle in my closet with …" She made a face. "A…with that rodent." She pointed at the squirrel, which had by now recovered and was gripping the bars of the cage. "They've done something with my cat. Look. In the closet. There's nothing but a smattering of hair. They've eaten my cat!"

The prince drew his sword. "It'll take but a second to verify that."

The squirrel threw himself against the back of the cage, his tiny heart pounding, his head shaking from side to side. "I didn't do anything," he stammered. But, of course, the prince was incapable of understanding squirrel-speak and heard nothing but the chattering of little squirrel teeth. Hastily, the squirrel scrambled for some of the Scrabble tiles scattered about the bedroom and arranged three of them.

"W*at*?" read the prince, baffled.

The squirrel strained for an "I," but couldn't quite reach it through the bars of the cage. Extending his middle finger (which everyone knows happens to be the longest finger on a squirrel's hand), he placed it in the appropriate position.

"Why, you little…" the prince raised his sword, ready to smash through cage and all.

"Wait!" said the princess.

"What the hell for?"

"No. That's what it's spelling. Wait."

The squirrel's head bobbed up and down.

"Wait for what?"

The squirrel gestured at the Scrabble tiles that he couldn't reach. With a growl that said he was fast losing patience, the prince kicked the tiles nearer the cage. The squirrel hastily arranged them.

"K*night?* What knight?" the prince demanded, while the princess, blanching, suddenly decided to make herself scarce.

There weren't enough tiles, so the squirrel got down on all fours, mocked a great shell of a back, and waddled around like a turtle with his tail tucked up under his belly. Then he stepped back as if to indicate a second character in his little game of Charades, arched a bowed leg over where the mock-turtle had been a moment ago, and went through the motions of holding reins and bouncing up and down as if at a full gallop.

"You're saying a knight rode in here on a turtle and slew my wife's cat? That's the most preposterous thing I've ever heard! What was he here for?" roared the prince, again raising his sword to put an end to the squirrel.

The squirrel scrambled for more tiles. Hastily, he arranged them, getting only so far as L-A-R before the prince scattered them all and kicked the cage across the room. "Guards!" he roared. A dozen of them were already crowded into the room, while a dozen others waited in the hallway. He could have simply turned and spoken to them, but he'd always been fond of bellowing that word. "There's a strange knight in my kingdom," the prince told them. "Find him. Immediately. Arrest him."

"What's the charge?" asked the Captain of the Guard.

"He's a spy," said the prince. "Kill him if he resists."

The guards saluted and charged out of the room in a great

clanking of weapons and armor.

It took but minutes to locate the Turtle Knight. And had they known, they could have found him even quicker by merely following the princess. When they surrounded him in the stables, she was still clinging to his arm, begging him to flee. He pushed her gently aside and placed his hand on the hilt of his sword.

"No!" she screamed. "They'll kill you!"

The smile that tugged at the corner of his mouth and the calm set of his eyes said that he didn't fear the twenty-four guards that had him surrounded. Nor did he fear death. The tune that his fingers tapped out on the hilt of his sword was a familiar one. His hands had at last found something they knew how to do.

"Please," she begged him. "Don't do this. I could not bear to watch them kill you."

The circle of guards drew tighter. The Turtle Knight paused, indecisive, his blade drawn just inches from its scabbard. A familiar song trilled in his blood, pounded in his ears, twitched along the tendons in his sword arm. But the princess had placed her hand on his wrist. The warmth of her burned through him.

"Put down your sword," she begged. "They won't hurt you. Please.

"Do it for me."

And that's how he came to set his sword down in the dust and surrender to the prince's guards. They knocked him down. Kicked him senseless. Stripped him of his armor. Bound him in chains.

And caged him in the dungeons.

– THE RESCUE –

The turtle was dressed all in black. (For legal reasons that should be obvious, we'll refrain from using the term "ninja" when referring to the turtle at this time.)

Nervous as he was around the turtle-who-was-not-really-a-turtle, the cat made several wrong turns as he led them through the underground tunnels and hidden passages of the Oakland palace. It seemed as if they'd been stumbling around in the dark for hours. The turtle was beginning to wonder if the cat knew where he was going.

"It's j-j-just up these st-stairs," stammered the cat, "and then through a s-s-secret panel that opens into a wardrobe." He scratched at his bald spots nervously. Apparently, in addition to the hair loss, the cat was developing a stress-induced skin condition.

Three wrong turns and two sets of stairs later, the cat finally paused before a wooden panel at the end of a long, dark hallway. "Through there."

The turtle found the latch for the secret door, opened it about an inch, and peered through the crack. This was a guestroom. Vacant at the moment. Followed closely by the scraggly cat, the turtle leaped from the wardrobe and crossed the room to the bedroom door. Through this door was a hallway, which the turtle recognized from her visit to the princess's bedroom. She made her way quietly down the hallway, sticking to shadows wherever she could. Were it not for the cat scratching himself against everything, they would have made not a sound at all moving down the hall. Before the princess's door, the turtle paused, placed the flat side of her head against the polished wood and listened, while the cat paced back and forth.

"Oh, I do hope we're not too late," moaned the cat.

The turtle opened the door and darted inside, nearly shutting the door on the cat's tail in her haste. The princess's room was empty. The dented cage with the squirrel inside was still on its side against the far wall where the prince had kicked it. When he saw them, the squirrel began darting back and forth, chattering inanely. The cat rubbed himself against the side of the cage, shedding more fur, mewling ecstatically.

"I thought I was a goner," said the squirrel, then repeated it five or six times as he shot back and forth across the cage.

"I went and found the turtle as fast as I could," explained the cat.

It took only a couple seconds for the turtle to pick the lock (another talent shared by turtles everywhere). The squirrel leaped from the cage and hugged the turtle. "Oh, thank you, thank you, thank you!"

"They'll be looking for you," said the cat. "I'm afraid you'll have to flee the city."

"Not a problem," said the squirrel. "There's a bus to Tijuana with my name on it. That's for damn sure." He dashed across the room, into the princess's closet—which was still a mess—and through the hole in the wall. They heard the faint clicking of his nails as he crossed the attic … then he was gone.

"You're welcome," said the cat, sadly, wistfully. He had thought their friendship important enough to at least warrant a goodbye. He felt as if part of him had just been ripped away.

The turtle gestured impatiently toward the bedroom door.

"Yes," said the cat, "I'll show you where to find him now. Thank you for rescuing my friend."

Back down the hall. Through the secret panel in the back of the wardrobe. Down many, many stairs, the walls and the air and the flagstones beneath their feet growing damper and colder with every step … they made their way into the dungeons. The air grew heavy and stale. The walls became drab with mold. The only light came from the squirrel's flashlight, which the cat had located in the princess's closet. The cat was more sure of himself now, less wary of the turtle-who-was-not-a-turtle. His ordeal was almost over and, besides, he knew these passages, had prowled them for mice his entire life. As they drew close to the cell where the Turtle Knight was being held, they could hear voices.

"It's the prince!" whispered the cat.

The turtle gestured for the cat to remain quiet and began to inch forward, keeping to the shadows.

The cat shook his head wildly from side to side. "Not me. No thanks. You're on your own now. I appreciate what you did for the squirrel, but this is as far as I go. Good luck." And the cat vanished back the way they had come.

"If you refuse to tell me who you are spying for," came the voice of the prince, "I'll be forced to find a means of making you talk."

"I am not a spy," came the reply of the Turtle Knight. His

voice sounded weak, muted by swollen and split lips.

The turtle crept closer, an inch at a time, moving with a silence and grace known only to turtles, until at last, in the flickering light of a torch, she could see where the knight lay beaten and bloody behind iron bars. The prince stood outside the cell, his breath wafting a fog in the cold, damp air, a heavy cloak wrapped about his shoulders.

"You're here to find a weakness in our defenses. Tell me who you're working for."

"I'm here for no one but myself," said the knight. "My reasons are my own."

"You're lying. And we *will* make you tell the truth." The prince crossed the room to a long, low object covered by a mottled tarp. "I suggest you tell me the truth now," he called back to the shivering figure in the cell. "Who sent you?"

"No one."

"Why are you here?"

The Turtle Knight struggled to his feet, his chains rattling. He brushed a bloody strand of hair out of his eyes, drew the rags that had been his undergarments a bit closer about him. "You know why I'm here."

"How could I know?"

"You know."

With a dramatic flourish, the prince whipped the tarp aside to reveal the device beneath. "With this, I will soon know everything."

The turtle had never seen such a device, but its purpose was clear. The table was pegged with holes. There were numerous stone blocks, cut to fit in the holes and serve as fulcrums, a point about which other blocks might move on tracks, powered by gears and cogs, cranked by wooden staves whose ends had been burnished by many a sweaty palm. There were sliding grooves and fitted clamps. Leather straps and brass buckles and gags.

It was a device for taking a man apart.

"You know why I am here," the knight said again. "I am not a spy."

"Say it then," said the prince. "If you're not a spy, then tell me why you're really here."

The Turtle Knight shook his head. "I will not. You'll have to ask her."

The prince did not ask to whom the knight referred. He only grit his teeth and traced a finger 'round the old stains on the surface of the torture machine. "You leave me no choice," he said.

"You have a choice," replied the knight. "Ask her. Ask her why I've stayed."

"She has nothing to do with this. It's you I'll have the truth from. In the morning," the prince spat, stalking from the room. "In the morning, you will talk."

The knight, exhausted, collapsed back into his corner of the cell.

The turtle rushed forward, picked the lock of the cell, and flung open the door.

"Hello, old friend," said the knight, as the turtle picked the locks on the chains.

The turtle nuzzled him, tried to get him to stand back up.

"I'm tired. So very tired."

The turtle tried to push him toward the door, butting the knight with her head, edging her great shell between the man and the stone wall.

"No," whispered the knight. "I'm not leaving."

"But you must," said the princess from the door of the cell, startling them both. "If you don't go, he'll kill you."

The knight struggled to his feet again, crossed the room, and stood before her. "You, and only you, can save me, Lara. He knows I'm not a spy, but he will execute me as such unless you tell him the truth."

"And what truth is that, Sir Knight?"

"That each time I tried to leave, you stopped me."

"But that is proof of nothing," she snapped.

"For you I have remained here. For you, Lara."

She turned away. "It's simply not true."

"You will stand there and say that you feel nothing for me? You will deny your heart and let me die?"

"I am not responsible for your fate, Sir Knight. Tell him whatever you choose in order to save your life."

"Not without your leave, m'lady. Only the truth shall pass my lips—and the truth would be best heard from you. Tell him the truth and ask him to spare me. Tell me the truth and I will do whatever you ask."

"There is no truth in this."

"Then you do not love me?"

"Of course not! I love the prince. He built this palace for me—"

"With this wretched torture chamber as foundation."

"—and bought me these fine clothes and jewelry and perfume. I am safe and cared for and cherished and..."

"While all I can offer is a life on the road, a bed 'neath the stars ... and my heart," said the knight.

"It's not enough."

"Then I will remain here," he said, returning to his corner.

"They'll kill you. Please. Go. While there is still time."

"Only you can save me," said the knight. "Tell the prince the truth."

"There is no truth!" she screamed.

"If you won't admit it to him, then at least admit it to me," begged the knight.

"You damn fool, run away!"

There came the echo of boots descending one of the stairwells.

"The prince has sent his guards," explained the princess. "In seconds, your one and only chance to escape will have passed. Please. Your turtle knows the way. Run for your life, good knight."

He shook his head. "No."

"He'll kill you!" she screamed.

"He can only kill me. He cannot kill what lies in my heart. I will love again."

She balled up her pretty little fists with their carefully manicured nails, crossed the room, and struck him several times in the face. "I hate you!" she wailed. Then she fled from the room.

Shaking, the knight wiped fresh blood from his mouth. The footsteps drew nearer. "Go," he told the turtle. "Save yourself, my faithful friend."

The turtle fled only so far as the shadows, where she crouched and waited while the guardsmen took up positions outside the cell. They immediately noticed the open cell door and the discarded chains. They beat the knight with the chains. Shackled him again. They slammed and locked the door. Hauberks and crossbows at the ready, they set up watch.

There was no way the knight could escape now.

— STICKS AND STONES —

"Do you remember," the knight asked the turtle in the frozen hours just before dawn, "where I got this?" And the turtle could see the shimmer of opal and lace in the flickering of the torches. Clutched in the knight's bruised and bloody hand. Evidently snatched from his armor as he'd been beaten and stripped. Hidden since then.

"Shut up!" shouted one of the guards, clanging his hauberk against the bars of the cell.

"It was a glorious day, wasn't it?"

The guard began to fumble with his keys so that he could unlock the door, go in, and beat the Turtle Knight again. A second guard stopped him. "Leave him be. The fool's just talking to himself. If we're not careful, there won't be enough left of him for the prince to torture."

The first guard laughed. "You're right. Let him rant and rave. He'll be screaming come dawn."

The Turtle Knight seemed not to even hear them. "We took the field ... won her heart."

Her eyes nearly closed now, the turtle remembered it all. The charge and the thunder of hooves. The splintering of lances. The great crashing of other knights toppled from their mounts and into the sawdust. The roar of the crowd. The sweet voice of the lady who had blessed the knight's entry in the tournament and placed her colors in his hand.

"I loved her, too," whispered the knight, his voice hollow and impotent in the barren cell. "Loved them all."

And the turtle took in the knight's great loneliness, tasted the curse that drove him, felt the love that only he could feel: true love. A love placed above all other needs for oneself. A love without measure or cost, without pretense or barter or debt. A love only the Turtle Knight knew. Given and never returned. Experienced and so often lost ... just so lesser loves might satisfy all the perfect little princesses and disillusioned queens. The ladies and the damsels and the sweet, chaste virgins. The farm girls and the tavern wenches. The thatchers' wives. The fair maidens. The castle debutantes. And as was often her want, the turtle reached deeper and felt the underlying affection that the knight felt for her: faithful friend, trusty steed, devoted companion. The knight did love the turtle. But not enough. Not enough to break the spell and return the turtle to its true form. Not enough to set her free and give her voice again. That old spell was just as strong today as the day it had been cast.

With a great sigh that almost gave away her presence, the turtle placed her head against the cold stones of the floor. A single tear broke from her eye, traced a glistening path down her weathered turtle cheek, vanished in the lichens and the moss that coated the dungeon floor. Vanished without a trace. Forgotten like a dream. Remembered only in the trail it left across the turtle's face, gleaming there in the torchlight like a scar.

Dawn came with no fanfare, no bristling morning sun—for no single beam could reach so deep in the prince's dungeons. Came without a trumpet's call to arms. Without the thunder of hooves or the rumble of explosives or even a princess's pleas to spare the knight's life. There was none to rescue him. None save the turtle.

But being just a turtle, there was nothing she could do but wait.

The prince arrived and ordered the knight dragged from his cell and strapped to the device. The knight did not protest, did not struggle. He seemed to have resigned himself to his fate. They could take him apart, but they could not undo him. When he was strapped in place, the prince leaned over him.

"Why are you here? Who sent you?"

"My heart brought me here," said the knight. "And my

heart's love bid me stay. It's the first organ to form, you know. Older and wiser than the rest of our constituent parts. Vessel of the soul ... and it's our souls that remember our past lives, our past loves. More people should listen to their heart."

The prince frowned at the knight's soliloquy. Seemed almost to hesitate. Then he gestured to the knight's right leg. "We shall start here."

His men set the blocks and the gears in place.

The prince turned the wheel.

And the Turtle Knight's bones creaked in protest.

He closed his eyes. Bit his lip. Made not a sound. When his leg snapped, the echo ricocheted throughout the dungeon like the crack of a whip. The turtle flinched, felt the searing heat of pain in her mind, reeled back from the sheer agony of contact. She blacked out for a moment ... while the knight ground his teeth, but held on to consciousness amid the bright floodlight of pain that lit every dark corner of his mind, exposing every memory, every love, every misery. From the black whirlpool in which she'd fallen, the turtle tasted them all, all the past moments of glory and grandeur and romance, even those dramas in which she had never played a part, and loved the knight all the more for them, knowing in each saga he'd followed his own advice. He had simply listened to his heart, no matter what it had cost him to do so.

"Why are you here?" asked the prince.

"Ask her," the knight whispered through the pain.

The turtle came back to dull, unending agony, even as they were setting the blocks on the knight's other leg. She closed her eyes. Focused inward. Let her mind sweep out over the castle until it at last came upon the princess all alone in her garden.

And the turtle fed the princess the knight's pain as the prince leaned against the hand crank and brought the stones to bear on the knight's left leg. By the time the princess arrived, the knight's leg had snapped. His scream—for even he could only endure so much—was drowned out by her own.

"Stop this!"

The prince turned from his task, the wooden stave of the crank spinning wildly out of his hands, unwinding all that tension from the knight's shattered bones. The wooden shaft was flung free, clattering across the cold stones of the dungeon.

"Do you know this man?" he asked his wife.

"This isn't right," she said. "This man is not a spy."

"How do you know this?" asked the prince.

"I don't," she said. "But surely he would have told you something by now? He's a vagabond. A drifter. A troubadour, a layabout, and perhaps a sellsword … but he's no spy. Can't you see that?"

The prince shook his head. "How is it that you see so much in him … my darling wife?"

And the princess didn't know what to say.

"His arms," said the prince to his men.

They moved to obey him, but it was obvious even their hearts weren't in this. Several of them had seen the princess and the knight together, strolling the market, near the city gates, perhaps even in the garden. This was no interrogation. This was the prince's jealousy at work.

The princess wrung her hands as the guards shifted the blocks to the knight's arm. "You can't," she begged her husband. "Not his swordarm. How will he live?"

The prince cocked an eyebrow. "How will he *live*? Until I hear the truth, he shall not even receive the mercy of a quick death."

"Tell him," whispered the knight.

She looked down at the knight. Saw the pain in his eyes. Felt its backlash through the conduit of the turtle's empathetic mind. The truth lay there on her tongue, bitter even as it was sweet. All she had to do was speak it. More, she saw that the knight cared more for the truth than for his own life … for even the truth might not save him now.

"Lara?" asked the prince.

Her knees trembled. Her hands were clenched in bloodless white.

The prince reached out and squeezed her arm, there where the sleeve of her fancy silk dress ended. She flinched in pain.

"Perhaps," she said, "his partner would know more."

"His partner?" asked the prince, taken aback.

"The turtle," said the princess, her arm a livid red. "I know where it is."

"No!" screamed the knight, for the first time struggling against the straps that held him to the device. Buckles popped and sprang across the room. Leather snapped. The knight surged up from the table, and it took four guards to haul him back down against the cold stone. The shattered bones in his legs ground together and unreal pain shot through the turtle, which shook in the shadows, fighting another blackout, fighting a pain so great she wanted to howl again, as she had done in the closet. But through the pain, the turtle drank in the knight's devotion and concern for her. Something surged in her blood, something as old and as powerful as time, something as rich as love and as true as a knight's promise. There was a glimmer of white in the shadows. The yellow glint of an eye that was hardly turtle-ish. The gleam of a canine incisor. Where before there had been the dry, reptilian odor of turtle, there was now the sharp musk of something mammalian, something that smelled of old kills and deep woods and moonlight.

"Don't do this," wept the knight, broken at last ... while the beast in the shadows waited, lips curled back and muscles taut, knowing nothing of fear, already anticipating the bloodshed.

"Bring your guards," said the princess to the prince. "I'll show you where the turtle is hiding."

They untied the knight and tossed him, broken bones and all, back into the cell. Slammed and locked the door. And marched up the stairs on the heels of the princess, who never looked back. Not even once.

No matter how badly she wanted to.

– WOLF DREAMS –

Far beyond the Oakland castle, deep in the forest, the wolf that had been a turtle paused beside a clear brook and allowed the knight to drink.

The knight lay there in his bloody rags, his face in the cool water, letting its chill leech away some of the fever and the pain. The last few days had been a blur for him. The wolf had rarely stopped. He could remember only brief episodes: moments of heightened pain, like the time his leg had become snagged in a root and the wolf had wrenched it from the splints, forcing a second setting of the bones; moments of unreal clarity, like the time he awoke with his face pressed into a bed of fragrant blue flowers, more beautiful than anything he had seen in the princess's garden, while the wolf lay collapsed beside him, beyond exhaustion from having dragged him from the castle dungeons; and moments of sheer, delirious fantasy, like the time he thought he saw Lara running alongside them.

"Sir?"

This had to be one of those latter moments. He must be dreaming. But, no, the wolf saw her, too. The knight could see the wolf watching the girl through hooded eyes, struggling with the need to sleep.

"Are you hurt?" asked the girl from the other side of the brook.

He wiped the water from his face, struggled to sit up on his elbows. "I'm broken beyond compare, girl. But I'll heal. I always do."

She was standing in sunlight, the forest breeze teasing her golden thighs with the ragged hem of her short shift. A poor girl. Mid-twenties. Dark of hair and eye. Full of lip. Lithe and buxom and fair. Her calves looked as if she'd spent her life running through the forest. Tentatively, she waded the water to kneel at his side, beads of water clinging to her bare feet. He lay mesmerized by the simple beauty of her ankles, her instep, her toes. When he looked back up to her face, he saw a fine net of scars across her throat, down one cheek, across her collarbone and fading into the sun-wrought freckles on her chest. He reached a tentative hand to trace the scars, but she flinched away from his hand—proof that the scars he couldn't see were worse. He ached to take it all away, to mend every fragile fracture in her heart.

"When was the last time you ate?" she asked.

"I don't remember," he told her.

"My home isn't far. A simple cabin that my father, a woodsman, built a long time ago. I lived with him there until …

until he died." The pain in her eyes said there was a story there, a story that the knight intuited was all wrapped up with those scars, both visible and not. Her need was as palpable as the leaves and twigs beneath him, as sharp and as painful as the jagged ends of broken bones in his legs. "I can take you there. I'll feed you. Check your wounds. You can rest and heal and…" She seemed to realize that she'd spoken at a breathless pace, nervous and unsure of herself. "My name is Tanya," she added. She looked expectantly from him to the wolf and back again, waiting for an exchange of information.

The knight glanced at his companion, dozing there in the tangled shade of an oak's exposed roots. He wondered what the wolf might be dreaming as her legs twitched in the carpet of leaves.

"Sir?"

And the wolf, with empathetic clarity, saw it all in a dream and fed it back to the knight as hope, as promise. If one spell could be broken, if one curse could be lifted … well, then so could another. Quests were meant to have endings, after all.

"I am the Wolf Knight," he told the girl. "Feed me, fair maiden … and I'll tell you the whole story…"

A thousand times these mysteries unfold themselves
Like galaxies in my head
On and on the mysteries unwind themselves
Eternities still unsaid
'Til you love me

–Sting, from "A Thousand Years"

SHEEPSKINS

The boy reminded Carol of Andy.

She was accustomed to it. In four years of aimless wandering, she'd run across dozens of runaway children, all of whom reminded her in some way of her dead son.

Carol found the boy about an hour before sunrise on Route 183 just north of I-70 and Hays, Kansas. He was shivering before a roadside diner, wrapped in a tattered black trench coat that fussed and flapped about him like a bevy of crows. He told her his name was Gil. Claimed he was waiting for someone, but his hightops were worn through and his faded jeans were slashed with the camo-striping stains of high grass. He looked to be fourteen or fifteen and in need of a meal.

The diner was serving its early breakfast crowd, but he wanted a burger and fries. When he finished the first hamburger, she bought him another. In no time, he'd put that away and was mopping catsup off the plate with the last of his fries.

"You want that?" he asked, pointing to her half eaten danish.

"Please." Carol slid him the plate. She wanted more coffee, but the diner's only waitress was swamped with tired truckers and belligerent vacationers. When Carol tired of trying to catch the waitress's eye, she focused on finding things about Gil that did *not* remind her of Andy.

The boy pushed the empty plate aside. "What do you want, lady?"

"It's Carol. Do I have to *want* something?"

"Everybody wants something."

"Oh? What do *you* want?"

He frowned and didn't answer.

"How about a ride to the nearest bus station and a free ticket home?"

"You rich or something?"

"Maybe."

"How do you know I won't bash you over the head on the way and take *all* your money."

"I guess I don't."

After that exchange, a silence fell between them while each reevaluated the other. Carol tried to guess where the boy had come from (Oklahoma perhaps; the accent fit) and how she might locate his parents to let them know he was still alive. How many times had she prayed that someone would call about Andy? Then, three months after her husband's fatal heart attack, she finally did get a call...

The boy broke the silence. "Thanks." He made to leave the booth.

Carol caught the dusty sleeve of his coat. "Wait."

"I don't need your help."

They'd all said that. She pictured Andy confidently turning down a stranger's help. Andy's eyes might have flashed in anger just like this boy's when a stranger laid a hand on him.

The chime on the front door rang, just as it had done half a dozen other times since they'd arrived. This time it was followed by a warhoop and a deafening gunshot.

Carol turned to find a thin black man framed in the closing door. A white cloud of plaster drifted down from a hole in the ceiling, salting his short-cropped hair and broad shoulders. He wore ragged jeans tucked into scuffed workboots. Dried blood clotted the hair just above one ear and what looked like a bullet hole had darkened his left thigh.

"Camillus of Veii!" he howled. "Show yourself!" The muzzle of the handgun swept over the diner's patrons. "I know you're here!"

"Brennus," the boy hissed, low enough that no one but Carol heard him.

One of several truckers seated near the door rose from his seat. "Look buddy—"

The stranger shot him in the face.

The diner erupted in startled protests, horrified screams, and the sound of chairs overturning. The waitress dropped a tray and dashed for the kitchen doors. Calmly, the stranger aimed the semi-automatic pistol and shot her in the back. The impact hurled the waitress through the swinging doors where she collided with the cook. He caught her in his arms, but when he felt the warm rush of blood down the front of his shirt he screamed and dropped her at his feet. The stranger shot the cook through the throat. The cook went down, gurgling like a severed septic line. The kitchen doors swung closed, hiding the corpses from sight.

"Quiet!" screamed the madman. The turmoil in the room died to terrified sobs. Most of the customers had crawled beneath the tables, Carol included.

Gil hadn't moved.

"Get down!" Carol whispered.

The boy didn't answer. His gaze was locked on the gunman.

"I know you're here," the madman repeated.

"What do you want?" asked another of the truckers. He was crouched beside the corpse of the first victim.

The madman stuck the gun in the trucker's face. "Do you want to die, asshole?"

The trucker tried to answer, but his voice failed him. He shook his head slowly. He was a big man, but the gaping muzzle of the pistol dwarfed him.

"Get up."

"Wha—?"

"Get up!"

The trucker got slowly to his feet. The madman put the muzzle of the automatic beneath the trucker's chin. The trucker's legs trembled, threatening to spill him to his knees.

"Have you ever seen a .45 rip the top off a man's head?"

The trucker opened his mouth, but all that came out was a whimper.

"Do you fear death?"

"Yes."

"Then well might you tremble, for I am death called Brennus. Three hundred and ninety years before the birth of your Christ, my Gauls sacked Rome. We raped; we pillaged; we burned. Men, women, children—we left nothing but corpses rotting in the sun. Then, for a change of pace, I sailed *with* Caesar against the Veneti in 57 B.C. The first known battle at sea and I was there."

"He's crazy," whispered someone behind the counter.

"I was there when they hung your savior from the cross. Sixty years later I massacred Romans at Camalodunum for Queen Boadicea. In the second century, I stood watch atop the first completed section of Hadrian's wall. I was at Aquileia in 340 when the sons of Constantine made war. In the fifth century they called me Alaric, the 'All-King,' and I ransomed Rome for five thousand pounds of gold, thirty thousand pounds of silver, four thousand silken robes, three thousand pieces of scarlet cloth, and three thousand pounds of pepper!"

Brennus threw back his head and howled at the ceiling. "I've fought a hundred wars, died a thousand deaths, and slaughtered millions. In the ninth century, I fought in all five campaigns between Rome and the Saracens, changing sides more than a dozen times as the mood took me. I owe allegiance to no man, not even this shell I wear now.

"Do you doubt me?" asked the madman.

"No," the trucker moaned.

"Then walk with me, mortal." Brennus grasped the trucker's hand and wrapped it about the handle of the .45. He shifted the barrel so that it lay beneath his own chin. "Step across the razor's edge and take a peek at the other side.

"Pull the trigger."

The trucker's trembling ceased. One corner of his mouth twisted sadistically. Without hesitation he squeezed the trigger. The gun roared and the top of the madman's head exploded in a shower of red, splattering bone and brain-matter across the suspended ceiling.

Rather than fall away from the trucker, Brennus's body clung tenaciously, hands twisted like talons in the trucker's leather jacket. The top of his head gaped like a ravaged egg as it lolled forward on his limp neck.

The trucker's hair seemed suddenly charged with static

electricity, for it rose as if lifted by a gentle breeze. He screamed and his eyes rolled back to shine an empty white. A second later, the corpse dropped away and the trucker stood alone, the gore-drenched weapon still clutched in his hand.

The trucker laughed softly, cruelly. "A rush like no other, eh Camillus?" Though the voice matched that of the trucker, the tone belonged to he who had called himself Brennus.

Gil slid to the very edge of the padded booth, leaning forward, tense. Carol clutched his knee, terrified the boy was about to do something that would get them both killed. She tasted copper where she'd bitten through her lip to keep from screaming. Her heart was pounding so loud she feared everyone would hear it. *Be quiet,* she begged, fearing any sound might draw attention to herself and the boy.

A woman huddled beneath a table with her two children began to say the Lord's Prayer.

The trucker kicked her. "You could at least get it right, bitch—

> *The lord is my shepherd; I shall not want.*
> *He makes me down to lie.*
> *Through pastures green he leadeth me the silent waters by.*
> *With bright knives he releaseth my soul.*
> *He maketh me to hang on hooks in high places.*
> *He converteth me to lamb cutlets.*
> *For lo, he hath great power, and great hunger.*
> *When cometh the day we lowly ones,*
> *Through quiet reflection, and great dedication,*
> *Master the art of karate,*
> *Lo, we shall rise up,*
> *And then we'll make the bugger's eyes water!*

—Ah man, Waters should have been one of *us*! Not one of these *sheep*." He grabbed the woman by the hair and dragged her out from under the table. Her children began to scream.

"Cam, I haven't enough bullets or time to kill everyone here. Show yourself." His eyes, rabid, scanned his cowering audience. They came to rest on the only person not visibly terrified: Gil.

"Remember when we fed on the blood of mortals such as these? We were the wolves, swift and silent in the night, and they the sheep upon which we preyed.

"Remember when I first invaded Rome? They agreed to pay me to leave, then whined and sniveled all through the weighing of the gold. I tossed my sword onto the scale and cried 'Woe to the vanquished!' Gods, but they raged about that. Then you showed up and routed my army from the city. Show me you haven't forgotten. Show me you're still the warrior who drove me from Rome."

He forced the muzzle between the woman's quivering lips. "Show yourself or I'll blow this woman's brains out. After her, I'll do her children."

Gil rose smoothly to his feet.

Brennus laughed. "You chose a child's body?"

"No choosing," Gil answered. "There was an accident and I was dying. The boy tried to help me."

"And your damn sensibilities kept you from killing him and changing hosts. You probably haven't even subjugated him. You were always such a wretched peasant, Cam."

"And you were always the butcher. Let the woman go."

Brennus shrugged and shoved her aside. He leveled the gun at the boy's face. "It ends here, my friend. Centuries of conflict between us. Acres of corpses left rotting in the sun to get at you."

"All because I ran you out of Rome over two thousand years ago?"

"Pah! What did I care about Rome? That's just where all the blood was being shed at the time. Did I care when they killed Hitler and forced me to move on? Did I care when they pulled the troops out of Nam? Inconveniences. Nothing more. No, I want you dead because you keep me from being unique."

"Then you'd better be certain."

"A slug through your brain will be certain. No one will touch you as you die."

The boy smiled for the first time. "What if I don't need physical contact to transfer?"

"You can bluff better than that, Cam. Of all our kind that I've met—"

"And slain."

"—I've never seen one who could make the jump without physical contact."

"The legends—"

"Children's stories. You know that as well as I."

"You'd better be certain," the boy repeated. "And there's only one battleground where you can be one hundred percent certain."

"You're an anachronistic bastard, aren't you?"

"Scared?"

Brennus bared his teeth in a feral grin. He extended his free hand, fingers extended and splayed. "Bring the boy with you, Cam. I'll show him what a real master's like."

Gil took the offered hand, fingers interlacing with the bigger man's. "I'll bring them all, butcher."

Brennus's grin faltered.

"All of them. They've been with me down through the centuries. Every last one."

Brennus tried to pull his hand away. The boy's coat flapped about his ankles as the larger man jerked him off his feet, but the boy hung on. Though the gun was trained on the boy's face, Brennus didn't fire.

Gil twisted his free hand in his opponent's hair and pulled their faces together. "You're right, Brennus. I suffer the same limitations as you. I can't transfer without physical contact and I can't leave a body unless it's dying. But unlike you, I've *never* subjugated a host. I've never discarded any of them either. They're all here within me, every last one."

"Let go of me!"

"Shoot me, Brennus. Take us in and let's see who's stronger, you or them."

Brennus dropped the gun so he could get a better grip on the clinging boy. With a great heave, he tore Gil from him and hurled him against the counter.

Carol watched the gun clatter across the floor. She wondered fleetingly if she'd know how to use it, then she scrambled out from under the booth on her hands and knees. Out of the corner of her eye, she saw Brennus plant a kick into Gil's side, slamming him against the counter again. Her fingers closed on the handle of the gun, but another hand batted hers away.

Brennus turned from the dazed boy to find the gun he'd dropped.

The mother whose children had been threatened pointed the weapon at the madman's chest. Her hands were shaking and from her trembling lips came a low keening.

Brennus held out a hand. "Give me the gun, lady." He took a step toward her.

"Don't..." Gil tried to say, but he couldn't get his breath.

Carol understood. "Don't let him get close!"

Brennus took another step. One more and he'd be within reach of the woman.

"No," she whimpered.

"Just give me—"

The roar of the .45 cut him off. He stumbled back against the counter, his black leather jacket suddenly slick with blood. Red saliva bubbled from his mouth and ran down his chin. He caught the edge of the counter and used it to stay on his feet. Blood pumped from the hole in his chest and splattered Gil where he lay on the floor below him.

"Shoot him again!" Carol screamed, but the pistol's recoil had startled the woman and she'd dropped it.

Brennus pushed himself away from the counter and took one wobbling step towards the two women and the pistol on the floor. It was obvious he'd never make it. He dropped to his knees and smiled at the boy. "Looks like we'll do it your way after all."

He fell across the boy, wrapping him in a crimson hug. By the time Carol reached the two of them, Brennus was dead and the boy was struggling to get out from under him.

She helped him up. "Are you alright?"

He nodded, but his eyes were glazed. In the distance there were sirens. "Got to go." He turned towards the kitchen.

"Wait!"

"No time." He pushed through the swinging doors, stepped across the dead waitress and cook, and started for the back door. She followed.

"Don't I get some sort of explanation?" she asked as they stepped out into a field behind the diner. The sun was just beginning to grey the horizon.

"Best you keep your distance."

"Why?"

He turned and she saw the pain on his face. "Because he's still here, you know." He struck his chest with one gnarled fist. "In me."

"And just who are you? Should I call you Camillus?"

"Call me what you will. The boy, Gil, is here. Just like every other personality I've given immortality these past two thousand years."

"I don't understand."

"We're not mortal, lady. From one host to the next, we hop-scotch through time. Normal procedure is to subdue—hell, with Brennus's kind, it's more like *destroy* the resident personality during a transfer. If the resident personality's too strong, it's normally abandoned and left to die when the next transfer's made. I never do either. Every soul I've occupied is with me, the whole clamoring lot of them."

"Dear God."

"That's why Brennus feared to kill me while we were touching. He knew I'd transfer to his mind, bringing all of them with me. He couldn't have withstood it."

"But he transferred to you?"

"It was that or die. He couldn't reach anyone else." The boy turned and ran out into the field. "Stay away from me, lady. I've got to come to terms with this new voice inside me."

Carol let him go.

When the police finished their questioning and released her, Carol got in her car and started north. She made a note to check her bank balance in the next town. The money from her husband's life insurance must be nearly depleted. She had no idea what she'd do when it was gone. Maybe it was time to go home.

But there were still so many Andys out there...

WISH ONE KNIGHT

Jeremy closed his comic book when he heard the front door slam.

Such a telling sound, this slamming of the door. The ten-year-old scrambled beneath his bed, taking the tattered comic with him. Familiar dustballs, a sock deprived of its mate, and a one-legged G.I. Joe welcomed him to his secret sanctuary.

"I'm home!"

Slurred words. Heavy, shambling feet.

Deke was drunk.

Again.

"Goddammit, where is everybody?"

Jeremy crawled further beneath the bed, its dark weight scant reassurance over his head. The room's corner was as far as he could go, pressed there against the peeling wallpaper and moldy sheetrock.

"I'm in the kitchen." Mother's voice. Apprehensive. Tremulous.

"Bring me a cold beer on your way out, Becky. I'm sweating like a goddamn hog." The worn sofa groaned beneath Big Deke Reynolds' weight. Loading trucks the last three months, Deke had burned off most of the excess he'd put on during his out-of-work period, but he was still a big man: six two in his stocking feet, nearly two hundred and thirty pounds on the scales at the corner drug store. Except for a beer gut, his bulk was all muscle.

Jeremy opened his comic.

Page eleven of *The Black Knight*: The villainous Jules de Monteret has kidnapped the Lady Joan de Vac. With her draped

rudely across his saddlebow, he rides through Dreadwood
Forest to his dark castle by the sea. In the dungeons below
Castle Torn, he chains her to a rack and prepares to torture from
her the information he seeks.

"Dinner ready?"

Nothing from Mother.

The sofa groaned again as Deke leaned forward, preparing
to head for the kitchen. "Did you hear me?"

"Twenty minutes," came a wee voice from the kitchen.

"Didn't I tell you I'd be home at five? I told you to have
dinner ready at five. Can't you at least have dinner ready when
I get home? Is that too fucking much to ask?"

The questions were, of course, rhetorical. Becky Reynolds
knew to keep quiet. She had come to fear this stranger in her
house, this man she once loved. Yet more terrifying for her was
the thought of where she'd be without him. Without so much
as a high school education, with her first husband long since
cold in the grave, dead of some unpronounceable disease that
struck but one in a million, she had no value outside that of a
mother and a wife. Housework was her sole profession, sex her
occupational hazard, and Deke her unforgiving employer.

"Where's that kid? Doesn't he know how to greet his old
man anymore?" The sofa groaned a third time, but it was just
Deke settling back. A greeting from Jeremy hardly warranted
getting up from the sofa. Of course, Deke wasn't Jeremy's real
father. For the last four years, Deke had been trying to replace a
man Jeremy could only vaguely remember. Mostly good times,
until Deke lost his job and the drinking started.

Jeremy settled in for the long haul, willing the drifting
dustballs to lie still and quiet. There mustn't be a single sign of
his presence. *That kid* had gone to ground and would stay there
until Deke's snoring blended with the voice of the Late Night
News.

Page Twelve of *The Black Knight*: The evil de Monteret's
questions are scoffed at by the lovely Lady Joan. "There was
never a treasure," she assures the villain. "You've been made
the fool, Monsieur. You chase dreams. A peasant's fantasy,
nothing more." De Monteret turns the rack and the Lady's

screams balloon across the colorful page.

Mother's cautious footsteps as she left the kitchen came to Jeremy more as vibrations than true sound. Until he heard them, he didn't realize he'd been listening for them. Awaiting the inevitable.

"The goddamn beer's not even cold!"

"But I put it in the fridge more than an hour ago."

Her whine ended with a sharp crack, the sound a pine knot makes exploding in a campfire. It was a sound Jeremy had heard all too often: the sound of Deke's hand on Mother's face.

"I asked for a cold beer. *Cold* beer! Can't you even get that much right?"

A sob. "I said I put it in the—"

"Listen to me, woman. The beer. Isn't. Cold."

"The refrigerator... it's old. You know—"

Another slap. Part of the ten-year-old wanted to slip out from under the bed and go help Mother. But a greater part of him, that part which remembered the pain of Deke's belt, fists, and boots, urged him to cower in his sanctuary.

Page thirteen of *The Black Knight* is an advertisement for Atlas Bodybuilding.

I'm a coward, Jeremy thought, not for the first time. *Kick sand in my face, and I'll crawl beneath my bed.*

Slap! "Here I am working all fucking day with those stinking goddamn niggers loading trucks for that Jew bastard, Silverstein." *Crack!* "All I ask is for my dinner to be waiting when I get home and for my fucking beer to be cold. Is that too much?" *Smack!*

Mother whimpered.

"Maybe you'd like to take your fat ass out on the street and try to support this family?"

"Please!"

"That's about all you're good for anymore. Just a piece of ass!"

Another slap.

"Here. I'll show you, bitch!"

Page fourteen of *The Black Knight*: Lady Joan refuses to divulge the location of the treasure. Monteret leans close and whispers more despicable methods of torture to her. Her face goes pale. Her bottom lip quivers. Whatever debasement Monteret has threatened appears to have hit home. The fable has reached its bleakest hour, for Lady de Vac is about to break and the treasure will only allow Monteret to wreak more misery and injustice on the kingdom. Now is the time for a hero. Now is the time for page fifteen where the Black Knight arrives, thundering down the dungeon stairs on his midnight charger, scarlet cape billowing like storm clouds, a gleaming yard of steel bright as lightning in his fist.

Where is Mother's knight? Who is there to save her?

"If not me myself," Jeremy whispered to the dustballs, "then there is no one."

"No! Please. What if Jeremy walks in?"

Jeremy believed in truths.

The truth that this wasn't really his stepfather, but rather some urban demon crawled forth from the sewers to possess Deke. A demon with many, many names: unemployment, inflation, foreclosure, eviction, deficit, debt, urban renewal, welfare, food stamps, economic depression...and the collapse of the U.S. oil industry, that dreaded beast which put Deke out of work, out on the streets, and, later, in the bars.

The truth that this demon had destroyed the loving, caring Deke, the man who had taken him to Disney World two summers ago, the man who had read him, a little bit each night over the span of a year, Tolkien's *Hobbit*.

The truth that this demon might also kill his mother.

Unless her Black Knight came forth to slay it.

Jeremy slid from under the bed, his comic rolled and clenched in his shaking fist. He went to the bedroom door, which opened, like every other room in the tiny apartment, on the living room. He opened it a crack and dared to put his eye to it.

The boy uttered a small, terrified gasp. His legs buckled, nearly dropping him to the floor.

Deke had Mother bent over the end of the sofa, one hand cruelly twisted in her short blond hair, the other holding her house dress up around her waist. Jeremy could see very little of his mother. Of Deke, he could see far too much. Deke's bare and hairy ass moved back and forth in quivering thrusts at the forward apex of which Mother's weeping climbed an octave. Between Deke's widespread legs swung wrinkled brown sacks. Like counter-weights on an old grandfather clock, they were keeping time with the raggedly metronomic thrusting of his hips.

Jeremy had heard as much as any other ten-year-old about sex. The scene in his living room did not match what he'd heard—unless rape was to be considered sex. Shaking uncontrollably, understanding that he had witnessed something vile, something that exceeded the hate and abuse levied daily on his mother in the form of beatings and curses, Jeremy closed his bedroom door. But he forgot to twist the doorknob, and the latch made a deafening *click* as it slammed home in the frame.

"The little bastard's watching us!"

A second later, Jeremy heard heavy footsteps. The boy dove for the bed and its comforting dark underbelly, but he was only half-hidden when the bedroom door burst inward to slam like thunder against the opposing wall.

"Come here, you little sonabitch!"

Deke's growl sounded very much like a drunken lion. He reached for Jeremy's exposed ankles, but his pants were still undone and they dropped down around his knees. He hauled them up, struggling to get them closed over his erection, then had to fight a stuck zipper and poorly sewn button. Under other circumstances, it might have been comical, but there was murder stretched like some rubber Halloween mask over Deke's face and insane hatred glistened shark-like in his eyes.

By the time Deke got his pants secured, Jeremy was huddled in his corner beneath the bed, shivering amid the dustballs and broken toys, clutching the rolled-up comic to his pounding heart.

"Come out from under there!"

Tears started down the boy's face.

"If I have to haul this goddamn bed outta' the way, I'm gonna' beat you so's you can't move for a month, boy! Now, get out here!"

Jeremy recognized the *truth* in Deke's words. He knew he should crawl out from under the bed. To stay would only aggravate Deke more. But he couldn't move.

"Fine. If that's the way you want it..."

There was a great squeal of protest as the bed moved, the sound of old wood dragged across linoleum, only slightly less hair-raising than fingernails on slate. Jeremy's dark sanctuary was invaded with light. A great beefy hand took him by the back of the neck and hauled him away from the moldy corner.

Held aloft by that one strong hand, Jeremy was turned to confront Deke's twisted countenance. Deke's grip was so tight, Jeremy feared his neck would surely snap.

"Did you like what you saw, you little pervert? Huh?" Deke reeked of beer and something worse. Something sickeningly sweet, like mildew or old urine. Jeremy instantly associated it with what Deke had been doing to Mother. "Answer me, boy!"

"Please," Jeremy sobbed.

"I ever catch you spying on me again, you little shit, and I'll—"

"Please don't hurt Mommy."

"What I do to your mother is *my* business. You understand me?" He shook the boy for emphasis, hard enough that Jeremy's teeth rattled. The boy's eyes were beginning to bug out and his face had turned crimson, suffused with so much blood he could taste it in the back of his throat. His lower lip was quivering and he'd bitten his tongue.

Where is Mother's knight?

Jeremy's previous thoughts taunted in a sing-song chorus through his mind, pounding in time to the beating of his heart and the racing of blood in his veins.

If not me myself, then there is no one.

"I won't let you hurt her," Jeremy croaked, trying to sound the way he knew the Black Knight must sound on page fifteen. His voice came out sounding more like the terrified squeak of a mouse caught between the paws of a cat, but it was enough to further anger Deke.

"Seems you're getting a little too big for your goddamn britches. Time I taught you a lesson, boy!"

As Deke's free hand drew back, Jeremy could see Mother's blood sprinkled like new rust across the knuckles. Jeremy hardly realized what he was doing until it was too late and the rolled-up comic book had smacked across the bridge of Deke's nose.

The comic proved poor substitute for a broadsword.

Deke gasped in surprise and fury. His eyes swelled to twice their normal size. The drawn hand, held open for a slap, closed into an angry, knuckle-white fist. The fist seemed to scream as it catapulted forward. It was only after the blow, replaying the image of the plummeting fist in his mind, that Jeremy realized it was he who had screamed.

In Jeremy's head there was a detonation of light, accompanied by pain like he'd never known before. His mind, stripped of reason and sensory input, latched on an image from one of any of a hundred films in the *Friday the Thirteenth* or *Nightmare on Elm Street* genre. In it, a man's face was split with a machete, a victim's head caved in with a fireman's axe, or a woman's forehead pierced with an iron railroad spike. There were a thousand variations, but *that* was the pain he felt. A bright implosion of agony that burned through his skull like a nuclear inferno and left him stripped, lifeless, hanging from a lance of chrome thrust between his eyes.

Infinite seconds passed. On some distant level, Jeremy was aware of the floor slamming hard against his back. His head hit the cracked linoleum with a dull *smack*, the sound a basketball in need of air makes on wet cement. Somewhere far, far away, Deke made more threats. Jeremy thought he heard his mother's voice crying from the living room, "Please don't kill my boy." There was a second blow that must have been a kick. Jeremy felt it wedge knife-like between his ribs. And then the door slammed shut.

Despite the pain, the tears, the blood trailing from his nostrils, Jeremy felt relief. He had survived another beating. He tried to sit up, but the room wouldn't hold still for it. Something was pounding against the inside of his skull in an effort to escape. Tentatively, he felt his nose, and whimpered as broken cartilage grated beneath his fingers.

When he was finally able to sit up, it felt as if there was a heated knife in his side. His neck was sore where Deke had held him.

All in all, he'd come out of it pretty lucky.

Jeremy heard Deke in the living room ordering Mother to hold still. A moment later, her weeping and Deke's hoarse moans whispered through the closed door and echoed off the barren bedroom walls.

Where is Mother's Black Knight?

The comic lay beside him, open to a curling page sixteen. A single scene occupied the entire page: The Black Knight standing triumphant over a shuddering Monteret. It was drawn from a ground-level perspective so that Monteret was but a cowering child and the knight was a tower stretched above him, the gleaming length of his broadsword a polished slide from tower to ground. In the background, Lady de Vac was still on the rack, but her head was raised and her eyes were fixated on her savior. Her eyes said it all.

"I can't do it alone," Jeremy cried. His tears ran a course parallel to the blood streaming from his broken nose. "I need your help, Sir Knight."

A light breeze, perhaps from beneath the door, rustled the page. From the other side of the door, Mother's weeping had quieted to a resolute sobbing, while Deke's breathing had become ragged and full of shuddering gasps.

"You've got to save us," Jeremy told the comic book image. "I'm calling you forth to right this wrong, Black Knight. I—" The boy stumbled over the words. What were you supposed to say in a summoning? What were the proper procedures for—

Blood!

Every summoning needs blood!

The boy leaned over the open comic and, despite the sharp pain and fireworks going off back of his eyes, he squeezed his broken nose. Fresh blood splattered across the page and was promptly absorbed by the cheap, dry paper.

But nothing happened.

Jeremy stared into the dark eyes gleaming through the knight's visor. "You *must* come!" He pounded the blood-dampened page with his fist.

Still, nothing.

Then, a single tear, like a tiny, pearl-shaped diamond, fell from Jeremy's eye and hit the page, soaking into the violet jewel in the pommel of the knight's broadsword. There was a moment of silence, as if all time had stopped. Gone were the sounds of Mother and Deke, the cars and people on the streets outside, the failing air conditioner in the living room window... everything. Gone.

The silence was shattered by a thunderclap that left Jeremy's ears ringing. The air above his bed parted, opening on some netherworld where damp stone corridors overgrown with green moss and black mold led off into dark recesses that screamed of hidden evil. The air that came through was fetid, foul with stale death and worse, unidentifiable odors. Jeremy had a second to wonder if this was such a good idea, then the gaping hole was filled with the Black Knight.

The knight stepped out onto Jeremy's bed, stooped to prevent his head and shoulders crashing through the ceiling. One of the bed's legs snapped beneath his weight. The bed tipped precariously. Legs braced, the knight didn't even notice. Behind him, the rent in time and space closed with a soft pop. The knight stepped down off the bed. He was now able to stand without stooping, although the scarlet plumes shooting from the top of his helmet were bent double by the ceiling. Where he had walked across the bed, there were grimy, rust-colored smears, thick and oily, like wet clay. The knight carried with him an odor of death. His armor was a lackluster ebony, splattered with old blood that clung like dried onion skin. Strapped about his waist were two weapons, longknife and broadsword. The broadsword's tip nearly dragged the ground; its pommel was tipped with a vermillion stone that glistened wetly.

From the living room: "Goddammit, I don't know what the hell that little bastard's doing in there, but as soon as I'm done, I'm gonna' kick his ass!" Deke's words were spaced around short, gasping breaths, as if he was speaking while exercising.

The knight's eyes, barely visible through the slit in his visor, were black as crude oil. The helmet seemed to contain its own field of darkness, cloaking the face within, leaving nothing but the eyes discernable. Those eyes studied Jeremy for a moment, then their intense gaze traversed to the door. Something in the knight's posture seemed to indicate a patient query.

"Yes," Jeremy whispered.

The knight hesitated but a second longer, and Jeremy could almost hear his thoughts as he considered the close confines of the doorway and compared it with the space required to wield the broadsword. He drew his longknife. The blade rasped like a hornet as it slid from its sheath. The iron was dark, the edge notched and worn, but the tip was finely tempered and, where the edge had not been misused, it gleamed silvery sharp in the feeble bedroom light.

He crossed the room in two great strides, the broadsword slapping metallic against his thigh, and with one kick split the door down the middle. The doorknob half pinwheeled out into the living room, spinning like some crazy top before it fell. It struck Deke across the back of his legs, just above where his trousers hung around his ankles, and he let out a yelp of pain. The hinged half clung tenaciously, swinging wildly on hinges that had pulled free of the frame and hung now by screws seated mere threads deep. As the knight stepped through the doorway, he hit it with his shoulder and it crashed to the floor.

Mother screamed.

The Black Knight strode through the living room, brandishing the knife on level with Deke's throat. Deke's pants saved him from the first cut. As he scrambled away, abandoning Mother across the couch with her house dress hiked up around her waist to reveal her pale buttocks, Deke tripped and fell. The knife whistled by, mere inches from his face.

Despite a quivering jaw and a keening not unlike Jeremy's earlier, Deke fought back. He clawed up the battered half-door beside him and, with a Herculean heave made possible by months of heavy lifting on the loading docks, slung it at the knight. The door caught the knight by surprise. Its weight not only carried him back several feet, it also knocked the knife from his hand. The heavy blade clattered across the linoleum, sliding to a halt in the bedroom doorway where Jeremy now stood.

Deke scrambled to his feet, fighting his trousers up over knobby knees and hairy thighs. There was no erection to get in the way this time. The knight's presence had taken care of that. Ignoring the difficult zipper and button, Deke held them up with one hand. With the other, he shoved his screaming wife aside so he could run for the front door.

The knight caught him about halfway there, driving him into the wall with a backhand. The knight's iron gauntlet opened up the side of Deke's face as easily as if it were rice paper. Deke hit the wall hard enough to leave an impression in the sheet rock, then he crumbled to the floor. As he sat there, blood seeping down his face to drench his dirty t-shirt, the Black Knight drew his broadsword and raised it over his head.

"No," Jeremy said, but his voice was barely a whisper.

Suddenly Deke was on his feet, ramming his shoulder into the knight's stomach. But the knight wasn't even moved by the tackle. He brought the pommel of his sword down atop Deke's head. Deke staggered back, more blood starting from his forehead. Deke's eyes, shiny and distant, met Jeremy's across the room. In them, Jeremy wasn't sure if he saw apology or accusation.

The sword flashed and blood flew in a wide spray, decorating the wall in violent red swathes of abstract art. Deke spun as if on a string, a gruesome ballerina tasseled with blood and intestines, until the blade came back and stopped him in his tracks with its length thrust through his back and out the upper part of his chest. Deke hung there while the Black Knight contemplated him like a crude man studying something he'd just pulled from his nose.

Were it not for Mother's screaming, the room would have been completely silent. The blood running down the walls and dripping about Deke's feet made not a sound.

"Fuck," Deke said in that silence, his final comment to world and family. The single word sounded thick and wet, like he was talking around a mouthful of raw liver.

Contemptuously, the Black Knight slung him free of the sword. Deke hit the floor like a sodden sack of dog food and lay dead, a loop of grey intestine strung out beside him. His eyes were open, staring accusingly in Jeremy's direction.

Jeremy's stomach heaved and he vomited across the floor, splattering the front of his shirt and his feet.

The knight shook his sword to clear it of blood. The viscous fluid splattered the floor in Rorschach patterns of red—crude images of women with spread legs, yawning chest cavities, and ravaged throats. The Black Knight said something then, the first word he'd spoken since he'd stepped out of that netherworld. The word was in a foreign tongue, but Jeremy interpreted the tone as contempt for an opponent too easily vanquished.

He glanced once at Jeremy, then turned to face Mother where she cowered, whimpering, on the sofa. Sheathing his sword, he stepped toward her. Mother screamed again.

"It's alright, Mother," Jeremy said from the doorway. "I called for him. He's here to help."

The knight reached out and caught the front of Mother's dress. With a single wrench, he stripped it from her body and tossed it aside. Mother huddled on the couch, one hand covering the dark hair between her legs, the other clutched across her breasts.

"No," Jeremy stammered.

The Black Knight looked back over his shoulder. The dark eyes blinked, polished onyx, hard and cold. He spoke again in that foreign tongue. Though the words themselves were a mystery, Jeremy knew the message: *To the victor go the spoils.*

Jeremy sagged against the door frame and sank to his knees. One knee landed in vomit, but he was beyond caring.

The knight knocked Mother's hand away from her crotch. He forced her legs open and slid between them, slapping her once when she tried to claw at his eyes through the visor. As she sagged back against the sofa, he squeezed one of her breasts hard enough to leave the imprint of his armored hand. There was blood there too, bright red against Mother's pale flesh. It was Deke's blood.

The knight began fumbling with the buckles at his waist.

Where is Mother's Black Knight?

From the apartment building's stairway came the sound of heavy feet.

Jeremy's hand found the cold iron of the knight's knife where it lay on the floor.

Mother's hands pounded vainly against the heavy armor shielding the knight's broad chest. He laughed. It was a cruel laugh, universal in all languages.

Jeremy staggered to his feet, his eyes on the knight's back, looking for an opening, his hand wrapped tight about the handle of the knife.

There was a pounding at the door. "Police! Open up!"

Still working at the buckles, the knight looked back over his shoulder at the door, just as Jeremy slipped the knife in to the hilt where breastplate and shoulder-piece met. Blood flooded hot over the boy's hand. The knight bellowed in pain. Jeremy ripped the knife free and drew it back to plunge it in again, but there was another clap of thunder and the knight was simply... gone.

The front door burst open and two policemen ducked through, indistinct blurs of blue and black to Jeremy. His focus had narrowed to the dripping knife in his hand, the only thing remaining of the Black Knight. Everything else was out of focus, elongated and disassociated with distance.

Guns leveled, the cops ordered him to drop the knife. Their eyes shifted from the red blade in his hand to the corpse on the floor.

Jeremy looked to his mother. She would tell them what had happened.

Mother was a gibbering mess, her eyes rolled back in her head, her hands rhythmically clenching and unclenching the sofa cushions. She no longer made any attempt to cover her nudity. "Please don't hurt me," she chanted again and again.

"Drop the knife, son," one of the cops repeated. The muzzles of their service revolvers seemed incredibly large, dark tunnels leading to another world.

Jeremy let the knife slip through his sticky wet fingers. It thudded to the floor. He wiped his hand on his pants.

"I can explain," he began as they cuffed his hands behind his back.

RHUESHAN'S PALLADIUM

(a Swords of Eire fantasy)

He awoke to pain and the rain threatening to drown him where he lay in the mud. Opening his eyes and straining to see through the downpour, he found that he had somehow managed to drag himself away from the main flow of the storm-flooded creek. If he expected to live much longer, he would need to move farther yet.

Though it had been hours since he'd fallen here—dawn was now painting the eastern skyline a bleary grey—the creek was still rising. Already it tugged possessively at his boots.

Moving was easier thought about than done. Any movement brought pain from the gash in his leg. Looking down, he saw the torn leather, the blood, and the ragged cloth he'd used to tie the leg off. How long had it been since he'd loosened the tourniquet?

He fumbled weakly with the wet knot, found that he couldn't get it loose, and wept in frustration. Exhausted with the failure, he lay his head back, feeling the mud's cold embrace as it sucked up around his head, filling his ears, blocking the dirge of the rain. He closed his eyes and the only sound was the coursing of blood through his veins and the hammering in his skull.

The hammering grew distant. Deeper. Melded into the rumble of thunder. His body floated on mercury waves, weightless, tossed by gentle winds.

And he dreamed.

The clouds moved in: dark; ominous; fast, like the roiling front of a black flood. Sheet lightning flashed in eerie, ice green as the clouds fought for air space. Seemingly timed with the collisions of the clouds, stronger bolts of lightning surged free to trace jagged, random lines of energy to the plains of Kilcullen. Borne on the strong, cool winds stirred up by the spring storm, thunderous rumblings echoed across the land.

Slowly, as if drawing the curtain on the final act of a play, the clouds hid the sun. King Duncannon's army watched as a dark shadow marched across Kilcullen's golden fields, crossing from the west, where it seemed to engulf their enemy, to the east, where it advanced up the gentle slope on which they stood in full battle array.

An omen, declared the optimists among them. The dark took the Kildare forces first; *we* will be victorious!

From where he sat his mount, lance and shield braced across the saddlebow, Glengaerif Callin saw it only as a storm, one that would make this final battle all the more unpleasant. At least the storm had lowered the temperature. But he feared the chill winds and sheet lightning meant hail. A cold pelting from above was one more distraction he didn't need.

Down the hill and across the glen, the massed forces of Cloyne Kildare took the darkening of the noonday sun for an omen in their behalf. Behind the advancing line of light-dark drawn on the plain, they charged. Their cries carried up the slope, setting Glengaerif's horse to dancing nervously.

"Easy," he bid the warhorse. "We'll be at them when Donegal signals."

As if he heard his name, the scarred veteran turned on his grey stallion and looked back at the seven thousand men behind him: three thousand footmen, pikes and shields forming a spiny wall at the army's front; two and a half thousand archers behind them, arrows nocked in their long bows of yew; and fifteen hundred horsemen. All seven thousand tired from the march from Duncannon's seat at Droichead Nua.

Even at this distance, Glengaerif could see Donegal Connaught's face as he surveyed his troops. The scar that ran from just below Donegal's right eye, across both lips, and over his cleft chin where his jaw was permanently disfigured, was a livid red. Donegal's eyes looked wild in the lightning flashes, and his mouth, showing what teeth he still had, was split in a feral grin.

From the hopelessly outnumbered army assembled behind him, the warlord looked to the king at his side. For what seemed like several long minutes, but could only have been seconds, the two men stared at each other, saying nothing. Below them, four thousand Kildare soldiers started up the slope on foot, while twice that many horsemen swung around each side to flank the Duncannons.

A farewell? Glengaerif wondered. No words were necessary between those two; they'd been fighting together since before Glengaerif was born. Duncannon, a man with a dream of peace and freedom who'd set himself as king to achieve it. Donegal, content merely to serve the king whose dream he deemed worth dying for. Together they'd achieved that dream.

For a time.

Nothing lasts forever, thought Glengaerif Callin. Looking downhill at the Kildare horde, he added: *Nobody lives forever either.*

The king sat up straight in the saddle and drew his sword. Lightning strobed and the wind lifted his pennant as he raised the sword over his head. His long grey hair, seemingly charged by the storm, stood out about him, hiding the thin circlet of gold he'd chosen to wear into battle.

The King's gesture needed no words. *To battle,* it said. *And take as many of them with you as you can.*

With a last smile to his king, Donegal Connaught threw back his head and howled at the black sky. Slicing the air about him with his sword, he led the charge down the hill...

Dawn had progressed little when he next awoke. However, the creek had risen to the point where it was now threatening to spin him around at the waist and drag him along with it. Only the suction of the mud held him in place.

He struggled for a moment to free his head of the clinging black ichor, then rolled over on his chest and began to drag himself away from the creek. As he moved, his right hand encountered cold steel and he clutched at it. It was the sword he'd dropped an eternity ago.

The blade hampered his worm-like progress, but he refused to abandon it. When he deemed himself far enough from the creek and could afford to stop and rest, he turned his attention to his leg.

The knots he knew to be beyond him. Placing the sword close to his side, he drew his dagger and slid it between the tourniquet and the leather of his leggings. The filthy cloth parted with no effort.

He howled as blood flowed back into the numb leg. Throwing back his head, he screamed at the heavy black clouds, ambivalent as they continued to dowse him with cold rain. The pain overcame him and he fell back, lost in a blanket of darkness that promised comfort, release, escape.

—from the pain, but not from the haunting of his mind.

Hours, days, an unmeasurable amount of time later, the armies pulled back to assess their losses.

Glengaerif didn't hear which side sounded the call to withdraw first. In the blood-heat of battle, he was as unaware of trumpet signals as he was of the passage of time. He only withdrew when a comrade got his attention by hauling on his horse's bridle. Still clutching his gory broadsword and battered shield—he'd lost the lance in the first few moments—Glengaerif joined the men remaining in his squad. As they dismounted to rest, the sky continued to spit forth its lightning, but no rain.

An officer was directing the wounded over the hill where a field hospital had been set up. Glengaerif sat back and tried to rest, but the rumble of the thunder wasn"t loud enough to drown out the moans of the wounded and dying on the bloody slopes below. When his eyes refused to stay closed, he took time to estimate the number of men still among the living. He was surprised to find that half his squad remained. Perhaps there *was* hope for a Duncannon victory.

He pondered wiping the fast-drying gore from his sword, but decided it was a waste of time and energy. Now that the red haze of battle was gone, the smell of all that blood sickened him. He was covered with it, though none of it was his own. At least he thought none of it was his own. He'd been in battles before where it was hours later that he realized he'd been cut.

Thunder continued to rumble over Kilcullen. Blended with its deep bass, Glengaerif noticed a new sound over the field: the cry of the carrion birds as they gathered for the feast. Circling above, they were nearly invisible against the black sky.

"We did a lot better than I thought we'd do," commented an out of breath rider beside Glengaerif.

Glengaerif tried to spit, but his mouth was too dry. "Nothing difficult about killing peasants."

"Eh?"

Donaughmore, Glengaerif thought. *I think his name is Donaughmore.*

"They're using peasants for footmen. No training. Pitchforks and harvest scythes for weapons." But their horsemen were another story. Remembering an old soldier who'd gotten close—way too close—Glengaerif added, "Their riders are damn good, though."

"Don't count out the peasants," someone spoke up from behind them. "Was a harvest scythe removed young Sean Tilgor's head."

Glengaerif was trying to place who Tilgor was when Donaughmore suddenly got to his feet. "Look!"

Glengaerif did, though with the slope of the hill such as it was, it wasn't necessary to stand. Across the corpse strewn lower slope, came three riders: a standard bearer, a soldier, and Cloyne Kildare himself. The standard bearer's lance bore two flags. Below the green and gold flag of Kildare, fluttered a simple flag of white.

"Whoresons want to surrender," Donaughmore laughed.

Ignoring this absurdity, Glengaerif watched as Duncannon and Donegal mounted and rode out to meet the three Kildares. They took no standard bearer; the boy who'd held that title lay dead below, an arrow through his throat. Duncannon's flag lay with the boy, trampled in the red mud of Eire's finest grasslands.

On neutral ground between the armies, the two groups met. Kildare's standard bearer held back as if acknowledging the absence of a counterpart. Separated by no more than ten paces, the other four held counsel, the two kings, as yet unmarked by the battle, and the two warriors, bespattered with blood and gore.

There was no way to hear what was said, but Glengaerif guessed that Cloyne Kildare was offering terms for Duncannon's surrender. Duncannon's stiff posture and shaking head was testimony to his answer. Donegal's left hand remained on his sword hilt the whole time as if he trusted none of it.

Finally, Duncannon spat something, indecipherable at this distance, but the vehemence in his voice was clear. Then the King spun his horse and started back up the slope.

"Wait!" shouted Kildare, so loud that his voice carried across the entire field. Duncannon ignored him, but Donegal had remained, intent on protecting his king's exposed back. Kildare pointed up at the crest of the hill.

"Your doom!" Kildare called after Duncannon's retreating back. "Look upon it, Clive Duncannon."

Glengaerif saw Donegal's expression first as the warlord's gaze went up the hill, past his waiting troops, to the crest. For a second, he seemed to falter, his horse backing up as if it too was affected by whatever terror waited above. Glengaerif looked back over his shoulder to see what could have struck the stalwart Eirelander so hard, but his view of the hill's peak was blocked by the milling horsemen and their mounts.

Donaughmore, however, had a clear view: "Gods protect us!"

Glengaerif lurched to his feet, things happening around him all at once. Below, Donegal Connaught bellowed, whipped his sword from its scabbard, and launched himself at Kildare. King Duncannon continued up the slope, eyes locked on the hilltop and whatever waited there. Donaughmore dropped to his knees, face pale and waxy, lance slipping from fear-numb fingers.

On his feet, Glengaerif spun to see what doom awaited.

"Ari Kirkmaugh," he muttered in fear and awe. Legend. He'd never expected to see them.

They filled the hilltop; only a hundred of them, but on their huge black chargers, side by side, their line stretched nearly a thousand feet long. Black armor, trimmed in scarlet. Billowing cloaks, ebony on the outside, crimson inside. Swords of black

iron held aloft in challenge or salute, Glengaerif had no way
of knowing which. Matching longknives belted about their
waists, not another weapon among them. Not a single lance or
bow. No shields; it was said they didn't need them. The sword
was their weapon. They needed nothing else—save blood for
the letting.

Dubh Aogail, they were called. The Black Death.

"Get up," Glengaerif hissed at Donaughmore. Behind him
he heard the ring of steel on steel. He looked back down the hill.

The Kildare soldier had moved to protect his king, cutting
off Donegal's attack. Above the heads of their struggling mounts
their swords met once more, then the Kildare pitched from the
saddle, his face destroyed in a shower of blood.

The standard bearer had also moved to save his king. With
a shout of triumph, he drove his lance for Donegal's midsection
while the Duncannon warlord was recovering from the blow
he had dealt the first defender. Donegal met the flag-bearing
lance with a desperate sweep of his blade that spared his own
life, but the lance sank into his mount's neck. With a scream
of pain, the grey stallion went down. Even as he fell with the
horse, Donegal turned his parry into a return stroke that passed
above the entangled lance and dashed the standard bearer from
the saddle. Arms spiraling, the young Kildare hit the ground in
a spray of crimson only a fraction of a second behind Donegal.
Donegal got to his feet; the Kildare did not.

Donegal tried to catch the standard bearer's horse, but the
terrified animal bolted away and he was left afoot while Cloyne
Kildare returned to his army.

"Get up," Glengaerif repeated.

"Their saddles," Donaughmore mumbled. He retched.
"Didn't you see? On their saddles, man…"

Below, the Kildare forces roared as one and charged
forward. Between their advancing line and the Duncannons,
stood Donegal Connaught. He looked up once and saw his king
retreating. He saw his own forces in disarray, startled by the
appearance of the mercenary Kirkmaughs. Though his king
didn't see, he raised his crimson blade in final salute, then ran
to meet the thousands of Kildares.

Glengaerif looked back to the Kirkmaughs on the hilltop and saw what had sickened Donaughmore. Tied across each Kirkmaugh saddlebow by the hair was an array of heads. The heads trailed wet ribbons of blood across the black saddle tack.

The wounded, Glengaerif thought, his legs going weak on him for a second.

The whole scene below had been a ruse allowing Ari Kirkmaugh's butchers to move into position behind Duncannon's army. Duncannon had ordered the wounded sent over the hill to safety, unknowingly placing them in the Kirkmaughs' way.

They shouted to him for orders, but Duncannon charged through his confused forces in silence, eyes locked on the black line atop the hill. Less than twenty feet away, he passed Glengaerif's position and continued up the hill.

Forgetting the shield and helm he'd removed but moments ago, Glengaerif caught up his horse's reins, kicked the whimpering Donaughmore, and sprang into the saddle. He wasn't sure whether the kick got Donaughmore moving or not. He never saw the man again.

As he charged up the hill after his king, lightning flashed and the rain suddenly broke loose in a blinding torrent.

Seeing Duncannon charging the wall of mercenaries, the soldiers behind him realized that the path their king had chosen was the only way out. Below them were still ten thousand Kildares. There, on the crest of the hill, was only one thin line of warriors. True, they were the legendary Dubh Aogail, but they were only a hundred men.

King Duncannon struck the black wall, his mount rearing as a Kirkmaugh charger lunged forward to meet it. Glengaerif was close behind the king. As black iron slid through the king's guard and plunged into his ribs, Glengaerif saw the baleful eyes, the scarred cheeks, and bloody lips of the Kirkmaugh.

The stories are true, Glengaerif thought, as Duncannon brought his blade down on the Kirkmaugh's head. *Some of them actually drink blood.*

The Kirkmaugh jerked his head to one side and Duncannon's blade crashed into the heavy armor plating protecting the mercenary's shoulder. Not a mortal blow, but still one that would have fallen a normal man. With a mad screech of glee, the Kirkmaugh ripped his blade from Duncannon's side and drew it back for a final blow.

Striking from the side, Glengaerif's stroke took the Kirkmaugh just below the chin. The head rolled away in the rain and mud; the body seemed to cling defiantly to its mount as Duncannon and Glengaerif passed.

The king looked back, finding himself accompanied by one young soldier quicker than the others to follow him.

For his troubles, Glengaerif was rewarded with a Kirkmaugh blade in his thigh. As the blade plunged through muscle, he cried out and nearly fell from the saddle. Then king and soldier were through the Kirkmaugh line, with a clear downhill run ahead of them.

Glengaerif was set to give his horse its head and make a run for it when Duncannon hauled back on his reins, bringing his horse about to reengage the Kirkmaughs. Glengaerif drew his own horse to a sliding halt, nearly fell from the saddle a second time as the injured leg failed to balance him in the saddle, and spun to join his king.

"Go!" Duncannon hissed, blood pumping from the rent in his shirt of mail.

The Kirkmaughs on either side of the fallen mercenary turned to meet the men who had passed their line. To the left, the Kirkmaugh's blade was red with blood from Glengaerif's thigh. Duncannon went for that one.

Fighting to hold his reins and stem the flow of blood from his thigh, Glengaerif followed his King back to the mercenary line. In the deluge of rain, Duncannon armies struck the line from the fore while Glengaerif and the king struck it from behind.

Blinking rain from his eyes, Glengaerif crossed blades with the Kirkmaugh on the right. It took but a moment for Glengaerif to realize he was no match for the mercenary. He was barely able to keep the black blade from his throat, let alone get through the other man's guard. Through the Kirkmaugh's black visor, he saw triple scars running vertically down the mercenary's cheeks, indicative of some rank, attesting to his prowess, promising no mercy.

Suddenly Duncannon joined the fight, allowing Glengaerif the freedom to turn the Kirkmaugh's blade aside long enough for the king to slip his steel through the scarred mercenary's heart. As the dead man splashed to the rain-sopped ground, the king indicated another corpse behind them, "I wasn't always so old." There was blood running from his mouth, down his chin. More blood was seeping from the gaping hole in his side. "There are tricks these butchers have never seen."

In the melee of combat, they had a few seconds. About them, Duncannon's horsemen, the first to reach the hill top, were engaged with the Kirkmaughs. They were losing badly.

"Your name?" the king asked.

But Glengaerif's attention had gone down the slope, past where the Duncannon foot soldiers were still climbing the hill, past where the Kildare horsemen were riding up, cutting down Duncannons from behind, to where Donegal Connaught stood, ringed by corpses stacked three and four deep.

"M'lord King," Glengaerif said, pointing downhill. "There."

"Donegal," the king whispered.

The Kildares were still trying to get at him, but it was hopeless. They were hampered now by the piles of their own dead which Donegal had laid in a protective wall about himself. As the Kildare footmen scrambled over the walls of dead to reach him, Donegal would cut them down, building his perimeter ever higher. Even with their long lances, the peasant footmen were no match for him.

They brought archers to bring him down.

Glengaerif and Duncannon watched, helpless to intervene, as Donegal Connaught died.

"M'lord, I am Glengaerif Callin. Come with me; we must escape."

The king, tears mixing with the rain pouring down his face, seemed not to have heard him. He watched as the Kildares hacked apart Donegal's arrow-ridden corpse.

"M'lord, I have family at Droichead Nua. We've got to warn—"

A Kirkmaugh rushed them, ending any further discussion. The massive charger cut between their horses, forcing them apart. Glengaerif swung at the mercenary, but his blow was easily, almost casually, swept aside. The Kirkmaugh's horse struck his own, causing his horse to stumble, and Glengaerif, unable to grip the saddle with his bad leg, nearly fell. He would have died then, open to the mercenary's next blow, but Duncannon attacked.

Duncannon's blow was a powerful overhanded one, meant to split the Kirkmaugh's skull wide open, but the Kirkmaugh parried the blow, allowing it to sink into the flank of his horse so he would have an opening at the King. Before Glengaerif could react, the Kirkmaugh thrust his blade through King Duncannon's throat. The king toppled from his horse, blood spewing from the fatal wound.

Taking the opening presented, Glengaerif rose in the stirrup on his good leg and brought his sword down with all his might in a crushing two-handed blow. Horse and rider went down, the charger suffering from Duncannon's blow, the Kirkmaugh with his skull caved in.

Glengaerif looked about him. Duncannon riders were dying left and right as the Kirkmaughs held their line. Black blades swept back and forth like harvest scythes, showering crimson trails in their wake. Hemmed in between the unmoving mercenaries and the relentless advance of the Kildares coming up the hill, Duncannon's army was being slaughtered.

The king had fallen. There was nothing to be gained by staying. Downhill, the way was clear, through the trampled grass, past the hastily organized field hospital where the helpless wounded had been murdered, and across Kilcullen Fields to Droichead Nua.

Other Duncannons who had somehow broken through had already reached the same conclusion. He saw several riders disappearing across the fields. If he hesitated now, he would be engaged again soon. Looking down, he saw that, despite the heavy wash of the rain, his right leg was drenched in blood. The leg had gone numb, hanging lifeless in the stirrup.

Glengaerif pointed the horse downhill and struck it across the withers with the flat of his sword. He looked back only once, and only then because the sight of the decapitated wounded at the field hospital was too much for him. What he saw behind him set his hand to trembling on the reins.

Two of the mercenaries had pulled away from the slaughter and were giving chase. Their cloaks flapped madly behind them as they came down the hill after him. Their blades of black iron, red with Eirelander blood, were held out before them, like the outthrust noses of hunting dogs.

Why were they following him, when they had ignored the other fleeing Duncannons?

They saw me fight beside the king, he realized. He crouched low over the saddle, urging the horse by voice, heel, and reins to give him whatever speed it had left.

The Kirkmaughs had mistakenly assumed him to be of some importance...

He awoke with a scream, certain that they were still after him. But when he raised his head and peered through the pouring rain, there was no one but himself. Looking down at his leg, he realized that during his last unconscious lapse the leg had been steadily bleeding. Alarmed, he looked about for the strip of cloth he had used as a tourniquet, but the rising stream had swept it away.

He stripped off his sodden mail so he could get at the soft wool shirt he wore underneath. The dagger was gone, lost in the mud, but he found his sword still close at hand. Using the yard of battle-dulled steel, he half cut, half tore a strip from his shirt to use as a bandage.

Glengaerif wrapped the bandage about his leg as tight as he dared, but not as tight as the tourniquet had been. The bleeding had slowed enough that a bandage should stop it. What he worried about now was losing the leg to infection. The Kirkmaugh blade had completely pierced his thigh, leaving a gaping hole in the front and a somewhat smaller counterpart in the rear. Gods alone knew what poison the black blade had left in his flesh.

He debated over the mail shirt for several minutes. It was still in good shape, having only one ragged tear where the Kirkmaughs had caught him on the cliff overlooking the now turbulent creekbed. He checked, the matching ache in his side

was little more than a bruise and some lacerated skin. The armor
had saved him from that one.

But of what further use was the armor? He was too far gone
to face even a single mercenary. Better to discard the weight and
make his best speed to Droichead Nua. Especially since he was
now likely afoot; unless by some chance his horse had remained
in the area after their fall into the creek.

Droichead Nua.

It was more than a name to him now. More than the place
he had called home since taking Jehnna as wife eight years ago.
It was his destination, his goal. Nothing mattered, save that he
reach Droichead Nua ahead of the Kildares.

Clive Duncannon was dead. His army lay slaughtered.

Cloyne Kildare's next stop would be Duncannon's home.

Droichead Nua.

...relentless, they chased him across the plains for several
long, bone-jarring miles. His horse had just endured hours on
the battlefield, and before that a three-day march to the site of
the confrontation. It was no match for the fresh Kirkmaugh
stallions.

After hours of chase, he realized the only advantage he still
had was to choose the ground on which he would make his
stand. He chose a muddy hill overlooking a small river whose
name he'd either never known or long since forgotten, some
unsubstantial tributary to the mighty Dunshaughlin River
which flowed through Droichead Nua. He hoped that he might
stand a chance of escaping by hurling himself and the horse
backwards off the cliff and into the river. As it turned out, they
did go over the cliff, but not quite the way he had planned.

Overhead, the moon tried in vain to cast its light through the
heavy cloud cover as he brought the gasping warhorse around
before the drop to the creek. He drew his sword and met them.

The Kirkmaughs came at him simultaneously, two on one.
Even as he parried one sword stroke, another bit at his side sending
links of chain mail spinning off in the darkness. Glengaerif
Callin knew his death was at hand, but he didn't flinch. His only
regret was that he wouldn't reach Droichead Nua.

Jehnna, he thought, as one mercenary blade hacked aside his guard and the other went for his throat, *I tried to come for you, but—*

The world pitched out from under him. He would later remember hearing his horse squeal and a curse from one of the Kirkmaughs. Together with the mercenaries and all three mounts, he plunged down into the creekbed.

There was the fall, a sinking feeling that left his insides twenty feet above him on the cliff face—or rather, where the cliff face had been moments ago. Then there was the wet crash as tons of mud collapsed.

Warmth. A luxury he hadn't felt since he'd left Jehnna and home. An all-encompassing warmth as if he were wrapped in a mother's womb.

And then darkness...He left a long trench behind him, dug by the lifeless leg he had dragged up the mud embankment. The top, and flat ground, was still ten feet away, but he had made it over half way. He'd make it the rest of the way.

At least I'm alive, he told himself. Which was more than he could say for the two Kirkmaughs who had gone down with him. One he found buried in the mud beneath his horse. The horse had broken its neck in the fall; the rider had died, choking on mud, trapped beneath the horse. The second Kirkmaugh had suffered a quicker fate; a jagged tree limb, long embedded in the mud, had ripped out his throat.

Glengaerif had suffered only superficial cuts, bruises, and a nasty blow to the head. Luck. Nothing else accounted for it.

With the Kirkmaughs dead, time was now Glengaerif's enemy. Kildare's next conquest would be Droichead Nua. Not that it would be much of a battle; Duncannon had left barely a hundred guardsmen there to maintain order in his absence. Every man had been needed at the Kilcullen battle. It was either win at Kilcullen or face a siege which Droichead Nua was unprepared for. Not one to meet his death starving behind castle walls, Duncannon had chosen to meet the Kildare army en route. They'd hoped for southern support: Maddock, Rohr, Oughtergard, Emery, any of the southern barons. Just *one* might have made the difference.

None had made the trip north to stand beside Duncannon.

Glengaerif had to reach Droichead Nua before Cloyne Kildare. Already he'd lost an entire night's march. But would Kildare push his men on through after the battle? Or would he stop to rest and tend his wounded? Glengaerif had to hope that Kildare would stop.

If so, Glengaerif had a day's head start. But that head start was worthless without a mount. In his condition, it'd take him weeks to reach Droichead Nua. Crawling.

At the top of the bank, his worst fears were set aside. Dutiful, trained to wait for its rider, the surviving Kirkmaugh charger stood in the rain. Head and tail hanging, streaked with mud, saddle torn and missing one stirrup, soaked through, the animal was a beautiful sight. Glengaerif wanted to scream his joy, but held it back for fear of scaring the horse.

Of his own horse, there wasn't any sign. Either it had run off or it was buried in the mud slide.Droichead Nua sat the Dunshaughlin River like some great spider, the spider's legs formed by the great bridges as they arched back and forth over the wide river. The main keep, Duncannon's palace, formed the spider's bulbous body. Its domed roof dwarfed the surrounding buildings. Gleaming spires and pinnacles towered above it all. The walls, broken in two places to accommodate the flow of the Dunshaughlin, defied any castle norms.

"You'll never defend it," Donegal had warned the king ages ago when they were just starting to build both the empire and its capital city.

"I don't intend to," Clive Duncannon had answered. "she's meant as a sign that the empire is reborn, the old tyranny overthrown. Nothing so grand has ever stood since King Rodric held court at Kiamina. With the towers I have in mind, we'll know of an enemy's approach long in advance. We'll fight our battles afield, not at home."

The king's eyes had sparkled with the dreams bursting within him. "Perhaps we'll even bring the south back into the empire. Oh, not by conquering them, Donegal; don't get that look in your eyes. Diplomacy will be our sword against the south. I'll make them barons, vassals to a great empire. I'll bridge the old disagreements and get trade goods flowing through Kiamina Pass once again."

A bridge. A *new* bridge. Thus had Droichead Nua been named.

Her towers now were streaked with black soot from the flames that must have arched hundreds of feet high earlier in the day. Even now, he could see scattered flames and the sky was filled with dark smoke. Her gates hung open, the courtyard beyond littered with corpses dressed in the red and gold of Droichead Nua's guard.

From a distance, Glengaerif sat the stolen horse and tried to reason what had happened. Kildare couldn't have gotten ahead of him. That big of an army would have left a trail even a tracker as inexperienced as he could have spotted. Kildare's army had to be somewhere behind him, either en route or still resting after their victory over Duncannon.

For fifteen minutes he watched for signs of life in the city, but the only movement was the languid rising of smoke and the occasional flicker of dying flames. Even the empire's banners were lifeless where they hung atop the battlements, the plains now still and quiet after the long spring rainstorm.

Finally, he put heels to the Kirkmaugh charger and started toward the open gates at a fast gallop. For the moment, the apprehension he felt, a cold claw gripping throat and chest, made him forget the sharp pain that shot through his thigh with every stride of the horse.

Without slowing, he passed through the gates and into the high-walled reception yard where he disturbed a score of carrion birds. The horse, already upset by all the smoke and flames, shied away as the birds took flight. Cursing, Glengaerif checked the horse's panic and got it moving, not straight down the main road to the high ivory bridge and the palace, but to the left on a much smaller street.

He moved quickly, down streets he knew by heart, taking sharp turns at speeds that set the nervous horse to fighting the reins. Ruthlessly, treating it as he'd treated no mount in his life, Glengaerif kept the warhorse under control. Turning one corner, he nearly ran down an old woman, the first person he'd encountered.

Though he called out and tried to show her his empty hands,

the old woman screamed and ran. He gave chase, but she could maneuver through tighter alleys than the jittery warhorse. He didn't dare dismount, for he wasn't sure if he could stand; and, if the horse bolted while he was afoot, he'd really be in trouble. Helpless, he watched as the old woman's rags disappeared around a corner and out of sight.

He got his bearings and started back on the path to his original destination, terror of what he would find still gnawing at his insides. It took another ten minutes to reach his villa.

Glengaerif was relieved to see that few of the buildings in this area, including his own house, had been burned. In addition, there were only a few bodies scattered about the rust-colored cobblestones of the streets. Grasping for any hope, he told himself those two observations meant the people this far into the city had had sufficient time to hide or flee.

Please be alright, he begged them.

The front door to his two-story villa was open, hanging to one side on half its hinges. As he forced the horse through the doorway, he called out her name. There was no answer.

The inside of the house was in shambles. Everything the looters hadn't wanted, they'd broken and scattered about over the floor. A small fire had started, burning most of the throw rugs in the wide vestibule, but it appeared to have been stomped out before it spread.

"Jehnna!"

Still no answer.

Trails of mud, blood, and soot led up the stairs to the second floor. The horse had no trouble navigating the wide marble stairway. At the top of the stairs, he had only to follow the same trail to where it led to the master bedroom. That door too had been busted down. Again, he forced down the horse's head and urged it on through.

A cry caught in his throat when he found her. He fell from the horse, beyond caring if it ran off. Numb to the pain in his leg, he dragged himself across the floor and gathered her cold, naked corpse in his arms.

Later, he would drag himself through the house, looking for survivors. He'd find his servants, cold and dead, the younger women molested like his wife had been, the older women and men simply murdered.

Sometime later, as the setting sun was beginning to throw long shadows throughout the silent house, a Duncannon city guardsman found him.

Lowering his pike, which he had been about to use on Glengaerif, the dirty soldier walked across the room and tore a spread from off the bed. He tossed it to Glengaerif. "Cover her, son."

Glengaerif drew the warm spread about them. Her cold flesh had warmed not at all during the long hours that he'd held her, instead her chill had spread into his own body. He had no idea how close he was to joining her in death, but the old soldier knew it on first sight.

"Someone saw you and sent me. Dangerous thing, riding that Kirkmaugh horse. We thought one of them had come back or never left."

Mention of the Kirkmaughs got Glengaerif's attention. "They were here?"

The soldier cocked his head. "Who are you? Where'd you come from, son?"

"Glengaerif Callin. I fought with Duncannon."

"And what of our king?"

Glengaerif pulled away from his dead wife, wrapping her carefully in the bedspread. "Answer my question first. The Kirkmaughs did this?"

"Yes. What of King Duncannon?"

"Dead. They're all dead."

"Except you."

"And a few others that ran at the end." Glengaerif tried to get to his feet, but failed.

"The Kirkmaughs fought for Kildare?"

"I need help," Glengaerif told him.

"So does everyone else in this city," the guard replied. He bunched his fist in the tunic he wore. "And everyone in these colors will be put to death when Kildare gets here." He bent and caught Glengaerif by the hair. "How far behind you are they, boy?"

"Can't say. Depends how long he'll rest his army before marching on after the battle. Evidently, he sent the Kirkmaughs on ahead."

The guard released him. "No. If he'd sent the Kirkmaughs to do this, they'd have stayed for payment. He's turned them loose. They simply saw Droichead Nua along the way and knew she was ripe for picking."

"Help me."

The guardsman looked down, studied Glengaerif's leg where livid red lines were already radiating out from the bandaged wound. Below the wound, the leg had turned a pale grey-green. "You're beyond help, son."

"I've got to follow them."

The guard shook his head. "Beyond taking vengeance as well. Even so, there's nothing you could do to them that would account for what they did to her."

"Not vengeance." Glengaerif shook his head emphatically. "They've taken something of mine."

As they rode south, heading for their stronghold hidden deep in Eire's mountain belt, the mercenaries found Duleek. The peaceful village sat amid the gentle hills, not quite a full day's ride from Droichead Nua. The men of the village were devoted to raising sheep and other livestock for the king. Their only weapons were the tools they used to work the fields and an occasional bow. Most of the Duleek men were in the fields cutting food for the livestock when the Dubh Aogail came upon them.

The peasants in the fields proved better adversaries than the Kirkmaughs expected. Ari Kirkmaugh lost two of his remaining seventy-three men to farmers. When it was over, he left his own dead with a hundred or so Duleek residents watering the crops with their blood.

In the village, they met little resistance: an old woman who stood in the street shouting obscenities until Kirkmaugh himself removed her head; three old men, retired from the wars that had put Duncannon on the throne years ago, who thought they still had what it took to stand and fight; a shop owner who fancied he could stand by and watch, and not be touched by the violence, then when attacked, proved that he did have some fight in him by attacking a mercenary with an adze; a whore that knifed one of his younger, overeager men; a mother who thought her son too good to join the chained group of boys they'd led from Droichead Nua; and one very good archer who killed four men before they stormed the bell tower where he'd hidden.

While his men worked to capture the sniper, Ari Kirkmaugh took the time to remove his hot armor. By the time his men had stormed the tower and brought out the Duleek archer, Kirkmaugh was comfortably seated in his cushioned field chair, shaded by a storefront awning.

The archer proved to be but a boy. Kicking and fighting against the arms that held him, he fought his captors as they dragged him to face Ari Kirkmaugh. The boy was bleeding from several cuts on his face, more blood was matted into his red hair, and he was holding his side as if the mercenaries had broken a few ribs, but he was still alive.

One of his men handed over the boy's bow and a nearly empty quiver of arrows. Comfortable in silken robes and soft doeskin boots, Kirkmaugh studied the boy's homemade bow of yew. It was smooth and carefully formed, made of many pliable yew strips bonded in an overlapping pattern. It was stout enough that many *men* might have trouble drawing it back, let alone this boy of fifteen or so summers.

"What's your name, boy?"

Unfaltering, the boy met the mercenary Lord's gaze. The boy's eyes were a bright blue, luminous against his dark skin and red hair. "You going to kill me now?"

Kirkmaugh smiled. The boy was afraid, but determined not to show it. Kirkmaugh respected him for that. "You make this?" he asked, still holding the bow.

The youth nodded toward the chained string of boys held nearby. "You like boys?"

The smile faded from Kirkmaugh's face, respect for the boy temporarily forgotten. "Captain, bring me one of the boys."

"Yes, M'lord."

A rather small, sandy-haired boy was unchained and

thrown to the ground beside the taller, older boy from Duleek.

Kirkmaugh pulled an arrow from the quiver on his lap. He nocked the arrow, drew the bow, and pointed it at the sandy-haired youth, whose eyes immediately doubled in circumference. "What's *your* name, boy?"

Shaking, the boy answered in a voice weak with fear. "Drew."

The mercenary Lord pointed the bow at the red-haired youth. "See how easy that was? Now, what's your name?"

A silent stare.

The butcher smiled, hiding any irritation he might feel. He shifted his aim back to the pale youth from Droichead Nua. "What's your name, Red?"

"You can call me that."

"I'd rather use the name you were given. Tell me now or I'll kill our good friend Drew."

"Cull Garvin."

"See, that wasn't hard. You make this bow, Cull?"

"Yes."

"Who taught you?"

"My grandfather."

"Is he dead?"

"Is now."

Kirkmaugh raised his aim, let the arrow fly over the heads of the two boys. For a few seconds all eyes followed the flight of the arrow, then it was lost against the darkening sky.

"Be as purposeful as that arrow, boys. Set your sights on a goal, however distant, and cut a straight path to achieve it. Let *nothing* stand in your way." He studied them both intently for a moment, then tossed the bow aside. Rising from the chair, he motioned for the captain to remove the terrified boy, Drew.

There was a tavern across the street. Ari Kirkmaugh started toward it, then looked back over his shoulder. "Follow me, Red."

Spotlighted by sunbeams cutting through the buildings across the street, the tavern's owner was swinging in lazy circles over the gaping doorway. The innkeeper was beyond complaining; Kirkmaugh's men had hung him. "They sometimes run out of things to keep themselves amused,"

Kirkmaugh commented as he held the body aside for Cull to enter the tavern.

The boy looked sick as he shouldered past the black-faced corpse.

They took a table. One of the serving wenches, a lovely blonde—Kirkmaugh's men knew his tastes—was cut out of a group of six huddled in a corner and sent to serve the mercenary lord and his guest. Shaking in fear, she set out two steins and filled them from a pitcher of ale. As she turned to leave, Kirkmaugh caught her by the wrist and pulled her onto his lap.

"Drink up," Kirkmaugh told the boy.

Cull ignored the stein.

"Lovely, isn't she?"

Cull looked away.

"What's her name?" Kirkmaugh asked, knocking the pitcher out of her hands. It hit the wooden floor and rolled away, contents foaming out across the old boards.

Cull ignored him, weary of the mercenary's fascination with names. But his eyes were drawn back to the blonde and, though he tried, he found he couldn't look away. She was beautiful. Cull had seen her around Duleek for years, but he'd never had the nerve to get this close to her.

"Answer me, boy!" Kirkmaugh drew a knife from his belt and held it against her throat. "There are others across the room. We can try till you find you know one of them?"

"Laenora," Cull answered with an apologetic look in her direction.

"She a whore?" Kirkmaugh asked, moving his knife from her throat to the ties on her blouse.

"Suppose so."

The knife slipped through the ties and they parted without a sound. The press of her breasts pushed the blouse open to reveal a deep cleavage. "You ever had her, boy?"

Cull's face blushed to match his hair.

"Never had her, huh?" He laughed. "Never had *any* is what I think." Still laughing he slammed the knife into the scarred wood of the table. His hand free, he reached around and pulled open the whore's blouse, revealing her naked breasts.

"Mine for the taking, boy." He caressed her, gentle, working the nipple so that it stood out firm and pink. "Any way I want it." He squeezed hard, till she cried out in pain. When he relaxed his hand, its imprint showed red and painful on her breast.

"Power, boy. The world is mine. I take what I want. I don't raise cattle. I don't grow corn." He stood and slammed Laenora down across the table next to the deep-thrust knife. "And I don't court women, boy."

The mercenary Lord ripped at her skirts. She struggled, clawed at him, and even tried for the knife, but it was buried too deep in the hardwood of the table. Though she pulled, she hadn't the strength to remove it. He slapped her hard enough that her head cracked sharply against the table top.

"What I want, I take." He smiled a feral, carnivore grin as he opened his robes and thrust himself into her.

Cull turned away, torn between more emotions than he had ever had to deal with separately, let alone all at once. He was repulsed by what he knew was wrong, but at the same time, he was excited by Laenora's soft pale flesh and the power that Kirkmaugh was showing him, power to take what you wanted, to taste the sweeter things in life. Like Laenora's sweet flesh.

Kirkmaugh reached out, caught the boy by the front of the shirt, and dragged him close across the struggling woman. Their faces were inches apart, Cull's bloody and flushed, Kirkmaugh's dripping sweat as he continued to thrust into the woman beneath them.

"Join us and you can have her next. Join us and the world is yours for the taking."

Cull swallowed bile, revulsion having won out now that he was face to face with this madman. "If I say no?" He found his hand wrapped around the handle of the knife.

"Then I leave your head on a pole."

"And if I jerk out this knife and thrust it into your black heart?"

Some of the humor left Kirkmaugh's face, but not much. "Let us hope your aim is true then, Cull Garvin, because if your first thrust doesn't kill me, I'll rip your throat out with my teeth and let you bleed to death all over this lovely woman."

Cull considered. The four mercenaries he had slain with the bow were the first men he had ever killed. He didn't know if he had it in him to kill up close; to thrust with the knife and feel Kirkmaugh's hot blood well up over the hilt and run down his hand; to see his eyes, so close now, register the shock and pain, and then the death.

His hand slipped off the knife.

Breathing heavily now, Kirkmaugh shook him. "We need strong young men like you, Cull Garvin. Join us. That's what all those boys are for. We have to replenish our numbers somehow. But you're different. They're weak boys; you've proven you're a man."

"I'll join you," Cull answered, knowing in his heart that he'd proven exactly the opposite. He was no man. He was a coward.

Kirkmaugh released him, letting Cull fall back into his chair. "You've made the right choice. Tonight, you will see how we reap the world."

Black eyes glittering like shards of evil incarnate, the mercenary lord looked about the room. "You men show those other ladies a good time. This will be a night this little town will always remember!"

Morning. Warm, naked flesh. Soft blonde curls tickling his nose.

The smell of blood.

Cull Garvin jerked up his head, knocking it painfully on the table under which he had slept. From the floor beside him, Laenora watched him with fearful eyes. Eyes that hadn't seen any sleep last night.

There was shouting outside. Orders were being given to mount up and get underway. Cull looked out from under the table. They were alone in the tavern.

Except for the bodies.

He wanted to vomit, but fought it back down. The girl was still watching him, wondering how long she had to live, wondering if he'd take her again as he'd done repeatedly throughout the long night.

"Garvin!"

He pressed a finger to his lips, begging her to keep quiet.

If he'd been thinking straight, he'd have known such a gesture was unnecessary. She had more reason for silence than he. The bodies lying still and cold on the tavern's floor had been her friends.

"Garvin!"

Closer. Only a matter of seconds before they found him.

Cull looked down at the nude woman he'd spent the night with. Even covered with the filth of the tavern's floor, he found her beautiful.

They killed all the others.

Power. The power to take whatever he wanted, whenever he wanted it. Taking her had been fantastic. He'd wanted her. And wanted her still.

But he didn't want her dead.

Quickly, he scrambled out from under the table. Kirkmaugh's knife was still embedded in the tabletop. He tore it free and ran to the nearest corpse, a brunette who'd once been quite beautiful. Taking the dead woman by the arms, he dragged her to one side. Where she had lain, there remained a puddle of blood. He returned to the frightened girl under the table.

She cowered, seeing only the wild look in his eyes and the naked steel in his fist. "Please—"

"No time," he hissed, pulling her out from under the table and forcing her over to the blood-stained spot on the floor. He thrust her down to the floor by the crimson puddle. "Lay here. No matter what you hear, don't move."

He smeared some of the blood on his hands and coated more of it on the knife. As he rose from Laenora, he heard boots behind him. He turned and started for the doorway.

An officer blocked his path. The officer grabbed him, one hand twisting his head back by the hair, the other hand clamping down like a vise on his wrist. "Are you deaf, boy?" the mercenary growled.

"Sorry, sir. Just finishing my business."

The officer glanced from the bloody knife to the blonde on the floor behind Cull. "Next time, boy, you finish your business *before* you sleep. Understand?"

Numb, Cull nodded.

The officer struck Cull's hand against a table and the knife clattered away across the floor. "No one said you could carry a weapon yet either, pup." He thrust the boy out through the doorway into the street, glanced once around the room, and followed.

When the last echoes of their departure had faded and silence reigned over the desolate little hamlet, Laenora gathered what remained of her torn clothing and ran from the tavern.

West of the village was a grove of trees and a small pond, a place where she had found solace on other, less oppressive occasions. As fast as her weak legs could carry her, she ran there now. She crossed the dusty street in stumbling, wide-legged strides, avoiding the array of obscene obstacles in her path. Her gaze was locked on her goal, refusing to acknowledge the bloated corpses littering the streets; yet in her peripheral vision, she was acutely aware of the fluttering clumps of black that were crows come for the feast.

She burst into the trees, a shivering, half nude young woman, too exhausted to cry, beyond caring whether she lived or died, interested only in escaping the cloying scent of blood and death that permeated Duleek. Collapsing in the clover at the edge of the pond, she let the smell of the ardent vegetation cleanse her nostrils. The sunshine, green-hued as it filtered through the overhanging trees, warmed her scratched and bruised flesh. Looking at the filth that covered her body, she felt as if an aura of death, rape, and destruction clung to her like some filmy garment.

Setting her tattered clothing aside, she slipped into the cold pond, disturbing its serene surface with a myriad of ripples. The ripples echoed out from her, each carrying away some of her misery and shame.

She'd been intimate with men before, more than she cared to count. Many of them had repulsed her. Some had even treated her badly. But it had never been like last night. And it had never carried with it such a fear of death.

She dove deep, letting the pond's numbing cold surround her, an embrace far warmer than that of the mercenary leader.

Drifting deeper beneath the surface and finally coming to rest on the soft mud bottom, she felt she could still feel Kirkmaugh's hands on her body, the steel of his knife at her throat, the repugnant strength of his flesh against and in her own.

I'll never be free of that, she thought. And immediately after: *They killed them all. Raped. Mutilated. And finally just murdered.*

Her lungs began to ache and she looked up through the spread of her blonde hair, watching the sun as it played across the pond's crystal surface. *Better to stay here,* a part of her urged. *There's nothing up there.*

There's air, she answered, but made no move to go up for it. Her lungs began to scream.

The opalescent surface shimmered in sunlight, belaying the chill that was anesthetizing body and mind. She felt suffused with the pure bright light, yet at the same time beckoned by it. It was as if the light was waiting for her to follow it on some journey.

The light suddenly went out and she let go, peaceful acceptance washing over her. *Depart,* she bid whatever soul, essence, or ethereal part of her would carry on after death.

But then the light returned, bright and clean, the pond as unbroken as new snow—except for a shadow that swept across its surface and then was gone.

One of them has returned, she thought. She kicked for the surface, suddenly determined that no further violence be performed on Duleek or its silent residents.

She broke the surface, taking in deep gulps of air as quietly as she could. A rider was just disappearing through the trees, heading toward the village. Heart and head pounding in unison, Laenora started for the bank.

She'd caught but a brief glimpse of horse and rider: a tall, lean man in plain, ragged leather clothing, no armor and little weapons if any, bent over a huge black charger. Most of the armor and gear had been removed from the horse, but enough remained to identify it as one of those ridden by the Kirkmaughs.

Scrambling from the water, she caught up skirt and blouse, and ran for the trees. From behind a weathered oak, she watched as he left the grove and started into town. Bent over the saddle, one leg bandaged and flopping limp against the charger's side, he appeared to be in worse shape than she. He held a sword in a worn scabbard across his knees with one hand. In the other, he held the reins in a white-knuckled grip as if the horse had been giving him trouble.

She stepped into her skirt and drew it up around her waist, then shrugged into the ruined blouse. He was gone from sight again as he started down Duleek's central street. As soon as she was sure he'd gone far enough that there was no chance of him seeing her, she followed.

From the corner of the blacksmith's at the end of the street, Laenora watched as the horse picked its way nervously through the corpses. Intent on getting the only weapon she knew of, the knife left earlier by Cull and the mercenary officer, Laenora decided she could get across the street and over to the tavern while the stranger's back was turned.

The rider ignored the dead townspeople, pausing only when he came across the dead Kirkmaughs. From the back of his horse, he stared at the dead mercenaries for a second; then, as if they confirmed all he needed to know, he suddenly turned the horse to leave.

And caught her as she started across the street.

Startled, the horse threw back its head and snorted, nearly tossing him from the saddle. He clawed at the saddle with his free hand and dropped the sword.

She was debating on whether her best chances lay in fleeing or going for the sword he had dropped, when he got the horse under control and called out for her to wait.

Something in his voice, an underlying assurance of good intent or a desperate plea for help, she wasn't sure which, made her stand her ground.

He seemed as surprised as she when she didn't run.

The stranger looked her over, appraising her tattered clothing, skirt in strips that revealed bruised thighs and shirt torn so bad it barely concealed her breasts. Looking down, she saw that her bare feet were caked with dirt and leaves from her run through the grove and into town.

"Are you all right, girl?"

"You're not one of them," she countered, making it a statement, not a question.

"Which way did they go?"

"South."

"Wicklow then."

She nodded slowly, trying not to think of Duleek's fate repeated at the even smaller village just half a day's ride to the south.

"What's your name?" he asked.

"Laenora."

"I'm Glengaerif Callin," he responded. "From Droichead Nua."

She cocked her head then, her eyes betraying some hope that justice might be served. "The king is on his way?" As soon as she said it, she realized that his condition probably meant just the opposite.

He gave it to her straight: "The empire has fallen. Duncannon is dead."

Her legs, already weak, went out from under her and she dropped to her knees. He *clicked* to the horse and brought it up alongside her. Leaning down, he offered her his hand. "I'd get down, but I can't stand on this leg," he explained.

She took his hand and allowed him to pull her to her feet. "That's it then. The great empire falls yet again into anarchy and ruin."

He shrugged tired shoulders, letting her cynicism pass without comment. But then, what could he have said?

Leaning against his uninjured leg, she studied him. He had an honest face, square cut, dark of hair and beard, with gentle brown eyes. It was a drawn, haggard face. He looked as if he hadn't slept in days. There were dark circles under his eyes and the set of his jaw told of the pain he must be feeling. There was a haunted look there too, as if he had lost as much or more than she the past few days.

"You're following them," she said, just realizing what should have been immediately obvious.

He looked away, knowing what she would ask next. His eyes swept the haunted buildings, the dead in the street, and the feeding buzzards. "Looks bad now," he told her. "But there are sure to be survivors, some that ran faster than the others, men in the fields who snuck away ... They'll be back. Duleek will live again and you'll be all right."

"They came through the fields," she told him. "Killed the menfolk before they could run."

"There'll still be those who had time to hide."

She pulled away, ran to where he had dropped the sword and brought it back. She handed it up to him. "You need me."

"You'll slow me down. I've only one horse."

"And only one leg," she countered. "My mother taught me to weigh my choices in life and make the best of what was available. When she died and I was left alone years ago, I did just that. I've managed to survive. Right now, I've weighed all my options; I want to come with you. Now weigh yours, Callin."

"You're better off here."

"I made *my* choice. It's *yours* we're talking about. You need me and I can help."

"You don't even know what I'm after."

Her eyes locked with his, unblinking, a pale blue as cold as ice. "I want them as much as you do."

Frowning, he thought about what she said. Finally, he sighed and waved her away. "Find some clothes then, girl."

From the room she had shared with two other girls above the tavern, she got clean clothing and shoes. Glancing quickly about the small room, she tried to decide what she couldn't afford to leave behind; she had no intention of ever returning to Duleek.

She decided there was probably little that he would let her carry anyway and settled on tying an extra set of clothing into a bundle she could easily carry over her shoulder. In the middle of the clothing, she rolled a whalebone brush, the only thing left of her mother.

As she was leaving the tavern, she spotted the knife where it had been knocked from Cull's hand by the mercenary officer. She added it, bloodstain and all, to the center of her bundle.

Outside, she asked to burn the tavern before they left. It was the only thing she could think to do for her friends. Glengaerif refused, telling her they hadn't time.

"I want to get to Wicklow before they leave," he explained. "Get up behind me."

She handed him the bundle of extra clothing and was about to swing up behind him when he pointed across the street. "That bow, are there any arrows for it?

She crossed the street and picked up bow and quiver, unaware that it was the same homemade bow of yew that Cull Garvin had used to slay four Kirkmaughs. She brought it back to him. "Seven arrows."

"Good. You carry the bow."

"But I've got my own things to carry."

He smiled. "Choices, girl. Carry both or toss your bundle." He reached down and pulled her up behind him.

"You're a hard man, Callin."

He shook the reins and started the horse moving south out of the town. "I've reason to be."

For a time, they rode without talking, and perhaps they would have continued in silence all the way to Wicklow were it not for her questioning. She started off by asking him about his leg.

Glengaerif looked down at the lifeless limb. It was only marginally better since the attentions of the guardsman at Droichead Nua. Although color had returned to the leg, the red striations were still there, a spreading infection indicating that even if it didn't kill him, he was sure to lose the leg.

He told her about the battle at Kilcullen Fields, the arrival of the Dubh Aogail, Duncannon's fall, and his escape.

"I don't understand how Duncannon could have let Kildare gather so much strength. Why wasn't Kildare stopped sooner, before he became a threat to the empire?"

"Winters north of the Meath River are harsh. Word reached us of Kildare's intentions, but Duncannon didn't think we could march in the dead of winter and arrive at Drogheda with any hope of winning. He had no idea that Kildare would spend all winter conquering his neighbors or that he would gather together such a strong force to march south in the spring."

They came upon a small creek and Glengaerif rode along

its muddy bank studying the tracks where the mercenaries had crossed.

"What are you looking for?" she asked.

He didn't answer, seemingly intent on finding one set of tracks among the many.

Perplexed, she asked herself why he'd be looking for a particular set of tracks. "You've a score to settle with *one* of them?"

He drew the horse to a halt, leaning down from the saddle to get a closer look. Then, satisfied, he urged the horse across the stream and up the muddy bank on the other side.

"Are you going to ignore me?" she demanded.

"Do you always talk so much, girl?"

"I've got a right to know what you're after!" she insisted.

"And what right is that?" He drew the horse to a halt and looked back at her petulant face.

"How can I help you if I don't know what you're after?"

He let out a long sigh and pointed at the ground to their right. "See those tracks?"

"I see *lots* of tracks."

"Lots of hoof tracks, but look closer."

She did, but couldn't really see anything other than the tracks left by the Kirkmaugh horses. Then she remembered the string of boys the mercenaries had been leading behind them. She studied harder, and yes, there they were, small footprints mixed in with the trampled hoof tracks.

Laenora met his eyes. "You're not after revenge. They've got your son."

He nodded once, turned around in the saddle, and started the horse moving again.

Hours later, she asked if they could stop to rest.

"No."

"Look, Glengaerif, I—"

"Glen's a lot easier," he interrupted her.

"Okay then, Glen. I need to stop. I've lost all feeling from the waist down, except for those parts of my bottom in contact with this damn saddle. I've got to get down and stretch my legs."

"Step off and walk," he told her.

"But we need to rest. And in case you haven't noticed, I
haven't eaten anything all day!" She was starting to sound
really mad now. "And I have to relieve myself!"

Glengaerif turned the horse aside to a small gully, let it pick
its own way down the loose gravel bank, and brought it to a halt
at the bottom where a small stream had once flowed.

"We'll rest here. There's dried beef and cheese in the saddle
kit behind you. I've got water up here in this skin."

"Thank you." She swung down from the horse and promptly
fell to the ground. Luckily for him, he didn't laugh.

When she'd managed to get some feeling back into her legs,
she got up and offered him her hand. "Let me help you down."

He shook his head. "I'll never get back up if I get down."

So he sat in the saddle while they took a short rest. He ate
a little meat, wouldn't touch the cheese, and drank the water
in long greedy gulps. Watching him eat, she realized for the
first time how sick he was. His face was ashen, dripping with
sweat, mouth drawn in a thin line. His eyes were puffy and
heavy-lidded, as if the very act of keeping them open took too
much effort. His leg was an angry red, swollen tight beneath the
bandage wrapped about his thigh.

"Your wife must be worried."

"She's dead," he answered flatly.

She didn't know what to say to that, so she said nothing.

"Kirkmaughs," he said, stating the obvious. "They went
through Droichead Nua before they came to Duleek."

"I'm sorry," she said, knowing firsthand the horror his wife
had probably suffered.

"We'd better be moving now."

"Her name was Jehnna," he said later and proceeded to talk
about her for an hour or more.

Laenora listened, pretending to be unaware that he was
crying softly. Bent over the charger's neck, his broad back shook
with silent sobs beneath her hands.

She was a good listener. Years in the tavern had taught her
that men needed more than sex. Sometimes they just needed
someone they could talk to.

Eventually he spoke of his son, Drew Callin.

"My mother was a whore," she told him, when it came time to take the burden of conversation away from him. "Never had a father—unless you count her customers, most of whom were simply wondering when they'd get a go at me."

From him there was no response and for a moment she wondered if he had passed out. Even his iron resolve had to have a limit. A moment later, he cleared his throat and spat, so she continued.

"By all rights, I should be dead," she explained. "But there was a boy—well, nearly a man. I suppose after that night, he is a man—or thinks he is. He was rough that night, treating me as if nothing mattered but the simple fact that he was able to possess me. As if he were drunk on the power he wielded over me. I thought for sure he would kill me; they'd killed all my friends."

It was her turn to cry. She made no attempt to hide it, expecting some sort of comfort from him. But he sat hunched over the horse in front of her, ambivalent to her suffering or too far gone to offer solace.

"I intended to kill myself," she wept. "How Mother would have hated me for that. But I had no choice—until you showed up."

"There's always a choice," he mumbled.

She shook him awake. "Smoke ahead."

Weakly, he raised his head. He'd been asleep for no more than an hour, having nodded off in the saddle. She'd been talking to him about her mother and the life they had led. Her only indication he'd fallen asleep had been when the reins slipped from his fingers. Reaching around him, she'd caught them up and taken over the job of guiding the horse along the well-trampled trail of the mercenaries.

He coughed, hacked up phlegm, and spat. "That'll be Wicklow. The butchers are already there."

She shivered involuntarily, remembering Duleek's massacre. "We can't be more than thirty minutes away."

He nodded silent agreement.

"What will we do?"

"Get as close as possible. Wait for nightfall. Then I'm going in after Drew."

"You can't even walk. And they're sure as hell not going to let you ride in there and take him out."

"I've no other choice."

"You've got *me*," she argued. "I'll go in and bring him out."

It took a while, but he found the tree he wanted, a century old oak that overlooked the little glen wherein sat the village of Wicklow. Leaving the sword tied to the saddle, Glengaerif hauled himself up into the tree dragging his dead leg behind him.

Had she been called upon to bet on him getting into the tree, she'd have sworn he couldn't do it. But Glengaerif proved once again that he possessed vast reserves just waiting to be tapped. Once he was settled, she passed the bow and quiver up to him.

"Will you be able to hit anything from up there?" she asked.

"There's a good bit of light," he answered. "Half of Wicklow's burning. I've got an open view of most of the street. Stay away from the northern end; the trees there block my view."

"Are you any good with a bow?"

"Passable."

"Thanks for the reassurance."

Again he surveyed Wicklow's single street. "I'd feel a lot better if I could see the boys. You're liable to spend all night looking for them."

"Wicklow's not that big, Glen," she responded reassuringly. "I'll find him."

"Just remember one thing, girl. You're there to get Drew. Not for revenge. Understand?"

Laenora looked away, clutching the knife concealed in her blouse. She'd slid it from the bundle just moments ago when he wasn't looking.

"Set them *all* free, but make sure they understand that they're to scatter in different directions. It's the only way *some* of them will escape."

"We've been over this a dozen times already."

In the darkness, it was impossible for him to read her face. He hated that, wishing he had more time with her. More time in which to learn he could trust her. "Make sure that horse is tied fast then, and go."

"You're sure you'll be able to get down from there?" There was concern in her voice, clear as the fires burning just beyond the trees.

"Long as the horse doesn't get free. You sure you know where to meet me?"

"If I can find the place." There was silence between them for a minute while he fought the urge to tell her yet again how to find the small canyon where they'd agreed to meet up.

"Good luck, Glengaerif Callin."

"Be careful, girl."

She slipped away into the darkness.

In the run from the surrounding forest to the huddled buildings of the village, darkness served her faithfully. Under its protective veil, she moved furtively to the outermost building, a ramshackle hut of scrap wood and thatch. From the hut's shadow, she surveyed the street, alight with the flames greedily devouring buildings less fortunate than this one.

There were too many men on the street.

And the string of boys was tied to a rail at its far end. The *north* end—where Glengaerif had told her he couldn't see.

The eastern side of the street was lined with shops, a tavern, and a two-story building that might be an inn. From the tavern drifted the hoots and hollers of Kirkmaugh's butchers at play and the screams of women who would not survive the night.

Laenora shuddered. Her heart was a heavy rock lodged in her throat, pounding to be let out. Her hands were damp with sweat and her legs trembled. Reaching inside her shirt, she pulled out the knife, only distantly aware that it nicked her flesh, starting a trickle of blood that seeped into her light wool blouse.

The inn—assuming that's what it was—was aflame, spitting sparks into the moonless sky. The flames, tossed in the light evening breeze, cast shadows that darted about the streets, dark demons gifted with the ability to change size and shape at will. Even from this end of the street, she could feel the heat. Those in the tavern had to be crazy staying so close. Any minute a spark, or the heat itself, might ignite the tavern, possibly—*hopefully!* she corrected herself—trapping the tavern's occupants inside.

Half the other buildings on that same side of the street were also in flames. Above the smell of burning wood, she caught another smell, repulsive acrid fumes that she chose not to think about. But the smell refused to be ignored. It caught in her throat as well as her nostrils, its foulness assaulting those two senses like the cloying air of blood which had surrounded Duleek. She fought down a wave of nausea.

The west side of the street was sparsely populated with buildings separated by twenty- or thirty-foot expanses of grass. It was through these gaps that Glengaerif would have to shoot the bow. Most of the buildings on the west side had not been set afire. Kirkmaughs were still searching through those, looting what meager belongings the people of Wicklow might have possessed. Occasionally there'd come a scream as someone who thought themselves well-hidden was discovered.

There were fewer corpses on Wicklow's street. Perhaps they had been forewarned by refugees from Duleek. If survivors of her village had run all night, they could have made it here hours before the Kirkmaughs who had spent the night enjoying the spoils of their conquest.

Laenora jumped as an agonized scream burst from the tavern, bounced back and forth between the buildings along each side of the street, and came echoing down to the town's southern end where she crouched in shadow. A second later, the scream was abruptly cut short.

She shook as chills ran up her spine. She told herself that it was still early spring and the night air was far too cold for the thin clothing she wore, but she knew the true roots of her discomfort.

Suddenly, the tavern door crashed open and Ari Kirkmaugh stood there, lit by the raging fire next door. In his arms, he held a nude woman. Limp and lifeless, she hung like a rag doll, her head lolled back to reveal a gaping red grin beneath her chin. Kirkmaugh tossed her into the street where she landed in an unnatural tangle of twisted limbs.

Laenora clamped her hand over her mouth, fighting back

the urge to scream. Bile rose behind her hand and she was forced to duck back behind the building, risking everything with the possibility that he catch the swift movement in his peripheral vision. Out of sight, she dry-heaved for a moment. The pain of doing it in silence brought tears to her eyes, but she needn't have worried, there was little chance of him hearing her over the raging fire.

Her hand was clenched so tight on the handle of the knife, it ached. Inside her, there awoke a beast, an animal that screamed for Kirkmaugh's blood. Her head swam with the hate that burned within her, causing her to reel on her feet.

"Hello, little lady."

She spun, brandishing the knife, to find a lean and hairy mercenary, stripped of his armor, clad only in short, baggy breeches of greasy leather, grinning like he had just found the prize of a lifetime. In his right hand he clutched a short sword, double-edged and gleaming a polished black in the firelight. His feral grin revealed yellowed teeth. Like some cur at table, he licked his lips in anticipation.

"We can do this one of two ways, love. You can drop the knife or I can cut off your hand. Doesn't really—What the hell!?"

There was a barely audible hiss as something cut the air inches from his head, close enough that he actually felt, more than heard, its passage. An arrow skipped once across the street, striking sparks off some stray stone, and was gone in the night.

"Son of a—"

Thunk! A feathered shaft seemed to magically appear on one side of his throat. From the other protruded a dripping crimson rod, tipped with a broadhead that twinkled like some tiny star come to ground.

He opened his mouth, might have screamed—although it was questionable whether he still had the facilities for it—but she lunged forward, plunging the knife to the hilt in his chest. He went down under her without a sound, still and lifeless, his eyes staring blankly up at her pale face.

She ripped the knife loose and stumbled away, shaking so bad she had to sit down against the wall. Clutching her knees tight against her chest, she ducked her head in her arms so she wouldn't have to look at his corpse and his empty, open eyes. Shivering, she sat like that for several minutes until she finally realized that she was wasting valuable time. At any moment, another mercenary could turn the corner and find the first one dead on the ground.

Five arrows, she thought dismally.

When she looked back around the corner, Kirkmaugh had disappeared. His place on the wide tavern porch had been taken by two of his men. The two were laughing loud enough to be heard over the fire and passing a half empty bottle back and forth between them.

For the time being, the rest of the street was empty.

Concealing herself in those shadows which tended to remain in place, Laenora began to work her way down the street. She'd covered more than half the distance undiscovered, amazed at her run of good luck, when a man came running from the home she'd just passed, shouting for her to stop. Halfway across the yard separating the two buildings, the mercenary suddenly spun about, clutching at something she couldn't see in the darkness. He sprawled into the grass, squealing like one of the pigs the Duleek innkeeper had raised and butchered for his guests.

A second man came after the first, hollering his name. For a moment, the second mercenary was confused. His eyes didn't register the now quiet form on the ground. In black armor, the dead man looked just like any of the other shadows cast like throw rugs between the buildings. Since he couldn't find his companion, he focused on her. Harmless, he probably thought, and started toward her. About the time he stumbled upon his dead friend, an arrow hissed out of the darkness and sank into his hip. He grunted and dropped to one knee, his hands grabbing for the shaft like it was some insect he could bat away.

He should have cried for help or shouted a warning, instead he looked toward the trees beyond the village, trying to spot his assailant. Glengaerif's second arrow crashed through the mercenary's tightly clenched teeth, shattered his uppermost vertebrae, and exited at the base of his skull.

The second mercenary fell over dead, almost on top of the

first. Laenora found she was getting used to death. Watching those two die, she'd felt only a cold detachment. No emotion, except a gnawing regret that it wasn't Kirkmaugh himself.

Two arrows, she thought, knowing they wouldn't carry her much further if she didn't get moving. With an almost reckless abandon, she ran the rest of the way through the buildings toward the north end of town. It wasn't until she had reached the last building before the one in front of which the boys were tied, that she had them in her sight again. When she did, she slid to a stop, nearly falling over her own feet.

Sitting beside the string of prisoners was the mercenary leader.

With the raging fire now so close, she could only hear fragments of his conversation. He was holding up his hands. The wide sleeves of his robe had fallen back to reveal his arms. Up to the elbows, they were covered with fresh blood.

"...never washes off..."

Shoot the bastard, Glen! She nearly screamed it out loud, so intense was her lust for his blood.

"...but who wants it to?"

Fighting down her hysteria, clearing her head enough to think, she remembered why Glengaerif could not put an arrow through Kirkmaugh's heart. She also recalled her promise. She held her ground, though the knife in her hand made involuntary thrusts at the air as she fought the urge to rush the mercenary lord.

Kirkmaugh got to his feet. She ducked further into the shadows, thinking he would return to the tavern, a course that would take him right past her hiding place. Instead, he said something to the boys, his words lost as the second floor of the burning inn collapsed. Then he turned and walked off around the building and into the dark woods beyond.

Follow him! screamed her hatred, and for a moment she actually ran past the boys. It was only their faces, turned up at her with eyes full of hope, that brought her to a halt and turned her back.

"Drew Callin?"

One boy raised his hand, eyes wide and terrified at being

singled out. She cut him free with the knife, noticing for the first time that it and her hand were covered with blood. She cut free the boy to either side of him and handed the oldest looking one the knife.

"Free them all," she told him.

Without question, the boy set to doing it.

"Listen to me—all of you. Run as fast and as far as you can. But all of you must run in different directions. Not all of you will escape, but if you scatter, there will be more of a chance. Do you understand?"

They nodded, silent, gaunt, faces red and haggard in the firelight.

She looked once at the empty darkness that had swallowed up Ari Kirkmaugh, thinking for a second about the opportunity she'd passed up. Then, with her bloody hand, she grabbed Drew by the arm. "Come with me."

She was faced with a serious dilemma: Ari Kirkmaugh had disappeared in the same direction Glengaerif had told her to go once she had freed Drew. *Improvise,* her mother would have said. *The world is full of more than just the obvious choices of black and white.*

"Who are you?" the boy asked as she hesitated indecisively.

"Quiet," she hissed, dragging them deeper into shadow. Two of the Duleek boys passed them and disappeared into the trees, unknowingly following Kirkmaugh's path.

Laenora cursed the boys: first, for going where the mercenary had gone before; and, secondly, for traveling together. *Split up,* she had told them. Perhaps she should have expected it. They were, after all, just terrified children.

She counted to five hundred, certain that was enough time for the two boys to run into Kirkmaugh were he waiting in the dark of the forest. Finally, she took Drew by the arm and ran across the short, firelit clearing and into the inky gloom beneath the trees.

They'd gone several hundred feet in a direction which she hoped was a true perpendicular to the town, when she decided it was time to answer his questions. The boy had held his tongue after that first question on the street—likely more than she could have done in his place.

Without stopping, she gave him the good news first. "Your father is waiting for us."

In the dark, she couldn't see his face, but she heard the sharp intake of breath and a choked-off sob. Relief. *Daddy's here and now all will be well*, perhaps. She braced herself to deliver the bad news.

But the kid possessed a sharp wit of his own and asked his second question before she could say more. "How bad is he hurt?"

They ducked under a fallen tree, knocking loose lichen and moss. *An easy trail to follow*, she realized, but only *after* they'd made the mistake. On the other side of the log, she paused to catch her breath.

"How do you know he's hurt?"

"He'd have come into town after me, instead of sending you."

That made her feel appreciated.

Even in the dark he seemed to sense it though. "Not that I don't appreciate what you did for me. I—"

"Thank me later," she cut him off. "Right now, we've got to find a canyon your dad told me about."

The fact that she hadn't answered his last question escaped neither of them.

The mercenary handed the bow to Kirkmaugh. "Found it beneath a tree. Also found blood in the tree, so he's already wounded."

"Tracks?"

"Good clear ones. Big horse. Easy to follow; we got a lot of rain the other day."

"Arrows?"

"None with the bow. He probably shot what he had and then ran."

A second mercenary materialized out of the gloom. Kirkmaugh recognized him as the officer he'd sent to track the escaped boys.

"They've scattered in every direction. I've got men tracking them now, Lord Kirkmaugh. We'll find them."

"Good. I want them all back here before dawn, so we can leave this dung heap." He turned the bow over in his hands, studying. "But I'm more worried about this archer. Find the new kid we brought out of Duleek. Bring him to me."

Cull nearly dropped the bow when Kirkmaugh thrust it at him.

"Your work?"

The redhead swallowed, beads of sweat suddenly popping out on his forehead. "It's my bow. The one we left in Duleek."

"Did you leave friends back there as good as you?"

Cull shook his head. "No. I was the best—damn near the *only*—archer in Duleek."

"This guy's as good."

"Better, M'lord." There was respect in the young man's voice that Kirkmaugh didn't care for in the least. "I paced off one of the shots he made."

"I don't care how good he is; he's without the bow now. I want him dead. Take four men and find him. Bring me his head before sunrise."

"I will."

The butcher smiled. "I know you will, Cull Garvin. Because if you don't, I'll have *your* head as a substitute. Show me I made the right decision when I let you live."

Drew caught her arm and pointed to a small creek. "That way."

"What?"

"They'll be following us. If we walk in the creek for a while, maybe we can confuse them."

She nodded, accepting his word that it was good strategy, hoping his father had perhaps taught him something of hunting, something that could as easily be applied to being *hunted*.

She stepped into the creek and started off through the calf-deep water in the direction they'd been heading.

"No. This way."

She shook her head. "Your father said to meet him—"

"I know, but they've got trackers. They'll see where we went into the stream."

"I thought the whole trick was that they wouldn't know where we got out?"

"Right. But they'll guess that we continued in the same direction and follow the creek till they find where we came out."

"So we go in the opposite direction and try to confuse them?"

He nodded, his face now visible as the moon climbed above the trees. It wasn't exactly a confident or optimistic face, but it was far from negative. He appeared sure of the wisdom of his strategy, less sure that it would work against men as experienced as the Dubh Aogail. She saw a lot of the father in his face, mixed with a fairer, more sensitive quality that she attributed to his mother.

Laenora waved a weary hand downstream. "I'm right behind you."

Drew found an overhanging shelf of rock and they used it to crawl out of the creek without leaving tracks. The forest had thinned out, replaced now with sparsely wooded hills and gullies, foothills of the broad mountain belt separating north and south Eire. There were enough rocky outcroppings that they traveled a hundred yards from the creek before they were forced to leave tracks in soft soil.

"Will that work?" she asked as he did his best to erase their tracks with a fallen branch.

"I don't know. I've never had to do this for real."

At that moment, she saw only the child in him. A frightened boy, bereft of his mother, worried about his father, scared, lost, hoping that he would do everything right and make his father proud.

As much as possible, they kept to rocky ground, leaving little, if any, tracks. It was slow going, but Drew insisted that it was better if they were late reaching his father than if they got there with Kirkmaughs on their trail. When they were forced to cross open ground, he took the time to cover their trail as good as he could. Looking back, Laenora found that if she studied the ground, she could still note their passage. Not wanting to sound negative, she said nothing to Drew.

Perhaps the trail is only obvious to me because I know where to look, she told herself.

But it was scant reassurance.

They had some trouble finding the small canyon Glengaerif had chosen as a meeting place until Drew had her repeat his father's directions. When she'd told him everything, repeating it word for word twice, he angled their course thirty or so degrees to the south and thus brought them to the arroyo.

The first thing they spotted was the horse, calmly munching sage grass. It eyed them warily as they came over the southern wall and slid down into the sandy basin. A creek had once flowed through here, cutting a wide shallow bowl into the earth. But it had been ages since any water had passed through, some ancient event having perhaps changed the creek's course.

"Where is he?" Drew asked.

She tried to keep the fear and worry she felt from showing on her face. Where indeed? "He was supposed to stay with the horse."

"Maybe he went looking for us?"

She realized she'd never explained the nature of his father's injuries. "He can't walk, Drew."

The boy accepted that without comment, his face stoically set as if he were prepared for the worst.

"Let's look around," she suggested.

It took only a moment to find him around a bend at the south end of the arroyo. He lay against the canyon wall, for the most part hidden in shadow. There were tracks in the sand showing that he had dragged himself over to the wall.

He was unconscious, slumped over the sword he'd carried ever since Duncannon's defeat. The quiver was there with its two remaining arrows. Of the bow, there was no sign.

Glengaerif's face was white in the moonlight, paler than she remembered. There was fresh blood soaked into the bandages on his thigh.

Drew knelt beside the still form and wrapped his arms around him. But the father did not awaken.

"What happened?" the boy asked, his eyes locked on the wound.

"Duncannon's army was defeated," she explained. "Your father escaped, but took that wound doing it."

Drew touched the angry red flesh above and below the bandages, his face twisted with concern over the heat he felt there. "It's bad, isn't it?"

"Yes."

"I'll be okay," Glengaerif suddenly mumbled. His eyes fluttered, fought their way open, and finally locked on his son.

"Father!"

"You don't know how good it is to see you, son." Laenora watched as father weakly embraced son. Glengaerif's hands were shaking, a symptom he'd acquired since she saw him last.

Drew hugged him back, fiercely, oblivious to the grimace of pain on his father's pale face. Both were crying: the boy openly with soft, uncontrollable sobs; the father silently, moon-glistening tears trailing softly down his waxy face.

Over the boy's shoulder, he met her concerned gaze. "Horse threw me," he offered as explanation for his current situation. "Probably damn tired of carrying me."

She said nothing, having guessed as much already.

"Mother," Drew sobbed. "They—"

"I know," Glengaerif said, holding the boy at arm's length where he could look at him. "Time for that later, son. Right now, we have to get out of here."

"We *weren't* followed," Laenora told him indignantly.

"Right! I did everything like you taught me," Drew added.

"I was followed," Glengaerif confessed.

Laenora moaned, legs already weak with exhaustion. Her eyes fell on the quiver, thinking of the accuracy of his shots even in the dark. Their present location might be easy to defend. "Where's the bow? We can make it expensive for them to enter this canyon."

"I dropped the bow getting out of the tree. And," he added with a shrug, "there are only two arrows remaining."

She flung her arms out, exasperated. "So, what now? I save your son. We meet you here. Surely you knew they would follow?"

"Get the horse."

"And what, the three of us get on him and outrun who knows how many Kirkmaughs?" After she'd said it, she saw Drew's face and knew her complaining wasn't doing any good.

"I've got a plan," he said calmly. "Just get the horse like I asked."

"I'll get him," Drew volunteered. He got to his feet and ran off into the darkness.

Hands on hips, she stood and stared at him, trying to think of something constructive to say, something that wouldn't sound so negative. But damn it, she'd thought it would be over once she'd gotten his son out. She realized now she'd been fooling herself. Even if all they'd done was steal the boy, the Kirkmaughs might have come after them to get him back and teach them a lesson. As it was, they'd killed three of them during Drew's rescue. No way Ari Kirkmaugh was going to suffer them that affront.

Glengaerif's eyes slipped closed. She thought for a moment he had lost consciousness again, but his eyes opened back up at the sound of Drew's light footfalls returning.

"Horse ran off," he said, sliding to a stop. There were fresh tears running down his face. He knew how important the horse had been. He and Laenora could walk out of the canyon, but his father needed that horse.

"Damn!"

Glengaerif said nothing, just closed his eyes, leaned back against the hard rock at his back, and thought for a second. She was wondering again if he'd nodded off, when he finally opened them and leaned forward.

"Over that hill just south of us there's a village. A very small village called Rhueshan."

"I've never heard of any place called Rhueshan."

"No reason you would have. There's a score of small villages scattered across these foothills, mostly goat and sheep herders, a few farmers—descendants of Kiamina. When the old empire fell, before Duncannon fought to build a new one, these people made homes in the hills."

"Will they hide us?"

"I grew up in these hills. My father was one of them; he even fought for Kiamina as a volunteer. Mention the name

Callin and they'll help you. My father's name was Rolph Evers Callin. They'll remember—"

Laenora cocked her head at him. "You talk like you're not going."

"I'm not."

"Father?" Drew was suddenly kneeling at his side.

Laenora shook her head adamantly. "This is foolishness."

"They can't be far behind me," Glengaerif explained. "Without me, the two of you have a chance of escaping. They'll find me and probably not even continue on into Rhueshan. Odds are they don't even know it exists."

"This was your great plan?"

He let out a long sigh. "My great plan did not include losing the horse."

"We're not leaving you!" Drew cried.

"You'll do what I tell you, son."

"And me?" Laenora asked. "You going to tell me I have to do whatever you say?"

"I'm hoping you'll see the sense in what I'm saying, girl. Save my son. That's all I'm asking."

"And leave you here?"

"I'm finished anyway."

She frowned, acknowledging, yet hating, the defeat in his voice. For a moment, she considered leaving him. She could take the boy and the two of them could start some sort of life in the hills. She could find some way to support them.

Whoring, she thought. *What kind of a mother figure would that be?* And on the heels of that last, she thought of her own mother, who'd left her daughter nothing better than an occupation handed down like old clothing.

She ripped the sword out of his weak hands and pushed it at Drew. "Get up, boy. We're wasting time here."

"I won't leave him!"

She smiled. "Who said anything about leaving him? We passed some saplings on the way into this canyon. Go cut two strong ones for a stretcher. Hurry!"

Taking the sword, he ran off, little spurts of sand kicking up behind his heels.

"You're a fool," Glengaerif told her.

They made the stretcher from two stout saplings laced together
with smaller branches and strips of cloth cut from Drew's shirt.
While they worked, Glengaerif complained about the time they
were wasting. He alternated between pleading with them to
leave him and cursing at them for staying.

When the crude stretcher was complete, they got him on it
and started over the hill that formed the southern end of the
canyon. Twice the stretcher came apart and it was all they could
do to keep from dropping him. Each time, they cut more limbs
from nearby saplings and wove it back together.

"You're leaving a trail a blind man could follow," Glengaerif
complained.

Neither of the stretcher bearers made comment. There
was nothing to say. Laenora was busy thinking of Duleek and
Wicklow's massacres repeated in the small mountain village
of Rhueshan; their fault, because they were leaving such an
easy trail to follow, a trail that would lead straight into the
village. Drew was too busy to think, struggling under half the
stretcher's weight, a weight he was too emaciated to carry, and
shivering in the damp night air now that he was shirtless.

Laenora spotted the village first. In the early hours before
daylight, there was no activity and only a few lights. Excited,
she pointed it out to them.

Glengaerif gave it only a cursory glance, he was more
interested in watching their backtrail. Just seconds after Laenora
pointed out the lights of Rhueshan, he pointed to lights coming
through the canyon behind them.

"Torches," he explained when the others looked confused.
"They're no more than thirty minutes back, tracking us by
torchlight."

"We can't lead them into Rhueshan," Laenora protested.

"We've no choice. Whether we lead them there or not, the
Kirkmaughs have found it now. We've got to go down and warn
them."

Rhueshan could barely be called a village. Its single street was lined with only seven buildings: the largest an inn whose swinging sign proclaimed it THE BEAR'S LARDER; a combination stable and blacksmith's, the doors of the stable decorated with the painting of a huge silver bear, so large as to seem unreal; a small stone building, well built, but ancient, the purpose of which she had no inkling; and four nondescript buildings she took for private homes, each unique, yet each alike in that they all bore some bear-like decoration.

"These people have a fixation for bears," Laenora commented as they set the stretcher down in the street before the hostelry.

"Careful," Glengaerif warned. "Don't offend them; they worship a bear."

"Worship bears?"

"Bear. Singular. One special bear."

The door to the inn opened, spilling light into the street. A tall, stoop-shouldered man, grey of hair and beard, stepped from the doorway and out onto the wide veranda, his boots making soft, welcome sounds on the old boards there.

"Late for travelers," he said, his voice hoarse and old. "I've got room though. And there's stew still warm back of the fire."

Mention of the stew just about made Laenora forget the danger behind them. She hadn't eaten since sharing Glengaerif's food the previous afternoon. And who knew when the mercenaries had last fed Drew.

"You've got trouble coming down on you," Glengaerif spoke up from the stretcher.

"Guessed that right off," the old man said flatly. "I'll send for the rangers in the morning. For now, it's warm inside, and you're half-starved and in need of a doctor."

"This trouble's close on our heels, old man." Glengaerif sat up, though it caused him obvious pain. "You haven't time to wait for any of Kiamina's rangers. Kirkmaugh mercenaries are trailing us. Kirkmaughs, do you hear? The Dubh Aogail. They've already left a trail of blood across Northern Eire. Unless you mean Rhueshan to be next, rouse everyone and get them hidden in the hills."

The old man swallowed. "I'll wake everyone. Should we hide you as well?"

"No. If they don't find us, they'll stay till they do."

The old man turned to go back into the inn, paused, and looked back over his shoulder. "Thanks for the warning."

"You owe us nothing, old man. Better we had not brought this trouble down on your heads."

A silent nod, acceptance of the unspoken apology, silent understanding; then he went back in and closed the door behind him. Inside, more lights came on and a commotion began.

"Why wouldn't you let him hide us?" Laenora asked angrily.

"The Kirkmaughs would have hunted them down, slain them as well as us."

"What are we supposed to do now?"

"Head south out of town," Glengaerif told her. "It's not far now."

"What's not far now?"

He pointed at the double doors of the stable. "He's not far."

The trail to the cave was steep; Laenora and Drew had to drag the stretcher most of the way. Slipping in and out of consciousness, Glengaerif told them what he knew of the bear. Though the night was cool enough to set both the others to shivering, especially Drew, Glengaerif's pallid face was covered with a sheen of sweat. His hands, where they lay folded across the sword on his chest, were visibly shaking.

"Rhueshan has worshipped Kenmaeri Aergiod for forty or fifty years. They look on him as a god, a god come to Eire in the form of a giant bear. In truth, he's probably nothing more than an old silver bear, long lived because of the generosity of the Rhueshanians. They leave him weekly offerings of fresh, raw meat, not to mention the day-to-day scraps he takes from their refuse pile."

We should have taken the old man's offer, Laenora thought to herself. *Glengaerif would have protested, but in his condition, there's nothing he could have done. Without a doctor, he's going to die soon. He's even losing his senses; in a second, he's going to tell us this bear will save us from the Kirkmaughs.*

"But it's an equal trade," Glengaerif continued. "Kenmaeri's presence keeps away mountain cats and the occasional wyvern, both a threat to the Rhueshanians' livestock. The larger cats have even been known to steal children in these hills."

"But of what use is he to us?" Drew panted.

"The Rhueshanians say that Kenmaeri knows a true son of the mountains. He won't harm us, but the Kirkmaughs on the other hand…"

And what does that say for a daughter of Duleek? she thought cynically.

Glengaerif had slipped back into unconsciousness by the time they reached the top of the hill. Before them, in plain sight, lay the dark mouth of the bear's cave. The opening was huge, and even from fifty feet away they could hear soft rumblings as if something huge slept within.

"What now?" Drew asked, as if she were privy to his father's crazy plan.

"I guess we go in and wake up the bear. 'Here bear, this is Glen Callin, a *true son of the mountains*; recognize him?'"

Drew didn't laugh. "Father knows what he's doing."

"And, 'Oh! By the way, there are some really nasty lowland types following us, sir bear. Would you mind—'"

Drew caught her arm and pointed downslope. "Look!"

At the base of the steep trail, just starting up, were their pursuers. Between the torches, the moonlight, and the grey luminance of the eastern skyline, there was enough light to see them.

"Only five," Drew whispered.

More than enough, she thought, as the black armored group started up the slope toward them.

Cull Garvin flipped the reins of his horse across the saddle where they wouldn't become tangled in the sparse underbrush while the tall charger fed. The horse shook its mane and snorted, pleased to be rid of its rider, as Cull walked over to join his men. Through the wye of his black helm, he looked up the hill and saw his prey: a woman and a boy kneeling over what might be a third person.

"They're dragging someone," one of the trackers commented. He pointed to parallel grooves cut into the side of the slope. "Looks like a makeshift sled or travois."

Good place to stand your ground, Cull thought as he surveyed the enemy's position atop the hill. But what weapons would they use? For all his studying, the woman and boy appeared helpless.

Without waiting for his order, the four mercenaries, experienced killers all, started up the slope. He realized again that he was only loosely in control. Ari Kirkmaugh had said take them, but he had never designated Cull as the leader of this small group. And they were all veterans, likely to kill him if they suspected he thought he held some control over them.

He was about to follow after them when a figure materialized out of the gloom. The newcomer took up a position straddling the trail between the mercenaries and their prey. He wore long, flowing robes of green and brown, natural colors like one might wear to blend in with the surrounding hills and forests. Beneath the robes, there was an obvious bulge that could only have been a long sword. It was hard to tell in the gloom, but Cull thought he also caught the glint of mail when the breeze tugged the stranger's collar to one side.

The four mercenaries fanned out, filling the breadth of the steep trail. To either side was loose rock, treacherous ground for fighting if a man wished to keep his legs unbroken. Further up the slope, a misstep might also mean a fall, possibly a fatal one.

"Turn back," the stranger said, one hand gripping the sword beneath his robes. Just like that: *turn back* —as if they would shrug their shoulders and leave.

The four mercenaries drew their blades and advanced. Cull drew his own sword, though there was no room left for him to get at the stranger.

Four of the Dubh Aogail. One stranger. It should have been quick, easy. It wasn't.

The stranger threw aside what proved to be a heavy cloak, a mottled garment meant for camouflage and hiding the mail and weapons beneath. Sword and knife flashed in the moonlight, silver arcs radiating from the stranger's hands. He didn't wait for the four mercenaries, but leaped forward to meet them, his attack so sudden and ferocious that one mercenary flew to the side of the trail in a shower of blood before Cull had taken a single step.

Though there was now room on the trail, Cull hung back. This gave the three veterans room to maneuver, and it was clear within seconds that the stranger was now fighting for his life. Three against one, especially three as well trained as the Kirkmaughs, was just too much.

A second later, another Kirkmaugh stumbled to his knees, dropping his sword to clutch at his spewing throat. The mercenary knelt there, for all the world looking as if he thought he could hold his windpipe and jugular together with his bare hands, then he pitched forward on his face.

Cull stared at the lifeless form, unbelieving.

The stranger retreated up the hill, moonlight playing now off two rents in his armor, one of which was leaking crimson. For the first time, Cull noticed the emblem on the stranger's right breast: a hawk with a broken lance held in its claws. The hawk held the lance together such that it appeared to be whole.

Kiamina.

It was the symbol of the old empire, the only government to have ever united North and South Eire. This then, was one of those lost soldiers who'd retreated into the mountains, one of those the peasants called rangers. Cull had heard stories, none of which he'd believed to be true, of these so-called rangers fighting for no better reason than their own misplaced concept of justice.

Cull moved up to take a position with the two remaining mercenaries. These were his men he realized, and he felt overdue shame at having held back so long.

Between the three of them, they cut the ranger down, though in doing so another one of the veteran mercenaries was injured badly. Clutching a nearly severed arm against his side, he was bleeding to death.

"Tourniquet," Cull ordered.

The unmarked veteran scowled, murder in his eyes. "He's done for."

Cull ignored him, turning his back though an inner voice screamed that it was ludicrous to do so, and started up the slope. "I'm going to get what we came for."

The crisp ring of swordplay woke Glengaerif. He struggled to sit up, but failed. "What is it?"

Laenora didn't hear him, full attention locked on the fight taking place on the slope. Here was something, someone, to hope for. Though she had never seen a ranger, she instinctively guessed this to be one. She had no idea whether he was here to save them or to prevent the Kirkmaughs from violating the bear's cave, ground the Rhueshanians probably considered sacred.

Drew knelt to help his father. By the time Glengaerif was in a position where he could see down the slope, the ranger was falling to one side, silver mail drooping from his torn chest. Even over the crunch of the body as it rolled downhill, they could hear the tinkling of chain links scattering across the rocks.

Glengaerif caught the boy by the neck and pulled him close. "Listen to me!"

The venom in his voice even turned Laenora around. She was shaking, having put the last of her hope into the ranger. Drained, she was sinking into despair, certain that they were all three just minutes away from death.

Funny how quick she'd been ready to end it all in that pond outside Duleek. Looking at Glengaerif and the boy, she realized what had brought about the change. She saw the two of them as a reason for living. Maybe they didn't share the same feelings, maybe Glengaerif would never care for her—*could* never have feelings for a whore after the fine lady he'd had for a wife—but she wanted to try.

"The cave, son. You've got to go in there. You've got to wake up Kenmaeri Aergiod. Make him mad—mad enough to chase you out."

The boy's eyes were wide with fear.

"Then you've got to run like you've never run before. You've got to lead him down the slope—and into the Kirkmaughs."

"I'll do it," Laenora burst out.

Glengaerif's eyes never left those of his son. "No. You've got to drag me off this trail and into that deadfall back there. Drew isn't strong enough to drag me by himself."

"I'll drag you aside and *then* go after the damn bear."

"No time."

It was true. They could hear the mercenary laboring up the slope, no easy climb in armor.

"I can do it, Dad," the boy said, teeth clenched on his lower lip so it wouldn't tremble.

"I know you can. When you run through the mercenaries, don't stop. Don't even look back. Run all the way back to the village and hide. Understand?"

Drew nodded.

"Go on then."

The boy swallowed, a tear breaking free to trace a path through the dirt on his face. He pulled away from his father and ran for the dark cave.

"Hurry, girl. You've got to hide us. Quick!"

The dark cave enfolded Drew like the clammy embrace of a drowned lover found after hours beneath the sea. A chill raced up his spine as he clenched his teeth together to prevent their chattering. His knees were weak, threatening at any moment to fold beneath him and drop him helplessly to the damp cave floor.

He told himself he wasn't afraid, that these symptoms were brought on by the cold and his fatigue. But when something shifted in the back of the cave, something larger than even the black Kirkmaugh chargers, and let out a sleepy growl, a deep, bass rumble that reverberated throughout the now-so-very-small cave, he wanted only to run.

His legs wouldn't move.

Had he been able to, Drew would have fled. For at that moment, he knew that death outside at the hands of the mercenaries would be quick, clean, simple, and almost painless.

On the other hand, death in this abysmal cavern would be violent, bone-crushingly bloody, and painful. Rhueshan's god would rend him limb from limb; the great claws—a glimmer of which he was sure he could see beneath the shaggy, shadow-spawned hulk at the rear of the cave—would disembowel him, allowing the great maw to plunge into his gaping chest cavity.

In excruciating pain, he would struggle helplessly as the bear tore organs from...

His knees hit the hard stone floor, the pain snapping him out of the fear-induced trance in which he had sunk. Drew Callin shuddered, taking in great gulps of air and letting them out as quietly as possible. In the moist air of the cave, his breath became great white clouds, clouds that for a moment obscured the sleeping mass in front of him, allowing him precious seconds in which to collect his wits.

Just a bear.

He got weakly to his feet and crossed the few remaining feet separating them. Fear now somewhat in check, he became aware of the bear's smell. It was an overpowering odor he could only label as beast. The cave reeked of beast; the air that wafted in his face with every breath the monstrosity took stank of beast; the smell of beast seemed to be pervading the very pores of his body.

Only a bear. Just a bear. Nothing more than a common, every day, lives in the gods-be-damned-mountains bear!

There was the glimmer of claws, long as the breadth of his hand, on paws capable of crushing his head like a melon.

Wake it.

There was its head, indiscriminate in the dark of the cave, except for the sheen of reflected light on ivory fangs and, above the teeth, a glistening blackness darker than the surrounding cave gloom—the bear's nose.

The boy took a deep breath, held it, and drew back his leg. With all his might, he kicked the bear in the nose.

Like a coiled spring, the great beast came to life, rising from the cave floor with snapping jaws and a roar that threatened to bring the entire cave down on Drew's head. When the ivory fangs clashed together without the satisfying feel and taste of crushed flesh and bone, the bear swept its gaze about the cave, looking for its antagonist. The bear's scathing black eyes gleamed of hatred, visible even in the cave's shrouded interior.

Drew was already plunging out the cave entrance, legs flying like never before in his young life.

Heedless of thorns and dead branches that tore at their exposed flesh, Laenora pulled Glengaerif back into the brush at the side of the trail.

"Hurry!" he hissed.

With a final desperate yank that caused him to bite through his lip in pain, she got them both back into the deadfall, concealed as good as they could ever hope to be in these barren rocks. A crunch of gravel told them at least one of the mercenaries had reached the top of the trail.

A few seconds, later the very ground shook with the roar of something terrible.

When he reached the top of the trail, Cull was forced to bend over, resting hands on knees, and try to catch his breath. It had not been an easy climb in eighty pounds of armor.

To his right, he spotted the man and woman, the man obviously incapacitated with a leg wound, trying to hide in a mass of dead tree limbs and thorny brush. No threat; he'd deal with them in a moment. The woman might even be worth spending some time with before they had to kill her—it was hard to tell what she looked like behind the deadfall. The man he would waste no time dispatching, but first he had to find the boy.

He spared a glance downslope to see that one mercenary had used a leather thong to tourniquet the other's wound, in spite of declaring the injured man as good as dead, and was now working his own way up the slope. The wounded man was leaning against a boulder, miraculously still on his feet.

They raise these bastards to be tough, Cull reminded himself. Most likely, the wounded man believed that if he lay down, a sign of weakness, they'd decide he wasn't worth taking back with them. Of course, there was no guarantee Ari Kirkmaugh would take the wounded man on with them when they left. And he sure couldn't stay behind. The locals would torture him to death for what had been done to Duleek and Wicklow.

That was when the air was split with the cry of something incredibly huge. And incredibly mad. The boy burst from a cave which Cull hadn't even had time to notice yet.

"Boy, stop right—"

The boy dove right between Cull's legs and hit the slope in a ball that sent him rolling and tumbling downhill. Cull cursed and was about to give chase, when the source of the bestial roar exploded from the cave.

Later, Cull Garvin would remember only bits and pieces of the encounter. He would never forget the size of the thing as it stood up before the cave entrance and roared its anger at the grey sky. It had to be twelve feet tall, easily more than twice his own height. When it came down on all fours, its shoulder was still higher than his own.

He would always remember how it looked at him, as if *he* had done something—had been ignorant enough to anger something of that size! It charged forward then, bellowing the same war cry he had already heard two times too many.

He felt his sword slip from a hand that had gone totally numb. With the beast bearing down on him, he was acutely aware of the sound the sword made as it hit the rocky slope and started to slide downhill.

Then the bear hit him, its paw like some gargantuan sledgehammer tipped with razors. Cull raised an arm to defend himself and caught the blow on that shoulder. There was immense, bone-crushing pain, the splatter of blood across his face, and the sky and ground seemed to spin about him. He was vaguely aware of impact somewhere off the side of the escarpment, a second blow of numbing intensity, and then nothing.

Blackness swept over him, welcome relief to escalating pain.

The rocks tore bloody scrapes across his hands, knees, and exposed back before Drew was able to regain his feet. Behind him he heard one very short scream, barely audible over the roar of the infuriated bear.

He didn't look back. In fact, he hadn't looked back once since kicking the bear in the face. He knew if he did, if he saw Kenmaeri charging down on him, his legs would turn to water and his heart would simply freeze up. He knew the bear was behind him; what mattered just how close behind it was?

Halfway between him and the bottom of the slope stood a second Kirkmaugh. Drew was wondering whether the same trick of diving between the legs would work again, when he noticed the man's face. The mercenary was looking beyond him, the eyes so big around they were a blare of white dotted with pupils made tiny in comparison, eyes locked on the beast now just mere feet behind Drew's heels.

Without slowing down, the boy plummeted past the frozen mercenary. Behind him he heard the ravenous roar of the bear again. This time, his will power failed him and he looked back over his shoulder.

The bear launched itself at the lone mercenary like some jungle cat. The mercenary got in one good slash with his sword; blood flew and the bear bellowed in pain and anger. Then the mercenary was crushed beneath the claws and teeth of the silver-furred monstrosity.

As the mercenary went down, so did Drew, his ankle twisting on a loose piece of rock. He sprawled face first on the trail, ripping hands and elbows. He rolled over.

And saw the bear take the mercenary's head in its mouth and crunch down.

He scrambled to his feet and ran, limping now on the twisted ankle. He made it to the base of the trail without further misstep, but it was only luck that got him there. He was no longer seeing the trail in front of him; all he could see before him was the Kirkmaugh's head crushing like a red melon, spilling brains and gore over the jowls of the bear.

He ran past the injured mercenary, who had by now fallen to his knees, weak from the blood he had lost. Drew gave him not a single glance as he plunged past and headed for Rhueshan, not once looking back again. It was only later that he'd recall hearing the last mercenary plead for his help; then, moments later, scream beneath the rage of Kenmaeri Aergiod.

Laenora hid her face against Glengaerif's chest as the bear vented his rage on the bodies of the mercenaries. Glengaerif could do little to comfort her, he was slipping in and out of consciousness, darkness slipping back and forth like a piece of black lace played across his face.

Ten or fifteen minutes went by with the bear on the trail growling and chomping on what she'd rather not think about. Sickened by the ruthless deaths, deaths they had orchestrated, Laenora found that vengeance was not the sweet she had expected.

Finally, the noise on the trail ceased and she heard the silver bear making its way up the trail to the lair. Peering through the network of dead branches, Laenora watched as the bear reached the top of the trail. It paused there, lifted its head as if testing the wind, and then turned to look straight at their hiding place.

With a huff like an old man clearing his throat, the bear lumbered toward the deadfall. Its lips were curled back from teeth still dripping with Kirkmaugh blood and guts. More blood was frothed across its silver chest and clotted with dirt around its four feet. There was a gash on its shoulder from which its own blood flowed. As it walked toward them, it licked the wound once or twice.

Reaching the deadfall, it stretched out one great forepaw and swept aside most of the brush behind which the two humans were hidden.

Laenora was aware of a soft, high-pitched keening, a whine synchronized with her own ragged breath and fiercely pounding heart. It took a second before she realized the noise was coming from herself.

Tiny eyes of midnight black, ringed by near-white fur that covered most of its muzzle, locked with her own. Kenmaeri studied her for what seemed like an eternity, its breath, blood-sweet, wafting across her face. Laenora sat motionless, now silent save for the beating of her heart which she thought like the hammering of a kettle drum. She was afraid to even breath for fear that might somehow trigger the animal.

Finally, the bear looked from her to Glengaerif, unconscious on the stretcher. It reached out, set a bloody claw roughly on his chest, and then looked back at her.

"Glengaerif Callin," she whispered. "He belongs here. His father was—"

The bear huffed again, dowsing her with a fine mist of blood and saliva; then snapped at her face, prompting a sharp, but quiet, scream from her.

Shut up, perhaps? Was he reminding her that *she* did not belong and by his grace alone would she walk away alive? Or was he just an insane old bear, longer lived than was natural, and beyond human rationalization?

Whatever the reason, Kenmaeri withdrew his forepaw, leaving blood and dirt on Glengaerif's chest, and limped back to disappear in his cave.

She remained unmoving, catatonic save for quivers that phased up and down her spine, for what must have been several minutes, awoken from the trance only when Glengaerif caught the thorn torn sleeve of her blouse.

"Listen," he instructed in a voice both hoarse and pathetically weak.

From somewhere down the slope came the soft moaning of a man in pain.

"Take it," he said, meaning the broadsword beside him on the makeshift stretcher. "You've got to finish him. If he manages to return to—"

"I understand," she said, taking the sword from its weathered scabbard and pushing her way through what little brush the bear had left. In fact, she'd understood it before he'd even mentioned the sword. But that didn't necessarily mean she felt capable of doing it. She only left as quick as she did to belay him telling her *exactly* what she had to do.

The sides of the steep trail were too treacherous for her to go directly down after the injured mercenary. Instead, she had to go to the bottom, stepping carefully around and over the remains of the Kirkmaughs. She paused long enough to assure herself that the ranger was dead. He lay ten feet off the trail, glossy eyes staring up at the brightening sky, his chest one gaping sword wound from which protruded the splintered ends of broken ribs. Though the bear had ravaged the bodies of the Kirkmaughs, he had not touched the dead ranger.

From the base of the trail, she worked her way through the rocks to the side and finally came upon the one mercenary still living. He lay among the boulders, black armor dented and scraped from the fall. He held one unnaturally twisted arm tight against his side. There was blood too, deep claw marks that had cut through armor to score his chest and nearly taken out his throat as well.

The mercenary heard her approach, and before the battered helm had even turned to see who it was, he asked for help.

His plea was almost enough to steel her nerves for the task at hand. Asking help of her! What gave him the right? What help, what mercy, what common decency had they shown the villagers of Duleek and Wicklow?

He turned then, his eyes betraying recognition—so he was one of those who'd used her in Duleek! A second later, recognition faded to dread as he spotted the naked sword clutched in her hands.

She wanted to smile, wanted him to see that it would be with pleasure that she murder him like he had done so many innocents. But it wasn't in her; she wasn't, after all, cut from the same cloth as they.

The six steps she took toward him were the hardest she'd ever taken in her life.

He did something very strange then for a man about to be hit with a broadsword. He reached up, removed his helm, and tossed it aside. She heard it clang across the rocks, making enough noise she feared the bear might return, then roll to a stop, and silence.

A light morning breeze tossed his hair, red in the rising sun.

"Where's the sword?" he asked when she returned.

"Left it."

"Dammit, girl, we might—"

"I said I left it! Leave it at that."

He frowned, but said no more, thinking that she was a very young woman to have been through all, and seen all, the events of the past few days. Dispatching a wounded enemy was always a difficult necessity to bear, a black sin that weighed heavy on the soul, perhaps more so for a woman. No matter that you were enemies a second before the wounded man fell, when it came to finishing him off, you were no more than a murderer. And he, your victim.

"I can't get you down this slope alone," she said finally, breaking the silence.

"Go to Rhueshan for help. It's warm here in the sun. I'll be fine."

She touched his face, her hand soft against his cheek above the dirt-stiff beard. "I'll hurry," she promised. "You just rest, and don't—"

She swallowed and blinked eyes that threatened to spill tears.

"Just don't die on me, Glen Callin."

"Farthest thing from my mind, girl."

Be quiet, she'd said. And, *Stay hidden until we've taken Glengaerif back to Rhueshan.*

Cull did as she asked—would have been a fool not to. When they were gone, the woman and boy walking on each side of the stretcher two villagers carried, telling the wounded man that everything would be all right now, he dragged himself back to the trail. Crawling was agony with his broken arm. Movement caused his broken ribs to grate together, sending knives of pain lancing through his body. But he made it to the trail.

And found that things weren't as bad as he had thought they would be.

The Rhueshanians had left behind all five bodies. The horses had scattered when the bear came down the trail, but he could see two of them grazing not far off in a barren copse of trees.

If he could reach the horses and somehow get into a saddle—a tree would probably do for that—he could go anywhere he chose. If he returned to the Dubh Aogail, they could set and splint the arm and wrap his broken ribs.

There was food and water on the horses.

Laenora had left him a sword—not that there was any shortage with the four dead mercenaries and the dead ranger, as well as his own sword near the top of the trail if he wanted it bad enough. Which he didn't.

The dead ranger!

Bring me his head, Ari Kirkmaugh had said of the midnight archer.

Well, Cull even had one of those to take back.

KIAMINA'S GHOSTS

(a Swords of Eire fantasy)

— What has Gone Before: A Recap of Recent Events in Eire —

Forty-seven years after the founding of the Kiamina Empire, the Emperor Rodric Orvellon was assassinated by unknown adversaries. With nearly as many suspects as there were fiefdoms in Eire, little was done to investigate the crime. Those with the means to undertake such an investigation were too preoccupied with the future of the empire and, more specifically, with what could be gained for their own noble houses. In the turmoil that followed Orvellon's death, with southern barons and northern lords vying for the throne, nomadic clans from the far west united under the leadership of the merciless Bheag Ai Duboil and invaded Northern Eire. Kiamina was the primary target for these marauders. Northern and Southern Eire failed to unite under a single leader, nor even to form viable alliances in time, and Kiamina was laid to ruins. Those who didn't flee into the mountains were slaughtered. Most of Kiamina's elite guard, the Rangers, were slain; what few did escape scattered into the mountains with no leadership. Kiamina's walls were torn down. Her wells were poisoned and her fields were set ablaze. Thus fell the first and only power to ever unite Northern and Southern Eire. Forty-seven years of relative peace was at an end, replaced by the vicious tyranny of Bheag Ai Duboil.

The barbarians established a strong defensive seat, a primitive fortress of hewn wood and mud which they named Khal Mani. Situated where the Dunshaughlin and Meath

Rivers empty from Lake Severn, Khal Mani commanded an expansive view of Kilcullen Fields and an enviably strategic position. Bheag Ai Duboil proclaimed himself Emperor of Eire. For thirty years the northern lords fought him individually and lost. There were hints that the barbarians had in their possession some dark power, a force summoned from beyond the temporal and physical borders of Eire. True or not, the rumor spread fear among Bheag Ai Duboil's enemies and lent his savages a fanatical ardor which, when coupled with their ruthless techniques, brought victory time after time.

Meanwhile, the southern barons refused to acknowledge Bheag Ai Duboil's claim to the throne of Eire and fought amongst themselves for rulership of the south, all the while suffering from the lack of northern trade goods which Bheag Ai Duboil's patrols would not allow through Kiamina Pass.

Eventually, a rebellion under the leadership of Clive Duncannon of Mandarlin drove Bheag Ai Duboil's forces from Kiamina Pass and secured a footing in the mountains there. Uniting with armies from Howth, Armagh, Devon, and Gairloch, Duncannon was able to cut off all supplies to Khal Mani. When Bheag Ai Duboil arranged with the city of Drogheda for supplies, Duncannon attacked that city from the sea, bombing the city into submission with ship-side catapults and dropping mercenaries behind the city walls with ingenious hot air balloons. His energies were then turned to Khal Mani, where it is said he left not a single man, woman, or child alive. A year after the rebellion began, the armies of Armagh, Devon, Gairloch, Howth and, reluctantly, Drogheda swore allegiance and proclaimed Clive Duncannon King of Northern Eire. The other great powers in the north were quick to follow. Duncannon built a great city astride the Dunshaughlin River and named it Droichead Nua, the New Bridge. Droichead Nua was to become a metaphoric bridge between new friends and former foes, between north and south, between what was and what could be.

Clive Duncannon would rule for twenty years, a peaceful period in which many reparations were made between north and south. For a time, it appeared there might once again be a united Eire, but in the far north, in bitter Drogheda, where nothing is ever forgotten or forgiven, Cloyne Kildare set himself on a brutal winter campaign to conquer his neighbors. In addition to conquering neighboring Gairloch and Armagh, Kildare conscripted all male peasants, young and old, forcing them to fight with whatever farm implements could be used as weaponry. Ravaging the land as he moved south, Kildare left nothing in his wake but starving babes and weeping women. Duncannon was slow to react, expecting Kildare to accomplish very little at the height of the vicious Eire winter. He underestimated the northerner's hatred.

By spring, Kildare's power was great enough to challenge Duncannon. He marched on Droichead Nua. Duncannon, refusing to have his great city destroyed by siege, marched out to meet Kildare on Kilcullen Fields. The armies clashed. Duncannon was defeated. [These events were told in "Rhueshan's Palladium."]

It is now late summer, nearly 100 years after the founding of the Kiamina Empire. Cloyne Kildare sits the throne in Droichead Nua, planning incursions to the south. In Southern Eire, one baron, Duncan Emery, urges the others to unite their forces and march north to save Duncannon. He is unaware that he is already several months too late. Regardless, he is unsuccessful, for the southerners trust each other no more than they do the northerners. By the time Emery has formed a substantial army comprised of his own sworn-swords and volunteers, word of Duncannon's demise reaches them. Emery opts for a defensive position in Kiamina Pass, where he hopes to hold Kildare back. Other forces, hiding in the north, seek defensive, as well as offensive positions of their own.

– ONE: ASSASSINS, KINGS, AND FALLEN HEROES –

Bodyguards flanked Cloyne Kildare as he strode down the wide marble hall to the bedroom suite formerly occupied by the late Clive Duncannon. The suite hung out over the Dunshaughlin, its single point of access this one heavily guarded hall and ultimately a door that weighed as much as a Red Sea breacher whale—a fortress within a fortress (though Droichead Nua wasn't much of a fortress situated as it was across the river). The guards lining the corridor came to attention and saluted him as he passed. Kildare ignored them, his violet evening robes billowing out behind him. The walls behind the guards were lined with rich tapestries, many of them pillaged during the fall of Khal Mani, more than twenty years ago. No one wove so beautifully as the wagon women of the western tribes. The cold stone floor was covered with a thick maroon carpet which appeared almost new. The carpet had seen very little use in the years that Duncannon had slept here. Since Kildare's coming, the carpet had begun to acquire the tinge of the gray clay that lined the banks of the river, tracked in on the boots of his guards.

Where did Duncannon station his guards? wondered the new king.

Kildare's guards were huge men, each chosen for size and ferocity, surpassed in sheer strength only by the two personal bodyguards accompanying the king. Many were horribly disfigured—some intentionally so. None were scarless. Each wielded a heavy, two-headed axe. The blades of these axes gleamed in the light of torches mounted on the walls. Each man was armored head to foot in gleaming steel plate. Helmeted. Visored. Plumed.

Beyond the guards, at the end of the hall, the double doors. Twelve feet tall. Thick as the breadth of a large man's hand. Solid hardwood, banded with iron. The last bastion for a besieged king.

But Duncannon had marched his army out onto the field.

"And there he died," whispered the new king.

The guards nearest the doors leaned their bulk against the wood, and the doors swung slowly, ponderously inward. "M'lord King, is there anything further you require this evening?" asked one of the two bodyguards.

"My manservant, Horace, where is he?"

The bodyguard hesitated.

The man-at-arms nearest the door bowed his head, helmet plumes dipping gracefully before the king. "M'lord, he arrived more than an hour ago and was instructed to wait in your room."

Kildare frowned at the bodyguard, who really should have known in advance if there was anyone waiting within the suite. What if an assassin were inside? How many of Eire's kings had already been lost to inept bodyguards? Kildare's cold stare was enough to chastise the man, for the bodyguard went down on one knee and lowered his head. Kildare debated drawing the slender stiletto at his belt and plunging it into the back of the man's neck, but he realized lessons need never be so severe that they provide martyrs for the survivors. Besides, it would ruin the luxurious carpet.

He turned toward the doors as if to ignore the man, but at the last moment paused, looking back as the bodyguard raised his head. The blue eyes behind the visor were soft with relief. "I'd like a woman tonight," instructed the king. "Lydia, the redhead, I think." He pulled at his lower lip. "And when she leaves tonight, you will see her back to her chambers ... and pay her ten pieces of gold from your own salary."

The bodyguard's eyes narrowed just before he bowed his helmeted head. Kildare smiled, made a mental note to tell Horace to remove the man to the regular guard unit, and stepped through the heavy doors, indicating with a flick of his wrist that they should be sealed behind him. Once inside, with the doors closed, he dropped a heavy iron bar in place. He was safe now. Duncannon may have been a fool when it came to designing Droichead Nua, but this one chamber, so deeply situated within the castle, suspended out over a three-hundred-foot drop to the river, was impenetrable.

"Horace!"

Kildare frowned. Normally his servant was waiting just inside the door. For a moment he wondered what to do with the heavy robe without Horace there to take it. Finally, he dropped it to the floor. On top of the robe, he set the fine gold circlet that he'd taken from Duncannon's brow on Kilcullen fields. That done, he crossed the marble vestibule in search of a manservant about to be severely chastised.

"Horace! Where are you?"

The sitting room, resplendent with its overstuffed divans and multicolored throw pillows was just beyond the vestibule.

Everything was carefully placed, arranged to appeal to the eye. There was no Horace.

He's getting on in years, thought Kildare, fingering the hilt of the jeweled stiletto. *Perhaps I should replace him.*

The main receiving area was empty.

Kildare checked the bath. His water hadn't been drawn. Perhaps the guards were mistaken?

Kildare checked a side hall where a long table provided a private dining room. There was seating for fifty guests, hardly necessary in a king's private quarters, but who's to say what Duncannon had in mind? Kildare generally ate there alone.

Finally, the only room left was the bedroom itself. It was the only room specifically off limits even to Horace. Kildare allowed no one within that chamber but himself. He didn't even take women in there. The mere thought of sex in the same bed where he slept disgusted him. His mind conjured up sticky sheets, wet with sweat and worse. Whoring was enjoyed in the sitting room, where those colorful cushions could be soiled and discarded at will—or anywhere else in the suite. He'd even put that long table to good use one night.

From a pocket, Kildare removed the bedroom's key. Unless there was a duplicate he didn't know about, this was the only key. As he unlocked the door, he had a fleeting thought that perhaps he should call one of the guards, but quickly dismissed it. There was one way into this suite and one way out. There were eighteen guards in the hallway outside. What had he to fear?

Kildare pushed open the door, expecting the room's usual darkness. Since no one was allowed in, there was no one but he to build a fire or light a lamp.

Every lamp in the room was burning brightly.

"Horace, you whore's drippings. You're a dead bastard now."

The room was empty.

Except...

Except the heavy gold coverlet had been thrown back from the bed. He had drawn it up just that morning. The sheets were still on the bed, drawn up snug over the goose down pillows. He had tucked them *under* the pillows. In the center of the sheets there was a bulge. There was something under the sheets. Something about the size of a water gourd.

From the bulge, radiating outward along the creases in the linen, the sheets were soaked in crimson.

"I'm safe here," Kildare stammered. He drew the stiletto and took a step forward into the room. *I should turn now,* he thought. *Run back through the main hall and remove the iron bar so the chamber guards can sort this out.* But no man appreciated a coward for a king. Though he'd hardly call himself brave, Kildare had made sure that he seemed that way often enough, generally at the risk of his own life. Courage and stupidity were not so very different. But it seemed safe enough: the room lay open before him, empty. Squeezing tighter on the handle of the stiletto, he took another step into the room. "Horace, whatever joke you think you're playing," he called, his voice climbing an embarrassing octave, Ait's your last."

He stopped at the side of the bed, caught the top corner of the sheet in one trembling hand, and ripped it back.

From the blood-soaked bed, Horace's dead eyes stared up at him as if to ask just what the hell Kildare thought he could possibly do to him now. The look on Horace's face was one of absolute terror. Or excruciating pain. Or maybe a little of both. The head looked to have been removed with one deft blow, the edges of the cut precise and regular—no ragged-edged chop job, this.

The king swallowed bile. His bed … of all places.

"Who did this to you, old boy?"

Behind him, the bedroom door squealed on its hinges and slammed closed.

Campian shifted the weight of the dead stag on his shoulders and stepped from the mottled green shadows out into the light of the trail leading down into town. From here he had a good view. Rhueshan had changed little since his last visit.

A single street dog-legged through seven buildings—the entire village—four of them little more than hovels. The majority of those who could be claimed as residents of the little mountain village lived in the surrounding hills where they could be near the animals they tended. And where they could easily hide when necessary. Of the two military forces which hid in the Kiamina Mountains, only one paid for what it needed from the villagers.

The largest of the buildings, the only structure in Rhueshan which could legitimately qualify for that title in most communities, was the Bear's Larder. The inn catered to whatever weary travelers happened to be traveling amid the bloodshed and war which had kept this part of Eire in turmoil for as long as Campian had been alive. This time of evening, the inn would likely be full of locals whose lust for ale and a rowdy time kept them alive in one of Eire's coldest climes. Not many men chose to live in the Kiamina Mountains.

So as not to alarm the villagers, Campian dropped the hood of his forest-green cloak, revealing his weather-worn face and close-cut gray hair. He opened the front of the cloak, allowing the wind to whip it back behind him so that they could see the red eagle emblem on the right breast of his silver mail. His face was known here, though it had been some six months or more since his last visit, but it was the emblem, symbol of a lost empire that, even 51 years after its fall, would ensure the villagers of his good intentions.

Claymore and quiver slapping against his back, long bow in hand, he strode down through the last thick cedars and into the village. There was a long knife, more short sword than dagger, strapped to his right thigh. There was another, much smaller knife at the small of his back, and the haft of some hammer-like implement protruding from one knee-high leather boot. All these weapons looked to have seen many years of use, from the burnished riser of the bow, to the stained leather wrapped about the ricasso of the claymore. Likewise, Campian had seen his share of use. There were scars crisscrossing his forearms and a small knot where the temple bone over his right eye had been broken. There were other old injuries hidden beneath his tunic, leggings, and mail. Though his weathered face spoke of age, his step was light, even with the 150-pound stag over his shoulder. Beneath the cloak and light mail, there was nothing but hard muscle. The sun played like mercury across the chain mail stretched tight across his broad chest. He stood six four,

weighed a good 240. The claymore on his back would have
dragged the ground behind a shorter man.

The children spotted him first. They remembered him,
especially the boys. Old soldier. Teller of tales parents thought
best kept from the young. He was already legend among the
children, this scarred veteran of a vanquished empire, even if
most of the children didn't really understand his past or present
situation. They swarmed him, shouting questions from all sides,
wanting to touch him, his weapons, the deer … He held up his
hands and frowned at them until he got their silence, a feat their
parents could have never pulled off so easily.

"One at time," he told them, smiling now. He liked the
children. A long time ago, a million years it seemed, he'd had
two sons of his own. They were both, like their mother, long
since laid to rest in the ruins of Kiamina.

"Ranger Campian, there's a stranger in the village!" one boy
shouted.

"I know. Where's he staying?"

"The Larder!" answered a dozen voices.

"Good, I'll go and see him straight away," he told them. "I
need to take this buck to Master Fallon anyway."

They hardly needed him to bring them game. Likely there
were hunters in Rhueshan who could stalk and shoot better
than he. Though Fallon, the innkeeper, didn't hunt himself,
there were always young men willing to trade fresh game for
ale. Truth was, rumor of this stranger in Rhueshan had spread
among the mountains and been picked up by the Rangers who
frequently called on the villages. Campian had heard there
was an injured man hiding here, last officer alive who'd served
under King Duncannon. It was this man that Campian had
come to see. The buck was mere courtesy.

The children followed him down the street to the inn,
hands tugging at the bow until he relinquished it to the care of
one little boy he recognized from his previous visit, other hands
stroking the soft hide of the deer, and still others plucking at
his cloak, his leggings, and the claymore. Their hands made
him nervous, but he endured it without comment. A word from
him and they would have stopped, but he allowed them their

curiosity simply because he knew it was more than that. He understood their need to touch, to verify, to assure themselves that he was real. He was here to protect them. He and all his Rangers, sworn to protect the descendants of Kiamina who had fled into the mountains and made themselves a home. When the children could no longer *feel* his protection, that would be the day they would begin to worry—the day reality broke in on their lives and threatened the barriers they'd built to keep from thinking about the violence he kept at bay. The day these children knew about men like Cloyne Kildare, Ari Kirkmaugh, and the like, was the day Campian was no longer doing his job.

He swore that day would never come while he lived.

Surrounded by his boisterous escort, Campian reached the broad veranda of the inn. Fallon was already there, drying his hands on a messy apron and scanning the deer with a merchant's eye for profit. Fallon was older even than Campian, with parched skin stretched tight over long bones and stringy cords of muscle and tendon. His frost white hair and beard were long and unkept. The apron tied around his waist didn't look to have seen a washing since Kiamina fell. Despite all that, Fallon was an honest, likeable man. If Campian found the innkeeper somewhat short on intelligent conversation—well, on intelligence in general—he was still an honest man who often went out of his way to help others. It was no surprise to hear that the strangers were staying at the Bear's Larder. Campian would have checked there first, even without the information from the children.

"Good day to you, Ranger Campian!" Fallon called from the veranda.

"And you, Master Fallon," Campian returned as he took the three veranda steps as one. The children remained behind, knowing better than to enter the inn without business there. Fallon was not known as a lover of children. More than once his broom had sent prying youngsters running with stinging bottoms.

"You children run along now!" the innkeeper bellowed, though they'd all gone quiet and were behaving far better than could be expected.

"I'll be out to tell everyone a story later," Campian promised, softening the innkeeper's dismissal. He cast them a wink that would have made Fallon frown even harder had the innkeeper seen it. "Get on now," he told them. "And," calling after their retreating backs, "mind you watch my bow." The children scattered, most in one group with the boy who'd been assigned the bow. Fallon turned and pushed open the inn doors, motioning for Campian to follow.

"Appreciate the meat," the innkeeper threw back over his shoulder. "Nice buck. Looks like he'd go at least a hundred and ten pounds."

"At least," Campian replied with a slight smile, knowing full well that Fallon was baiting him. Fallon knew good and well how much the buck weighed, knew it better than Campian though the Ranger had been carrying the damn thing for two hours. They walked through the front hall—only a few customers occupied the scattered tables and benches—and through another set of swinging doors to the kitchen.

"Just toss the buck on the butcher table there."

The instruction wasn't necessary; this wasn't the first game Campian had brought the innkeeper. The table was scarred and streaked with old stains; it wobbled drunkenly when the heavy deer hit its surface. With the deer off his shoulder, Campian stretched and surveyed the kitchen, renewing an old vow never to eat at the Larder. It was quite possible that the butcher table was the cleanest thing in the room.

"Been awhile since we last saw you," Fallon commented, already sharpening a knife to start on the deer. "I don't suppose this is a social call though."

Campian shook his head. "You've got some visitors I need to talk to."

"Figured as much."

"What can you tell me about them?"

"Well, one night they appeared on my doorstep: a woman and a boy dragging a wounded man on a stretcher. I thought they wanted help, but it turned out all they wanted was to warn us of trouble."

"Warn you?"

"Yeah. They had Kirkmaughs on their trail, were worried about having led them to Rhueshan." The innkeeper began stripping the hide from the deer; Campian had already gutted it in the field. "Good man. Honest. Hates taking what's not his, like room and board here. His name's Glengaerif Callin, claims to be Rolph Evers' son."

"You believe him?"

Without hesitation, Fallon nodded. "Yeah. Man was in really bad shape, but his first concern was warning us. Five of Ari Kirkmaugh's butchers came through town not an hour behind Callin. Hadn't been for that warning ... well, you know the answer to that better than anyone. Most of the villagers fled into the highlands; I hid under the porch."

"Fallon! What if they'd set fire to the place?"

The old man shrugged his shoulders and smiled a mostly toothless grin. "I'm too old to be running off into the hills every time there's trouble, Ranger. Didn't matter though. The mercenaries were in a hurry to catch this Callin fellow and didn't do the usual rape and pillage here."

"Interesting. After they warned you, what'd they do?"

"They went up to Kenmaeri's den. I'm sure you've already heard that part of it."

"I was told the old bear killed the mercenaries," Campian said skeptically.

"Believe it. I saw the bodies myself. Kenmaeri didn't leave us a lot to bury."

"Who are the woman and the boy?"

"Boy's his son, Drew. I have no idea who the woman is."

"Wife?"

"Doesn't appear to be." Fallon had the hide drawn up around the head of the deer. With a larger knife, he started working at separating the head. "They're staying in separate rooms. Sometimes, though," and Fallon shielded his mouth with the bloody knife as if imparting a secret, "I think she'd like to be more to him than she is. Know what I mean?"

Campian didn't, but held his tongue, and Fallon went on to explain anyway.

"She stares at him when he's not looking. She doesn't know

I've seen her, mind you. Not that I'd be the only guy hereabouts watching *her*. She's quite a looker. But like I said, I think she's interested in this Callin guy. You can tell from the way she's been taking care of him—uh, I guess you might not know about his injuries."

The Ranger shook his head.

"I could tell right off that he was going to lose that leg."

"You amputated his leg?" Campian asked, thinking of just exactly what that would mean to a soldier.

"Well, not me personally. No way these old hands..." He held them up for inspection, dirty nails, gnarled knuckles, streaks of blood and deer fat running down his wrists. "We got the cutter from Southridge to do it. Cutter did a real fine job. Can't say as Callin was pleased though."

"I can imagine."

"I figure that's the problem between him and the woman. Maybe she is his wife—and still wants to be from the looks she gives him—but he doesn't feel up to it anymore. Know what I mean?"

"What room's he in?"

"First of the five at the top of the stairs," Fallon answered as he dug the knife in between the deer's vertebrae, working it back and forth. "The woman's in the second."

"And the boy?"

"Shares the room with his father." The deer's neck separated with a wet snap. The innkeeper wiped his bloody hands on his filthy apron and held one out to Campian. "Thanks for the deer."

Campian stared at the offered hand for a long minute, finally settled for slapping Fallon on the shoulder. "You're welcome."

Turn, Kildare ordered himself, but his legs refused to move. Behind him he heard the slow tread of the assassin. His main regret at that moment was that he would never get to conquer the rest of Eire. He had so wanted to see those pompous southern lords kneeling before him in the blood of their wives and children.

The footsteps came to a halt. Kildare suspected then that he was meant to hear every step. He was meant to feel the hot breath of the assassin on his neck. Anger overrode his terror. He spun around, lashing out with the stiletto. A black-gloved hand casually turned the blow aside and snared his wrist. The blade was taken away from him. Kildare found himself face to face with a man he had previously only met at court in Drogheda and on the battlefield … and in his nightmares.

Ari Kirkmaugh.

The mercenary planted a boot in the king's chest, shoving him back onto the blood-soaked bed. Horace's head bounced a foot in the air and came down with a sickening *plop!*, lifeless jowls and cheeks slapping obscenely. Kildare's weight created a crimson valley in the soft down mattress. After its initial bounce, Horace's head rolled down the slope of that valley toward the king.

Kildare screamed as the head came to a stop against his shoulder and Horace's blank eyes met his own. He tried to scramble away, but Kirkmaugh placed his foot on the king's crotch and pinned him painfully to the bed. The mercenary leaned forward, applying more weight on his foot, and set the tip of the stiletto against Kildare's throat.

"Let's not scream again, M'lord King. I don't think your screams will carry to the guards in the hall—Horace was proof of that—but I'm not one to take unnecessary risks." A grim smile wrinkled the scars on the mercenary's cheeks. Legend had it he'd made those scars himself as boy, proof that he feared nothing, not even disfigurement. Most Kirkmaughs wore the same scars with pride. "Risks are for patriots and zealots," Ari Kirkmaugh postulated. "I'm more of a businessman myself."

Kildare shook violently.

"Sorry about Horace. He said no one was allowed in the king's bed chambers. Said he was going to call the guards."

Kildare stared at the head. Horace's eyes were like stagnant black pools, infinitely deep, beckoning…

Kirkmaugh reached past Kildare with his free hand and ran it through the blood congealing on the sheets. Then he slapped the king across the face, bringing Kildare's attention back to the front. Kildare felt the blood on his cheek, cold and sticky. He could smell it. The mercenary smiled at the red handprint he'd

left across the king's face. "Maybe I should have been an artist,"
he chuckled.

Kildare finally managed to find his voice—or at least a
squeaky approximation. "Don't kill me," he croaked.

Kirkmaugh responded with a short, contemptuous snort.
"Relax, M'lord King. Don't go losing your head." He removed
the knife from Kildare's throat. "Horace lost his." Kirkmaugh
thrust the knife into the servant's right eye socket, through
the dead brain where it stopped with an audible *thunk* against
the back of the skull. He picked the head up from the bed and
studied it, removing his boot finally from Kildare's crotch. As
the king sat up, the mercenary flung the head from the knife
and across the room with a flick of his wrist. The head hit the
far wall, bounced off like an unripe melon, and rolled across the
floor where it came to rest behind a large chest, mercifully out
of Kildare's sight. However, from the bottom of that same chest,
there was a widening puddle of blood. Somehow Kildare had
missed that little detail earlier.

The king bit through his lower lip, using the pain in an effort
to snap back some measure of composure. He could feel Horace's
blood dripping from his chin. He suppressed a whimper and
tried to make himself think. What did Ari Kirkmaugh want?
If he'd been paid to assassinate the king, surely he would have
done so immediately.

Kirkmaugh caught the king by the front of his rich tunic
and hauled him to his feet.

"What do you want?" Kildare managed to croak.

Kirkmaugh responded with a cynical bowing of the head.
"M'lord King, 'twas you who sent for me."

"You're early," the king stammered.

The mercenary threw back his head and laughed at the high
ceiling. "That's all you can say? I'm early?"

"Why are you doing this?"

Kirkmaugh dragged the king across the room and planted
him in an overstuffed chair. Setting his hands on either arm
of the chair, he leaned down close. "I want you to understand,
Cloyne Kildare, bastard lord of Drogheda—"

"I am king," Kildare responded bitterly, "king of all Eire."

"Kingslayer maybe," Kirkmaugh hissed. "I want you to understand that, king or no, you do not own me. You do not own the Dubh Aogail. The next time, you request my presence, you do not demand it. Understand?"

"I am king of Eire," Kildare retorted weakly.

"You're no king of mine." With the tip of the stiletto, Kirkmaugh jingled the coins in the purse at Kildare's belt. "There is my master."

Kildare nodded silently, eyes locked with those of the man he still wasn't sure wouldn't kill him.

"Then we have an understanding?"

"Yes."

"Good." Kirkmaugh shoved back from the chair and paced the room, picking at his nails with the stiletto. "Relax now. We have business to discuss."

Kildare tried to will his heart to slow down. Momentarily it did seem as it if ceased trying to pound out through his chest, but he was still having trouble breathing. His eyes strayed to the chest against the far wall.

"Oh, Horace is quite comfortable. No need to fret about the old boy."

The king found a spot on the wall that needed his attention.

"What did you need to see me about?"

Deep breath. Shudder. The king scrunched his face as he tried to recall what reason could have possibly driven him to request the presence of this madman.

"Come on, out with it. I haven't got all night." With that same bloody hand, Kirkmaugh pushed long strands of unkempt, black hair out of his eyes. The man was old, as old as Kiamina even, but there was not a hint of gray. Some people whispered that Ari Kirkmaugh was not a mortal, that a sorcerer's spell kept him forever young. Others whispered that he was a changeling, and at night he flew as a dragon, matching the symbol emblazoned on his chest. The emblem originated with Kiamina, symbol for the Dragon Guard, that elite group of Rangers who had sworn to protect Orvellon. But Kirkmaugh had taken the emblem with him when he betrayed the empire, had taken it and made it the standard for the Black

Death, changing the standard's emerald green to a charcoal black.

"Three things," Kildare finally stammered. "First, I need some insurance with Howth. There are rumors that he is preparing an army to attack me from behind while I battle the South."

"Shall I bring you his head?" The mercenary's grin was unnerving.

"No. I said I need insurance. Give the north one more martyr and those holdfasts who have remained neutral will unite at my back. Howth has a daughter. Find her. Take her. Lock her in Drogheda. With her life in my hands, Rorvik of Howth is powerless."

Kirkmaugh nodded. "A thousand gold coins."

"Fine."

"Consider it done. Your second request?"

"A bit more complicated. I want these damn Rangers obliterated."

Kirkmaugh snorted. "They're nothing, Kildare. A rabble-band of old men hiding in the mountains somewhere."

"The people identify with them," Kildare countered. "And they're not all old. Many young men have sought them out and joined their ranks. They remember Kiamina—if not the empire, then at least what it stood for."

"The Rangers are too disorganized to pose you a threat."

"Maybe, but why take the risk? You said yourself that risk was a vice for patriots and zealots." Kildare met the mercenary's gaze, most of his fear in check now, some of his former authority restored in his eyes. "I, on the other hand, am a usurper, much like any good businessman."

Kirkmaugh laughed.

"Besides, the Rangers are an effective guerilla unit. If they're not checked, they will whittle at my army, weakening and demoralizing my forces."

"This one will not be easy. The Rangers are as well hidden in the Kiamina Mountains as my own forces. They will be difficult to locate."

"But you'll do it?"

Kirkmaugh nodded. "Consider it done."

"Payment?"

"We'll settle on it later. What is the third thing?"

"Duncan Emery is raising a force to head mine off in Kiamina Pass."

Kirkmaugh frowned. "A poor site for an offensive engagement. Assume that he has already taken up a defensive position. He will have the upper hand, count on it."

"That's why I need your help."

"I'll not send my men into the pass to pave the way with their blood. Find someone else."

"There is no one else. You've made sure in the days since Kiamina that no other mercenary force survived."

"We are not a suicide brigade."

Kildare raised his hands in surrender. "I have something else in mind. I want you to go to Emery. I want you to take Emery's money to fight me. When the armies engage, I want your men to strike from within, route Emery's forces, and help us take the Pass. I will pay you twice what Emery pays; thus, you will be paid thrice over for that engagement."

Kirkmaugh slapped his thigh with the blade of the stiletto and chewed on the mustache that hung from his face like blackened fangs. From the look on his face, he was swallowing something sour. "I don't like it."

"What's this? Scruples? At this stage in the game?"

"Who will trust us after this?"

Kildare laughed. "Who trusts you *now*?" He regretted the comment immediately as the mercenary crossed the room and thrust the stiletto deep into the back of the chair, inches from the king's throat. The chair rocked back on its legs, then fell heavily forward, propelling the king out and onto the floor. Kirkmaugh savagely jerked the knife free and dragged the king to his feet by the hair. Kildare was certain he was going to die.

"Wait!" squawked the king. "It doesn't matter, Kirkmaugh. As long as I'm alive, the Dubh Aogail will want for nothing, certainly not bloodletting."

"And how long do you think you will live, King?" The title literally dripped disdain coming from Kirkmaugh.

"Long enough, I hope."

Kirkmaugh pushed the king back into the chair.

At that moment, there came a knock on the doors in the main room.

"You were expecting someone?"

"I asked them to send a woman."

"Blonde?"

"What?"

"Will she be blonde?"

"Uh, no. I asked for a redhead."

"Damn." Kirkmaugh slapped the king playfully on the cheek. The dried blood there flaked and drifted into the king's lap. "Next time, I'll let you know I'm coming, Cloyne. You can call for a blonde, and we'll have a great time."

Kildare fought back a wave of nausea at the thought of sharing a woman with this monster, at the sound of his given name from Kirkmaugh's lips. He struggled for something to say, but Kirkmaugh's shifting reactions, ready to slit his throat one minute and lamenting over a whore the next, had left him too confused.

"And now, I really must be going." He reversed the stiletto and slapped it handle-first into the king's trembling hand. Quickly, he crossed the room and yanked open a shuttered window. Outside that window, Kildare knew, there was nothing but the long drop to the Dunshaughlin River.

"Do we have a deal?" Kildare called as the mercenary leaped to the window sill.

"We have a deal."

"On all three counts?"

Kirkmaugh looked back from the edge, his face set in cold lines. "Just don't forget that I am your single most valuable asset, M'lord King. I will bring you the Rangers' hearts. I will give you the daughter of Howth. And I will see that Duncan Emery falls in Kiamina Pass.

"But if you ever betray me ... history will record my greatest villainy as the way in which you died."

And then he was gone. Just like that. Out into the night, as if he'd simply dropped. Kildare sprang to the window and looked, but there was nothing in sight. Far below, the Dunshaughlin reflected a smooth, dark velvet spotted with stars. Not a ripple. Above and below the window: smooth stone for no more than ten yards before the walls cut back to join with the main castle. No one. Not a sound.

Kildare closed the shutters, dropped the latch, and ran to let in the guards.

Campian rapped softly on the first door at the top of the stairs. He had only a second to wait before a boy opened the door a crack and looked out. "You must be Drew Callin."

The boy spoke back over his shoulder. "There's a man here. A Ranger."

"Let him in."

Drew swung the door open and stepped aside, motioning for Campian to enter. Once Campian was inside, the boy closed the door behind them.

The room was simple, with only a few pieces of furniture, the principal item being the bed on which Glengaerif Callin lay. There was also a chest, a washbasin on a wooden tripod, and a chair the integrity of which Campian was of no mind to test. The boy took the chair, perhaps fearing that Campian might actually try it. The chair protested with a loud creak, even under Drew's insubstantial weight. Campian took a seat on the chest.

"I apologize for intruding at a time when I know you need your rest," Campian began.

"The last few weeks I've had more rest than's good for any man," Callin answered. "What can I do for you, Ranger?"

"My name's Campian—"

"The same Campian who *commands* the Rangers?"

Campian smiled. "The same, though I'd be the first to tell you that we have a very poorly defined chain of command. I give general guidelines and establish occasional objectives, but for the most part the Rangers are an independent lot."

"Pleased to meet you all the same." There was disbelief in Callin's eyes. He was buying none of Campian's assessment of the Rangers' organization or lack thereof. "My name's Glengaerif Callin, friends call me Glen." He motioned to the boy, silent and watchful from the rickety chair. "My son, Drew."

"And the woman you were traveling with?"

"Laenora. She's either in her own room or out about the town."

"Wife?"

"Friend."

"What are you here for?" the boy blurted out, his impatience with the adults' cat and mouse game having overcome his former composure.

"He's here about the Ranger who died on the trail below Kenmaeri's den," Callin said from the bed.

"In part," Campian admitted. "He was a good man. I knew him well. His name was Brandon and he left behind a wife and a little girl."

"My condolences."

"But I'm really here to learn more about you, Callin."

"Glen."

Campian let his eyes assess the man for the first time, trying not to linger overly long on the empty stretch of bed that marked a missing limb beneath the sheets. What he saw was a man who was beaten. A man who had given everything he had and wanted to be left alone to die. "You fought at Kilcullen Fields for Duncannon?"

"Second calvary under Donegal Connaught."

Campian nodded appreciably. Connaught had been Duncannon's right arm. The soldiers assigned to Connaught were the cream of the crop. "Officer?"

"Just a soldier."

"Stories I hear say you were more than that. Other soldiers fleeing the battlefield attracted little interest. But the Kirkmaughs chased you all the way here."

"I was with Duncannon at the end. Bad luck, nothing else. The Kirkmaughs mistook me for someone important. Later," and Callin glanced at Drew, "it became a personal thing."

Campian thought he understood that. Stories were that the Kirkmaughs took young boys, raised and trained them to replace their numbers. "What of Droichead Nua?" Campian asked.

"The Kirkmaughs were there long before Kildare's army. Citizens who didn't flee were slaughtered." Callin choked back something that tried to well up in his throat, swallowed something substantial, something that hurt immensely. For an instant, his eyes went misty. A second later, he regained his composure. "Whatever was worth taking, they took. By the time I got there, they were gone."

"With your son?"

"Yes."

"Where does Laenora fit into all this?"

"I found her in Duleek, a little village south of the river. Again, the Kirkmaughs had been there first. She had nowhere to go. She came with me." He swallowed again. More bad memories. "Without her, I'd be dead somewhere."

The door swung open. "And that's as close as he's come to thanking me yet."

Campian rose to meet her, extending a hand. "M'lady Laenora, I take it. Campian of the Kiamina Rangers."

She set her fine, pale hand in his rough, dark one and allowed him to bring it to his lips. She smelled of spices and soap, something flowery, and pure woman. Her eyes, which did not flinch from his own, were a deep blue. Striking. Piercing. He couldn't find the right words.

"Ranger Campian. I must apologize for intruding, but the walls between these rooms are paper thin."

"That's quite all right, M'lady. I would like to hear your version of all this as well." He realized he was still holding her hand and, reluctantly, let it go. He indicated the chest where he had been sitting; there was room for two.

"My version doesn't differ from Glen's, Ranger."

"I did not mean to insinuate that it would, M'lady."

She smiled and touched his arm. "Please, call me Laenora."

"Very well." It had been a long time since he'd been touched by a woman. Campian chided himself for acting like a school boy. He wondered if his face was flushed. He wondered if she knew how striking she was and if she knew how uncanny was her resemblance to the Orvellon line. Rodric Orvellon had three daughters when an assassin took his life. Those daughters were supposed to have died in the sacking of Kiamina, but who could say? If one of them did escape, then her daughter, Orvellon's granddaughter, would now be about Laenora's age. If Laenora were of Kiamina blood, she was rightfully heiress to the old empire and, therefore, Campian's liege.

Campian chided himself again. *Quit weaving fairytales, you old fool. Nothing of Kiamina remains, save her blackened ruins, now turned rookery for ravens and mice. And,* he added, *a bunch of tired old men who think they're still Rangers.*

But he knew that fairytales had a way of building momentum, of living long past those who invented them. Myth was a greater motivator than any allegiance. Men will go to war for a dream. Die for an ideal. Kiamina was the stuff of legend. There were lords, northern and southern, who had sworn allegiance to Kiamina, but had remained neutral ever since. An Orvellon at the forefront of a rebellion against Cloyne Kildare could make all the difference.

There was a confidence about her, a regal composure as she sat beside him on the ancient chest. The way her eyes met his. Whatever she had been through, first in Duleek and later with Glengaerif Callin, it had forged in her a strength and a surety and a sheer physical presence that he couldn't quite put a name to.

"Ranger Campian?"

Her hair was golden blonde, face delicately featured, eyes that deep, remarkably clear blue. The dress she wore, borrowed perhaps from a local woman, was simple, a single faded shade of mauve. It had been cut for an entirely different figure, one with a lot more middle than Laenora, but she'd belted it with a wide leather belt that accentuated her slim waist, ample bosom, and shapely hips. In a gown cut specifically for her, Campian had no doubt she could stall hearts. As it was, she caught his breath, and he found his hands sweating like a young courtier's, instead of the grayed old warhorse he was supposed to be.

"Ranger?"

With an embarrassed start, he realized he'd been staring at her for several minutes, while everyone else was staring at him. He shook his head. "Forgive me, M'lady—"

"Laenora," she corrected him.

"—but old as I am, I can't recall when last I looked upon so beautiful a woman."

She smiled. No blush. Just the smile. "Thank you, sir."

From the bed, Callin cleared his throat. "Is there anything else we can tell you, Ranger?"

Campian ignored him. "Laenora, might I inquire about your parents?"

Her smile faltered. Her eyes hardened. "My parents are long dead, Ranger."

Campian ducked his head briefly. From her tone it was obvious that he'd hit a nerve. "Forgive me if I've been inconsiderate. The reason I inquire is that you bear a striking resemblance to the Orvellon lineage."

She laughed. "My parents were commoners, Ranger. Nothing more."

Callin pushed himself up from the pillows and struggled to a sitting position. "I fail to see the reasoning behind this line of questioning."

"Perhaps there is none," Campian muttered. "Forgive me for intruding on your memories, Lady Laenora." He turned to Callin. "A few more questions and I'll be gone. I need to hear about Brandon's death."

"He tried to stop the Kirkmaughs," Drew blurted out.

"On the trail," Laenora explained. "He interceded on our behalf. Glen was in no shape to do anything. Your man killed two of the Kirkmaughs before they killed him."

"And then the Kirkmaughs took his head?"

All three of them looked taken aback.

"What do you mean?" Callin asked.

"Exactly what I said. Brandon's body was found below Kenmaeri's den, minus his head. There were the bodies of four Kirkmaughs and nothing else."

"There were five Kirkmaughs," Callin said.

"So I've been told," Campian acknowledged. "What became of the fifth one?"

Callin glanced at Laenora. Laenora studied the floor. The boy looked lost. Callin finally looked back to Campian, but did not hold that gaze. "Perhaps other Kirkmaughs came along and found one of their men wounded," he suggested. "Or perhaps one of them crawled off."

Someone is lying, thought Campian. But why? "The Kirkmaughs rarely salvage their wounded," he told Callin, "and my men could have easily tracked a wounded man."

The room was silent for what seemed like several long minutes.

Campian spread his arms. "Whatever happened, we know one mercenary survived. The fact that there have been no more Kirkmaughs visiting Rhueshan looking for you, Callin, leads me to believe that he took Brandon's head as proof that he'd gotten his man."

Callin bowed his head. "Then that's one more that I owe your man. If there's anything I can do for his family…"

"I'll check." Campian took a deep breath. "There's more, though, that you can do for Eire. I know you need time to rest, time to heal, but there's a war going on out there. Duncan Emery will attempt to hold Kildare at Kiamina Pass. He'll need men like you."

"The war's over for me," Callin replied bitterly.

"You're wrong."

Callin slapped the expanse of sheet where a leg should have been. "My days as a soldier are over."

"That doesn't have to be true. At the very least, there's a lot of tactics and strategy locked inside your head. And unless I travel north of the Meath and find survivors of Kildare's campaign against Armagh and Gairloch, you're the only man I have who's actually seen his army in action." Campian got to his feet. "You can lay there and waste away—"

"You don't know what I've been through!" Callin interjected.

"—or you can try to help." He hated baiting the man, but this was no time for pulling punches. "Looks to me like you've enough leg left to sit a horse. I'd be willing to bet that the saddler here in Rhueshan could design a saddle that would work for you. You sit there and think yourself a cripple, and a cripple's what you'll be."

Callin was a bright red, but he said nothing, merely stared with a fierce anger.

Laenora got to her feet. "I'll see you to the door, Ranger." Her tone had changed as well.

They stepped out into the hall and she pulled the door closed behind them. "That was cruel."

"You love him?"

Now she did blush.

"Then save him from himself, M'lady."

Her eyes moistened. "I'll try."

"Good enough." He touched her arm. "I might need your help as well."

"What can I do?" she asked doubtfully.

"Men need something to rally around. A symbol. A sign of hope."

"What does that have to do with me?"

"M'lady, you look to be a princess of Kiamina, Rodric Orvellon's own daughter."

Her eyes went cold. "My family name is Maendelton, Ranger. I'm Laenora Maendelton. I'm no princess."

"M'lady—"

"I never knew my father," she rasped, her voice dripping acid. "I doubt my mother even knew who he was. My mother, you see, was a whore in Duleek. And you can imagine in what profession she apprenticed me." Then she was gone back into the room, slamming the door behind her.

"Shit," cursed the Ranger.

"Trouble with the lady?" called Fallon from the bottom of the staircase. Campian hadn't noticed him there.

"You could say that." He came down the stairs, face knit in a frown.

"So, apologize next time you visit."

"I'm not sure there'll be a next time," Campian replied.

"What?"

Campian gripped the old merchant's shoulder. "We've all got to do what we can, Fallon. The Rangers ... well, we've shared these mountains with mercenaries long enough. We've decided it's time to root out the Kirkmaughs."

Four guards had taken up positions by the window and the bedroom door. The chest containing Horace's body and the offensive head had been removed. The mattress from the bed had been dragged out and a replacement was being sought. Lydia, the whore who'd expected to spend this night on her back, was down on her hands and knees scrubbing bloodstains from the floor. Kildare was admiring her ass and wondering if he could do it with guards so close by. Now that the excitement was over, he felt randier than he had in ages. But the guards were a problem. Still, there was no way he was going to dismiss them. He was wondering if he would even be able to sleep tonight.

Kirkmaugh had pushed too far. Who did he think he was? "I am king," Kildare hissed vehemently, pacing the floor, "and he will rue the day he forgot that." The guards remained stoically at attention. The girl ducked her head and scrubbed harder. Oh, yes, Kirkmaugh would pay. But first there were things Kildare needed Kirkmaugh to do. The Howth girl. The Rangers. Duncan Emery. Conquest of the South. After that ... after that, Ari Kirkmaugh's head would be permanently mounted on a pike in an airtight glass case that would be displayed ... Where? Some thought was going to have to go into that.

In a mirror, Kildare checked his face, searching for blood that he might have missed earlier when he'd washed up in the basin. He felt filthy and wanted a full bath, but how was he to bathe with guards nearby? His hair was in a disarray, the curly blond tresses having come unbound when Kirkmaugh had yanked him about by his hair. He was trying to gather the stray strands together when the room suddenly dimmed.

The four guards raised their battle axes and looked about for the source of the sudden change. There were six lamps spaced about the room. All appeared to be burning normally. But the room continued to dim.

"Stand fast," Kildare ordered.

"M'lord, perhaps you should leave," one of them suggested.

"I said stand fast. Move and you will die."

"M'lord?" The guards shifted in confusion, none of them

knowing what was going on, none of them obeying his order. The girl slipped beneath the bed.

The room continued to darken until each corner, each piece of furniture, each juncture of wall, floor, and ceiling held a deep, menacing shadow. The only light that remained haloed the lamps, impotent and dim, struggling to stand its ground against the encroaching blackness.

One shadow moved, separating from a dark corner like a puff of smoke, gliding across the room on nonexistent legs. As Kildare sank to his knees, the menacing point of darkness came to a stop just over his head. A second later there were two malevolent red eyes, glowing like hot embers within the darkness.

One of the guards near the window bellowed a war cry and launched himself at the dark. He'd barely covered three feet when there was a wet explosion and what was left of him splashed across the ceiling, the walls, the shuttered window, and the floor. The girl screamed. The other guard by the window, covered with his companion's blood took one step to the side, whether to fight or flee, no one will ever know. He exploded as well, ripped from within as if he were an overinflated sheep's bladder kicked about by children. Most of him wound up running like jelly from the walls and the ceiling, but something of him remained standing for several horrifying seconds. A rack of bones draped with scraps of tissue and flesh. A cage of splintered cartilage encasing perforated organs and fast escaping fluids. The caricature stood there for a moment, then collapsed in upon itself, forming a shattered pile of jagged bones and red meat, topped with a blood-drenched skull.

Kildare raised a warning hand to the two guards by the door. "Hold your ground," he commanded. One of them dropped his axe and went to his knees. Amazingly, the power that now controlled the room allowed it. The other guard simply closed his eyes and stood there, trembling.

From beneath the bed, the girl made not a sound. Her eyes were wide and her lips were quivering, but she hadn't looked away. Her face was spotted with the blood of the first guard to die.

"Greetings, Master," Kildare whispered.

"You've had a visitor this evening," replied the dark. The voice, oddly enough, was feminine.

"Yes. I want him dead. After he completes the tasks I gave him, I want him dead."

The eyes flashed brighter. "We'll have further use for Ari Kirkmaugh," boomed the darkness. "He dies when I say we're through with him."

"But he—"

"Silence!" The mirror on the wall cracked. The girl screamed and both surviving guards went down on their bellies and covered their heads with their arms. "When the time is right, I will take care of Ari Kirkmaugh. I made him. I can just as easily *unmake* him."

Kildare trembled. "Yes, Master."

"You have another matter which must be seen to. There is a Ranger." The eyes dimmed and then flashed a brilliant orange. "Campian."

"They say he leads the Rangers," Kildare volunteered. "An old man, one of the *original* Rangers. He must be over seventy years old by now. How can he threaten us?"

"He will find something in the ruins of Kiamina, something with the potential to be your undoing."

Spitted on a stick over Campian's small fire, a rabbit smoked and sizzled, dripping fat into the flames. Campian relaxed nearby, far enough so as to be out of the fire's primary radius of light, but not so far that he couldn't enjoy the mouth-watering aroma of the roasting meat. He'd killed the rabbit with the bow shortly before finding the small gully in which he'd made his camp. The gully was a good location, blocking the fire from view in all but one of the four compass directions. Still, he would put out the fire when the rabbit was done. Such cautions were second nature to him. Sharing the mountains with Ari Kirkmaugh's butchers had instilled in him a certain wariness. He knew them better than he cared to, knew Kirkmaugh himself, from that day long ago when the mercenary had handed the crown to Bheag Ai Duboil.

There were forces at work back then, forces that had nothing to do with strong arms and sharp steel. The wagon people of the Western Plains had brought something with them when they came to take Kiamina. Something dark and unholy. Whatever it was, it had the power to bring the dead back to life and to strike dead the living. Even now, with that evil long shut away on the Dorinthian Isles, Campian did not care to think about it. Just thinking about such a thing gave it power.

Suddenly something moved in the trees to the east. There wasn't a sound, so much as a *presence*. Campian rolled into the underbrush to his left, taking the bow and his quiver of arrows. The claymore remained atop his folded cloak by the fire, but he had the long knife on his thigh. Campian was surprised, for he had taken every precaution to conceal both camp and trail. He regretted having removed the cloak. His mail stood out in the moonlight like a discarded mirror, whereas the mottled cloak had hidden him from enemies on more than one occasion.

He was nocking an arrow to the bow when someone called out.

"Your rabbit smells fantastic, Campian!"

Campian slid the arrow back into the quiver and got to his feet. "That's a good way to get yourself killed, Avram."

From the shadows emerged a tall, slender man, wrapped in a cloak to match Campian's. "You'd have to see me first, old man. Rolling around out there, making more noise than a sow in heat, shining like a plump autumn pumpkin under a full moon, what chance do you think you'd have of avoiding my own arrow?" Avram pulled back his hood, revealing a face that couldn't have seen more than twenty summers, eyes that had yet to see war.

"So, *you've* become the teacher now, eh?"

"Comes a time in every man's life, old man," chuckled the youth.

They squatted together near the fire, exchanging more friendly banter.

"Rabbit smells delicious," Avram observed.

"He's probably got a friend out there somewhere," Campian responded wryly.

"Looks nice and fat. More than enough for one skinny old man."

"You'll get your share when he's done, youngster."

The banter between them was old, comfortable. Avram had come to the Rangers eight years before as a boy. His mother and father were dead, victims of some catastrophe which he'd never chosen to discuss. The boy asked to become a Ranger. They'd looked him up and down, studied the tear-streaked dirt on his face, and told him to go home. When he told them that he had no home to go to, they gave him an empty hut and told him his training would begin on the morrow.

"What did you learn in Rhueshan?"

"The stranger did fight for Duncannon, but he's no officer."

Avram shrugged. "No need to release that fact. We tout him as Connaught's senior man and send him to Emery to help raise support in the south. Who's to know the difference?"

"There are other complications. He's lost a leg. And, more importantly, the fight's gone out of him."

"But—"

"He's not our man, Avram." Campian considered sharing his speculations about Laenora Maendelton, but decided to keep them to himself. Now that he was away from her and had time to think more clearly, he wasn't so sure that she wasn't right and he had lost all his senses.

Avram shrugged again. "Well, we're no worse off than we were before."

Campian drew the knife from the small of his back and cut a leg from the rabbit, passed it hand to hand while it cooled. Avram drew a knife from his boot and helped himself to something from the other side. "Don't look so glum," he told his old teacher. "You haven't heard *my* good news yet."

Campian met the younger man's gaze across the fire. He'd sent Avram with several others to search for Kirkmaugh's mountain retreat.

"No, we haven't found them yet," Avram volunteered. He wiped rabbit juice from his lips and smiled like a wolf. "But we followed an eleven-man party most of the way to Droichead Nua. They're on their way back now."

"Then we can follow them back into the mountains and see where they go."

"That depends." Avram helped himself to more of the rabbit. "Which do you consider more important, finding their home or killing Ari Kirkmaugh himself?"

Campian didn't need to think about that. "Without Kirkmaugh, they're nothing."

Avram nodded. "That's how I thought you'd feel." The wolf's grin again. "Kirkmaugh himself is leading this party."

Campian tossed aside the rabbit's leg and began gathering his things. "Why didn't you tell me right away?"

"Hey, I know you, old man. You wouldn't have let me eat if I'd told you first. See, you're already running off, and you haven't even eaten yourself."

"How many men do you have following him?"

"Only three."

"We need more."

"No time," Avram answered.

Campian frowned. "Five of us. Eleven of them. Those are poor odds, Avram."

"Poor for a direct confrontation," Avram agreed, lifting his bow from the ground beside him, "but not for an ambush."

"All right then," Campian agreed, but his face betrayed his concern. He'd never told Avram about Kirkmaugh in the old days, in the days of Kiamina. He'd never told the boy that his respect and fear for Ari Kirkmaugh sprang from the fact that he'd already killed him once.

Lydia's hands were shaking as she tried to take the carrier pigeon from its cage. What she'd seen this day had taken years from her life, sucked the energy straight from her very soul. She felt vile and dirty, used like she'd never felt before. And she felt vulnerable. In every castle draft she thought she felt the return of that thing whose name she prayed she would never know. Legend spoke of it—*her*, actually, for the one thing all the tales agreed upon was that this demon Bheag Ai Duboil had conjured long ago was female. Legend spoke of her as a thing made of blood sacrifice and the wind off the glacier cap, of things brought up from the bottom of Devil's Bay where man had long ago drowned his gods. When Duncannon had overthrown the western horde at Khal Mani, he and his general, Donegal Connaught, had somehow imprisoned this spirit and hidden her away where no one was to ever find her. But now it appeared that she had somehow found a way to again influence Eire's future.

Lydia feared to even think of her, for fear the demon might somehow sense it and return. It took all her courage to come here to the roof where the birds were hidden, to write what she'd seen in the usurper's bedchamber on the tiny slip of paper and fit it inside the metal message band.

The bird shied away, its wings beating a staccato frenzy against Lydia's outstretched hands. Lydia snatched at it and very nearly injured it in her haste. She wanted nothing more right now than to hide in the chambers she shared with the other women who lived to serve Kildare's prurient needs. She wanted this deed done and behind her. It was the single most dangerous thing she would ever do.

Finally, she had the bird. Dragging it from the cage, she used the small metal tongs to clamp the band about its leg. Then she hurled it into the sky. As the bird exploded in a beating of wings and shot toward the rising son, Lydia said a silent prayer that it reach Duncan Emery in time.

– TWO: FRIENDS AND FOES –

In the days immediately following the fall of Kiamina— while the fires set by Bheag Ai Duboil's raiders smoldered in the surrounding woodlands and occasional screams could still be heard from within the walls as survivors were ferreted out of hiding places and hauled to the chopping block—those who fled into the hills spent their days avoiding capture and their nights speculating about what had happened. Second only to speculation on who had actually killed Emperor Orvellon was conjecture on why Campian, the emperor's warlord, hadn't been there when the attack came and how Ari Kirkmaugh, Captain of the Dragon Guard, had betrayed him.

There were those who said that the evil force which Bheag Ai Duboil had brought from the west had manifested itself as a beautiful enchantress who bewitched Kiamina's champion and led him away on that fateful night. While Kiamina burned, they whispered, Campian bedded an ancient force so evil that surely his soul was sacrificed in the bargain. For this reason, there are a few in the mountains who still whisper silent prayers to Ungarduhn, Eire's god of the underworld, whenever Campian is around. "Pray do not take him now," go those desperate prayers, Anot while I'm standing near."

Others thought Campian had been kidnaped by the traitor Ari Kirkmaugh, kidnaped and later set free rather than simply killed because the two had been friends. It's said that Kirkmaugh had been the one to show the barbarians the secret ways into Kiamina, up through the catacombs beneath the mountains. Some say they saw him that night, there among the enemy, in his black armor with its dragon crest. After the battle, when Kirkmaugh offered Campian a choice, the opportunity to serve with him or to die, it's said that Campian chose death, but Kirkmaugh set him free anyway.

There were even a few who whispered that Campian had been somehow to blame. Some who thought he'd also been involved in Orvellon's assassination. Still others who said Campian had seen the end of the empire in a dream and had simply fled into the night.

But the prevalent theory, and the one still whispered in the mountains to this day, is that Campian was betrayed, that the thing which came between Ari Kirkmaugh and him is the one thing sure to destroy any lifelong friendship between two men: a woman. And that woman was Regina ... Campian's wife. Some say he caught her in bed with Ari Kirkmaugh, while his two sons slept just two rooms away. Others, that he merely found letters from one or the other. It's well known that Campian was dedicated to the empire, that his wife and family had long been placed in a secondary role. Most understood that Kiamina would not be what it was without Campian and his Rangers. Most made allowances. But was it fair to expect Regina to make such sacrifices? Bereft of the companionship she needed, she'd found it elsewhere. Her loneliness and passion had been the ruin of them all.

It's the stuff legends are made of. And legends have a way of growing over the years, robbing scope and depth from the very tragedy about which they're drawn. And this legend had at its core the very fall of Kiamina, the only event on which every holdfast in northern and southern Eire had ever focused their attention. Some of it was speculation, but much of it was fact.

The Kiamina Mountains stretch the breadth of Eire, east to west, the rugged granite slopes clotted with dense scrub brush and wind-twisted trees. The mountain peaks reach thousands of feet high, *tens of thousands* in the range bordering the southern edge of the Dunbar Valley, capped with snow and carved by spring runoffs and the incessant wind. Between these peaks lay bowls of rich soil, trapped millennia ago when the mountains were pushed toward the clouds by the shifting of tectonic plates that had now gone stable and quiet. In these fertile valleys grow towering pines, oaks so tall that they'd barely noticed while Bheag Ai Duboil's fires chewed the lesser trees and then passed by, and stands of hickory and ash so dense a man could not pass through without turning sideways.

In three such trees hung Avram's men.

The Rangers' own swords had been used as crosspieces to which their wrists had been bound. Their bellies had been opened and their intestines pulled out and spilled down about their legs and the tree trunks. Their genitals had been removed. The bottom of the feet of one of them had been burned. One was missing his eyes. Only one of the three appeared to have been dead before he'd been hung up. The other two had taken several hours to die. All three had been ravaged by crows and other small animals.

"They should have known better than to confront the Kirkmaughs on their own," Avram moaned. "I told them to keep their distance and wait until I got back." He paced an erratic circle around where he and Campian had put the three corpses side by side, wrapped in their Ranger cloaks. This wasn't the first time Avram had seen dead men. It wasn't the first time he'd seen Kirkmaugh and his butchers torture a man to death. But it was the first time those men had been under his command.

Campian had already circled the area, studying the ground. "They didn't disobey your orders," he told the boy. "The Kirkmaughs knew they were being followed. They doubled back."

"I *want* them, Campian. I want the lot of them. Every last murdering one of them!"

Campian grabbed the younger man firmly by the upper arm. "Listen to me, Avram. We'll get them, but we'll do it slowly, cautiously. Right now, I need you to check your rage and think. Unbridled anger will get us both killed here. These aren't peasants or even common soldiers we're dealing with. It's the Dubh Aogail, the Black Death, and they know these mountains as well as we do. The last thing we need is to rush into a trap. Do you understand?"

Muscles stood out on either side of Avram's jaw. He looked as if he were about to crush his own teeth. But he nodded, and then growled, "But I will see these three men avenged, Campian."

"That you will. But it'll be done my way."

Ari Kirkmaugh pulled at his mustache and debated his next move. His men had located the trail of two other Rangers and backtracked them to where a small fire had been built in a narrow gully. There were the remains of a mostly uneaten rabbit which the insects had already claimed as their own. The coals of the fire, just beneath the surface, were still warm to the touch. The careless and uncharacteristic way in which the camp had been abandoned meant the two Rangers had left in a hurry, perhaps to rendezvous with the three men that Kirkmaugh had already dispatched.

Hard as the mercenaries had tried, they'd been unable to wring information from the Rangers they'd tortured last night. It had been pure luck that they'd stumbled upon them in the first place. Kirkmaugh had planned on returning to his own stronghold, three days to the west, to make arrangements for carrying out Kildare's other two requests before concentrating on the one that dealt specifically with the Rangers. The misfortune of these three Rangers had restructured his priorities. And now there were two more. Five Rangers was four more than he'd been able to get his hands on in the last year—and his men had summarily dispatched that one near the village of Rhueshan.

He'd sent one of his men on ahead with instructions to set the kidnaping of Howth's daughter in motion. Another he'd sent east to scout out Emery's position in Kiamina Pass. That left him with eight men to track down these two Rangers. If possible, he wanted to take them alive. Though he held little hope that torture would reveal the location of their main force, he was too much of a businessman to pass up the opportunity.

"M'lord Kirkmaugh," one of his men said, stepping forward, "might I be so bold as to make a suggestion?"

Kirkmaugh rose from the remains of the campfire and frowned at the mercenary. He rarely asked his men for anything other than their sword arms. Even his captains understood that there was only so much latitude implicit in his orders. Innovation and enterprise were just as often punishable as they were rewardable. Democracy was not a concept that fit into his military framework.

While Kirkmaugh debated whether to dispatch the man on the spot, hear him out, or simply tell him to sit down and shut up, there came a silent hiss in the air. It was a sound no mortal ear should have been able to hear, but Ari Kirkmaugh had seen the far side of mortality, had seen it and come back. He jogged his head to the left without consciously taking the fraction of a second required to plan the move. An angry hornet swept past his ear, nicking his lobe with razor-edged fangs. The mercenary who'd wanted so much to make a suggestion spewed blood on his lordship's armor as a feathered shaft slipped under his chin and through his throat. The mercenary stood there a moment, eyes wide, fletching protruding out from just beneath his chin, then he toppled over backwards. Before he ever hit the ground, Kirkmaugh was gone, disappearing into the underbrush.

Another man screamed and went down. The others followed Kirkmaugh's lead, diving into the nearest foliage. Even so, one man grunted and plowed face first into a stout oak, the shaft and head of an arrow protruding out just above his breastbone.

"Stay down!" Kirkmaugh bellowed at the remaining five. Then, "Shut up!" he ordered the wounded man, squirming about an arrow that had tacked his right arm to his shoulder and then to a tree limb. For the moment, the man was standing up and in plain view. An obvious target, but the archers—Were there two or three? More?—were ignoring him.

They know I'm watching, Kirkmaugh thought. *Know I'm trying to figure out where those arrows came from.* He had a general idea from the first arrow that had nearly taken him in the back of the neck, but the slopes rising above the tiny grotto were dense with foliage and rock outcroppings. There were a million places for an archer to hide.

"Did anyone see anything?" he asked. No one had. The wounded man was moaning and trying to work the arrow free of the tree. "Be still," Kirkmaugh told him, "or I'll kill you myself."

A hawk screeched. The wind rustled the leaves on the trees. A mosquito buzzed past Kirkmaugh's ear, found his neck and proceeded to dine. Kirkmaugh remained motionless.

Several minutes passed and then an arrow rustled through the brush and sank into the ground a foot to Kirkmaugh's right. Another one sank into a clump of berries where no one was hiding. The archers were probing. Senseless—they could only have so many arrows. Kirkmaugh would wait if he were in their position.

The sun rose in the sky. The man tacked to the tree was growing weaker, having trouble now staying on his feet. Were the situation reversed, Kirkmaugh knew he would use the injured man to draw the others out. The fact that his assailants weren't trying that told him that they knew the tactic wouldn't work on the mercenaries. It told him that he'd located the other two Rangers.

A couple more random arrows fell out of the sky to punch holes in the brush.

One of his men cursed and rolled about. "Be still, you idiot!" Kirkmaugh hissed at him, but a second later the man was up and running, and Kirkmaugh saw why. There was a shaft protruding from his shoulder. The archers were changing positions up in the hills, finding new vantage points from which they could see the mercenaries.

The man took five steps before an arrow slipped in just above his hip, down through his pelvis, and out through his thigh. Legs tangling, the mercenary went down out in the open, where he lay and bellowed in anger and pain.

"On three, we scatter," Kirkmaugh told the four remaining. "Try to regroup near the falls below Filson's Creek." He counted then, quickly, not wanting to give the archers time to spot his own location. Then he was up and running, leaping like a deer through the brush, dodging tree trunks and placing as many of them as possible at his back. Behind him, another man cried out in pain.

Avram felt for a pulse. "This one's dead," he told Campian. There was no sense trying to work the arrow free; it was embedded too deeply in the tree trunk.

"This one's got some life left in him," Campian responded as he danced back from a desperate sword swing. The mercenary couldn't get up, not even onto his knees, but he'd drawn his sword and planned to sell himself dearly if he got the chance.

"Not for long," Avram muttered, drawing his own sword.

Campian stayed his arm. "Wait." He knelt just out of range. "You want us to help you?" he asked the injured mercenary.

"I just want you to come closer."

Campian smiled and shook his head. "Hurts?"

The man responded by trying to worm his way closer. The head of the arrow protruding from his thigh dug into the forest floor, slowing him down, causing him to cry out in agony. Despite this, he inched closer.

"I'd keep your distance," Campian advised, placing his hand on the hilt of the long knife at his side. "For the moment, you're alive. Tell me what I want to know and I promise you'll stay that way. We'll see that you get help."

"Kill me now, Ranger. I'd rather that, than listen to your lies." The mercenary took the head of the arrow in hand and tried to snap it off, but the arrowhead was too sharp to hold and there was very little shaft to grip.

"Where will Kirkmaugh go?" Avram demanded.

"To the home of the whore that birthed you," snarled the mercenary, "where he'll cut her from chin to crotch and pack your dismembered head inside!"

Avram stepped forward to dispatch the man, but Campian restrained him. Somewhere nearby, a wolf howled. "We leave him," Campian said. Another howl answered the first. "Leave him for the wolves."

The mercenary clutched his sword and said nothing.

Kirkmaugh frowned at the wounded man. "You going to make it?"

The mercenary nodded. To admit that he might not would seal his fate. Ari Kirkmaugh wasn't known to show compassion to the injured. More than once, he'd dispatched those who slowed him down.

Kirkmaugh took the shaft of the arrow protruding from his man's side and, without warning, pushed it on through. The wounded mercenary bit his lip, but did not scream. He stood there, eyes unwavering, blood running down his chin and out from under the hand clutched at his side, but he did not cry out. Kirkmaugh studied the man for a long minute, then finally nodded curtly. "Make a fire and heat your knife. See if you can stop the bleeding." Then he turned to the other three men he had left. "They'll be tracking us. They'll attempt to ambush us again."

"Should he be allowed to build that fire then? Won't that just draw them to us?"

Kirkmaugh smiled and picked at the dried blood on his ear. "It'll certainly make it easier for them. But I expect they'd find us anyway. None of us hid our trail when we ran."

"Then, shouldn't we—"

"Shut up," Kirkmaugh told him. "I want them to find us."

"M'lord?"

"I'm not fond of being hunted," Kirkmaugh growled. "I'm much more comfortable as the hunter."

"To hunt," said the wounded man softly, nervously, "you need bait."

Kirkmaugh smiled. "That you do."

There was no moon. Clouds had swept in from the north to cover the stars. There was just that beacon-like fire, flickering among the trees, silhouetting the four men who sat around its orange glow, casting phantom shadows through the woods.

"There's one missing," Campian whispered from within the folds of his mottled cloak. The Rangers had already deciphered enough of the trail to know that, of the original ten with Ari Kirkmaugh, two had broken from the group before the ambush. Four men had fallen in the ambush itself. That left four, plus Kirkmaugh himself. There was no way to tell if the mercenary lord was one of the four seated around the fire.

"Maybe we wounded one, and he died en route," Avram replied. "We could have missed his body. And we did find blood on their trail."

"Maybe," Campian muttered. "But I don't like it."

"We sneak in close," Avram suggested. "We can be among them in seconds. They'll never know what hit them."

Campian shook his head. "You ever know Kirkmaughs to be this careless before?" He sniffed the wind, and in the silence that followed his rhetorical question they both listened to the wind rustling the leaves, to the sound of night insects. Nothing seemed amiss. Except that missing man.

"Then let me go, and you wait here as backup. I can be on them and take off all four heads before they even look up from that fire, Campian."

"Better to whittle at them with the bows."

"The trees are too thick," Avram countered. "You really want to try that shot in the dark?"

True, it was tricky. Between the swaying trees and the eerie shadows cast by the fire, they'd be lucky to kill even one of the mercenaries before the others disappeared in the darkness. And the ruins of Kiamina were just over that next series of hills, more cover for this cat and mouse game. Plus, they'd still have the same problem, a missing man who might be slipping up through the underbrush behind them right now.

"I can do this," Avram insisted.

"We'll give it a few more minutes," Campian countered.

So, they did. The wind picked up. More clouds moved in until not a single star broke the blackness overhead. A possum found them, his red eyes giving him away as he peered down at them from an overhead bough. An owl hooted. Occasional shifts in the wind brought snatches of indecipherable conversation from the Kirkmaughs, but other than tossing more wood on the fire, none of them moved.

"Okay, *I'll* take the four around the fire," Campian whispered, breaking their long silence. "You cover me."

Avram shook his head. "Bad idea. You're the better archer, old man. It's not necessary that I kill all four of them if I get the others to stand. You'll have a better shot at them once they're on their feet. Those I don't kill immediately will stand to brace me. You drop them with the bow."

Campian's dark eyes were unwavering in the folds of the cloak. "When did I become the better archer?"

Avram laughed softly. "Why'd you think I wanted to share that rabbit, old man?"

Campian said nothing.

"And," Avram added, "you know I'm quieter than you. I can get closer to them before I have to break cover and strike."

"I don't like it."

Avram shrugged and slipped his bow and arrows out from under his cloak. The bow he set aside, the quiver of arrows he passed to Campian. There were only three left, one less than the number in Campian's own quiver. "Just watch my back, old man. I'll take care of the rest." And then he was gone in the night, his cloak taking up the shadows and rendering him invisible in the gloom.

Campian placed three arrows near at hand, nocked another, and did what he hated most. He waited.

The young Ranger took his time, for it was caution that bought silence, and it would be silence that insured surprise when he sprang into that circle of light around the fire. Campian knew he had thirty minutes or more to wait, but knowing that didn't ease the tension knotting his insides. There was something wrong. He could feel the trap gathering around them. Ari Kirkmaugh was no fool. They were being set up.

Campian began to wish he had some means to call Avram back. This was a mistake. He was about to slip the arrows back into his quiver and crawl through the underbrush after the younger man, when something moved to his right.

Cursing himself for an old fool long past his mental prime, Campian shifted quietly onto his side to that he could peer into the gloom toward where the sound had come from. From this position, it was extremely difficult to draw the bow, but he did so, muscles trembling as he held it and waited for the sound to repeat itself.

A second later and it came again: something or *someone* slithering through the underbrush. Campian adjusted his aim and waited, though the muscles of his shoulder and arm were beginning to scream from the tension. He reminded himself for the thousandth time that he was too old for this. What he needed was a nice little cottage somewhere high in the mountains, with a fat little wife who baked and talked to him at night when the nightmares kept him up. What he needed —

Avram's cry split the night and, though he didn't dare turn to look in that direction, Campian could imagine the young Ranger suddenly leaping into the firelight from out of the brush and the shadows, his broadsword whistling in a great arc that would take at least one Kirkmaugh head. The other Kirkmaughs would spring to their feet, campfire blind, startled and confused. Campian had agreed to drop as many of them as he could when that happened, but he wouldn't be able to with his attention focused elsewhere. For the moment, Avram was on his own. It appeared, however, that Campian's aim was focused in the right direction as a dark phantom rose from the undergrowth and drew what appeared to be a part of the surrounding forest in a long arc.

Campian let his arrow fly as the sound of clashing swords broke the silence that had followed Avram's cry. The sudden release of the tension in his arm and shoulder caused the old warrior to roll over on his back, and he didn't see the arrow pierce the forest shadow. By the time he'd rolled back to his side, the phantom was gone and an errant shaft of firelight revealed Campian's arrow quivering in the trunk of a tree.

Nocking another arrow, Campian rose on his knees. Avram was holding two mercenaries at bay, swords flashing like falling stars in the firelight, the ring of steel on steel brittle and crisp in the damp night air. The other two mercenaries lay slumped beside the fire, unmoving. There was a gourd-shaped object sizzling in the campfire, its surface bursting with blackening blisters, flames already retreating down into the smoldering, moss-like tangle on its upper surface. Over the flames flashed the swords of the three combatants. Whatever advantage the Ranger had bought with his surprise attack had been short-lived. These were no average swordsmen. These were Dubh Aogail. And Avram was hard pressed to hold two of them at bay.

Campian drew and took aim on the nearer of the two mercenaries, but as he went to release, the phantom rose again from the darkness, half again as close to the fire as he was before. This time Campian saw that the man's weapon was nothing more than a small sapling, stripped of branches and leaves over a small stretch in the middle to allow for a riser, but otherwise a camouflaged extension of the forest. The arrow that came fishtailing at Campian's head was much the same, a crude and hasty weapon. Accurate enough, though, in the hands of this mercenary. Campian rolled to the side to avoid the missile, forced to let his own arrow fly wide of its mark.

He was scrambling for a new vantage point when he heard Avram cry out. When he raised his head to peer through the foliage, he saw that the young Ranger was down.

One of the men in the firelight turned to address the darkness. "Your friend is down, Ranger. Caught him just below the groin and opened an artery. He's bleeding to death."

"Don't listen to him!" Avram yelled. But there was fear in the young man's voice.

Nothing moved in the forest. The phantom with the crude bow had disappeared.

"Throw down your weapons and step into the light, Ranger. I'll let you put a tourniquet on this man."

"No!" Avram yelled. "Kill the bastards! Kill them now." More fear in his voice. Campian could imagine his confusion.

He probably hadn't seen the phantom archer. He was wondering what had happened to the aid that Campian was supposed to give. Why hadn't the old man shot the mercenaries?

The Kirkmaughs leaned on their swords and waited. "He's bleeding out pretty fast, Ranger."

Campian set his bow aside and slipped the claymore from his back.

"No!" Avram yelled. His voice was noticeably weaker.

Campian braced his legs beneath him, gripped the claymore by handle and leather-wrapped ricasso, took several deep breaths. There'd be no cottage or fat wife. He knew that. He knew that this was probably where it all ended. Seventy years and he'd come to this stupid mistake in a forest he'd once thought he ruled.

One of the mercenaries lifted his sword and ran his fingertips through the dark blood running down its blade. He opened his mouth to make some taunting remark, but that was when Campian exploded from the forest and split his head down the middle with sixty-six inches of claymore.

At its widest point, the Kiamina Pass is as wide as a thousand war horses standing shoulder to shoulder. At its narrowest, a point just three hundred rods from where it spills down into the grass of Kilcullen Fields, a point from whence an army has an expansive and determining view of the approach from the north, a hundred amply-supplied men could hold it against an army ten times that size. It's here that northern and southern Eire had clashed time and again throughout history. It's here that more than one tyrant had established a toll on trade goods flowing between the two hemispheres of Eire. Until the founding of Kiamina, ownership of the pass had always been in contention, and more blood had been spilled to occupy, take, and hold the pass than any other spot on the world.

It's here that Duncan Emery, with his small southern force, hoped to stall Cloyne Kildare's conquest. Too late to join Clive Duncannon and defeat the usurper, the southern baron now hoped only to protect his homeland just south of the pass. His home would be the first to fall when Kildare's army marched again. Kiamina Pass was the only spot where he stood a chance of holding him.

He had nearly a thousand men, three hundred of them mounted, six hundred of them with at least some training. It seemed an insignificant number against the ten thousand men Kildare had marched away from the scene of Duncannon's demise. Emery's army was decently armed, but poorly stocked. The southern barons did not expect to see anything out of the north for many years to come and were therefore reluctant to send precious stores north for Emery. As for sending soldiers … well, some had told him he was crazy, that the smart thing to do was swear allegiance when Kildare came south through the pass, and others had replied that they needed every soldier they had to defend their own homes. It went unsaid, but Emery knew that most of his neighbors were hoping he would weaken Kildare's forces enough to ensure them of, if not a victory, at least a stalemate in the years to come. The other southerners had, more or less and without it being a conscious consensus, agreed to sacrifice him.

Emery's camp stretched south from that narrow point of Kiamina Pass, that place dubbed Blood Gap by men who had fought to hold it before. The camp was a ragged line of tents, campfires, and livestock pens, now besieged by the snores of the eight hundred men not on watch or scouting the surrounding hills.

For Emery, however, there was little sleep. What time he did use to rest was in the heat of the day, when he could see for himself that nothing moved on Kilcullen Fields and knew that he had hours before anything spotted on the horizon could reach them. Nights he spent pacing the wooden palisade they'd erected across the Gap, watching the tall northern sage grass rippling in the wind, waiting for the watch fires his scouts would set if anything moved out there in the dark, wondering how much warning he'd have if Kildare's men got to his scouts before they gave that warning. On nights like this, nights with no moon and those thick, black clouds obscuring the stars, he would stare out into that impenetrable darkness and forget to even breathe.

"M'lord?"

Emery turned from the wooden barrier to find one of his scouts waiting at attention. "What is it?"

The man extended a hand encased in gloves made of the same black deer hide that covered the rest of him. It was an assassin's garb, but Emery's scouts had taken to wearing it to hide themselves out in the fields and in the surrounding hills where they were watching for Ari Kirkmaugh's butchers. In the palm of the scout's hand lay a dead pigeon, its gray feathers spotted with blood. The bird's right leg, where it would have worn a band, was missing.

"Do we know whose it was?"

The scout rolled the bird over so that Duncan Emery could see the red paint on its tail feathers.

"Our source inside Droichead Nua?"

"Yes," the scout replied. "The bird came to us same as the others ... dropped by a large raven."

Emery looked away. This was the third such bird delivered to them. One of the other pigeons had been dispatched from Howth and might have meant Emery had allies to the north. Now there was no way to tell. The other pigeon had come from home and a subsequent bird that had gotten through revealed that the first had been nothing more than an update on siege provisioning being done there. All of the pigeons had been killed and robbed of their message by a large raven. With the Howth pigeon, several of his men had actually seen the raven strike the carrier from the air, ripping away the leg and the message band before dropping the body into camp.

"Orders, M'lord?"

Emery shook his head. What orders was he to give? There was no way to contact their operative in Droichead Nua. No way to know what the message had said, whether it boded good or ill for Emery's force in the pass. He'd set himself to wait and meet Kildare's army head on. And that was what he would do.

"M'lord?"

"We wait," Emery said softly. "We wait and see how badly they want to advance to the south." He glanced up into the dark hills. "And we hope the man I sent up there after Kirkmaugh is successful."

The second Kirkmaugh struck a brutal blow as Campian's sword became entangled in the sternum of the collapsing mercenary. Campian twisted to avoid the blow and it glanced off his side, sending links of silver chain mail spinning off in the firelight. There was pain, but it wasn't accompanied by the wet, warm feeling of gushing blood, and Campian counted himself lucky. Cracked ribs he could live with. To avoid the mercenary's return stroke, however, the Ranger was forced to relinquish the claymore as the dead man pulled it from his grip.

Campian drew the long knife at his side and met the next stroke. The knife was solid, but never intended to stand up to such a heavy blow. Campian knew it wouldn't last him long. He danced back, nearly tripping over Avram, who lay in a puddle of blood, hands clamped about a gushing wound in his thigh. Avram's sword lay nearby. Campian tried to pick it up, but the mercenary pressed him fiercely. The Ranger was forced back toward the dark trees, each ringing blow from the mercenary's broadsword leaving deep indentations in the knife's edge. Then, there came a rustle of leaves behind him, and Campian had time only to flinch before something clubbed him over the head.

He went down, sparks igniting the boundaries of his vision. He tried to turn and raise the long knife, but the same crude bow that had clubbed him over the head lashed out and struck his elbow. His arm went numb and the knife dropped to the ground. Still, the Ranger tried to get back to his feet. The sapling lashed in again, slipping under his chain mail shirt to rap loudly against his hip bone. Campian's right leg went out from under him and he pitched face first into the dirt beside Avram.

"I suggest you stay down this time, Campian."

He knew that voice. He hadn't heard it in decades, but he knew it. Knew it from his nightmares. Knew it from memories, both fond and foul. Campian rolled over on his back. The rough-hewn end of the sapling bow was shoved under his chin, gouging his throat and pinning him to the ground. Campian's gaze followed the length of the shaft until he found the man at the other end.

Ari Kirkmaugh.

Kirkmaugh and the other man dragged Campian to his feet and slammed him against the nearest tree. Campian's arms were wrenched back behind the tree and bound, causing the Ranger to nearly cry out at the sharp pain that shot from elbow and ribs. There was a drum going off in his head and blood running down his neck from where Kirkmaugh had clubbed him.

Avram abandoned his thigh wound and fumbled for his sword—but when he removed his hands, blood sprayed from the gash in his thigh. Despite this, he might have still tried for the sword, but Ari Kirkmaugh stepped in and kicked him away from the weapon. Avram clamped his hands back around the wound and waited, hooded eyes shifting from the two mercenaries to Campian and back again. His face was pale in the firelight. His eyes had taken on a glassy sheen.

Kirkmaugh tossed his crude bow and several arrows on the fire. "Won't be needing this anymore," he remarked lightly. "Guess if I ever become cowardly enough to use a bow as a primary weapon, I've got two fine Ranger bows to choose from." He pried Campian's claymore from the dead mercenary by the fire and held it up for inspection. "Now that's what I call a sword, Campian! Most men would throw out their back swinging this whore's son."

Campian said nothing. He tried to test the strength of his bonds, but when he pulled against them, needles of pain radiated out from his elbow.

"Only a man of your size could use such a thing," Kirkmaugh remarked. "Though I don't see how even you could expect to exact any sort of finesse with it."

"Turn me loose and I'll be happy to demonstrate," Campian said softly.

"No doubt," Kirkmaugh laughed. He slung the heavy claymore out into the dark forest. It disappeared into the foliage with an anticlimactic rustling of leaves. Kirkmaugh picked up the long knife next and inspected its battered edge. "Now this might have been worth keeping if Landry hadn't put such a beating on it." He hurled it out into the woods after the claymore.

Next, he retrieved Avram's sword and those belonging to the fallen mercenaries, and he sent them out into the darkness, too. The man he'd called Landry was then ordered to drag the three bodies away from the fire.

During all of this, Campian waited against the tree and Avram remained silent on the ground, blood seeping out from around his hands.

When the bodies had been removed, Kirkmaugh told Landry to check Campian for other weapons. The mercenary removed the armor-piercing hammer from Campian's boot, but didn't find the knife in the small of the Ranger's back where it was pressed against the trunk of the tree. He handed the hammer to Kirkmaugh.

Kirkmaugh knelt beside Avram and studied the seeping wound. "Hurt?" he asked, rhythmically slapping the war hammer against the palm of his hand.

Avram said nothing.

"Ari…" Campian began.

"If he speaks again without permission," Kirkmaugh told his man, "cut him somewhere. I don't care where, but make sure it's not fatal and make sure it hurts." Landry drew a dagger from his belt and gave Campian a grim smile.

"You're bleeding to death," Kirkmaugh told Avram. "You know that, don't you?"

"Much the way your mother bled on the night I bedded her," Avram hissed.

Kirkmaugh laughed. "I like a good sense of humor. Not sure this is any time for you to be joking though, son. You realize you'd probably already be dead if you weren't applying pressure to that artery, don't you?" He suddenly lashed out with the flat-headed side of the hammer and broke Avram's right hand. Avram cried out, drawing back his hand. Blood pumped from the wound in his leg.

"No!" Campian screamed.

Landry reached out with the knife and slashed away most of Campian's left ear.

Kirkmaugh looked back over his shoulder at the writhing Ranger lashed to the tree. "Ouch! That *had* to hurt."

Campian said nothing. His teeth were clenched and he was breathing heavily through his nose. There was blood pouring from what was left of his ear. He looked like a wild animal, restrained but untamed. Ready, at any moment, to rip free and strike. His blue eyes had gone nearly black. He'd forgotten the pain of his broken ribs and bruised elbow and was straining against his bonds with all his might. The ropes were holding.

"You know what I want," Kirkmaugh said. He turned back to Avram who was now trying to grip the thigh wound with his broken hand. Kirkmaugh reversed the hammer and put the pike side of it right through Avram's hand.

"Ah!" Avram screamed. "I will rip your bloody fucking head off!"

"That," said Kirkmaugh, "is unlikely." He rose, leaving the hammer embedded in Avram's hand, hanging there like some weapon the Ranger was too daft to use. Avram might have pulled it loose, but that would have meant releasing his wound with his good hand. The wound pulsed a metronomic flow of blood out onto the ground, keeping time with Avram's heart.

Kirkmaugh turned to Campian, motioning Landry aside. "Tell me what I want to know and I'll let you tend to his wound."

Campian bared his teeth and growled like a feral dog. Chords stood out on his neck like bowstrings. Blood vessels had burst in his eyes. He pulled against the ropes that held him to the tree with every ounce of his strength, the tendons and ligaments in his arms and back popping like green wood tossed on a fire.

"Your man is bleeding to death, Campian. You know what I need to hear."

"He won't tell you," Avram said weakly. He'd been sitting up, but now he slumped over and curled into a fetal position, hammer-impaled hand and injured leg drawn up against his chest. The flow of blood from his thigh had visibly decreased.

Kirkmaugh glanced meaningfully back over his shoulder at the dying man. "You can save him," he whispered to Campian. "Tell me where the Rangers are based."

"I'm sorry, Avram," Campian moaned.

"Not your fault," Avram whispered. He sounded as if he

were speaking from another room. "Just be sure and kill that bastard for me."

Kirkmaugh cocked an amused eyebrow at Campian. "Haven't told him everything, eh?"

"He's told me enough," Avram hissed.

Without looking away from Campian, Kirkmaugh said, "Is that so? Did he tell you about Cahlindra, the witch that the plainsmen brought from Devil's Bay? Did he tell you how he killed me just before he slept with the witch? Or that I was born again from their passion?" He smiled at Campian. "In a way, my friend, you're the father I never had."

"I'd sooner sire a sewer rat," Campian spit.

"Did he tell you it was me who slit Orvellon's fat throat from ear to ear? That I did it for Cahlindra?"

Looking over Kirkmaugh's shoulder, Campian saw Avram release his wound, take the hammer by the handle and rip it from his hand. Kirkmaugh and Landry were focused on Campian. They didn't see Avram struggling to get his feet under him. Campian considered saying something to stop the boy, but it was already too late. Kirkmaugh would let Avram bleed to death no matter what Campian did or did not say. And Campian himself was as good as dead, for he had tested his bonds until every muscle in his body screamed in agony, to no avail. Better Avram try to make it to his feet and sell his life as dearly as possible. Better a quick death than more of Kirkmaugh's torture. The old man stifled a sob that came from some forgotten part of him that seemed only just recently restored. It was Glengaerif Callin's beautiful Laenora that had reached inside and reminded him what it was to feel again. It was a rabbit shared around a campfire that had reminded him he still had friends. Campian let his eyes fall to the dragon emblazoned on Kirkmaugh's breast. He stared and focused on his hate, letting the love that would betray his friend wash away. He would grieve later, when it was safe to do so. If there ever was a later...

"Nothing to say, Campian?"

The boy needed time to get to his feet. He needed the mercenaries kept distracted.

"Tell him why you really killed Orvellon," Campian growled. "Tell him how you went to him because I dismissed you from the Rangers, how you begged him to take you back, but he refused. So you murdered him. Tell him," Campian added for Avram's ears, "how you stained the reputation of the finest men in Kiamina, how you were unfit to wear the eagle, let alone that dragon. Tell that boy that he's twice the man you'll ever be, Ari."

Kirkmaugh uttered a strained little laugh and would have made some reply, but at that moment Avram surged to his feet and struck with the hammer. Kirkmaugh jogged his head to the side at the last instant, and the pike, missing its intended target, whistled past his ear and sunk with a metallic *chink!* down through the armor over his left shoulder. Kirkmaugh bellowed in pain. Snatching a black dagger from his belt, he spun and plunged it to the hilt in Avram's breast. The young Ranger fell past the stumbling mercenary, right into Campian. He clung there, blood bubbling from his lips.

"Campian...?"

"I'm sorry, Avram. I'm so sorry..."

"Argh!" Kirkmaugh roared again, ripping the hammer from his shoulder.

Avram wrapped his arms around his old friend, clinging, struggling to stay on his feet. "Kill him ... for me. Okay?" His hands found the small knife in Campian's belt. He slipped it out and sliced the ropes holding Campian to the tree, just as Kirkmaugh, with a forest-rending howl of rage, sank the hammer into the top of the young man's skull.

Avram crumbled at Campian's feet and Ari Kirkmaugh stood there, blood gushing from the hole in his shoulder, teeth bared in pain and rage. When Campian reached out and plunged his thumb deep into the shoulder wound, the mercenary was taken entirely by surprise.

Using the wound as leverage, Campian drove the smaller man backward off his feet and shoved him into the fire. Kirkmaugh went rolling through the flames, howling with fury and pain. He came up on the far side of the fire, flames licking at his unkempt hair and clothing. Landry, who had sheathed his sword earlier when he'd taken out the knife, rushed forward, brandishing the bloody weapon. Campian took the knife thrust along his forearm, a long jagged gash that he barely felt through all his other injuries. Inside the mercenary's guard now, Campian caught the man by the ears. Dragging the mercenary's head down, Campian raised a knee, shattering the man's nose in a spew of blood and cartilage fragments. As Landry stumbled back, Campian ripped his ears from his head. The mercenary screamed. The scream was short-lived, for Campian slipped behind the man, wrapped an arm around his head, and broke the man's neck as if it were nothing more than dry kindling.

There was a sharp, metallic rasp as Ari Kirkmaugh drew his broadsword. The only comparable weapon in reach was Landry's sword—as fate would have it, trapped beneath the dead mercenary's body. Campian had less than a second to make his decision. Scramble for the sword and probably die when Kirkmaugh leaped the fire and caught him struggling to pull it free. Or run.

— THREE: BLACKENED RUINS AND ANCIENT GHOSTS —

Dawn cleared the mountains bordering the western range of Kiamina Pass and lit the cobbled roads that wove through the crumbled towers and breached, blackened walls below. From a hill overlooking the western wall of the city, Campian's gaze swept down over the broken battlements. He looked on the shattered homes of people he had once known and shops where he had taken his wife. He flinched away from thoughts of what mummified remains now occupied the bunks in the barracks where troops he had once commanded had died in their sleep. He found it hard to fathom the ruthless act that had turned the stables, which had once housed Kiamina's finest equine stock, to ash, blackened timbers, and charcoaled bone. Strangely enough, Orvellon's palace appeared mostly intact, the only sign that it had been taken from within, the black streaks of soot on the walls above the windows. A pennant still flew from one turret, though it had long been bleached of color and was now little more than a single tattered strip of cloth wound about the pole like an old bandage. Rats and crows moved through the rubble and bones below. The wind sighed through the rubble-strewn streets, whistled past a lance standing from the nigh-empty armor of a long dead guardsman, rustled a scrap of clothe here, the long dead hair of a woman's skull there. Nothing else.

Aching sword arm held against his broken ribs, Campian limped down the hillside and through a gap in the wall. One side of his head was caked with dried, black blood. His forearm was wrapped in a bloody rag. His eyes were wild and furtive.

Much of the city lay underground, for Kiamina had been a place of cellars and dungeons, passages and tunnels and great subterranean halls. Campian's own home had been three levels down, just south of the palace. He'd only been here once since the fall. Once to find his wife and sons dead. Three trips to the surface to bury them in the hills, picking his way through the thousands of dead and the crows feasting in the streets. One last trip to collect what few belongings had escaped the plainsmen and the fires that had swept through the underground after they'd gone. He'd never come back.

Until now.

The streets were littered with crumbling skeletons whose disintegrating digits still lay claim to weather-ravaged weapons. Most of what he disturbed with the toe of his boot crumbled away. What remained, an ivory sword handle here, the splintered shaft of a lance there, was useless. If he hoped to find anything with which to battle Ari Kirkmaugh, he would have to go below. He had no doubt that Kirkmaugh would be close behind him.

The cistern in the market square was full from whatever mountain spring still supplied water. Campian struggled through the vines that had claimed it, wiped leaves away from its stagnant surface, and plunged his face into the frigid water. Immediately, the pain from his ear tripled. Fresh blood ran pink with the water streaming off his head. He was dizzy with pain. Stumbling back from the cistern, he sat down heavily in the dust. A crow called. Campian imagined the bird having waited all these years for his return. Like a dog to its own vomit, the walking carrion comes to the table at long last. Grimacing, he regained his feet. He took a few drinks from the cistern, then proceeded west through the city.

Beneath the arch Orvellon had ordered constructed in honor of the city's tenth anniversary, lay an entrance to the Galleria of the Ancients, a large, subterranean hall where those merchants who could not afford the more expensive shop space above ground had once gathered to barter and trade, decorating the gargantuan support columns below with rich tapestries and furs, stacking crates of vegetables and dried meats to the ceiling. Though the arch appeared unscathed, the entrance itself was clogged with vegetation that had now spent several decades separating the cobblestones.

Campian was tearing a way down through the dense foliage, when an iridescent green tree adder raised its ugly head, flared its neck, and hissed at him. The snake's eyes glowed violet in the morning sun. Its forked tongue was so small and fast that its existence was more suggestion than reality. It was impossible to tell the snake's full size, as its body vanished into the foliage, but it was large for an adder, fattened on rats and having existed without enemies for who knew how many years in the ruins of Kiamina. Campian jerked his hand back, but he was too slow. The adder struck. Fangs penetrated the arm that was already bruised and cut. The pain of the bite was so minuscule that Campian wanted to laugh and ask the heavy clouds above, "What next?"—but he knew the snake was venomous.

Stumbling back from the vine clotted entrance to the underground, the Ranger acknowledged that Kirkmaugh now had one more advantage.

He sucked at the tiny puncture wounds, spitting out the bitter venom. He didn't have a knife to bleed the damn thing. The amount of venom he was able to extract without cutting was probably minimal, perhaps not even worth the effort. And there were those who argued that it didn't matter. Once the adder's venom penetrated the skin, it was taken up by surrounding cells and hustled through the blood stream faster than most could bring themselves to cut anyway.

He tried to recall what he knew of the tree adder. Whether anyone he'd ever known had died from a bite. He recalled men who'd hallucinated and one who'd dropped into a coma from which he'd recovered five days later, thin and emaciated, dehydrated and sore, but alive. The venom was lethal to smaller animals, perhaps even to children, but a grown man ought to be able to survive it.

Campian passed by the Galleria entrance in search of other access to the underground. Adders were known to congregate. Best to avoid that stand of brush. The venom compounded itself, each dosage approaching some level of lethality; it wouldn't do to be bitten again, by that snake or one of its relatives.

A hostelry had crumbled from the heat of the fires that had taken the massive stables nearby, collapsing in on itself to reveal a dark basement. The hostelry had primarily served those who came to trade and show horses; thus, the basement provided underground access to the stables and to training arenas below. Campian cautiously climbed down a splintered cross beam into the rubble. There were several holes in the stone floor, gaping blackly on lower levels. He walked carefully around these, working his way across the basement to the splintered remains of a stout wooden door, beyond which lay a tunnel to the stables.

The underground wasn't as dark as he'd feared it might be. Everywhere, there were holes and crevices through which sunlight struggled to assert its influence. It was more a world of shadows than of darkness, a world where there seemed always to be something lurking, watching, waiting to pounce. The floors were cluttered with destruction, with grim reminders that people had once lived here, that they had, in fact, died here. Once he accidentally kicked the skull of child, wincing as the gruesome object clattered down the hallway. The semi-dark only served to cloak these remains in macabre garments of umbrage. And the shadows concealed many death traps. Twice he slipped as stones shifted out from under his feet and sank away into the darkness below. He found the well-preserved shaft of a guardsman's lance and used it to probe the floor ahead of him.

The stables were damp and musty, the heavy wooden walls separating the stalls now crumbling black logs held together by the lack of any disturbance. Everything still standing looked as if it was just waiting the right moment to collapse, as if a gaze was all that was needed. Horse skulls, their eyes as empty and black as the frequent pits in the floor, lined the length of the room like barracks soldiers standing at inspection. Ancient saddle tack hung from the walls, leather so old it crumbled, most of it wrinkled and fire-hardened. Campian moved quickly through the stables. Several mounts of his own had been here when the stables went up. The place stank, not so much of death and old smoke, but of some injustice that had since been forgotten. It was as if the musty, cloying air was suppressing the real odor of the place, as if all that was needed was the right memory to lift the stench, like dust in the wind, up from the floors.

Leaving the stables, Campian thought he saw movement behind him, just a flash of white out of the corner of his eye. However, when he turned and stared into the darkness, there was nothing there.

His heart was beating erratically. His head was ringing. And every muscle in his body ached. He was having trouble breathing, a symptom he attributed to the paralyzing effect of the adder venom. The tips of his fingers seemed to be going numb.

Beyond the stables, the armorer's. For twenty minutes, he dug through the rubble of the forge, the bellows, and racks that had once held hundreds of weapons for sale. There was nothing. Bheag Ai Duboil's marauders and subsequent vandals had stripped the place clean. Buried in the long dead ashes of the forge, he found a fifty-inch length of rough-hammered steel, black and soot encrusted, with but the bare beginnings of an edge. It would have eventually been a sword after a hundred more sessions of tempering and folding and pounding. It was crude for a weapon, but it was all he could find.

While he was pulling the sword blank free of the crumbled remains of the forge, he saw the ghost again, closer this time, a diaphanous white specter in the deep gloom of the tunnel he'd followed from the stables.

"Come ahead," he whispered, surprised to find his own voice laced with madness there in the dark. He sat and wrapped one end of his makeshift weapon with cloth torn from the shirt he wore under his mail. He took his time making sure it was well fastened with wire that he found in the ruins. All the while, watching. Waiting. But the phantom came no closer. When he was done, he at least had a suitable handle for his weapon. He could hold and swing the makeshift sword without ruining his hands. He took a couple practice swings, groaning at the pain in his arm and ribs. The sword was too heavy for its length, completely unbalanced, and suitable for little more than clubbing a man to death. It hurt him to even lift it.

"Come ahead then, ghost," he called to the dark tunnel, his voice cracking with insipid laughter. "Let's see what we're made of."

Nothing. Just the wind sighing through the underground. The distant dripping of water. The sharp taste of the adder's venom in the back of his throat and the hammering of his blood in his one good ear.

From the armory, Campian took a wide underground concourse known as the King's Way toward the palace sub-levels. Though he didn't look back, he knew the ghost was there. He could feel its eyes on him, its icy breath raising the hairs on the back of his neck. He was leaning on the makeshift sword, its tip clanking loudly on the stone floor with each step he took. It sounded like someone buried alive, tapping the crypt ceiling with a heavy ring in the hopes that someone might hear him. The phantom at his back was Death, called in to collect his due, whether the buried man was ready or not.

Campian acknowledged that he might be hallucinating. The fact that he was able to recognize this fact was very little comfort to him.

Beneath the palace, a major battle had been fought on the King's Way. Helmet-encased skulls, dented shields and armor plate, the broken shafts of weapons, boots and visors and rib cages cupped like empty fish traps cluttered the boulevard. Small bones crunched under his heel. Broken femurs and collarbones clattered ahead of his boots. Heads had been stacked against one wall beyond a clear area where there sat a trio of rust-hued, deeply scarred chopping blocks. The vertebrae-trailing mound reached nearly to the ceiling, forty feet overhead, stretched at least sixty feet along the wall, and was fifteen feet deep. The bodies that went with these heads had been stripped and stacked like cordwood against the opposite wall. They were now only a tangle of bones, like a barricade of dead wood in the forest, their individuality surrendered to time and the rats.

Beyond the major debris of the subterranean battle, Campian came to the five winding stairways that led up into the palace proper. Four of the stairways were cluttered with the bones and armor of those who had fought a last-ditch effort to contain the enemy below ground, but the fifth had been cleared to serve as monument. On each of the steps to the surface there sat a single skull, the personal servants, friends, retainers, and family members of Emperor Rodric Orvellon, from least to most important as Bheag Ai Duboil must have viewed them. Orvellon's wife's head decorated the top step. His three daughters the steps below that. His councilors, his aids, all the way down to his personal valet on the bottom step. Somewhere in that hierarchy there was a vacant step, the one that Bheag Ai Duboil had reserved for Campian. Campian had seen it all, years ago when he'd come to bury his wife and sons, when the steps had sported heads and not just skulls. The heads of people he had known. People he had sworn to protect. He'd sat on that vacant step and wept with guilt and anguish and failure. Then, he'd done what he came to do, and he disappeared into the mountains. Eventually, years after Duncannon had taken Khal Mani, other Rangers who had survived the fall of Kiamina had sought him out. Old loyalties die hard.

Campian did not ascend the stairs this time. He pressed on past the palace toward the officers' quarters and residential districts to the south.

The ghost followed quietly.

Much of the residential section had been wood: simple frame structures wedged into the natural volcanic fissures that undermined Kiamina; apartment complexes descending as much as thirty levels down. A great deal of these structures had burned—the flames dying out, perhaps, when their need for oxygen exceeded what was available—but much of the underground in this area had escaped the fire. What remained was a complex warren of passages and rooms where there was sometimes a floor and a roof, four walls and a logical layout, but just as often there was not—just fragmented domiciles with indecipherable floor plans, spilling one into the other in all three dimensions with no apparent rhyme or reason. His own home had been spared most of the fire, losing just a few intervening walls between his family room and a third level causeway that ran from the palace all the way to the subterranean ponds just this side of the city's southern walls. Campian stopped there, in the home he hadn't seen in so many years, found an old overturned chair beneath the rubble and an inch of dust, and sat down to await the ghost.

When she didn't immediately come to him, his head settled back against the chair, his eyes slipped shut, and his heart slowed to a belabored rhythm. The venom whispered a death song in his veins. He passed out.

White lace and Dorinthian silk. Buttons of polished ivory imported from South Benabi. Gilded thread shipped all the way from Port Chafi. He'd paid the surface merchant a small fortune for the materials, but looking at Regina in the dress she'd made, it was well worth it. Campian hadn't seen her this happy in years. She pirouetted before him in the new dress, eyes all bright and sparkling, her fine blonde hair floating about her face ... so very bright against the fire-blackened wall of their family room.

Fire?

Something was wrong.

"Regina?" He rose from the chair—or tried to. His body felt as if it weighed several tons, as if every muscle had been cut and left impotent.

His wife smiled down at him. "What is it, my love?" Suddenly, her teeth blackened and spilled out into his lap. Her hair curled as if from a great heat, withered and disintegrated. Her eyes retreated into her skull, leaving her cheekbones and occipital ridges protruding from flesh that had gone ashen, flesh drawn as taut as the hide on a marching drum. "You've been a long time coming home, Campian," rasped the skeletal visage.

"This isn't real," Campian croaked, thinking of the

adder's venom, of how exhausted he was. "I'm dreaming this. Hallucinating." He tried to lift his hand from the arm of the chair. If he could gouge the wound on the side of his head, he thought, that would surely wake him from this nightmare. But his arm just sat there, unresponsive.

Regina leaned close, and the cloying, magnolia-sweet odor of the grave accompanied her words. "Was she worth it, Campian? Cahlindra, the witch, was bedding her worth all of this?"

Flashbacks struck like summer lightning, swift and brutal, burning their images into the retina, shaking the soul with their thunder. A younger Campian battled Ari Kirkmaugh in the timber above Kiamina. Lifeless in the chair, Campian felt again his hatred for this man he'd once called friend, the man he'd caught in bed with his wife, the man who'd slit the throat of the emperor he'd sworn to protect. Images and sounds strobed his senses: the clangor of steel on steel; the hoarse gasps of exertion; and, ultimately, the soft sigh of last breaths. Kirkmaugh slid back from Campian's bloody sword, his expression torn between pain and disbelief ... and something else. Remorse? Anguish? Maybe it was relief and release, because the man hadn't been entirely under his own control. He'd been seduced by two women. First, by Regina, lonely and bored, and more than susceptible to the easy charm Ari had wielded in the days of his careless youth. And then Bheag Ai Duboil's witch, Cahlindra. She'd sent him to slay Orvellon, using the young warrior's anguish and anger at being routed from the guard to capture his mind. She'd sent him to meet the barbarians in the mountains and show them the secret ways into Kiamina, but Campian had tracked him through the mountains and killed him first. At the time, he'd never even heard the name Cahlindra.

To think of a thing, to recall such a power, isn't far removed from a conjuring.

His dead wife's skull wavered before Campian's eyes, transformed, became the beautiful face of Cahlindra. Her hair was a long and luxurious cinnamon. She was naked, save for a white silken sash thrown carelessly over one shoulder and bands of gold intricately spiraled about arms and thighs.

She smiled that perfect smile and her eyes gleamed violet like the tree adder's. Campian's flashbacks were still going off like fireworks, some of them real experiences and others suppositions and mysteries. Juxtaposed over Cahlindra's face, Campian saw the witch standing amid a ring of candles, arms raised as she worked some twisted conjuring. Smoke swirled about her. The sky split open and poured forth a fiery miasma of copper and gold, boiling above her head. From this orange, molten cloud two totems appeared, symbols that Campian knew well. The Rangers' red eagle, same as the emblem emblazoned on his breast. And the dragon, symbol of Orvellon's elite guard, the unit over which Campian had placed his best friend, Ari Kirkmaugh.

Watching this, Campian realized, for the first time, that perhaps Regina and Ari had never had a choice in the matter. The failings that had brought down Kiamina might have been human enough, but Cahlindra had been there from the beginning, had been at the heart of it all.

The witch before him showed pearl white teeth, and the juxtaposed image faded, eagle and dragon whirling into a chaotic mist. She spoke then, but in the minuscule time between her smile and her words, Campian remembered the forest and the death of his friend.

Spitting blood, Ari Kirkmaugh had clutched at Campian's cloak, trying to say something before he died. At the time, Campian had been unable to understand him. It came to him now, clearly.

"I'm sorry, Campian."

But that morning, he'd simply twisted out of Kirkmaugh's death grip and collapsed into the thick fall leaves, exhausted and suffering more than one injury himself, where he lay, panting, fighting the emotions that sought to overwhelm him. He'd just killed his best friend. He'd just killed his wife's lover. Below him waited not only his family problems, but an empire without its emperor, a city in chaos. For the moment, he let his eyes close and simply chose not to think about any of it. He might have even slept. To this day, he's unsure.

She came up from the ground, through the leaves and the

moist humus, smelling of earth and musk and elementary, natural things. Her breath was sweet, like honeysuckle. Her hands were as soft as doeskin. Her lips on his neck were warm and moist, and when she kissed him ... when she kissed him, he tasted flowers and mountain springs and fresh honey. He tasted passion and desire and things he had set aside to help Orvellon build his empire. Something not unlike the adder's venom—though this is another realization that comes to him only now—slipped down his throat. Euphoria. Aphrodisia. He remembered looking into her eyes just before she mounted him. They were as blue and cold as the Glacier Cap. He remembered her laugh, as cruel as it was beautiful. She rode him and he thrust back, never asking who she was or where she came from. For the moment, it was enough that he feel pleasure rather than pain, that he feel this basest lust rather than emptiness. He told himself that it really didn't matter. It was all a dream from which he'd awake shortly. He'd look at his friend and his wife across the dinner table, laugh and tell them all about it. And if their eyes betrayed the least guilt—if, perhaps, there *was* something between the two, even if it had never gone beyond words and dreams—he would smile at them both and pretend not to notice. Better his wife and his best friend love each other behind his back than an empire crumble, than he lose them both. But he wasn't dreaming. And when he poured his seed into her and she howled at the blackening sky, he knew that everything had changed forever. He tried to push her off of him, but the leaves and the loam and the forest swept up about him, wrapping him in a dreamless dark.

Later, he woke chained to a tree. Cahlindra was gone. Kirkmaugh, wounds closing beneath a paste of something the witch had concocted from saliva and semen and the gods alone know what else, sat waiting the arrival of Bheag Ai Duboil. Campian tried to talk to him, but Kirkmaugh would not so much as turn and acknowledge that he could hear him. When the barbarians came, Kirkmaugh left Campian there, straining against the chains. Kiamina was taken by surprise. Afterward, Kirkmaugh offered Campian life in his service or death. Campian chose death. Eyes a flat, lifeless black, Kirkmaugh had stared at him for several long minutes, while Campian waited the death blow. It never came. Kirkmaugh unlocked the chains and let him walk away. Campian had gone below, into the smoking city ... where he now found himself again, sitting before the witch who had contrived it all.

And the witch spoke: "He's coming for you, Campian, and this time he *will* kill you."

Campian stared into her sapphire eyes and said nothing.

"I can help you."

The makeshift sword stood against his knee, but his hands would not obey him when he told them to pick it up.

"Look at you." She ran a cold finger down his stubbled cheek. "Old and weak, hurting something awful. You turned me down all those years ago, Campian. Even after I seduced you, you walked away."

Somewhere something clattered, metal on stone, a breastplate kicked from one level to the next perhaps, or a shield someone had stumbled upon. The witch vanished, and Campian's hand, straining for so long to reach the sword against his knee, leaped from the arm of the chair and knocked the weapon over with a crash.

At least he thought that the witch had gone. A second later, she whispered in his ear. "You could have ruled Eire with me, Campian. Fool! Ari will spill your blood in these ashes."

He turned, but there was no one there.

From somewhere down King's Way came the sound of running footsteps. Campian picked up his weapon and surged to his feet. His head spun and his vision blurred. For a moment, he thought he was going to pass out again. The witch laughed in his good ear.

"Curse you, bitch!" he hissed. "If you've such a longing to see me dead, then do it yourself." Then, a sudden intuition: "You can't, can you?" Duncannon's men had imprisoned her and hurled her into a volcano in the Dorinthian Isles after the sacking of Khal Mani. From there she must have found some means of reaching out in recent years, of influencing world events once again, but her strength was tenuous at best. Perhaps in proximity of her summoner, she would possess more strength, but here in the ruins of Kiamina she was no more substantial than an ill breeze.

And as soon as he realized this, her chill presence was gone.

That was when Ari Kirkmaugh came crashing through the blackened wall, hacking madly with his broadsword, his bloodcurdling scream shattering the grave-like silence of the ruins.

Campian raised the length of untempered iron and met the mercenary's onslaught. The finely crafted broadsword struck sparks from the coarser weapon. Repeated blows drove Campian back and through the wall that separated his family room from the bedroom he'd once shared with Regina—the same room in which he'd walked in on the two of them. Feet tangling in the remains of the wall, Campian went down. Kirkmaugh pressed the advantage, spraying saliva as he hacked mercilessly at the fallen Ranger. Campian scrambled back like a crab, sparks and chips of iron raining in his eyes as he fought off the other man's blows. The bare frame of his bed halted his retreat. The mattress was nothing more than black ash on the floor. By scrambling beneath the bed and out the other side, Campian was able to regain his feet as Kirkmaugh leaped across the bed in pursuit. The mercenary's next blow removed at least ten inches from the tip of Campian's weapon.

Bellowing, Kirkmaugh pressed harder, beating the larger man back into a corner. Campian hurled his weight backward, crashing into the juncture of the two walls, but they held, untouched and unweakened by the fire. "No escape this time!" Kirkmaugh yelled, raining blow after blow. Sparks and chunks of metal flew with every ear-shattering clash of the blades. As Kirkmaugh's wild blows were deflected left and right, they tore plaster from the walls. The plaster dust clung to the fresh blood flowing from the wounds of both men. Powdered with dust, they both looked even older than they were. Kirkmaugh looked Campian's age. Campian looked ancient, a weathered extension of the ruined city standing over his head.

It was all Campian could do to hold his enemy at bay. His hands were numb from the adder venom and from absorbing impact through the crude sword. Every muscle in his body ached. His head was ringing. His vision was blurry. The exertion left him gasping for air and with every heaving breath it felt as if his broken ribs were puncturing his lungs. Blood ran from the gash in his forearm and soaked the rags wrapped as handle about the sword. When the unfinished blade snapped down the middle, he was certain he was dead. He saw the same truth reflected in Kirkmaugh's mad eyes, saw nothing but hatred and satisfaction there as the mercenary drew back his sword for the final blow.

Then the floor suddenly groaned and pitched out from under them both.

They fell one level, crashing down through the fire-damaged floor and into another apartment. Kirkmaugh was the first one to regain his feet, heaving chunks of plaster and shattered timbers away from him. He'd hung on to his sword. Without hesitation, he lunged for Campian with the blade drawn back. Campian had managed to cling to one half of his former weapon. He threw it at the mercenary. Kirkmaugh flinched and turned his head away as the twenty some inches of steel clanged off his breastplate. Then his foot tangled in an unidentifiable piece of charred furniture and he went down.

Campian scrambled out of the way as the mercenary fell, launching himself toward the splintered remains of a door. He crashed through, rolled several yards into a burnt shell of a room before that floor gave out and he dropped again. He was slower to recover from this second fall. He lay there for what seemed like several long minutes until he heard Kirkmaugh moving on the floor above him. A second later, the mercenary came crashing down after him. Campian got to his feet and stumbled through a hole in the nearest wall. The room beyond was nearly pitch black, its ceiling in place. He crossed it blind, stumbling over several furniture items until he came up against another wall. As his fingers explored its texture, he realized his mistake. This was a stone wall.

Kirkmaugh's silhouette filled the hole in the wall. He was breathing as heavily as the Ranger and it appeared to take considerable effort to lift his broadsword. "You can't run from me forever," he panted.

Campian didn't have the breath to waste on answering. He was having trouble breathing as it was. He stretched his arms out, exploring the rough contour of the wall in both directions. When he felt nothing, he side-stepped several feet to his left, exploring further.

"I can hear you, Campian," Kirkmaugh whispered, stepping through the hole and into the room. His blade caught the faint light and threw it about the room; then he stepped away from the hole and was lost in the darkness.

Campian's fingers found a frame set in the wall. Beyond the edge of the frame, the smooth, recessed surface of a wooden door. He ran his hands across the face of the door, seeking a knob or a latch. When he found the knob, he turned it only to find that it was locked from the other side. He tugged at the door, eliciting a noise that made Kirkmaugh snicker, "Not as quiet as you were in your youth, my friend," but both door and lock were solid.

He raised his throbbing right forearm, blood-soaked and bandaged and swollen with pus where the snake had bitten him, and drove it down on the knob with all his strength. The pain that shot through his arm made him cry out. Kirkmaugh reacted to the noise by advancing into the room and taking a wild swing with the broadsword. Campian felt a kiss of cold air as the blade hissed past him in the dark. The knob was hanging loose, half torn from the door, but the door was still locked. Ignoring the pain, Campian raised his forearm again and brought it down with all his might. One of the two bones in his forearm broke with a subdued little snap. The knob came away from the door and clattered across the floor. Campian shoved his fingers through the hole where the knob had been and pushed out the lock assembly on the other side. The door yawned free of its frame, swinging inward. There was nothing but pitch black on the other side. As he pulled it open, he heard Kirkmaugh draw for another swing with the broadsword. Campian ducked and the blade whistled by overhead, catching the door and ripping it from Campian's hand. Campian lunged forward through the open doorway into the blackness beyond.

And plunged downward.

Arms flailing, he struck a floor about ten feet down and crashed right on through. Something raked his face—the remains of another sub-level?—and he kept falling. Finally, he was brought to a bone-jarring halt amid debris that ripped at his exposed flesh and bruised every other surface of his body, even through the mail. He lay there for several seconds, trying to pierce the darkness about him, and then the floor shrieked and pitched out from under him again. He fell, crashed through another floor, fell again, was brought up short and buried under debris following him down. He lay there fighting to remain conscious, wondering if there were any bones in his body that weren't broken. He couldn't move. It felt as if there was a ton of broken lumber and plaster piled on top of him. Not even Ari Kirkmaugh wanted him bad enough to chance descending into this madness and, even if he did, he might never find him buried under all the rubble. Then this floor fell out from under him, too, and he howled with maniacal laughter as he plunged further into the catacombs beneath Kiamina.

Kirkmaugh lit a rag and let it fall down into the pit beyond the door, watched as it sank sub-level by sub-level until it caught on the jagged end of a broken beam and hung there, casting its flickering orange glow throughout the shattered bedrooms and exposed terraces of Kiamina's underground. There was no sign of Campian. He was buried somewhere below, who knew how many levels deep, his neck likely broken. Kirkmaugh hated the uncertainty of the situation, but it wasn't safe to descend further into this nightmare warren. That he'd ever lived in such a death trap himself seemed impossible to him now. It was, he acknowledged, another lifetime.

"Campian!" he called down into the hole. Then he sat and listened as the echoes circulated and came back up to him. There was no other sound.

He'd lost the scabbard for his sword. It didn't matter. The blade was all but ruined after its workout on that length of iron Campian had scrounged up. He tossed it aside, and then made his way carefully across the dark room, through the hole in the wall, and off in search of access to the surface.

Consciousness surrendered to the body's demands that its pain be felt, rising back to the surface of the Ranger's mind. Campian awoke with a groan, followed by a hollow whimper. He tried to move. Placing weight on his right arm was a big mistake. The pain nearly caused him to black out. At first it seemed he was crushed beneath an imponderable weight and could not move, but when he moved his legs to see if either was broken, he discovered that he could slide forward on his belly, leaving most of the rubble tented over the spot where he'd lain.

He scrambled forward through the darkness, crying out each time his broken arm came in contact with something. His chain mail caught on the rubble and eventually he was forced to unlace it and scramble free. This process took nearly twenty minutes, limited as he was to using only one arm and the cramped quarters. By the time he was free of the rubble, he was exhausted. He might have lost consciousness again, but he wanted to see where he was. A pouch with flint and steel hung from his belt. He held the flint between his knees and it took but a minute to light a ragged strip of cloth torn from his jerkin.

The flame consumed the tiny strip of cloth quickly, but for a few seconds there was enough light that Campian could see where he was. He was in one of the city's libraries. All around him were shelves and shelves of books and scrolls. The fire had obviously stopped short of this level.

Fumbling in the dark, Campian pulled several volumes from their shelves. He tore pages out to build a small fire. As the flames climbed higher and the darkness retreated to the very corners of the room, Campian saw that it wasn't a library at all. It was some sort of museum. The books he was burning were probably worth a fortune. The walls were hung with paintings no one had seen in decades. Broken sculpture littered the floor, along with glass from display cases Bheag Ai Duboil's butchers had long ago pillaged. There were moldy tapestries and shattered vases, ancient coins, discarded scriptures, and the bones of a long dead curator slumped over his desk.

There was a door at the far end of the room, but before heading that way Campian checked himself over. His arm was broken, but the rest of him appeared intact. Bruised and battered, cut and punctured and torn, but he was alive.

He took one of the largest volumes he could find and started for the door, tearing out a page and lighting it as each one burned down. It was a difficult process because he only had full use of one hand. He managed by tucking the book, spread open, under his broken right arm, and using his left to pull free pages. He burned his arm slightly each time he did this, because he was holding one burning page at the same time he was pulling another free, but the pain was so minor it didn't rise above the rest of his injuries.

The exit door was unlocked. He was opening it when he saw the painting hung just to the right of the door. Something about the lay of the hair. Something about the eyes. He raised his flaming pages for a better look. He blew away the dust that clung to the painting's surface. The plate set in the painting's frame read, "Princess Galewyne Orvellon." It was Rodric Orvellon's eldest daughter's eldest daughter.

The face in the painting, however, belonged to Glengaerif Callin's lady friend, Laenora Maendelton.

West of the ruins, in concealed grottos and cedar-choked caves, there were several exits from the Kiamina underground. Once these exits had been guarded, but those guards were long dead. And what was the use? Few remembered they existed. Even fewer knew how to find them.

Ari Kirkmaugh crawled from one of these caves, squinting in the afternoon sunlight. There was blood on his face and blood still running from the hole in his shoulder. His hair was singed and his clothing was burnt. He was coated with plaster dust and streaked with soot. He was limping. He was exhausted. And he was hungry enough to eat the first animal he could get his hands on.

But he was alive. Which, he thought wryly, was more than could be said for his opponent.

Just the other side of the nearest hills lay Kiamina Pass. He had no intention of approaching that area in daylight. Duncan Emery's army would be firmly entrenched there by now.

Kirkmaugh planned eventually to meet the southern baron, but not looking like this. He would sneak across the pass after the sun went down and make his way through the mountains on the other side to his hidden stronghold. This left him now with several hours in which to rest, which was exactly what he planned to do.

"Rough day?"

Kirkmaugh jumped at the voice from behind. Too late for any kind of offensive move, the mercenary displayed his empty hands and turned around slowly. He was confronted with a dour soldier in unmarked chain mail, sitting quietly on a displaced boulder. The stranger wore a broadsword and knife belted at his waist, neither of which had he drawn. His weapons and clothing were neither cheap nor extravagant. A sword for hire, Kirkmaugh guessed. A rogue and thief perhaps. Kirkmaugh realized that he was unarmed save for a small dagger. Even if the stranger were not a thief, the black dragon on Kirkmaugh's breastplate might be reason enough to kill him.

"I've nothing worth stealing," Kirkmaugh said softly in lieu of greeting.

"You insult me, M'lord," called the stranger, leaping down from the boulder.

For a moment, on landing, the stranger was off balance. In that moment, Kirkmaugh drew his dagger and lunged forward. The stranger didn't seem surprised. He turned the dagger on a leather guard wrapped about his forearm, caught the mercenary's wrist, turned him, and kicked his feet out from under him. It happened so quickly, that Kirkmaugh was taken off guard. One minute he was thrusting for the stranger's heart, and the next he was on his back with the stranger's knee on his chest and his own blade at his throat. This was no common brigand. The man had training, serious training.

The stranger smiled down at him. "I think we should start over." He reversed the dagger, slapped the handle in Kirkmaugh's palm, and backed off. "My name," he said, "is Kevlyn." He extended a hand and cocked an eyebrow.

Kirkmaugh ignored the offered hand and got to his feet on his own. "Kevlyn what?" he asked. "And what is your business?"

"Just Kevlyn," replied the stranger. "A soldier, nothing more. And my business, M'lord Kirkmaugh, is finding you."

So, he already knew who he was dealing with. "Finding me?"

Kevlyn nodded. "I've been sent by Duncan Emery, M'lord, to barter for the services of the Dubh Aogail in Emery's stand against Cloyne Kildare."

Kirkmaugh suppressed a grin. It was turning out to be one hell of a day.

South of the city walls, half a dozen springs spill out from beneath Kiamina to trickle down out of the mountains and into Kilgari Woods. Out of a crevasse, from which one of these springs bubbled, crawled a caricature of a man late that evening. He was tall and would have been incredibly broad-shouldered if he wasn't hunched over broken bones and wounds which seeped and throbbed. He was covered in blood and ash. His clothes were in tatters. He was limping. Tucked under one arm was a rolled canvas.

Once outside, he blinked at the sunlight and cursed a raven in a nearby tree. The raven merely cocked its head, studying him. For several minutes the two stood staring at each other. Finally, the raven took to wing and vanished to the East. The man turned and walked in the opposite direction.

He hadn't gone very far at all when six horsemen came upon him. The lead rider leveled a crossbow and ordered him to stop. When the beaten man raised his eyes, he saw the colors of Cloyne Kildare, the usurper. He was too beat to put up a fight when they took the painting and bound his wrists.

They tried to run him behind the horses, but he was spent. They dragged him for a while, until it became obvious that he'd be dead before they made it out of the mountains, let alone all the way to Droichead Nua. Kildare hadn't given instructions to bring the man back alive, just to be sure and bring back what he brought out of the ruins, but the soldiers knew that with Kildare it was best not to take chances. There'd be plenty of time to kill the Ranger later. So two of the soldiers were designated to double up, and the prisoner was thrown over a mount.

He drifted in and out of consciousness as they skirted the western walls of the city and proceeded north. Sometimes he thought he was still trapped beneath Kiamina. Sometimes he thought he was dead and wondered why he should have to continue enduring so much pain. Once he asked his captors about the painting, but that only got him kicked in the head. Mostly he hung there in a stupor, lost in a world of agony and despair.

He lost track of time, but suspected he was awake for less and less of it as the ride went on. He wondered briefly whether a man could will himself to die. He thought about his heart just stopping, but it went on beating. After this little experiment, he happened to look up at the saddle of the horse. Regina was there, her leg casually thrown side-saddle over his shoulders, her long white dress trailing over the horse's withers and flank.

The ghost smiled down at him. "Just a little further," she said.

"The painting...?" he asked.

And someone kicked him again.

Sometime later, he was aroused as the horse bolted. It was dark and there was a lot of yelling. Steel rang on steel. A body hit the ground and was trampled beneath Campian's mount. Someone caught the mount's reins and tried to pull it into the dark trees beside the trail they were on, but a second later the man was spinning out of his saddle, blood bursting dark and wet from a gaping wound in his neck. Campian's mount reared, spilling him to the ground. He cried out as he came down on the broken arm. Then he curled into as small a shape as possible as horses' hooves thundered past.

There followed several minutes of horses stomping, swords clashing, and the cursing and dying of men. When it was over, someone dismounted beside him and turned him over. The young soldier was wearing a Ranger's cloak and a face masked with concern. Beyond the Ranger, mounted on a horse, his partial thigh situated in a custom stirrup, was Glengaerif Callin.

"Campian?"

The old man tried to smile. "That bad, eh?"

"Worse."

Several others dismounted, but Callin remained in the saddle, his face occasionally eclipsing the moon as his mount shifted. Someone cut Campian's hands free and began to wrap the broken arm against a short pine bough.

"There's a painting," Campian told them. "Find the painting."

"We have it," Callin assured him.

"Good." He closed his eyes for what he thought was just a minute, but when he awoke there was a small fire and blankets and a million stars overhead. Glengaerif Callin was sitting beside him.

"How are you holding up, old man?"

"I'll live. There was a painting..."

Callin set a hand on the Ranger's shoulder. "We have it, Campian."

"Have you looked at it?"

Callin nodded. "She won't believe it," he said.

"Doesn't matter," Campian replied. "Everyone else will."

"She won't go along with it."

Campian reached out with his good arm and slapped at Callin's stump. "None of us are finished, Callin. You being here proves that. She'll do her part."

"How can you be sure?"

"Because," Campian said softly, "you'll ask her."

DO THE WALLS COME DOWN?

(a Swords of Eire fantasy)

Helmet plumes streaming crimson behind him, the mercenary captain rode through the assembled army to where Ari Kirkmaugh sat his rough-hewn field chair. Seeing the open hills beyond the warlord, the horse fought the reins. Even the horses were tired of sitting outside Maddock's walls of impenetrable stone.

Captain Fenrey drew his mount to a halt before the man he'd sworn allegiance to as a boy, the man in whose service he would one day die. That passing would be a grim, red death with no one likely to notice his departure, but what else was there for him? War and death were all Fenrey knew. He had a home with the Dubh Aogail—the Black Death. Ari Kirkmaugh's raiders were a cruelly disciplined war machine controlled by the heaviest purse. The assorted cutthroats that comprised its ranks were his brethren. What did it matter that he feared Kirkmaugh more than any other man alive?

"Report," Kirkmaugh hissed ere the captain had even touched the ground. At the sound of the cold voice, rife with venom and contempt, the warhorse shied away. For a moment, Fenrey thought he would have to face the embarrassment of not being able to control his mount, but a sharp jerk on the bridle checked the animal's flight.

"M'lord,"—sharp slap of open hand against the hilt of the long sword at his hip; traditional salute over which Ari Kirkmaugh had killed forgetful men—"we've finished the siege towers. At first light we'll place them."

Kirkmaugh rose from his field chair, a frown screwing his face into what could only be described as a snarl. His eyes bored a hole into Fenrey, a sulphurating wound through which Fenrey felt Kirkmaugh could see his beating heart, and reaching in, could crush it if he felt the whim. "Captain," Kirkmaugh rasped, "tell me what you see over my shoulder."

Fenrey swallowed visibly, straining to keep the fear he felt from showing in his eyes—the only part of his face visible through the wye of his ebony helm.

The hill Kirkmaugh was referring to bore the same lone rider who'd been sitting there all day. Astride a tall, heavily-built horse, the mysterious watcher was presently silhouetted by the fast-setting sun. "He's still there," the captain answered.

"Pah!" Kirkmaugh spat. "Incompetent fool! Look beyond. Look at the sky. What do you see, Fenrey?"

Not *Captain Fenrey*, just *Fenrey*.

"Storms," he answered, trying to sound calm, confident. "They'll cross the plains quickly," he added, swallowing again. "Likely be here before dawn."

"Then move the damn towers while you can! By morning the ground will be so wet they'll sink in the mud where they stand."

Fenrey bowed his head so Kirkmaugh could not see the humiliation in his eyes. He was grateful for the helm that hid his reddening cheeks. "It will be done, M'lord."

"And the catapults?"

"They'll be finished by midday tomorrow."

"*Tonight*, Fenrey! Tomorrow you won't be able to move them!"

Kirkmaugh stepped forward, filling what little space had separated the two men. His next words were spoken softly and seemed to rasp like hardened steel across bone. "If they're not finished by first light, Fenrey, the crows will have your eyes for breakfast." Then he waved his hand in an exasperated gesture of dismissal and returned to his seat to brood.

But Fenrey didn't leave. "M'lord, what of the rider on the hill?"

"Forget him," Kirkmaugh answered without looking up.

"We've more important things to worry about. One man is certainly no threat to us."

Having grown weary of the saddle, Kevlyn dismounted. He took a seat on a boulder and chewed the last of the dried meat he'd begged from villagers to the north. The horse stayed near, war-trained to stay as long as its rider breathed; but more than that, it seemed content just to munch the moist, tender spring grasses on the hill.

The cube-shaped rock sat the hilltop like a lone sentry, last guardian of the retreating sun at his back. Dunn Meara it was called—Laughing Rock. Stories, all of them older than he, were told of the origin of the rock's name and how it had come to sit alone atop the hill overlooking Maddock Castle.

But the memories Dunn Meara brought to Kevlyn's mind were not of laughter and happiness. On this hill there'd been only tears, bitter accusations of betrayal, and that heart-wrenching farewell.

As the first raindrops began to hit the back of his neck, he drew his sword from where it hung down his back. Like the chain mail and leather trappings he wore, the sword was old, dirty, much used. Laying it across his knees, he idly ran his thumb along the dented edge and studied the scene spread out below him.

Maddock Castle was like a fresh-turned anthill, aswarm with Ari Kirkmaugh's butchers. Armor of black, trimmed and plumed in scarlet. Flowing capes darker than a moonless night with linings of blood red. Weapons forged of black iron. These were mercenaries with whom he was all too familiar.

As he watched, several hundred men worked to move three siege towers across the fields. Three towers to assault the three walls of the castle. Her fourth side was a natural barrier, the towering cliff face of Linn Gaul. Impregnable. Well … almost.

Kevlyn would be going in that way tonight.

He caught his head nodding, chin coming to rest against the battered mail across his chest. He'd dozed on and off in the saddle during the day's vigilance, but he was still days, weeks even, behind on his sleep.

On the southern slope bordering the fields—which had yet to be planted, such had been the timing of Kirkmaugh's siege—five catapults were being assembled to replace the seven Kirkmaugh had originally brought from his Silver Mountain stronghold. Those seven were nothing more than black ash now. The previous evening, Kyle Maddock's midnight raid had removed that problem.

But Kevlyn knew that Kyle's greatest problem still remained: food. How much did they have left in winter stores? How long till they were forced to negotiate terms of surrender with the mercenaries? And did they know Ari Kirkmaugh was not one to keep his word? Whatever terms Kirkmaugh allowed the Maddocks wouldn't amount to spit once the castle gates were open and his butchers were inside.

Kevlyn planned to be inside the castle before Kyle Maddock reached that impasse.

The sword on his lap was a symbol of power, of authority, of trust and honor. His father had given it to him years ago, just as he had done for brothers Kyle and Kyri. It was a symbol of family, of belonging.

But the blade looked old. And so did he.

Neither were all that old in years. It had been only eight years since he'd left the safe haven spread out below him. But in those years, it seemed he had aged a lifetime.

The siege towers would soon be in place. The rain was moving in slowly—no hope yet that the fields would turn to mud and prevent the Kirkmaughs getting them in place.

Still, the towers were a minor problem that Kyle would know how to handle, just as he had the catapults. Towers could be dowsed in oil and set afire, all the easier since, unlike catapults, they were within reach from the walls.

Inside the castle, they might not be aware of how hopeless their situation really was. They might not have heard of Emery's defeat in Kiamina Pass. When the spring monsoons passed, Cloyne Kildare would proceed south, conquering everything in his path, including Maddock Castle. The only chance the Southern Lords had of staying alive was to unite and confront Kildare. And they were not about to stop fighting each other.

The scene below was proof enough of that.

Only Emery had been willing to abandon all and meet the Kildares in the north. If he'd been able to reach King Duncannon at Kilcullen Fields, the two might have defeated Kildare. But Duncannon fell before Emery could get there. Subsequently, Emery was caught in Kiamina Pass and destroyed without ever setting foot on Kilcullen's golden grasses. Only a few men had escaped to warn the south. Each survivor had scattered for home.

And where was I to go? Kevlyn asked himself.

Unbidden, he remembered holding Holly, here on Dunn Meara, when last he had seen her, eight years ago. From about his neck, he had pulled a chain, his only personal possession aside from the sword his father had given him. The delicate silver chain held a small ruby jewel, shot through with fine tracings of gold. The gem was a natural pendant, hourglass shaped with a near-perfect hole in one end.

Bloodstone. The rock of life. Finding a shard of the gem at all meant good luck. Finding a piece formed as a pendant by nature should have guaranteed him harmony the rest of his days.

It hadn't.

He hoped it had brought her better luck, but looking down on the siege forces massed about Maddock Castle, he knew it wasn't so.

"Take this," he'd told her. "If ever you need me, send it. No matter where I am, or what I'm doing, no matter what has passed between us, I will come."

"Don't do this, Kev," she'd cried.

"There's nothing here for me. Da and Kyle blame me for Kyri's death. I've got to leave."

She never sent it, he told himself.

Though Ari Kirkmaugh's Black Death had been paid to lay siege to Maddock Castle—the same Kirkmaughs who'd left Droichead Nua, Duncannon's stronghold, as well as a score of northern villages, in fiery ruin—she never sent for him.

Though over the years, throughout the uncountable wars, the stench of death on him had gotten so bad he'd prayed with all his might for her message just to have a reason to leave the bloodshed and return...

Though his heart had ached for her and he'd hated himself all those years for the weakness that drove him to leave...

She never sent it.

"What now?" he had asked himself after Emery's fall at Kiamina.

Home, the sword, his only link with the past, had bidden.

So here he was. Home. Only to find a thousand enemies between him and the castle gates. And once inside—for he had no doubt that he could get *in* the castle—death would have him surrounded.

He'd eluded that grim lady far too many times already.

The rain began to come down in large, cold drops. In the distance, the darkening sky flickered alight with fierce flashes of sheet lightning, as yet too distant to be heard.

Fate had brought him here. Just as fate had maneuvered Ari Kirkmaugh. Old debts unsettled between them.

Fate had also contrived to bring them all together at this specific time. It was the heavy spring rains that would get Kevlyn in the castle.

Like the nexus of his life, Maddock Castle beckoned.

When Kevlyn reached a point in the hills where the horse could go no further, he removed its saddle and gear, and set it free. As he watched the roan gelding disappear into the darkness, he realized there were other things he no longer needed. As lightning flashed and the heavy rain pelted him, he removed all but his sword and his soft leather under-tunic. He tore the sword's sheath from its belt and discarded the wide band of leather. Carrying the sheathed weapon in his hand, he started the last leg of the ascent to the catchbasin above Maddock Castle, leaving a pile of armor and battle-trappings behind him in the rain.

He wished he could shed the reality, the stigmata, of war as easily as he had shed its accouterments. He knew it was impossible; the sword he refused to leave behind was proof enough of that.

The natural chimney was smaller than he remembered it, but then he had been sixteen when he was here last. He had once traversed the vertical chasm easily by bracing feet and back against the opposing walls of marble; it would not be so easy now.

He was forced to toss his weapon up ahead of him, wincing as the scarred scabbard and sword clattered on the rocks above. Then, bracing back, knees, and elbows against the sides of the shaft, he made his way painfully to the top.

Fifteen minutes later, Kevlyn stood in the wind and rain on a plateau above the chimney. The rain washed the blood from his knees and elbows, soothing the bruised and torn flesh, but it was bitter cold. Shivering, he collected his sword and continued on.

He crossed the plateau and found the gully he was looking for. Six feet deep, it ran across the plateau and then down through a narrow passage of towering monoliths, carrying with it a steady stream of water. Kevlyn slid down the side and stood in the knee-deep flow. Following the frigid stream to where it plunged down between the towers of stone, he met a sight that caught his breath just as it had always done.

The stream plunged straight down, a sixty-foot drop, into the Catch. A hundred feet across and immeasurably deep, the catchbasin was Maddock Castle's power. When holdings to the south rationed water during the long dry months of summer, when their crops perished for want of water, when their children cried hoarsely through the long hot nights, Maddock Castle had water to waste.

The deep pool was fed by nine different streams carrying water down from the mountains, some natural, but many guided to the basin by Maddocks far older than Kevlyn, or even his father, Thorin. Decades had been spent shaping the waterways that flowed down from the mountains, shaping them so they contributed to the Catch, contributed to Maddock power.

A natural aqueduct—dry now, but within the hour the downpour of rain would raise the water level—channeled the water from the Catch down through massive Linn Gaul and into the castle where it emptied into a man-made tank. The aqueduct remained dry most of the year, conducting water to the castle only during the early spring runoffs and monsoons. But the water provided during those wet periods was enough to last Maddock Castle throughout the rest of the year.

Do it, Kyri! Dive! What are you afraid of?

The boy's words, high-pitched and taunting, leaped unsummoned from deep-seated memories in Kevlyn's mind. Like dropped crystal, they echoed sharply about the basin. His memories were suddenly a well, tapped surreptitiously while his guard was down, now spewing forth like a geyser.

Across the deep pool, perched on the edge of a cascading waterfall, Kevlyn imagined he saw a small boy, eight years old, naked, shivering with cold or fear. Or both.

I've done it a hundred times, little brother. Don't be such a coward!

Kevlyn shook his head, dispelling the unwanted memory, clearing his head of the haunting voices. How many times had he remembered that day? How many times since that day had he played it over in his mind and begged his younger brother to ignore his taunts and go home without diving into the catchbasin?

But Kyri *had* dived. Atop the waterfall, a sixteen-year-old Kevlyn had stood and applauded him, triumphant in getting his brother to overcome his fear. But the applause and the triumph had quickly faded when Kyri did not return to the surface. Kevlyn had plunged into the water after him, had dove again and again beneath the surface looking for him until he was so tired, he had to rest in the aqueduct lest he drown as well.

He remembered the long walk down the aqueduct to find his father.

Father. Kyri ... your favorite ... is dead.

It was my fault.

They never found the body. Somewhere, at the bottom of the abyss they called the Catch, Kevlyn could picture him: waxy white skin stretched taut like the inflated pig's bladder they'd played with as boys, eyes that had lost their iridescent hue, blue lips drawn back from a mouth gaping like some suppurating wound, face frozen in a rictus of pain as water had filled his lungs ... and an accusing finger.

All your fault, Kev.

Dawn was just beginning to turn the eastern horizon from black to grey when Kevlyn crawled out the castle-end of the aqueduct. He swam the tank to the far side where a stone stairway circled up to the tank's rim ten feet above the aqueduct opening.

Atop the tank, he stood for a moment, cold, wet, and bone-tired. He was in the castle now.

Home.

Taking an identical stairway down the outside of the tank, he reached a courtyard. Without hesitation, he opened a nearby door and started down a corridor he could have navigated in the dark. There was no need though; the corridor was well lit with evenly-spaced oil lamps.

Her door was unlocked. He stood for several minutes with his hand on the doorhandle, sword set aside so he could hold a borrowed oil lamp in the other hand. What would she think, awakening to find him, filthy and wet, standing over her bed?

With a last glance up and down the quiet, empty corridor, he pushed open the door, stepped through, pulled the sword in after him, and closed the door softly behind him.

"Holly?" he asked, voice trembling.

Silence greeted him. Holding the lamp aloft, he saw the room was empty. Her things were gone.

She was gone.

Of course. What possible reason had he given her for staying?

He crossed the room to the bed, stripped of covers, but still equipped with the mattress on which she had slept. Laying the lamp on the bedstand, he curled up on the bed, feeling more alone and lost than ever.

The mattress was old and musty, but it was the softest thing he'd slept on since leaving his own bed here in the castle. Shivering, he slept.

He was awakened by his stomach's painful demands for food. Stiff and sore, he got unsteadily to his feet. From the heavy drumming of rain on the roof and the rumble of thunder across the fields, he could tell the spring storm had not abated during his sleep, even though it must now be at least noon.

The lamp he'd brought in earlier had gone out, throwing most of the room in shadow. In those shadows, he imagined he saw his family waiting to pounce. Even Mother, dead of a plague when he was only ten, was there. He shook his head, wondering just how far gone he was on the road to madness.

He stumbled to the door, legs not quite awake yet, the right one aching where a lance had pegged him to the ground four years ago. It wasn't the only old wound bothering him, but it was certainly the most painful.

Without thinking to check the hall, he grabbed the door handle and swung it open. An old man in the corridor spun around and uttered a startled shriek as if he expected Kirkmaugh himself to be sneaking about in the castle. Water from the bucket he carried sloshed out on the cold stones of the floor.

It took a moment before the old man's eyes focused on the bedraggled intruder. Even then, he had to look twice.

"Master Kevlyn?"

The smile that split Kevlyn's face was genuine. If there was one face other than Holly's that could have made him feel at home, it was this old man's. Cook, physician, and storyteller, Hap Tulone was as integral to Maddock Castle as the very stone itself.

"It's me, Hap."

The old man stepped closer, touching Kevlyn's shoulder as if he needed proof. "After Kiamina Pass ... we thought you dead, lad."

"Most are."

Hap looked him over. "Not too far from it though, eh? I'm on my way to the kitchen. Come with me and I'll fix you something before I take food up to the walls."

More than anything, Kevlyn wanted to sit again in that warm kitchen, safest place he'd ever known, with Hap's food and tales. "Thanks, but first I want to see my father. With the siege going on, I'm not sure where to find him."

The sad look that crossed Hap's face made Kevlyn think

at first that his father was dead. "Guess you wouldn't know, having been gone all these years," he explained. "Your father's not doing too well. He took ill four years ago and hasn't been up much since. Bedridden, mostly blind, he rarely even remembers who I am. Most of the time he's not in his right mind. Spends a lot of time talking as if your mother were there."

"Take me to him."

"Same room as always. Forgotten the way? I've got to get food up to the men on the walls. They've been fighting off those towers all morning." The old man smiled and touched Kevlyn again as if still in disbelief and requiring the simple contact to dispel his last doubts. "When you're through, there'll be food on the stove, lad."

"There always was, Hap."

Halfway to his father's rooms, Kevlyn heard and felt the first impact on the walls. Ari had gotten his new catapults in place. The shock of boulders battering at the heavy walls of Maddock Castle was disconcerting enough, but Kevlyn knew that was only part of their intended use. Outside they'd already be raining death on the courtyards. As a psychological weapon, demoralizing the besieged with rocks, hot oil, burning faggots, and other missiles dropped from above, they were far more effective.

It would be night before Kyle could venture out to destroy those catapults. That meant a long exhausting day trying to pay attention to the battle while watching the sky. And when Kyle finally did get out to attack the catapults, the Kirkmaughs would not be so easily taken a second time.

Only the face, though somehow older than he remembered or even imagined it would be, told Kevlyn that the emaciated form on the bed was his father. The heavy blankets did little to hide the wasted condition of the man who slept beneath them.

For several minutes, he just stood there listening to his father's ragged breathing, remembering a much more powerful man, one who could have met Ari Kirkmaugh in the field and come away, if not the victor, at least no worse than he'd left his enemy.

Moved by unforgotten feelings of love and respect for the old man, Kevlyn reached out and tentatively touched his hand where it lay across the sunken chest. Awakened by the touch, Thorin Maddock's eyes opened. Though he'd been prepared for it, Kevlyn shuddered to see the sightless eyes, milky white and devoid of all the fire and fury he had long associated with his father.

"Who's there?" Thorin asked. No fear, just an exhausted sort of curiosity.

"It's me, Da."

"Kyle? Why aren't you at the walls?"

So the old man knew of the siege. Perhaps Hap had exaggerated his senility.

"It's not Kyle. It's—"

"Kyri?" There were suddenly tears in those dead orbs. "My God, son, I'd almost given you up for dead. Where have you been?"

"Da, it's Kev. I—"

"Sit, Kyri. Talk to me boy; you've been gone so long."

"I'm not—"

"Hold my hand, son. Your brother will be so happy to see you!"

Not knowing what else to do, Kevlyn took the weathered hand in his own and squeezed it gently. The old man returned the squeeze, closest thing to affection Kevlyn had experienced since he had left home.

Behind him, Kevlyn heard the door open. When he pulled his gaze away from his father's face, he found Kyle standing in the doorway.

"Hello, Brother," Kevlyn greeted him softly, flatly, testing the air between them.

Father tried to sit up in bed, his face all aglow. "Kyle, come see who's home. It's Kyri, son! I told you he'd come home when he heard of the trouble."

"Get away from him," Kyle ordered, hand on his sword, twin to the one Kevlyn had left leaning just inside the door. There was still hatred in his voice. Time had not softened the barrier between them. He was soaking wet and his armor was streaked with rain-diluted blood, some of it his own. His right side bore a ragged tear in the armor, deep enough to have reached flesh, maybe even bone.

"Come see, Kyle!"

"Da, it's not Kyri," the elder son answered. "It's Kevlyn."

"Kevlyn's dead," Father replied, his voice like ice. "Get away from him."

Kevlyn released his father's hand and moved away from the bed. "I've come home, Kyle. Don't begrudge me that."

"It ceased to be your home the day you left."

"You mean the day you ran me out."

"Kevlyn's dead," the old man repeated like some prophesy of doom.

"I want you out of here."

Kevlyn made for the door, stepping around his unmoving older brother. "I'm leaving."

"I wasn't talking about this room; I mean out of the castle."

"You'd send me out to my death?" So long as the storms continued, there was no way back up the aqueduct. The only way out was through the castle gates.

"This evening you can steal away in the dark," Kyle answered. "Same as you did eight years ago."

Pausing in the doorway, Kevlyn picked up his sword and waited, wondering how deep his brother's hatred ran. "I could use a meal and a few supplies. Provided you can spare it, Brother."

"You know where the kitchen is. Hap can feed you and fix you up with what provisions you'll need. By dark I want you gone. And stay out of my way till then."

Kevlyn nodded his head as if acknowledging a great boon. Truth was, he'd have gotten the supplies with or without his brother's leave. "One other thing," Kevlyn asked, hoping to gain at least something of value from the chance encounter with his brother. "Where can I find Holly?"

Kyle looked away. "Let it go, Kev." His voice had suddenly softening as if he really cared about the man he was sending out of his home.

"I can't. I—" But Kyle slammed the door in his face, leaving

him standing outside the heavy door, shaking with emotions
he'd long ago forgotten how to deal with.

Though the kitchen was empty, Kevlyn found food and warmth,
just as Hap had promised. He took roasted beef and fresh bread
from the hearth and went out to sit at one of the long, scarred
tables in the great hall. In better times, it was here the Maddock
clan took their meals. From Maddock and his sons, to the lowest
servant, everyone held an equal place at table.

Well, that was *almost* true. When Da sat down to eat, Kyle
and Kyri had always taken the seats to either side of him.
Kyle's right to be close and privy to all the information that
ran through Thorin Maddock. For it was Kyle, eldest son, who
would one day assume Thorin's place. That day had obviously
come during Kevlyn's long absence. And Kyri, youngest son,
always reminding Thorin of his dead wife, his right to also be
close because it was he that Thorin loved most.

Despite those uncomfortable memories, the kitchen, more
than any other place in the castle, made him feel at home. *I've
really come back*, he acknowledged, but wondered what that
meant. Holly was gone. Where, he couldn't even get his own
brother to tell him. There was nothing left for him here.

But had there ever been?

Kyle had always had Da's attention when it came to making
sure someone could take over the land. Kyri had always had
Da's affection.

All Kevlyn had ever had was Holly. In that, if nothing else,
he had won out over his brothers.

It was here, as a child, that he'd first met Holly. She was the
daughter of a traveling merchant, one of those that owned no
property save what would fit in his wagons as he traveled from
holding to holding selling his wares. Her father had come to sell
wines. His trip took him north where he met his death at the
hands of common thieves. Holly, along with what servants and
bodyguards escaped, with nowhere else to go, had come to beg
shelter of Maddock Castle, simply because it was the last place
they had stopped and thus the closest.

Fate. Again.

"Kev?"

Please, he begged his hallucinating mind. *No more. Enough ghosts. Enough memories.*

But the shadow that fell across the long table came from no ghost. Nor the smells in the warm kitchen air: the tactile essence of sunshine on golden tresses and clean, soft skin.

Heart lodged in his throat, he turned ever so slowly, certain that there'd be no one behind him. Equally certain that when he found the room empty, his mind would snap, like the string of a bow drawn too tight.

The rain had stopped and the sun was fighting its way through the dense cloud cover outside. Thus, when he found Holly standing nervously near the hall's southern entrance, she was framed in a bright splash of sunlight piercing in through the large windows. Her hair was golden fire, awash in the sun's rays. Her eyes, an eerie emerald, made him think of seas he had seen in his travels. Before leaving Maddock Castle, he had never quite found an adequate comparison. Her pastel gown matched her eyes, set off by pale yellow slippers.

To his embarrassment, he found that he couldn't make a sound. His face, he knew, must look ridiculous: mouth open, eyes fighting between tears and wide-eyed amazement, and a hot red flush spreading across neck and cheeks.

She smiled, but it was not the same carefree smile he remembered. Not the smile she'd given him as young lovers when they'd spent the long hot summers chasing each other across the downs and then resting, out of breath, in each other's arms beneath a shade tree. The fields had been theirs, shared only with the wild horses they occasionally saw there. Faking ignorance to the violence that abounded in their world and the safety they could only have in Maddock Castle, he'd promised her he'd one day build her a home amid the tall grass in Linn Gaul's shadow.

Her smile said she was glad to see him, but nothing was the same. She'd changed, grown in more ways than he would ever ascertain; she was no longer the wild young woman he'd played at love with.

And the smile that he returned, though he tried his best,

probably conveyed some of the changes in him. The bloodshed. The pain. The years he'd spent fighting for hopeless causes and just one more day of life.

"I thought you were dead," she finally said, doing what he could not and breaking the heavy silence between them.

He looked away, fighting for words to convey what he felt inside. He was in turmoil, wanting to hold her, yet terrified she'd reject him. And maybe, just maybe, there was a small part of him that was terrified that she wouldn't.

He suddenly realized how filthy he was. His trip through the aqueduct had left him clean, but the layered dust on her bed had left his skin ashen. Looking at her fine gown of pale green silk, he knew that even if he had the courage to do so, he couldn't hold her. On her gown, his filth would sit like all the blood he'd shed since last they held each other at Dunn Meara.

At the far end of the hall, there was a shallow trough of water meant for washing. He rose and went to it, still searching for the words to tell her why he had come home.

"Duncan Emery and most of his followers fell at Kiamina Pass. We failed, Holly. Cloyne Kildare waits only for the rains to pass before he marches south." With his back to her, he pulled his shirt off over his head.

"But you escaped."

He tried to believe that she didn't mean it to sound like an accusation. "There were others." He cursed himself for the direction their conversation had taken. Emery's demise was not what he wanted to talk to her about. Nor did he want to tell her that Maddock Castle was doomed even if it did somehow survive Kirkmaugh's siege.

Her footsteps echoed softly as she crossed the room to stand behind him. "Why, Kev?"

"Why?" he asked, knowing full well what she meant. Knowing, as well, that she had brought the conversation back on course. With a wet sponge he began to clean the dirt and sweat from his body.

"Why come home now? After all these years?" There was anger in her voice.

He stared at the cold, grey stone wall in front of him,

remembering how, as children, they'd always hated being kept inside. "Still visiting the downs, Holly?"

"There's no one to go with. I haven't even been outside the castle in years."

He reached out and traced the lines in the stone with his fingertips, thinking of her trapped within the castle, a prison as surely as his own self-imposed exile had been. He remembered how they'd talked of living without unfeeling stone between them and the world, how they'd laughed and said they would bring the walls down.

He let out a long sigh. "Do the walls come down when you think of me?"

She reached out, took hold of one shoulder, and spun him around.

And saw the scars.

A look of horror on her face, she carefully touched the worst of them where it ran from his left shoulder across his chest.

"You can't live by the sword without it leaving its mark on you," he told her.

She looked up, tears building in her green eyes. "So much pain," she whispered, the tears starting down her cheeks.

Dropping the sponge, he held her close.

"I've come back for you, Holly. I know nothing stays the same, but—"

"Kev," she pulled away.

"It can work."

"We can't even get out of the castle!"

"I can get you out."

"How?"

His eyes betrayed him as his gaze darted to where his sword lay on the long table. There was, after all, only one way out of the castle now.

"No," she said, having no idea what he really intended, but sensing it could mean his death. "What we had is gone, Kev."

Refusing to believe her, he pulled her close again. And for the first time noticed the fine silver chain about her neck.

"It was over the day you left, Kev. I don't love you anymore."

"I don't believe you," he said. His eyes followed the twin

halves of the chain to where they met between her breasts. There, like blood against the pale beauty of her cleavage, lay the gem he'd given her long ago. She thought it hidden, and it would have been were it not for the way he held her.

There was a sound at the door and she pulled away.

Kyle Maddock stood in the doorway, his blade nearly drawn, his face red, and his eyes ablaze. "Holly, get out of here."

There was an easy, comfortable air to the way he ordered her. Things finally clicked in Kevlyn's mind. The way Kyle had seemed almost sad when he had said to forget about Holly. The way Kevlyn had found Holly's room empty. It all fell into place.

Holly started for the door, but Kevlyn caught her arm. "The girl I knew took orders only from her heart."

From across the room came a soft rasp as Kyle drew his weapon.

Holly raised her gaze to meet Kevlyn's stare.

"Do you love him?" he asked, releasing her arm.

She swallowed, caught in a situation where truth or falsehood would hurt. Then, ever so softly: "Yes."

But she loves me as well, Kevlyn thought. *Else why wear the bloodstone all these years? I could ask her that. I could.* He looked across the room at his brother.

But I won't.

Perhaps she saw all that transpire in his eyes. Perhaps she was simply listening to what her husband had told her. Or maybe she just realized that this scene had been played to completion. Kevlyn would never know. She turned and left the hall.

But just before she crossed the threshold and left his life forever, he fancied he saw her reach to her bosom where hung the ruby pendant. For just a moment, he thought he saw her fondle his gift.

Then she was gone.

"Too far, Kev."

Kevlyn shrugged into his shirt, only marginally cleaner than he had been a few minutes ago. He crossed the room and picked up his own sword from where it lay on the table.

Nervous, Kyle raised the point of his blade. "By nightfall," he said softly. "I want you gone by nightfall."

Kevlyn drew his blade, admiring how the fine sunlight played across its battle-polished surface. A Maddock blade, forged here in this castle of ore taken from the surrounding mountains. As battle-scarred as he himself. A weapon born to defend those he loved, to serve the lord of Maddock Castle. Yet in all its years, it had only served other lords in faraway lands, in battles that mattered little to those here at home.

Home.

He turned and crossed the room in long, sure strides, causing Kyle to come on guard. Stopping in front of his older brother, Kevlyn knelt and placed his naked blade lengthwise at Kyle's feet.

"I pledge my weapon and my life to your service, Kyle Maddock. Ask, and I will lay down my life for you and your hold. Your orders alone will I follow. In honor, let me serve you."

Kyle stepped back from the offered blade, surprise and anger written across his face. "As well as you served your last master at Kiamina Pass, Kevlyn?" Then he turned and was gone down the corridor.

The lull in the rain and the sun's appearance lasted briefly— perhaps fifteen minutes. But in that short span of time, Kyle's men managed to set one of the three siege towers afire by soaking it in oil. Crackling madly, the damp wood burned where it rested against the wall. The raging flames blackened the surrounding stone, but otherwise did little damage to the castle. The heat was enough to drive back any attempt the Kirkmaughs might have wanted to make to save the tower.

From a high rampart, shivering in the wind now that the sun had gone back behind the clouds, Kevlyn watched the tower burn. It seemed to him that the flames knew only hunger, an overwhelming desire to consume, caring not at all for war or the principles of its combatants. There were times when he had been like that fire. Hell, he had even fought for Ari Kirkmaugh for a time.

Below, in the fields of mud surrounding the castle, Kirkmaugh pulled most of his forces back for an evening respite, leaving only enough men to defend the two remaining towers.

On the walls, the Maddocks took the opportunity to rest, tend their wounded, and gather up their dead. For the time being, they simply watched the remaining towers. Sentries posted on the walls watched for the mercenaries to return.

Only the catapults remained active, battering the walls and raining death in the courtyards of the castle. If not for their sporadic noise and the distant rumblings of thunder, all would have been silent.

As silent as Kiamina Pass after the Kildares had finished off Emery's wounded.

Kevlyn remembered it vividly. With a handful of survivors, he had watched as Cloyne Kildare's pikemen had stalked through the gore of the battlefield, seeking out the wounded, both theirs and the enemy. For their own, there was the stretcher and medical treatment. For the enemy, there was only the quick, merciless thrust of the lance or misericord.

Gripping Kevlyn's arm, strong as a vise, another soldier had held him fast lest he give away their position. "We can only die with them if we go down there."

"I can't stand here and watch them die," Kevlyn had protested.

"It's over, lad. All we can do is try to warn the south."

"But—"

"Go home, Kevlyn Maddock."

And how had he come to be away during that final battle in the pass? Not through any disloyalty or cowardice as Kyle had insinuated. He would have died with the others, serving Duncan Emery—had he only been there. But Duncan had sent a handful of men scouting in each direction. "Why?" they'd asked, for everyone knew where the enemy was: advancing up through the northern side of the pass. "I don't want to be caught by surprise. It'd be like Kildare to send men through the mountains and catch us in a pincer movement."

So they'd gone out, though none of those sent believed Emery's reasoning. Before he'd left, Kevlyn had gone to Duncan. He'd wanted to ask, but Duncan had stopped him with a smile and: "You've never questioned or failed to follow my orders, Kev. Don't start now."

And he had shaken Duncan Emery's hand for the last time.

And gone, only to return later and find the carnage in the pass and all their hopes of holding off Cloyne Kildare seeping into the rocks and sand with the blood of Emery's army.

You see, dear brother, I served my master to the end. For whatever reason, he wanted some of us to survive. My only sin is being one of those he chose.

The rain began to come down again, just a slow drizzle for now, but certain to pick up.

And you, Ari Kirkmaugh. Where were you that day in Kiamina Pass? When the Kildares charged and you stood amidst our ranks, paid with Emery's money, what happened?

He began to shiver in the cold rain. Despite having only wet wood, the mercenaries were building fires for the night. Though two or three hours remained before sunset, it was already almost dark. Their fires bit at the gathering gloom, belching white smoke into the air, for all the world looking like the carrion pyres that day in the pass.

What happened, Ari? All I know is when I watched from above, your men were among the living, while all of Emery's were dead.

Old debts unsettled between them.

A bloodstone kept, worn, but never sent.

The ties of family and blood, no matter how frayed or broken.

A promise: *If ever you need me…*

He rose and went back inside the castle. There were three things he had to find.

The Maddock sentries spotted him on the battlements, a rain-soaked man in tattered leather shirt and breeches, burdened with two sacks like one might use to carry potatoes or corn meal, a length of heavy rope, and a sword. One sack appeared to be significantly heavier than the other, for the man struggled with it slung over his shoulder.

Before the sentries could stop him, the stranger had tied sword and sacks to one end of the rope and lowered it down the wall. The outside wall.

With leveled crossbows, they surrounded him, expecting some sort of mercenary trick. Ignoring them, he made the topside end of his rope fast to a metal ring set in the stone buttress.

Rope secured as if he intended to climb down among the Kirkmaughs—whose attention he had succeeded in capturing—he turned to the sentries. "I am Kevlyn Maddock. Fetch my brother, Kyle, if you doubt me, but don't interfere."

Then he took up the rope and began to scale down the outside of the castle wall. In the fields below, a mercenary ran to find Ari Kirkmaugh.

"What do we do?" one guard asked.

"I recognize him," another answered. "He *is* Kevlyn Maddock."

"Even so, I think we should get Kyle."

Already alerted to the activity on the wall, Kyle arrived a moment later, in time to see Kevlyn reach the halfway point in his descent. "Fool!" he called down.

Kevlyn looked up and smiled. "You told me to leave."

"I said to slip away in the dark. This is suicide!"

"What do you care?"

"Argh! Get back up here. Now!"

Below, Kirkmaugh archers were taking aim.

"If I start back up, they'll surely shoot me, Kyle."

Kyle cursed. "Climb up now; they're poor shots." It was common knowledge that Ari's butchers rarely used any weapon other than the sword.

"No."

Kyle drew his sword. "Climb up or I'll cut this damn rope!"

Ignoring him, Kevlyn continued his descent.

Kyle sheathed his weapon, realizing the futility of the situation. As if Mother Nature were acknowledging that something was about to happen, the rain ceased all together.

"Captain Fenrey, hold your archers." It was Ari Kirkmaugh himself, drawn away from his meal to investigate the commotion. Straining his eyes in the fast-gathering twilight, Kirkmaugh studied the man who was slowly making his way down the wall.

Only those closest to the legendary butcher saw the smile that spread across his face. "Let him approach."

Kevlyn reached the ground, gathered up sword and sacks,

and walked through the mud to a clear spot not ten yards from the archers and their leader. On the field and on the castle battlements, audiences were gathering. The evening air was full of whispers: rumors that sprang from the minds of the more imaginative, questions from those who would admit they didn't understand what was going on, and warnings from the wary.

It's some kind of trick, was the predominant opinion of both sides.

As Kevlyn set sword and sacks at his feet, he heard the heavy rope drop to the ground at the foot of the wall behind him. Kyle's concern had been genuine—but limited. He'd cut the rope once there was no chance of Kevlyn returning up it.

Ari greeted him with a smile. "Missed you in the pass."

"Some of us were scouting the hills," Kevlyn answered blackly. "We had no way of knowing the ambush would come from within."

Ari shrugged his massive shoulders. "We're a weapon. Bought and paid for, nothing more."

"Emery bought and paid for you."

"I got a better offer."

Kevlyn turned his back to the mercenary chieftain and knelt to open the lighter of the two sacks.

"You're no different, Kevlyn. How much are they paying you here? From the looks of those rags, it can't be as much as I paid you that year you rode with us."

Kevlyn rose, holding the open sack in his left hand. "I'm *nothing* like you."

"Hah! You rode with us, fought at my side. I thought you were a friend—"

"Almost seemed I was ... until Kiamina Pass."

"You're one of the few outsiders I've ever allowed. You know how we operate. Young boys are stolen and raised to be one of us." A pause then, while the mercenary considered what value there was in honesty. "I liked you."

"I only joined because Duncan ordered me to," Kevlyn confessed. "He knew he needed help and he thought I could get close to you. Thought I could ensure your support." With his right hand, Kevlyn reached into the sack, pulled out a handful of stone-ground flour and began to trace a large circle of white in the mud. "I told him you were good for the battle so long as you were paid in advance. Well paid. You betrayed us, Ari."

Kirkmaugh's eyes were following the development of the white circle. "Whatever they're paying you, Kevlyn, it's not worth this."

"They're *not* paying me."

"What then?"

Kevlyn ignored him until the ring, a twenty-foot diameter circle of white, was complete. Then he tossed aside what remained of the flour and picked up his sword. Standing in the ring, he drew the blade and flung away the scabbard.

"My full name is Kevlyn Maddock. You betrayed me and my lord, Duncan Emery, to our enemy, Cloyne Kildare. You were pivotal in bringing about our defeat in Kiamina Pass. You have laid siege to and assaulted my home. According to the laws you set when you established this mercenary clan, I challenge you for its leadership."

Kirkmaugh laughed. "What makes you think I won't order these archers to cut you down right now? Only a member has the right to challenge—"

"You've already admitted to my being one of you. Challenge has been issued, Ari. The circle is drawn."

"You're a fool, Kevlyn," Ari hissed. He turned to Fenrey. "Have my things brought out. Bring torches so we can see. And get him whatever he needs; he's not even armored."

"There's nothing further I need," Kevlyn told Fenrey.

Across the muddy fields and atop the castle walls, more men gathered to watch as word of the confrontation was spread throughout both armies. In the white circle, clenching his sword in ropeburned hands, Kevlyn waited patiently for servants to bring Ari Kirkmaugh's armor and weapons. It took only a minute for them to return; and, with their help, it took but another minute for him to don his ebony breastplate. He ignored the rest of his armor and even pushed aside his red plumed helm when they tried to sit it on his head. He did, however, take up a small oval shield of iron for his left arm. The weapon he chose was a long, two-handed broadsword, unmarked and finely tempered, antithesis to Kevlyn's tarnished and battered family blade.

"You know the rules?" Kirkmaugh asked as he stepped into the circle.

There had only ever been one. "Step out while your opponent is still breathing and you're dead."

The mercenary nodded. "My archers will see to it."

Sloshing through the ankle-deep mud, the two men came together at the circle's center. Naked steel flickered in the torchlight, bright shimmering from the mercenary blade, dull glow from the Maddock family weapon. There followed the crisp, clear ring of steel on steel, a song already over a thousand years old, signaling bloodshed and death. In the dancing light cast by the windblown torches, the fast-moving swords left gossamer silver trails etched in the retina of the spectators, like the wet strands of a spider's web against the morning sun.

For several long minutes, the two men tested each other, neither getting fancy, neither taking chances, just feeling each other out, ascertaining the other's capabilities and limitations, determining where an opening might exist, what quirks of the opponent might be used against him.

It took Kirkmaugh only those few minutes to determine that Kevlyn favored his right leg. His balance, when leading to that side was poor; he was off his center, often overextending. When Ari was satisfied that it was no ploy, he made his move, allowing Kevlyn's blade to slip by—actually urging it on by sweeping his own sword along its length. As Kevlyn's blade passed, overextended, Ari slammed the small shield into his opponent's shoulder, driving him forward into the mud.

Kevlyn hit with a splash, his blade nearly wrenched free as it plowed into the soft earth. He was thinking *roll!*, knowing that Kirkmaugh wasted no advantage, when he felt the sharp bite in his side and knew he'd been hit. Ignoring the pain, he rolled, hearing heavy splashing as Ari pursued him across the circle.

To continue the roll would mean his death so long as Ari was on his feet. Kevlyn reversed, sweeping out with his sword in the hope that he might catch Ari in the legs. He didn't cut him, but he succeeded in tangling himself up with the mercenary warlord and dragging him into the mud with him.

Both men scrambled to their feet at the same time, dripping thick mud, searching for the opponent. Kevlyn felt warmth amid the pain in his right side: blood. He didn't have time to check the severity of the wound; Ari came after him.

Thrust. Parry. Slash. Thrust. Riposte. They danced a waltz of death, blades seeking flesh and blood.

With the shield, Ari had a definite advantage. Within the next two minutes, Kevlyn was also bleeding from the right forearm and left thigh. He stumbled backward from a barrage of deadly swordstrokes and tried to pull himself together.

Think! He spots my weaknesses, uses them to his advantage.

Kevlyn stumbled forward, off center again with the bad right leg extended.

Ari smiled behind the mud on his face. His eyes, seemingly as dark as the armor he wore, gleamed like black onyx in the torchlight. He slipped to Kevlyn's side as the Maddock warrior stumbled forward, swept his blade out and up, intending to bring it down in a devastating blow that would end the duel, when he suddenly felt a searing bite of pain as the point of Kevlyn's blade slid neatly through his calf and into the mud. Kirkmaugh howled.

Fully aware of his opponent's blade arcing overhead, Kevlyn turned his stumble into a lunge. He dived into the mud, ripping his sword from Ari's leg—doing more damage than it had on entry—and rolled clear of the bellowing mercenary.

Virtually hamstrung, Ari went down on one knee. Blood pumped from his right leg, spotting the dark mud with vivid scarlet.

Kevlyn got to his feet, his own blood flowing from side, forearm, and thigh. Without hesitation, he went after his wounded opponent.

Kirkmaugh blocked Kevlyn's first stroke, but the second slammed across the armor on his shoulder, numbing his right arm. Kevlyn's third sword stroke took the sword from Kirkmaugh's hands and sent it skidding through the mud. The weapon came to a halt, nearly concealed in the mud, half in and half out of the white circle. Kevlyn drew back for a blow that would take Kirkmaugh's head from his shoulders.

Ari dived forward, ramming his heavy oval shield into Kevlyn's bad leg. Both men went down, Kirkmaugh on top. He brought the shield down across Kevlyn's face as hard as he could and was rewarded with a bright stream of crimson that shot from Kevlyn's nose. Then he was scrambling over the dazed man and making for his sword where it lay in the mud.

Kevlyn blinked blood from his eyes, rolled over, and pushed himself up from the ground. He got to his feet in time to see Kirkmaugh retrieve his sword. The mercenary somehow got his ruined leg under him and got to his feet. He stood there, wobbling unsteadily, back against the circle's edge.

Kevlyn charged.

Kirkmaugh parried Kevlyn's overeager blade and returned a blow of his own that tore a hunk of meat from Kevlyn's shoulder. Ignoring the jarring blow to his shoulder, Kevlyn thrust. His blade caught Kirkmaugh in the chest and slid harmlessly across the black breastplate. Kirkmaugh brought his shield down across Kevlyn's extended swordarm, hoping to break bone.

Sword slipping through numb fingers, Kevlyn tried to back away. Kirkmaugh's blade flashed high in the torchlight, hung for an incredibly long second at the apex of the stroke, and then came down, hissing as it cut the damp night air.

A great swordsman will tell you that in the heat of battle there is no time for conscious thought. Normally, the eyes see, pass the information on to the brain, and the brain tells the muscles to react. And yet there are times when survival hangs on faster reaction. Kevlyn's sword met the downfalling mercenary broadsword, stopping it from splitting his skull open, but it was pure reaction, like a child pulling his hand away from a hot stove for the first time. There was no conscious thought, only the near instantaneous reaction of the human survival instinct. The same instinct kept the sword clutched in his unfeeling hand, numb from the blow Kirkmaugh had delivered with his shield.

Knowing he wouldn't be on his feet much longer, Kirkmaugh relentlessly pressed his attack. Hacking madly, he pressed Kevlyn back, beating down his guard.

And then Fate played her hand, chose her side in the duel.

The Maddock blade shattered, leaving Kevlyn holding the hilt with no more than five inches of jagged blade.

Still grasping the shattered hilt, Kevlyn stumbled backward as Kirkmaugh's blade screamed past, missing his face by mere inches. Kirkmaugh followed, already tasting victory, when his leg failed him and he fell.

As the mercenary fell, Kevlyn plunged what remained of his sword into Kirkmaugh's right armpit where the black breastplate ended. He tried to wrench it free for another thrust, but the two men collided and went down in a tangle of limbs. Kevlyn lost his grip on the shattered Maddock blade as his head slammed against a rock concealed beneath the mud. Head hammering, Kevlyn had enough sense left to clasp his hands together in one double-sized fist and strike the mercenary off him.

Kirkmaugh's sword spun away in the torchlight to land, spear-like, in the mud. Waving in the wet ground like a metronome, the mercenary blade stood a good four feet outside the white circle.

While Kevlyn tried to shake the gathering blackness from his pounding head, Kirkmaugh scrambled for his weapon. Dragging bad leg and arm, he reached the edge of the circle, looked once at his archers to make sure they had no intention of shooting their leader, and reached outside the circle for the quivering sword.

An arrow slapped into the mud, barely missing his extended hand. Enraged, Kirkmaugh looked up, but none of his men had drawn their bows. Atop the wall of the castle stood Kyle Maddock, nocking another arrow to a longbow.

"*Your* rules, Kirkmaugh!"

The mercenary rolled over, expecting to meet his enemy, but Kevlyn was still on the ground. Ari's leg felt dead, lifeless. When he tried to get up on it, there was no response. Only its numb weight assured him it was still there. All the pain he felt was now centered in his right arm and chest. Looking down, he found the protruding handle of Kevlyn's sword. He wanted to pull the dreaded instrument of his destruction free, but feared he'd bleed even heavier if it were removed. His head was reeling, darkness threatening to push in from the sides of his vision.

There was a buzzing inside his head, like a thousand angry hornets racing back and forth just behind his eyes. Almost too late he forgot about the knife he carried in his right boot.

Kevlyn got to his feet, wiping mud and blood from his eyes. The mercenary was struggling to stand and fumbling in his boot for something.

Ari got the knife out and lurched up on one foot. He found himself too weak to stand though, and was falling even before Kevlyn slammed into him. He tried to thrust the knife into Kevlyn's unprotected gut, but he lost the knife somehow. Too late, he realized Kevlyn had taken it. And then he saw the blade plunging toward his throat. He saw a fountain of blood gush out from under his chin as the knife sank deep, felt the warm flow between breastplate and chest. The ground slammed against the back of his head. And he knew no more.

Leaving the knife where he'd planted it, Kevlyn rolled off the dead mercenary and stared at the dark sky. The low-hanging clouds seemed to be moving incredibly fast. In sinister waves, they washed across the sky, erasing everything, leaving a dark void where they'd crossed.

He was vaguely aware of someone approaching.

A face.

Two faces for a moment; then by sheer will, he got his eyes to focus.

Fenrey.

"What makes you think I won't kill you?" the captain asked. Kevlyn felt a sharp edge against his throat. Small pain, barely discernible through the haze of his mind.

"Wait," he croaked.

"Wait?"

"I'm not done."

Fenrey laughed. "You look *done* to me."

"Help me," Kevlyn croaked. "Get me on my feet."

Fenrey thought for a moment. "Guess I can kill you just as easily after I hear you out." He grabbed a handful of leather shirt and dragged Kevlyn to his feet.

"How much were we paid to destroy Maddock Castle?"

Kevlyn asked, leaning heavily on the mercenary captain.

"We?"

"I'm your leader now."

Fenrey dug his knife into Kevlyn's abdomen. "A short-lived one, I'll bet."

"How much?"

"I don't know," Fenrey answered, his voice heavy with impatience. "Ari has a man—Delsworth. He worries about finances."

Kevlyn tried a more direct approach: "How much would it take to turn the Kirkmaugh mercenaries around?"

Fenrey laughed. "Buy us off? The way Kildare did at Kiamina Pass?"

Kevlyn nodded.

"You haven't got enough gold."

"Name your price."

Fenrey did, expecting the figure he quoted to be outrageous.

Kevlyn indicated the second sack he'd brought down from the castle. "There's twice that much there."

Fenrey rushed to the sack, tore it open, and sighed with near-sexual ecstasy at the sight of the gold. With his back to Kevlyn, he listened to the sound of the gold coins raining through his fingers.

Kevlyn stumbled to the nearest archer, took the man's longbow with nocked arrow. The mercenary stepped back, making no move to stop him. For the moment, with Ari dead in the mud, confusion reigned.

Kevlyn drew the longbow, fighting against the encroaching blackness as he tried to aim. "Break camp, Fenrey. We've been paid."

Fenrey got to his feet, drawn sword still in hand. He turned slowly, reluctant to look away from the open sack of gold. "Sorry. I definitely think you're done now—"

Kevlyn shot him. There was dull *chink* as the arrow penetrated the captain's black armor at such close range. Fenrey fell over backward to land with a splash beside the sack of gold. He struggled with the arrow in his chest for several long seconds while his legs kicked about in the mud. Then he was still.

Kevlyn tossed the longbow back to its owner, a young man with wet red hair and startling blue eyes. "*You're* captain now. My order: break camp."

A moment of indecision passed through those blue eyes. Kevlyn knew the man was trying to decide whether he should nock an arrow and kill him where he stood. If he decided to, there was nothing Kevlyn could do.

Got to help him make the right decision.

"What's your name?" Kevlyn asked. He wobbled on his feet, close to falling. Drawing the long bow had taken the last of his strength.

"Cull Garvin."

"Think I can fill Ari Kirkmaugh's place, Cull?"

"Perhaps."

"Think *you* could?"

"No." A moment of silent thought, then the youth smiled. "But I'll make a damn good captain."

"Then carry out your orders, Captain Garvin."

Cull bowed his head, "M'lord." He turned to the mercenaries gathered about. "Break camp! You heard Lord Maddock. Move it! We march in two hours, you dogs."

Kevlyn put one hand on the new captain's shoulder to steady himself. "You'd better get me to a tent before I collapse." He hated admitting to weakness, at any moment the young mercenary could turn wolf and rip out his throat, but he didn't see as he had any choice. Better to ask help of one man, than fall down in front of the entire army.

"Hold up a bit longer." Cull nodded toward the castle where the gates were swinging open and an iron portcullis was raising. "Want me to handle it?"

"No. Just help me over there."

Cull shook his head. "Let them come to us."

A dozen men came out of the castle, but only one walked across the muddy field to where Cull and Kevlyn waited. Stopping a few feet from his bloody brother, Kyle glanced briefly at the gold being loaded on a cart.

"How much of our coffer did you steal?"

"For her life, I would have taken it all," Kevlyn answered.

Kyle could discover later that he had taken only half the Maddock fortune. It was not the sort of thing to say in front of Cull Garvin.

"For *her* life?"

"Make no doubts about why I did it."

Kyle looked taken aback. "I thought—"

"That I did it for you? For Da? I don't owe you two anything. You should owe me for this." He waved a weak arm at the corpses lying silent in the mud. "But the only payment I want is for you to go back and straighten out the lie you told eight years ago."

"Lie?" the older brother stammered. His voice sounded perplexed, but his eyes betrayed the truth of Kevlyn's intuition.

"You told Da it was me who died that day, and Kyri left to fight in the north. That's why he thought I was Kyri this morning. That's why he insisted I was dead."

"Kev, I want … I mean it's time we made amends."

"Go back to your castle, Brother. Cull, take me somewhere I can rest." The two mercenaries started away from the tall dark walls of stone.

"Take care of yourself, Kev."

Kevlyn looked back over his shoulder one last time. "You take care of *her*, Kyle Maddock."

In the light of the torches, the two brothers locked eyes. In Kevlyn's burned an unspoken threat. Yet a second later, the eyes softened, just enough for Kyle to see and know. Then the expression was gone and the mercenaries, captain and lord, had turned away.

Once out of earshot, Cull asked what direction they were heading.

"North," Kevlyn answered. "The war is to the north, Captain Garvin."

About the Author

Brian A. Hopkins is a four-time winner of the coveted Bram Stoker Award for excellence in horror literature. He's also been nominated for the International Horror Guild (IHG) Award, the Nebula Award, and the Theodore Sturgeon Memorial Award. Of the many stories he's written in collaboration with longtime friend, David Niall Wilson, the three bizarre westerns included here are his favorites. Brian lives just east of Oklahoma City with his wife and a pack of wild dogs. As a life-long student of the martial arts and warfare, he has an unmatched collection of weapons of every sort and strives for accurate and riveting depictions of combat in his fiction. In his most recent work, the short novel "La Belle Époque," set in Paris in the year 1900, he challenged himself to write the knife fight to end all knife fights (available in Voices in the Darkness, edited by David Niall Wilson). To learn more about Brian, seek him out on Facebook, where he wastes far too much time, https://www.facebook.com/bahopkins3/

Bibliography

Something Haunts Us All (1995)
Cold at Heart (1997)
Flesh Wounds (1999)
The Licking Valley Coon Hunters Club (2000)
Wrinkles at Twilight (2000)
These I Know By Heart (2001)
Salt Water Tears (2001)
El Dia De Los Muertos (2002)
Lipstick, Lies, and Lady Luck (2004)
Phoenix (2013)

Meet the Artist

Paul "Johno" Johnston lives in the beautiful southwest of western Australia. He's 48 and a stay-at-home father to three young boys. His hobbies and passions include photography, drawing, and crafting. The cover art used here of the red shield and axe is a composite piece, combining his artist and editing abilities with photographs of his hand-crafted items. Paul says, "I live and breathe everything art."

Curious about other Crossroad Press books?
Stop by our site:
http://store.crossroadpress.com
We offer quality writing
in digital, audio, and print formats.